OF STARS & LIGHTNING

Melanie Mar

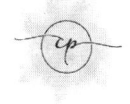

Conquest Publishing

A Conquest Publishing Original

Conquest Publishing

https://conquest-publishing.com

Copyright © 2024 Melanie Mar

Cover Design: Abigail Baia

Edited by: Brittany McMunn

Map Illustration: Victoria Diaz

All rights reserved. No part of this publication may be reproduced, distributed, or transmitted in any form or by any means, including photocopying, recording, or other electronic or mechanical methods, without the prior written permission of the publisher, except in the case of brief quotations embodied in critical reviews and certain other noncommercial uses permitted by copyright law.

Print ISBN: 978-1-962739-14-6

eBook ISBN: 978-1-962739-13-9

Any references to historical events, real people, or real places are used fictitiously. Names, characters, and places are products of the author's imagination.

DEDICATION

*For the ones who can't seem to find the light
at the end of the tunnel—
sometimes that light is you.*

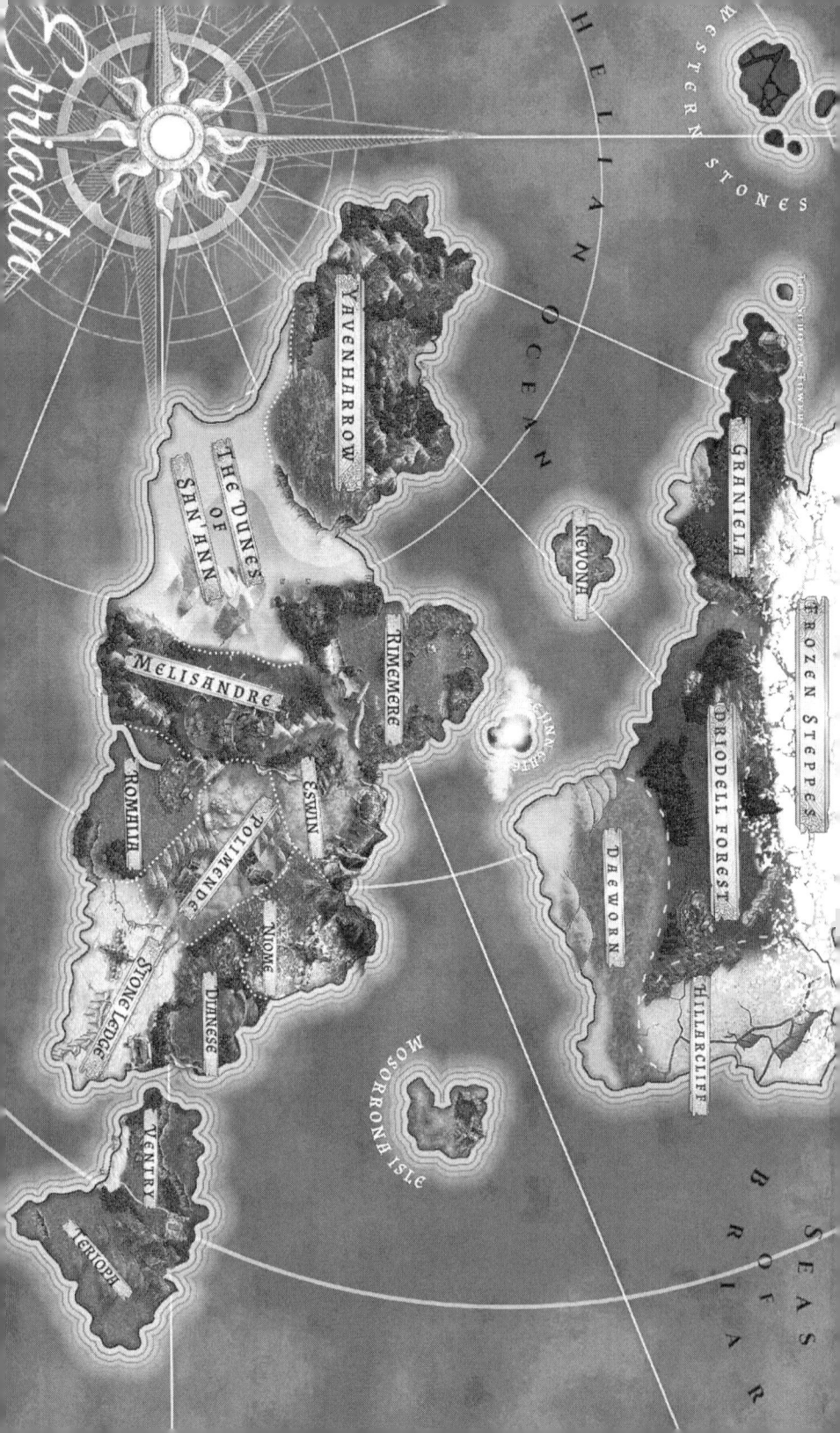

CONTENT WARNING

This is a dark, adult fantasy romance. Certain topics and themes may be difficult for some. Reader discretion is advised.

Mention of suicide.

Violence, blood, and self-harming tendencies.

Murder.

Heavy mental health themes.

Mention of SA.

Use of hallucinogens.

CONTENTS

Prologue		3
1.	Chapter One	7
2.	Chapter Two	21
3.	Chapter Three	30
4.	Chapter Four	42
5.	Chapter Five	52
6.	Chapter Six	62
7.	Chapter Seven	71
8.	Chapter Eight	80
9.	Chapter Nine	87
10.	Chapter Ten	101
11.	Chapter Eleven	104
12.	Chapter Twelve	112
13.	Chapter Thirteen	122
14.	Chapter Fourteen	134

15.	Chapter Fifteen	143
16.	Chapter Sixteen	155
17.	Chapter Seventeen	165
18.	Chapter Eighteen	174
19.	Chapter Nineteen	185
20.	Chapter Twenty	200
21.	Chapter Twenty-One	209
22.	Chapter Twenty-Two	220
23.	Chapter Twenty-Three	228
24.	Chapter Twenty-Four	232
25.	Chapter Twenty-Five	240
26.	Chapter Twenty-Six	247
27.	Chapter Twenty-Seven	256
28.	Chapter Twenty-Eight	269
29.	Chapter Twenty-Nine	281
30.	Chapter Thirty	290
31.	Chapter Thirty-One	298
32.	Chapter Thirty-Two	305
33.	Chapter Thirty-Three	314
34.	Chapter Thirty-Four	323
35.	Chapter Thirty-Five	331

36.	Chapter Thirty-Six	344
37.	Chapter Thirty-Seven	348
38.	Chapter Thirty-Eight	364
39.	Chapter Thirty-Nine	376
40.	Chapter Forty	394
41.	Chapter Forty-One	400
42.	Chapter Forty-Two	408
43.	Chapter Forty-Three	422
44.	Chapter Forty-Four	429
45.	Chapter Forty-Five	436
46.	Chapter Forty-Six	447
47.	Chapter Forty-Seven	450
48.	Chapter Forty-Eight	454
49.	Chapter Forty-Nine	461
50.	Chapter Fifty	470
51.	Chapter Fifty-One	476
52.	Chapter Fifty-Two	487
53.	Chapter Fifty-Three	492
54.	Chapter Fifty-Four	497
	Epilogue	500
	Of Seas and Storms	512

INTRODUCTION

Light Magic

Magic stemming from the 5 gods. Given to specific bloodlines upon their Awakening, Kept by blood offerings to the Wielder's respective god.

Dark magic

Not bloodline specific. Gifted by Loumallet from the Void itself. Taxed through the keeper's soul, paid for not by blood, but by essence.

Flora Goddess of Land and Blood. (Flo-ra)

This deity's holy temple is located within Rimemere. Erriadin's first god, born from a drop of sunshine falling from the skies. A fair and kind god, with an ancient wrath if provoked.

Aquarene Goddess of Water and Wisdom. (Aqua-Reen)

This deity's holy temple is located within Rimemere. Erriadin's second god, born from Flora's tears. A pensive god, unyielding to excuses. Prefers her children to keep their bloodlines pure.

Winderlyn God of Wind and Justice. (Win-dur-lyn)

This deity's holy temple is located within Rimemere. Erriadin's third god, born of Aquarene and Flora's prayers. An impatient and finite god. Prefers blood offerings directly from the neck and has no mercy for traitors.

Emberdon God of Fire and War (Em-ber-dohn)

This deity's holy temple is located within Rimemere. Erriadin's fourth god, born from Flora's wrath at her defiant siblings. A temperamental god who requires regular blood offerings from his children. Known as the most brutal sort of light magic.

Warren God of Wards and Souls (War-ren)

This deity's holy temple is located within Rimemere. Erriadin's fifth god. Origins unknown, much like his volatile magic.

Loumallet Keeper of Dark Magic (Low-ma-let)

This god has no temple. This god is not recognized by the holy laws, nor is it one Wielders pray to. Gifter of Shadows, father of Jinn.

PROLOGUE

They watched her in silence.

She strode from table to table, an easy smile on her full lips and a gentle gaze in her emerald eyes. Although she physically looked so different from their Queen, the girl before them moved with the same swiftness, the same sense of urgency.

After several orbits around the dusty, loud tavern, she settled behind the wooden bar, returning to whatever book she had been reading the past four days.

"What do you think?" Nina asked, lowering her face to her cupped hands while she watched the girl.

Cas shrugged. "There's no way to know for certain until we speak to her."

They continued assessing the golden-haired girl, her smile alone captivating the table of sailors she returned to serve.

Nina sighed. "If she is who we think...how did *they* know?" She held up the crumpled-up letter, its edges folding and cracking with the movement.

He plucked it from her hands. "That's the question, isn't it? How did whoever sent us this letter find her when we couldn't for years?"

"I have a bad feeling about this," she whispered, tugging forward the black hood of her cloak to further conceal her face. "I don't like that we don't know who found her."

Cas tapped the wooden table before them, the motion sending small bursts of dirt adrift. "The faster we get her out of here, the better."

"Tomorrow," Nina echoed. "We will do it tomorrow after the other two come back from scouting the area."

He nodded.

The crunching of boots on the tiled floor made them both reach for their daggers and lock eyes. And although no physical threats loomed near, Cas's breath hitched slightly as he glanced over Nina's shoulder.

"Greetings, travelers."

They both stiffened at the bright, rich voice that seeped like honey around them.

"Did you two desire anything to drink? The ale here in Yavenharrow is absolutely exquisite."

Nina didn't move, trying her best to keep her breathing steady.

Cas smiled slightly, but carefully averted his gaze to the ground. "We are okay, thank you."

"Well, holler if you change your mind, my Lord."

Without any further conversation, the girl walked past them and moved to the next table, offering them the same script before once again returning to the bar.

She seemed so comfortable, so sure of her place in this world of hers.

And they were about to destroy it.

Cas lowered the letter to the table, exhaling a sigh of relief.

Nina trailed the words, although they had been engraved in her mind for weeks.

Your Princess is in Yavenharrow.

ACT ONE

*Once upon a time, a girl lost her way...
so she forged her own path instead*

CHAPTER ONE

Live, Love, and Eat Stew

Sol knew two things for certain: the stifling, humid Yavenharrow heat might kill her, and her knives were dull.

Steady. Breathe. Throw on an exhale.

She repeated Leo's guidance in her mind, adjusting her form and stance with each mental instruction.

The forest grew silent as Sol rolled her shoulders and sent the blade flying. It sang through the air and slammed proudly into the evergreen she aimed for, but just as she began to smile in triumph, she angled her head.

The knife didn't hit the bull's eye.

"You're getting lazy, Sunny."

Sol frowned and wiped at the sweat on her brow with a sleeve, then eyed Leo as he stepped up beside her. "I need to sharpen them. They always miss when they're dull."

"Knives aren't sentient." He gave her a casual smile. "Last I checked, weapons are only as good as their wielder."

In a smooth dance, he retrieved an arrow from his quiver, nocked it into his bow, and shot it right into the hilt of her dagger, all without taking his golden eyes from her face.

Sol looked from the tree to her now broken knife on the forest floor. "You owe me a knife."

It's not like it was the first knife that had succumbed to Leo's lessons, but it was the first time it was one of her favorites. She brought her mother's old knives out to play this time, hoping Irene's spirit would gift them some luck on their hunt.

It hadn't.

Surely the animals were scarce due to the season—Yavenharrow spring was dreadful. The animals felt it. The town felt it.

Sol also felt it as she gathered her belongings from a nearby cluster of stones, the hairs that strayed from her braid smeared to her neck.

By the time she and Leo made it out to the Hunter's Lands, Yavenharrow's best hunting ground, the sun burned overhead, but the promise of rain lingered on the horizon, making the breeze sticky and humid.

"I keep begging you to let me get you all metal ones instead of flimsy wooden ones," Leo said, also collecting his bag of weapons. "But every time I offer, it's like I've said a personal insult." His tanned skin was flushed, and his short, ebony hair was glued to his forehead with moisture as he took her bag from her hands and retrieved his arrow from the tree bark.

Before Sol could protest, he led the way deeper into the woods, forcing her to swallow her remarks and follow.

Typically, she accompanied her best friend on hunts to practice her aim, never really engaging with the "killing" part of the activity. She often provided snacks and miscellaneous anecdotes about the herbs they came across, some so obscure her aunt Lora would send her right back to pick them for her tonics and salves if Sol ever recounted the discoveries to her.

She plucked interesting things from the forest regardless, the last of her finds being a cluster of poison berries from a Sadenberrie bush—that had been a fast and valuable lesson from her aunt the second Sol placed them on the dining table.

Sadenberries and blueberries were unfortunately very similar.

They continued their walk in companionable silence until the familiar trickle of the Jasen Lake signaled the halfway point of the land, and usually their landmark to return to town. Anything further than the lake was too unexplored for either of their skills.

Leo halted, forcing Sol to shift sideways to avoid a collision. "What is it?"

He shook his head. "I hadn't been out here since..." His eyes flashed and his grip tightened around his bag of arrows.

Sol looked back to the river knowing exactly the memory it brought.

It had been here that they found Holden. Holden, Yavenharrow's most seasoned hunter and explorer, was always known to be prowling the lands for whatever adventure Erriadin gave him next.

Two weeks ago, though, the town had been shocked speechless when the details of his death spread like a plague. The shops in the town square began to close at dusk instead of midnight, and the taverns at midnight instead of dawn. Sol hated seeing her lively town gloom in terror at the realization that one of their own had been murdered doing what he loved most.

Also, what he was best at.

Second best, and now owner of Holden's archery shop, Leo made sure to answer all the questions the townsfolk flocked him with—to the best of his abilities.

"Is it true a beast slayed him?"

"We heard his insides were missing."

"Someone said he had no blood when they pulled him out of the Jasen Lake."

It had truly been a nightmare of a week.

Sol placed a hand on Leo's forearm. "It wasn't your fault."

"I know."

"Do you?"

He sighed. "I do, but it will always feel like it was."

Instead of being with Holden that day, Leo had been with Sol, helping her home after a difficult shift at the Hound. If his death was anyone's fault, it was that wretched place for keeping her so late they weren't there to walk him home.

She tugged Leo forward and knelt by the water, gently tracing the ripples with her fingertips. "What do you think did it?"

He sat beside her, gaze far away. "Not anything human."

"An animal?" Sol shivered. Mountain lions were common around Yavenharrow. Bears sometimes wandered from the mountains, too.

"None that we've ever seen before."

She dropped the subject. The edge of emotion in his voice was something Sol didn't want to push.

Leo must've felt the same, as he said, "Do you work today?"

Of course she did. There wasn't a miserable day she didn't work at that Inn, and though she despised it, it was the only place in town that took her in with minimum questions and respected her desire for privacy. Even her mother had remarked on its sleaziness when she was alive, which had made Sol all the more curious to know what went on behind the doors of Yavenharrow's primary stop for travelers, sailors, and anyone else who desired a taste of the town's oldest kind of fun.

Now that she knew it was nothing of interest, she wished she could bop her younger self in the head for even approaching the place to begin with.

Five years later and she had yet to find anything better.

Picking up a lonely stone to toss over the water, Sol sighed. "Unfortunately, I do."

"Do you want company?"

"I'm fine."

Leo shook his head, outstretching his arms. "Please quit that wretched place. Keelin treats you terribly, and it's always filled to the brim with scummy people."

She shrugged, "Those scummy people give great tips."

"I can fend for us just fine, you know. Or you can take Lora's allowance she's been trying to give you for years."

"I want to finance my own education."

"She loves you, Sol." He leaned closer. "She says she makes good money selling as a healer, let her take care of you."

Sol had this discussion often with him and Lora. She knew she should just sit at home, tend to the gardens, and take the coins given to her. Unfortunately, Sol couldn't do it. She had tried, truly. But the unease stillness caused her was the sort she didn't want to take the time to decipher.

Boredom called to the mind. The mind called to memories, and her memories had claws.

Sol had only ever really wanted to study, entranced by all the lectures Leo recounted after his days at the town school. Unfortunately, her mother had been against her attendance despite all the tantrums and pleas Sol made.

"*It's too dangerous,*" Irene would say. "*You're too special.*"

Whatever that meant.

The prohibition to study only made Sol get her thirst for knowledge sedated through other ways, sneakier and more unfiltered. She dared say the stories she heard from the citizens made her a different sort of educated.

Sol sighed. "Keelin pays well. I'll quit when I can afford a ship to the Scholar Towers."

Leo rolled his eyes. "It's compensation for the abuse of labor."

She shook her head and flicked the flat stone over the lake. "It's an overnight shift anyway. You have morning duties in the town."

Stocking shifts were Sol's favorite, though still dreaded. She could at least pick at the food and bread undisturbed as she organized the shipment of ale and vegetables for the week.

Leo splashed water over his face. "Even more of a reason to have someone else there. You shouldn't be alone at night."

"Lora was gonna swing by after her rounds so we could walk home together." Sol nudged his shoulder. "Plus, I can take care of myself."

He nudged her back. "Holden probably thought the same thing."

Sol and Leo parted ways a few hours later, ultimately deciding squirrels and lazy birds were not worth prowling the forest, especially as it still held an air of eerie mystery.

Leo made his way back to his cottage, neighbor to Sol's, to help his sister prepare for what he swore was going to be a rainy evening.

Before he let her go, though, Sol had to promise she would stop by on her way home, if only to let him know she was alive. He even bribed her with the promise of fresh stew.

Sol took the long way to the Hound Inn, deciding to prepare for what presumably was to be a boring night. She detoured to the Yavenharrow Archives, the town's epicenter of knowledge and folklore. It was also the town's oldest building, and history claimed it had been some sort of temple for the gods long before civilization bloomed on the continent. It was a domed, stone-carved monstrosity in the center of Yavenharrow, its entry archway depicting Erriadin's gods.

The original legends, the ones her mother sang as lullabies, told the origins of the four gods, the Creators, and gifters, of all magic. In all illustrations and statues, they were in a frozen dance, the males showcased their physical strengths while the females gazed at each other as if they knew secrets Erriadin didn't. Later came the fifth and most mysterious god, one most of Erriadin still only spoke about in scattered whispers. Irene was devoted to him, though, constantly sharing how his blessings were worth more than all others combined.

Sol had thought her mother liked Warren the most because he was objectively the most handsomely illustrated in the folklore.

As Sol collected the memories and passed the stone deities, she swore Emberdon, god of fire, followed her with his beady, ruthless eyes. The structure shone in the sunlight and the wooden doors of the Archives creaked open as a group of students made their way out, arms full of books, and faces bright with smiles.

The smell of worn parchment and leather greeted her, prompting a satisfied inhale while she made her way inside. The only way time passed in the place where it all stood still (the Hound), was with a good, long romance novel. Another benefit was she could later trade it with Mina, Leo's sister, for whatever she managed to find.

Sol traced a finger along the bookshelves, leaving behind a clean trail while dust flew, when a book title made her pause.

Angling her head, she plucked it from the shelf.

Myths, Tales, and Truths of the Southern Continent: Light Magic and its History.

Sol smiled.

Erriadin's Southern Continent, further south than Yavenharrow, was famous for its stories—and secrets. Tales of magic the Southern natives possessed were widely sung around fires and festivals. The one story told the loudest was the legend of a city with rough, hilly landscapes and crowded streets paved with the densest stone, fiercely loved by its Queen and her people. The stories whispered of the city of Rimemere mostly warned of the Light Magic Wielders who walked among it, taking up residence in a giant castle stark in the middle of the city.

The bedtime stories meant to lull children to sleep sang of the sweet, elemental magic they held, while the stories meant to discipline, and spook told of the way they despised humans. In fact, they coveted their abilities so much that most of their bloodlines only married known Wielders.

Sol's mother had told her so many stories she wondered if somehow she had traveled there. But every time Sol asked, Irene would laugh and tuck her into bed.

The memory squeezed at her chest, and by the time she left the Archives, she decided to take one final detour.

She walked through the bristling streets, smiling at the vendors and children as they chased each other around the Old Square. Yavenharrow, though difficult with its weather, was a lovely town.

Anything a person might need, Yavenharrow had it. It was the advantage of living in a port town, one Sol had never taken for granted—what they lacked in finery and luxury, they made up for in culture.

Past the vendors and markets toward the edge of town, the cobblestone funneled into the Yaven Ports. Ships were docked as usual, ready to take sailors on their quests or transport whatever item the Northerners fancied.

This month, to Sol's dismay, it was quilts. The fools had purchased most of the town's supply of wool and fur blankets, leaving the thinner options for them. It wasn't a huge concern since summer solstice was next, but Sol still liked stocking up while they didn't cost a whole week's coins.

Sol looked around for any and plotted to negotiate for one but settled with free seafood samples instead. She didn't only prowl the shops with plots to snag cozy things, but also to greet the regular vendors who would set up across the docks. Most of them were regulars at the Hound, so remaining on their friendly side was advantageous. For tips, and free seafood, of course. Blue crab meat melted on her tongue, and she suppressed a sigh as she plopped a spiced shrimp in after it. The food almost made her want to stay in Yavenharrow.

Almost.

Exploring Erriadin called to her a little louder.

She swerved toward the beach, passing the sleeping ships, and evading the busy fisherman as they ran around the docks. Past the docks was a thin, rickety ladder that led to the sands, then to a path she could walk in her sleep. Sol made to step unto the sand, eager to feel its familiar warmth.

But she halted.

Her mother's grave was far enough from the water the waves never reached it but close enough to the sea from the small grassland bordering the beach to always feel the salty breeze. There had been no point in securing a burial plot at the town pantheon since so little of her mother's body had remained after the murder. So, she and Lora had burned her remains and buried the ashes at the beach, the place her mother loved the most.

No one except Sol, Lora, and Leo visited. So, it was startling to see a figure looming.

The block of stone on the ground served as a memorial and was completely covered by a cloaked individual. Sol saw their hands shifting through the patches of lavender and moss she had planted around it.

A small part of her, the logical side, told her perhaps she should turn and visit another day. But that pesky, defiant side pulled her forward, hands gripping her books harder in case she had to use them as weapons.

Salty sea water sprayed at her face, blurring her vision so that her steps turned sloppy—and noisy—as she descended the walkway.

The stranger peered over their shoulder. "Who's there?" The voice was firm and foreign with a slight, deep Southern accent that piqued Sol's interest.

Still, she stopped a healthy distance from them. "I'm afraid that's the question I should ask you." Her voice shook, betraying the nonchalant facade she attempted to play.

A smile pulled at the man's full lips as he stood to face her.

Yavenharrow was filled with people from all edges of Erriadin since it was a town for travelers. However, most long-term citizens kept to brown eyes, black hair, and carefully sun-kissed skin, all the total opposite of Sol. It wasn't often she saw features like her own, so when the man removed his hood, she couldn't help but stare.

Pale ringlets fell around his forehead, stopping just above a set of pine-green eyes. Unlike Sol's, his had specs of silver so intense, she could see them from where she stood a few steps away.

He motioned to the tombstone, a small carved stone with her mother's initials. "I'm sorry. I guess this belongs to you?"

Sol nodded and clutched her books against her chest.

"I was walking to the docks and saw this lovely bed of lavender, you see." The man held up a stem of lavender, plump and violet, and deliciously fragrant. "Then, after I plucked it, realized it was a grave and—" He ran his fingers through his hair in an obvious nervous tell, making Sol relax.

She cleared her throat and said, "You may take more if you'd like. The animals around here love to steal when they're fresh blooms anyway, so there's always chunks missing."

He knelt beside the bed of lavender and thyme, the impossible agricultural feat finally successful after she had begged Lora to bring back soil from the Driodell forest. The myths surrounding its ability to grow anything proved true. The herbs had been her mother's favorite and offered a sort of comfort Sol hadn't been able to match with anything else.

"I have a journey North and heard lavender helps with seasickness," he remarked, plucking another stem, and easing it into his pocket. "If this doesn't work I'm afraid I'll perish before I reach the Western Stones."

Cautiously, Sol knelt on the opposite side. "You're better off trying ginger for that. Or Belladonna. Can't throw up if you're asleep."

A roar from the docks interrupted the man's laughter. Fishermen waved and rang their bells, signaling the departure of a ship.

The man sighed, "That's me, I'm afraid." He surveyed her, and Sol instantly regretted dropping her guard.

Yavenharrow men weren't the kind of people to have conversations and not plan to take it further, she had learned that the hard way. But the man made no move forward or change of expression. Instead, he stood, brushing the sand off his leather breeches.

"Well, it was nice to meet you." He angled his head. "What's your name?"

Sol's breath hitched.

That had been Irene's only rule. *"You never tell anyone your full name, Sunshine. The only ones who can know are people you wholeheartedly trust. Even then, think twice about it."* She didn't remember the first time her mom told her this but recalled it constantly throughout her life and had yet to break it. Sol could only use her first name, the shortened version of it that most people knew her by anyway.

Still, she tried her best to avoid even giving that.

"Stella," she lied, giving him the name of her favorite of Leo's goats.

The man nodded. "Stella," he repeated the name slowly. "Star."

Sol shrugged. "My mother liked the sky."

Another booming horn vibrated on the beach, prompting the man to sigh. "Yavenharrow natives are very impatient." He winked, "See you later, Stella."

Sol watched him leave, still entranced by his demeanor and cool features. If she had to guess, she would say he was from Niome, or Ventry, somewhere deeper south where their features were common.

The evening had cooled as the clouds continued to darken, so much so Sol could barely see through the haze and rain. She looked down to her mother's herb garden, spotting the bare spec where the man had plucked the stems.

Shielding herself from the oncoming rain with her satchel, she quickly scooped up some dirt and stray leaves to cover it, to save the soil from becoming unsavory for when she planted a fresh batch.

Just as she dug her fingers into the ground, hot pain sliced through them.

"What the—" Sol cursed as she yanked her hand against her chest, sure she had hit some sort of thorn.

She inched closer.

No, not a thorn.

Sol pulled at the metal chain, freeing it from beneath the sand and dirt. It was a curious necklace, loud and resplendent despite the gray air. A pendant in its center sparkled as she held it to her face, the shape of a six-pointed star made of delicate golden strips. It reminded her of the birthmark on her back, the one she had shared with her mother and the women before her.

A booming horn made her flinch and clutch the thing, then swirl to the ports.

As the rain began to pour, Sol swore the mysterious man lingered over the edge of the now sailing ship, and with an uneasy feeling, she realized he hadn't told her his name.

CHAPTER TWO

AT NIGHT, ALL THINGS BITE

Sol found herself exhausted before the night even began. She battled with the notion of throwing the necklace into the Helian Ocean, but the pendant was pretty, so she vainly decided to keep it.

Yavenharrow at night was lovely, a sight she enjoyed with more ease when whispers of murders weren't around, but she still took the scenic route —with her hand wrapped around a knife.

Sol walked back into town the way she came, thankful the heavy rain lasted only a few minutes while she took cover beneath the roof of some bait shops. About two miles behind the Archives, the Inns began on either side of the road, then after the Inns were the taverns and bakeries.

Sol had learned the taverns in the town were rowdy, but fun before midnight. After that, the people became feral, thirsty for way more than just the ale. But she had learned the ones to dance at and the ones meant for talking, and even Leo enjoyed the occasional dark ale, though he wouldn't admit it.

Smiling to herself, she gazed up at the inky sky to look at the stars. The town was silent, serene as night settled. Only the soft rumble of the taverns and late-night eateries vibrated across the cobblestone, evidence her home lived and thrived and enjoyed.

Sol wasn't a fan of the stillness, it made her mind wander, and her skintight. She needed life, a purpose, something to remind her that anything was possible in a world that liked to make things impossible. Yavenharrow fulfilled some of that incessant need—but not enough.

The rain had stopped completely by the time Sol rounded the corner to the Hound, the smell of dewy grass clinging to the air. Her workplace was a solitary building, constructed from a mix of sandstone and clay. There were a few stray windows from the second and third floors lit with soft, amber candlelight, the only indication the place housed travelers.

Her footsteps echoed atop the pavement of the thin walkway as she passed the front lawn. She was about to push the doors open when a series of whistles made her halt.

"Hey, Keelin," Sol said, not bothering to look behind her at her boss.

Sol knew what she would find: one of the most devastatingly handsome men she had ever seen with cyan eyes that seemed to pierce her soul. She had almost not taken the job when he offered it to her for fear she would never be able to tear her focus away from him, but he offered her a generous schedule and free food whenever she had breaks. Plus, never asked for her full name, something all other places had asked for. He had only asked her to do a full turn, then threw an apron at her.

"You're soaked," Keelin observed, stepping up beside her and leaning his back against the door.

Sol shrugged. "It rained."

"Not very professional to come to your shift in wet clothing, lovely."

She cut her gaze to him. Even in the dim light, she could see his smirk. "Good thing it's just me the whole night in there with no one to complain, huh?"

He smoothed his crimson tunic and said coolly, "I didn't say anything about complaints." He finished the sentence with a sly wink. "Good thing I ran into you. I've been meaning to tell you I will be docking your pay."

Sol blinked. "Is this because I came in wet clothes?"

"It's not personal, Sol." He tugged at a stray thread from the sleeve of his beige blouse. "The trade on the Northern borders is slow. People in town are paranoid about Holden, so our business is slow. I have to find cuts somewhere."

"Find them somewhere *else*."

A smile bloomed on his lips. "Ah, Sol. I do love when you banter with me."

"I'll quit," she said, crossing her arms. For a second, she meant it. She would quit and take the savings she already had to board a ship. Well, a boat, with how expensive ship travel was. Would she have enough for her and Lora?

Would a boat survive the Helian Ocean?

A boat wouldn't get her to the Scholar Towers.

"I sure hope you don't, Sol. You're a favorite, you know, and way more competent than the others."

"You can't cut my salary, Keelin." Sol braced a hand on the door, suddenly wishing Leo was with her.

"I have to."

"I'll stay longer, then. Work more shifts."

"Take it up with the rest of them." He began walking away, catching up to a woman by the street Sol hadn't noticed before.

"I'm the barmaid and waitress. You can't seriously think it's fair to underpay me," she called after him.

Throwing an arm around the woman and leading her into the cluster of taverns down the road, he said, "Nothing is fair, Sol. Truly, I'm sorry."

Sol watched him fade into the night for a moment, trying to decide how to react. But after the day she had, she decided she would deal with it later.

She kicked the wooden doors open, wondering if maybe picking a god to worship and devoting to them would perhaps improve her luck.

To sedate the thirst for vengeance, Sol decided to leave small inconveniences for Keelin scattered around the tavern while she worked.

She set her satchel down on a nearby chair while concluding that her first mischief would be switching the cucumbers with the squash, so when the cooks went to make vegetable stew, they would find soggy cucumbers in their pots instead. She tossed her hair into a knot, then examined the space, searching for the boxes that usually waited for her in the lobby.

Thinking perhaps Keelin had taken them to the back for her, she began her waltz to the kitchen. The gentle crackling of the fireplace sizzled after her, the soft scent of burning bark wrapping around her in a warm hug, providing a much-needed change from the humid, rainy—

Sol stopped.

She turned back toward the fireplace, bracing her hands on her hips as a dreadful feeling spread through her.

The fireplace was lit.

Everyone knew never to leave it on, the routine to extinguish it was second nature after a close call years ago.

"You should really tell whoever owns this place to lock the doors, you know."

Sol screamed, slamming against a table behind her. She struggled to keep it and herself standing as she clutched the wood, her heart hammering in her chest.

There were four people sat around the large table in the center of the room. Two men and two women, obviously foreigners based on their demeanor alone. They sat gingerly along the rectangular table, their expressions equally nonchalant. They seemed like part of the background, somehow, as if they materialized from the shadows themselves.

"Anyone could just come in here and steal things," one of the women said, the voice the same as the one who had spoken before. She had long, raven black hair that fell in a braid over her chest, the color mirroring her eyes. She, just like the others, had on a black bodysuit, and a pair of twin swords peeked from behind her shoulders.

Sol glanced at the others, and her stomach fluttered with nerves as she realized the quartet all fashioned different weapons.

Maybe Holden *had* been killed by a person. A strange, heavily armed person.

"We are not going to hurt you," the other woman said, her glowing green eyes gleaming while her auburn hair shone against the firelight. Her skin was delicately pale, a stark contrast to her surroundings, as she extended her hands in front of her in what seemed like a gesture of peace. "We just want to talk."

Sol took a careful step back, the bottom of her worn skirt nearly making her stumble.

Talk.

That's what all killers said before they did way more than talk.

What could they possibly want from the Inn? Money? They picked a poor place for that. Holden had money, though. And he still wound up dead.

"We—we're closed," Sol stammered, carefully inching toward her satchel.

Her knives. She had her knives there.

"Fortunately, we aren't here for mediocre food," the dark-haired woman said, leaning back in her chair. "And if you think anything in that bag of yours will help you avoid us, you're mistaken."

The man next to the red-haired woman, the tallest of the bunch with deep tawny skin, shot a look at the girl. "Gods, Sawyer.".

The dark-haired woman—Sawyer—shrugged. "Just saving her the effort."

Sol knew she didn't have many options. Lora would tell her to run.

So, she did.

Shifting on her heel, she stumbled back to the entrance and threw the doors open, knocking over some chairs in her way. She heard soft murmurs, then footsteps following.

Faster.

Faster.

Sol ran down the cobblestone walkway that led into the street, then propelled into the night. Tears flew from her eyes as the footsteps behind her grew closer. Veering to the only place she felt safe, she turned down an alley she knew would lead to the beach.

"Godsdamn it," a male voice mumbled from behind as she evaded the holes and puddles along the narrow space. The air burned in her lungs. The smell of sweat mixed with rotten food filled her nostrils until the salty spray of the ocean greeted her as she launched herself onto the docks.

Now what, genius?

Sol wondered what she had done to offend the gods when a large hand wrapped around her bicep, stopping her from heading onto the sweet, beautiful beach.

"No—stop it!" She planted her feet on the ground and clawed at the person's forearm. "You can take anything you want from the Inn, just let me go!"

The man pulled her against his chest, his forearm wrapping around the front of her shoulders. "You are weaker than anticipated."

Sol panted, continuing to twist and fight her way out of his grip as he dragged them off the docks and back to the road. "Why are you doing this?" she ground out. "Please, leave our town alone!"

Sol knew once they were done with her they would move on to the next victim, continuing their search for whatever they wanted. No. She had to survive somehow, to spare others from such a fate. To tell Holden's family she knew what happened.

"Relax, we won't take long," the man said, his voice too close to her ear.

We won't take long.

Panic coursed through her at the statement, enough so she did the only thing she remembered Leo telling her to do during this sort of hold.

She bit the man's arm.

Hard.

He let out a string of curses and released her, knocking her to the ground. She flinched as her knees collided with the solid wood of the docks, then slid away before swirling to face him. Her breath caught and for a moment she let herself still. The man's eyes were moonlight and storm clouds on a foggy winter morning. The strangest shade of silver stared back at her.

He furrowed his brows as he held his forearm. "Really?"

"What do you want?" she asked, her voice barely a whisper. "Why me—why Holden?"

The ships docked behind her swayed with the waves, softly clanking against themselves as a gust of wind blew a chill over Sol. She didn't dare tear her gaze away from the man, not even as he straightened.

He was perhaps a full foot taller than her, his black suit reinforced with dark armor, and a black and purple cloak hung grazing over his boots.

He angled his head. "Who?"

"He was a good man!" She pushed herself back with her heels, scooting away from the weight of his glare. "Holden had a family. A wife."

"I don't know who that is, Sol. If you just come with me, we can explain—"

Sol.

Her jaw tightened, the sound of her name on a foreign mouth sending shivers through her bones. "How do you know my name? Who are you?"

"Come and we will explain—"

"There's no way in hell I'm going with you."

Sol sprang to her feet and fumbled her way to the beach where she had been what seemed like years ago. Before she was able to jump from the docks onto the comfort of the waiting sand, the man threw his arms around her waist.

"*PLEASE*," she begged, kicking against him. Her feet were off the ground, and with a sigh, he threw her over his shoulder.

"Irene would've had a sword out by now," he mumbled.

Sol didn't know if it was the adrenaline or if she did it out of spite, but without giving herself time for regret, she shoved her entire weight sideways, throwing the man off balance and sending them both tumbling into the frigid, hungry ocean.

CHAPTER THREE

A Thing of Nightmares

The crash into the water awoke all her senses as she kicked upward to breathe. With a gasp, Sol swam to the nearest ship, the moonlight her only guide in the sky. Waves pushed her until she finally grabbed a stray rope, then secured it around her wrist while she gathered her wits.

Perhaps she'd be lucky, and the assailant wouldn't know how to swim. Maybe he would sink to the bottom of the Helian ocean, and though she would have to process killing a person, at least she saved herself.

A small laugh escaped her trembling lips. She outsmarted a kidnapper. Lora and Leo would never believe her.

"I would've let Alix come after you had I known you wanted to go for a swim."

Sol whined and hugged the ship, the small glimmer of triumph fading. "Please, *please* just go away."

The man laughed and swam up beside her. "I guess this is our fault for not explaining ourselves sooner." He spat out water. "But in our defense, you didn't give us the chance."

"Cas?!" A female voice resonated from the docks above them.

"Down here, Nina," the man—Cas—called out. Steps vibrated along the wood before the delicate, red-haired woman peeked her head over the edge of the railing, scanning the waters for them. Nina sighed, relief flooding her features. "Please tell me you can swim," she said, her eyes focused on Sol.

In response, Sol swam away from them.

"I don't think so." Cas grabbed her shirt, then her waist once again. Sol made to fight him off, but this time his grip was rock solid.

Sol stilled. Something was different about the sensation. Instead of his arm warming her, it was colder than the water itself. She looked down and for a moment thought perhaps this whole encounter was a nightmare.

Seeping from his arm were tendrils of black, swirling ropes, securing her tightly against his torso. No—as Sol looked closer, they weren't ropes at all, but shadows, dying the blue ocean black as if paint seeped from around them. The moonlight directly above shone on the darkening water, and Sol gasped as the spirals of ink shimmered, like a billion stars winking in the night sky. Speechless, she ran a hand across the water's surface, the mist clung to her skin as she lifted her fingers in front of her. It danced in the air, breaking apart into hundreds of tiny droplets before floating away on the breeze.

Although logic told her she should be scared, a sense of wonder filled her instead. She turned to look at the man who held her. "What are you?"

Cas only gave her a small smile before jerking his head toward the rope ladder hanging from the dock a few yards away. "The ocean is unsafe at night. Let's talk outside of it."

"Cas..."

Sol looked up to find Nina staring ahead to the horizon beyond them, her loose hair almost brushing against the crashing waves as they rose to meet her.

"Get the fuck out of the water, Xanthos," another voice called from above, the woman named Sawyer.

Sol couldn't see her, but the seriousness in her tone made her follow Nina's line of vision.

They swayed with the current as a sudden drop in temperature made her shiver, and the birthmark on her back burned as if lit on fire. Sol grimaced at the pain, but when she caught sight of what Nina saw, only a numbing horror spread through her body.

Cas's grip tightened around her as he whispered, *"Stay still."*

Her mother hadn't only told Sol stories of Rimemere and its magic. She also told her stories of the wicked creatures that resulted from it, from the greed and thirst for power the Light Magic Wielders had developed. Upon their discovery of Dark Magic, they unwittingly invoked darkness into their lands.

The story Irene told best was the one of a lone Fire Wielder who had been so thirsty for power and respect that she opened the gate to the Void itself to get it. And though her wish was granted, the gate remained open, letting the dark pit's most sinister and bloodthirsty creatures invade Erriadin: the Jinn.

And that was exactly what stared back at Sol through the waves, just as macabre as the illustrations Irene sometimes showed her in a feeble attempt to scare some discipline into her. It didn't work back then. It had instead piqued her curiosity and sharpened her ability to sneak around into their book collection to read about them in the middle of the night.

The Jinn had been a strange myth back then.

What floated in the sea before her was the truest physical representation of the Void itself.

Its beady, bulging eyes hovered directly over the water's surface, completely soulless and totally black. Instead of hair, it had strands of what looked like yarn sprouting from its waxy, wound-covered scalp. Its skin was pallid and a sickly shade of blue as if it had never known the comfort of warmth. Beside it, another head emerged from the water, then another.

And another.

"Great," Cas said.

Before Sol could let out the blood-chilling screech bubbling in her throat, the water beneath them rose, carrying them higher and higher until they were level with the dock. Wordlessly, Cas tossed her onto the paneling of the dock floor where Nina grabbed her arms with haste.

Sol coughed and shook herself from the woman's grasp. "What is going on?" she cried, still trying to process the water, the people, the creatures—

"Shhhh." Sawyer strode up beside them, her drawn swords reflecting the torches lining the bait houses behind them. "If you talk, they'll want to talk, too. You don't want that."

Nina pulled Sol up gently and gave her a kind enough smile she decided not to protest. "This wasn't how I wanted this to go, Princess."

Sol blinked through the mental fog.

Princess?

Nina looked back to the sea, and Sol felt her breath catch as more lifeless, glazed eyes appeared from the water.

"Alix." Cas still sat on the massive wave as if it had turned solid.

The other man from the Hound stepped forward from behind Sawyer, giving Sol a small nod before waving a series of maneuvers with his hands. Instantly, the ocean responded, funnels of water wrapping around him and carrying him to Cas.

Both the men nodded at their companions in some sort of silent understanding before plunging into the Jinn-infested waters below.

Swallowing the lump in her throat, Sol said, "This isn't real."

Beside her, Sawyer laughed. "Better get used to it."

Stepping closer to the edge of the dock, the woman rolled her neck and crossed her arms over her chest as she looked out into the ocean. In a smooth motion, she swung her arms open as they burst into an amber blaze all the way down to the edge of her swords. She illuminated the darkness around where they stood. The Jinn simultaneously turned their attention to her, like pests to a flame.

Cas and Alix landed on ships on opposite sides of the waterway, Alix with water swirling around him and Cas with the curious dark mist hovering by his feet. The ships swayed from the impact.

"I need you to stay with me, Sol," Nina whispered before tucking Sol behind her. "I know you're confused, but I need you to trust us right now."

A shimmer of iridescent light cast the dock in an otherworldly light prompting Sol to glance down. The woman's arms shone the purest green, so bright it was almost blinding. The very planet seemed to respond, the distant trees behind them rustling and straining as their branches extended past them, braiding into a single, solid limb. It morphed into a bridge, connecting the dock to the two ships the men stood on.

Sawyer jumped onto the makeshift bridge and joined Cas on the ship to the left.

Just when Sol thought her nightmare couldn't evolve into anything more terrifying, the Jinn emerged from the ocean, slowly ascending into the air, and hovering above the waves. All of their attention was directly on Sol but the one at the front of the formation snapped it away momentarily to face Sawyer.

"Fire Wielder," it hissed, its voice strained and rasped, but unnervingly loud.

"Yes, ugly?" Sawyer replied, her torso still ablaze as she took a spot next to Cas.

"You and I have unfinished business, Sawyerlyn," the Jinn said, its mouth widening into the most unsettling grin. A set of purple lips stretched across its face's entire bottom half. Where its nose should be were only two slits, and within its horrible mouth sat sharp, needle-like teeth.

A sob escaped Sol.

Immediately, the Jinn cut its eyes to her. It took a slow inhale. "Girl with the golden hair, we haven't seen you before."

"Don't let any live this time, Alix!" Sawyer bellowed, but the Jinn ignored her. It cocked its head in a purely serpentine motion then inched closer to where Sol stood in her fear. "You smell of stars and lightning, girl with the golden hair."

Sol's birthmark ignited. It felt like ant bites and sparks of flame, first in the center then spreading over her entire back.

She gritted her teeth but failed to suppress a pained yell. She clawed at her shirt and skin, hoping something would give to release the agony.

"Sol!" Nina caught her mid-fall and slowly guided her to the floor. "What's wrong?"

"*Yarrrroooow,*" the multitude of Jinn hissed, all narrowing their attention on her.

Sol could barely see as they floated forward, her vision blurred with pain.

Instantly, Nina stood, casting stray rocks and boulders toward the creatures.

Sawyer threw spheres of fire while Alix captured the fallen within his deadly waters while they burned to ashes.

Pain.

Sol's head pounded and her lungs were filled with cement as she crawled toward the small patch of trees nearby, the sound of battle echoing around her. She briefly heard Nina call Cas, then he was beside her, his hand on her shoulder.

"Come on," he said, pulling her to her feet. "You're not used to the Jinn, it's likely your magic reacting to them."

Sol's head spun and she tried not to fall as she swayed forward, but sensing her disorientation, Cas scooped her into his arms.

She tried to say she didn't have magic, but her mouth wouldn't move.

"Please don't fight me this time," he mumbled.

While they slid along buildings and alleys, the pain slowly subsiding, Sol tried to process the night's events.

Magic.

Magic.

When she was a child, Sol would pretend to have magic. She would dance all around the outskirts of Yavenharrow, holding red and orange scarves that would be her fire, carrying around jugs of water she would toss in the air, then try to control the splatters. Irene found it heartwarming, but Lora had always complained she stained their rugs.

Sol never cared about the stains or the stares she would get when she and Leo chased each other around the yard, pretending the breeze came from their palms, and the flowers grew with their touch. All she knew was how her mother's eyes brightened when she spoke of magic, and Sol believed every word Irene spoke of it until the very day she died, when that piece of Sol died with her.

That younger version of her would have been elated. Would have stayed on the docks to at least kick rocks at the Jinn if it meant helping the Wielders. But she wasn't young anymore, and the odds of the night being anything other than a terrible omen were slim.

Additionally, Irene always mused about how the Wielders remained around Rimemere and the deep south since their deity's temples stood within the kingdom. It made no sense for any to be so far from their home.

Or wanting anything from her.

"Stop," she said, kicking against her captor until her feet were firmly on the ground.

They were in an alley behind the jewelry and dress shops, a district she frequented often with Leo's sister. A solitary chimney huffed smoke into the air, hazing the corridor and the storefronts beyond.

Sol blew out a shaky breath and whispered, "What is happening?"

Running a hand through his wet, ebony hair, Cas sighed and leaned on the wall beside her. "We planned on easing you in, but I guess there's no better way of understanding a threat than for it to try to kill you."

"Are those really Jinn?" Sol breathed, bracing a hand against the stone wall. "How did they know my surname? No one knows it."

Her mother had made sure of that. Irene didn't so much as have Sol's full name printed anywhere, and she never uttered it herself. To protect their names was the sacred rule amongst their family, and though Sol had wondered why, the look Lora and Irene would give when she asked would make Sol not question it too long.

Sol had only heard her full name once, without her paternal surname since she might as well have sprouted from Irene alone.

She shook her head. Not the time to curse her absent father.

"You know what they are?" Cas asked, intrigued.

She looked up at him, stifling a flinch at his silver eyes. "I've heard of them."

"From your mother?"

Sol narrowed her eyes. "How do you know so much about me?"

Screeches pierced through the moment of silence, prompting the man to turn his attention toward the beginning of the alley where chaos surely unfolded beyond.

Curiosity, and perhaps impulsiveness, getting the better of her, Sol jogged to it, looking over the edge of the half-wall separating them from the way they came.

How the town remained dead was beyond her. She would've run out into the night to see what the commotion was as soon as it reached her, and it was that same thirst for adventure and knowledge that gnawed at her in that moment. She felt her chest tighten slightly at the thought of the people she had left behind to fight.

Flashes of amber shone in the distance, as well as the splash of waves. The ground beneath them shook, even the dirt seemed to drag toward the tide.

Accepting these people would have already killed her if they truly wanted to, she dared ask, "Why are they here?"

"Who?"

"You people and those demons."

Cas let out a small laugh, but looked to the commotion as well, leaning over the wall. "We are here for you. I don't have an answer for your second question."

"Why are you so vague—"

Cas slammed his arm against her chest, crushing the wind from her lungs as she collided against the wall to their backs. Sol shut her eyes and groaned at the impact before she clung to his arm when she realized why.

The Jinn were even more terrifying up close. This one's hair fell out in chunks, leaving spots of oozing, scabbing tissue around its head. Its blue skin was oily and seemed to melt from its very bones like a candle's wax. It only had a split moment to smile from ear to ear before Cas impaled it with a dagger to the forehead.

But the thing didn't move. In fact, Cas's hand seemed to suspend within it as if the dagger had met jelly instead of skull. He groaned and attempted to dig the knife deeper, but it only sliced further into nothing. The thing did, however, move its black eyes from Sol to something beside her.

"Sol—" He tightened his arm around her torso too late, a second too slow to save her from the putrid, pointed claws that grabbed her.

They pulled her from Cas, and she let out the loudest scream she had as the talons stroked her hair and neck. If she hadn't been so petrified, Sol was sure she would have vomited at the smell.

"I'd recognize the Yarrow *stench* anywhere," the creature purred behind her, its hot breath slicing across her cheek. "My master will be so pleased to know we finally found Irene's daughter hiding in this filth of a town."

"Release her." Cas's voice was low and full of deathly promise as he angled his sword toward them. "Now."

"I'm quite surprised you didn't recognize my illusion, Casimir." Sol whimpered as the Jinn cackled. "Distracted by the Princess?"

"Your kind's biggest downfall is how much you fucking talk."

Sol was torn from the creature's grasp as a ray of fire catapulted their way, colliding straight into the Jinn's face. It shrieked, lunging at Sawyer who swiftly pulled a sword from the sheath on her back and sliced the thing's head clean off its grotesque neck.

This time, Sol did vomit.

She slumped over arms and hurled on the sidewalk, trying to clean the Jinn's smell and words, and face from her body.

"We all reacted the same way at first," Nina said calmly, rubbing circles on her back. Sol coughed and nearly hurled again at the sight of the gooey, black liquid oozing from the creature's unmoving body.

"Up until a year ago, I distinctly remember you throwing up every single time we kill these things, Nins." Through teary eyes, Sol looked up to find Sawyer standing over them. "I think she only stopped doing it because she drinks anti-nausea teas weekly."

"Their blood smells disgusting. I don't know how any of you stand it," Nina countered, helping Sol to her feet. "Are you alright? Are you hurt?"

Sol shivered then angled her head to look past Nina. Cas knelt by the alley wall, his hands tracing something on the ground. He held up his fingers, a translucent substance clinging to them.

"Cas?" Alix strode past to stand next to him. "What happened?"

"I've never seen a Mind Slayer play with tangible illusions," Cas said, a muscle in his jaw twitching. "But this one managed to construct one."

Behind her, Sawyer said, "They don't. Their illusions are only visual."

Standing, Cas wiggled his fingers, the substance he retrieved from the floor shimmering in the moonlight. "Apparently not."

CHAPTER FOUR

She Was Their Queen

The strangers decided to only answer two of the myriad of questions Sol asked on their walk back to the Hound. The first response was confirmation the four of them were Light Magic Wielders. To Sol's annoyance, they didn't provide further information on the topic. The second one was the Mind Slayer they encountered had been a startling anomaly.

Sol asked if the Jinn lived amongst them and if the human race, as a collective, was just ignorant, which prompted a laugh from Nina before she responded.

The Earth Caller explained how Jinn were typically confined to their island a lonely, deserted, piece of land off the coast of Rimemere, where the sinister gate to their world lingered. Alix added they also typically dwelled around Rimemere, drawn to its magic.

Sawyer commented the Jinn were now being found all over Erriadin, from the Lower kinds all the way to the Mind Slayers, which was apparently the branch of Jinn no one enjoyed encountering.

With each kernel of information, Sol's nausea increased. They were almost to the Hound when she dared ask a final question, her chest in knots.

"Why are the Mind Slayers the worst ones? Aren't they all bad?"

They stopped at the beginning of the dusty, cobblestone walkway, the candlelight from within the guest rooms illuminating their path.

Alix's face tensed, his sharp features outlined amber from the reflections. "They are experts in deception and illusions and can mess with the mind. The other Lower ones aren't as cunning."

"Not only that," Sawyer added, tossing her braid over her shoulder. "They enjoy making their victims suffer. The more confused and terrified they are, the better. Sick bastards."

Sol's stomach dropped.

The Fire Wielder frowned in response. "Please don't throw up again."

Sol bypassed the group to place her forehead on the double doors, inhaling the woody scent until her dizziness subsided. These creatures were all over Erriadin. We're here, in Yavenharrow, where Leo and Lora and all her people lived.

The thought jolted her back to the present.

She shoved the doors open, remembering her aunt was meant to meet her inside. If Lora had been outside during the attack, if she had somehow gotten caught in the crossfire—

Her aunt rose from a worn, leather loveseat, a mug in one hand and book in the other. She blinked her lovely brown eyes causing wrinkles of age to crease her forehead as she examined what Sol could only assume was her appearance.

Lora said, "Gods, what is that all over you, Sol?"

Sol ran and crushed her in a hug. Lora was almost a foot shorter and comfortably plump, a combination that made her endlessly popular and approachable. Further than that, though, it made her very soothing.

Sol dropped her head on her aunt's shoulder and sunk into her warmth. "Lora, are you okay? Did you hear what happened? Did you *see* it?" Her voice was frantic and laced with panic.

Lora patted her back. "Hear what, dear?"

Before Sol could spill the night's horrors, her aunt chuckled beneath her. "You four were supposed to wait for me."

Footsteps sounded behind her as the Wielders walked into the Hound, chairs scraping the floor's wooden panels as they presumably sat.

"We thought we had it handled," Alix mused. "But then she decided to run."

Sol whirled around, lips pursed and mind racing. "I don't think my reaction was inappropriate."

Her aunt patted her back. "We taught her well to be wary of strangers."

Sol looked from person to person, from Nina's assessing gaze to Cas rolling his arm as if in pain. Sawyer had her feet on a table, and she tugged on her braid with a bored look.

Sol took a deep inhale and pushed aside her fear and anxiety, looking at the strangers as she stepped in front of Lora. "Someone better explain what's going on."

She wondered if, instead of a nightmare, the day's events were an elaborate joke.

It could be a trick of sorts; festival magicians could do as much. Sol had seen it herself during the solstice and equinox celebrations when foreign psychics and people who claimed to have magic would charge almost a whole day's pay to showcase their mirages. This could be that.

With that idea in mind, the panic subsided slightly, and Sol slid her attention to Lora. "Is this a joke?"

As if considering her answer, Lora angled her head and looked toward the peeling wallpaper along the ceiling.

"Children, it's late," her aunt said finally, leaving Sol standing alone while she neared the Wielders. The four of them gave her gentle smiles, even Sawyer, whom Sol had only seen scowl. "Head on up to the rooms, I'm sure Sol's boss won't mind you all taking two for the night."

Sol frowned, bracing her hands on her hips. "Lora—"

"Sol and I," her aunt cast her a glare, "will be going home where I will explain things. We will regroup here tomorrow."

Besides the fact Keelin would bite her head off for letting people into guest rooms without consulting him, Sol also didn't want to leave. She wanted answers.

Quickly.

"I'm not going anywhere until someone tells me what's happening," she said, frustration rising. "I deserve an explanation, after almost dying and all."

"You almost died because you decided to jump into the Helian ocean," Sawyer remarked.

Nina, who had been admiring a small firelight atop the mahogany table, gasped. "Sawyer!"

"That was his fault," Sol scoffed, pointing at Cas who narrowed his eyes at her. "For his size, he toppled over quite easily."

"Children," Lora warned, turning back to face Sol. Her aunt's eyes gleamed in the firelight. "Enough. Sol, show them to their rooms, then meet me outside." After sensing her hesitation, Lora added, "They won't bite."

Sol crossed her arms. "Not until I'm told who they are."

It was Nina who stepped forward, an apologetic smile on her face. "You are correct. We didn't introduce ourselves."

She nudged Sawyer forward. "My name is Nina. This here is Sawyer. The man you apparently almost drowned—impressive by the way—is Cas. And lastly," she wrapped an arm around the bronze-skinned man who smiled down at her, "is Alix. We can't give you our full names due to...well, Wielder laws, but these are what we go by."

Lora sighed and sat on a chair to the right, plopping her head on her palm. "Don't say I didn't warn you to wait, Sol."

But Sol ignored her, foot tapping on the wooden floor. "And you all broke into my place of work because?"

"Because, like I said in the alley, we are here for you."

Sol cut her gaze to Cas. "What could you possibly want with me?"

"Your mother, Sol," Lora said, tapping her nails on the table. "The stories she told you weren't myths. They were memories, things she lived through."

"What do you mean?"

"I mean, Sol, your mother was from Rimemere. And so are they."

All five pairs of eyes watched her, surveying her reaction. The silence was only filled by the soft patter of rain that had once again started while the occasional flash of lightning illuminated the shadows dancing along the walls. Through the open doors, the soft scent of a patchy rose and lily garden blew in with a cool breeze. Sol didn't know if the sudden chill was from said breeze, or from the words her aunt had spoken.

Sol narrowed her eyes. "You expect me to believe that?"

"After seeing us literally fight creatures from the Void itself with our magic, you still don't?" Sawyer asked, standing. "I can toss a ball of fire your way if that helps."

Her face tensing, Nina glared at the woman. "Sawyer."

Sawyer wasn't wrong, to Sol's annoyance. She had been so mesmerized by their magic out there, but then on their walk became progressively suspicious. There was no way. There was just no conceivable way.

So, Sol said, "Sure. Do it."

Nina looked horrified, but Lora laughed, then said to no one in particular, "She has some trust issues."

"Do *not* toss a fireball her way, Sawyer," Cas warned with a glare. He stood at the edge of their group, but slowly inched closer, as if ready to subdue her.

"Relax, Cassie." Sawyer rolled her eyes and stepped forward, walking to Sol.

As she neared, the space seemed to heat, the fireplace and candles themselves almost flaring. Sol was a few inches taller than Sawyer, but it still felt like she had to look up at her as they stood face to face.

One of the stories her mother would tell was about how each Wielder was gifted their magic. Often, both of their parents had magic. At fifteen, children would undergo a ritual to see which side of their bloodline would pass on to them, to see which god would bless them, if at all. Sol was always marveled at the fact that typically the child's personality mirrored their element. Fire Wielders were hot-headed, Water Dancers calm. Earth Callers were level-headed, Air Singers a bit of it all.

Looking at Sawyer now, that story didn't seem as unbelievable. The woman smiled at Sol, but not kindly. Sol held her stare and prayed to the gods she looked more confident than she felt.

"Although you look nothing like me, I can see how we are related, I suppose," Sawyer whispered, then from her fingertips flicked a string of fire her way.

Sol braced for the singe, almost craving the physical confirmation it was real, but a shimmering wall of violet static erupted in front of her face, causing the flames to disperse with a puff of smoke.

Sawyer huffed. "You're no fun, Cassie."

The violet static vanished. Sol watched the rays disintegrate before her eyes, then cut her gaze to Cas. His hands were wrapped by purple lightning. "Do not burn our Princess on our first meeting."

Sol looked from him to Sawyer.

Although you look nothing like me, I can see how we are related, I suppose.

Then back to Cas.

Do not burn our Princess on our first meeting.

Okay.

"You all can take rooms 54B and 53A. Keys are in the drawer behind the bar. If anyone asks, you're Lora's guests. Not mine."

Without waiting for responses, Sol strode past them, shouldered the half-open doors into a swing, and took an inhale of the cold night air before bending over to steady herself. She vaguely heard the Wielders attempt to follow her, saying something about the Jinn and the dangers of being alone.

But not even the fear of being out alone in an apparently Jinn-infested planet fazed her at that moment, not as the revelations swirled in her mind, interweaving with every story and too-vivid folklore her mother had told her. She dragged herself forward, forcefully taking in bits of air so she wouldn't faint.

Sol felt all synonyms for stupid.

She should've connected it. Her mother had described the Rimemere waters, how the castles gleamed in the sunlight that seemed to always be a shade of lilac...she should've known the stories were real.

A soft clicking beside her gave away Lora's presence. "We didn't tell you for many reasons, Sol."

Sol tried replying, but her tongue was useless as she simply continued with one foot in front of the other, starting her two-mile journey home. The taverns continued their songs, louder and more erratic than usual as midnight approached. Had they not heard the commotion? Had it only been her world that seemed to unfurl at the seams?

"If it's any consolation, I knew nothing of their world either until I married your uncle Axel," Lora continued.

Sol kept walking but tentatively slid her in a silent beckon to proceed.

"I lived in Hilarcliff at the time. It was closer to the Driodell forest where most of the healing herbs grew. Axel came to see me there and begged me to travel to Rimemere to heal his sick sister."

"My mom?"

Lora shook her head. "Your aunt, Melanese." Slowly, she looked back toward the Hound, then returned her attention to Sol. "Sawyer's mother."

At that, Sol halted.

Lora sighed. "She's Mel's only daughter, your cousin, and the only other Yarrow still alive, besides you."

"Sawyer is my cousin?" Sol said slowly, more to herself.

Family.

More family.

Despite the inner battle, Sol glanced back to the Hound as well.

"I traveled with Axel to Rimemere, despite me not believing it even existed to begin with," Lora continued, chuckling softly. "And the rest...well, you know the rest."

Sol turned back to face her. "And did you?"

"Did I what?"

"Heal her."

Lora peered over her shoulder, as she guided Sol forward, the moonlight outlining her aged features in silver. Her eyes saddened slightly. "Only for a little while."

They neared their cottage now, its familiar outline a spot of comfort in the sudden sea of unknown. The sound of their steps resounded in the night, and a wind rustled Sol's unbound hair. As they reached the pathway into their home, still achingly cold with her mother gone, Sol paused.

She blinked a few times and asked, "Why did that man call me Princess? I may not know him, but he doesn't seem like the type to be sweet."

"Who? Cas?"

Sol shrugged. "I think."

Lora laughed, the sound easing the knots in Sol's stomach ever so slightly. "No, that boy is quite the opposite of his father."

Her aunt's smile faded as she grasped Sol's hands. Sol studied the amber specs within her eyes as Lora said, "He said what he did because your mother wasn't just from Rimemere. She was their Queen."

CHAPTER FIVE
The Land of Light Magic

Lora made her sit in the center of their living room with nothing but the cold floor beneath her. After Sol had nothing but her nails to mess with, her aunt spoke.

And Sol listened.

Lora told tales of her past and everything in between, and Sol simply...listened. She was engaged in the stories at first, but about halfway through and an hour in, she had just focused on a spot on the wall, tracing the delicate cracks and peeling wallpapers with her gaze as the stories swam in and out of focus.

Rimemere was the primary domain of the Wielders as it held the temples of the Original Creators, the gods who granted them their magic.

The Rimemere natives mostly lived in the center of the kingdom, students of the royal houses within a castle made of stone and marble, while the ones not affiliated with nobility, or those without magic, staggered around the hilly outskirts of the territory. The Rimemere Wielders trained since children to master their gifts, tutored by experienced militia or top apprentices of their element. There were only a handful of Wielder bloodlines left, the Yarrows being the oldest recorded.

Others who had competed closely were wiped out by war, or enemies. Ivet Yarrow had been the matron of her bloodline, establishing order and law during the land's infancy. From her, all her direct descendants had been gifted the magic of Warding—creating ripples in time to shield themselves or others. Sol's mother had mastered the blessing so immensely she had been one of the most respected and feared Queens to ever rule.

Sol stopped listening after that. She tried to regain focus multiple times, but jumped into an unbelievable sentence, then into another even wilder one. She refused to register it. Refused to let this new identity sink its claws into her.

Because then it made the madness real.

Still, a small part betrayed her. The part of her that whispered of all the wonders her mother told—recounted—and begged her to accept the possibility it might all be real. Despite the magic she had seen that night, Sol still couldn't quite believe it.

The final straw had been when Lora said, "And you are the direct heir to the throne."

White noise danced in her head. Static clouded her vision.

Sol had never so much as led a shift at the Hound. The idea of leading a kingdom seemed extremely foreign. Not to mention, she had no magic. What would they say of her, especially if her own mother had been such a force to be reckoned with?

Her mother.

She was a stranger.

Sol met her aunt's gaze through the haze. "My mother lied to me."

Lora sighed, the wooden chair she situated in front of Sol to sit on groaning. "She couldn't tell you, Sol. If she told you, it meant she'd have to Awaken your magic, and she couldn't do that."

"She lied to me."

"She had to." Her aunt stood, walking to Sol, and kneeling by her side. Gently, she grasped her hands. "I know there are a lot of answers we owe you, dove. I know. We will answer them for you. Your mother loved you more than anything in the world, and she chose to protect you until the very end."

A moment of swollen silence passed.

Then Sol whispered, "Why am I being told this now? What do I have to do with anything?"

That was clearly the question Lora wished to avoid. "I wish I could continue to honor her wish and keep you here, hidden and away from everything she fled. But I cannot. Not with the Jinn in Yavenharrow, not with them and everyone else knowing you exist. You're the heiress to the throne, Sol. You're needed to restore balance in Rimemere." Sol's breath hitched. She couldn't focus as she braced herself for what she knew was coming. "And that's the safest place for you," Lora finished.

"No." She felt her body shake, her vision blurring with unwelcome tears.

"I will meet you there, dove." Lora took her chin in her hand. Her eyes were clear, focused. If she had any fear or reservations about the plan of action, she didn't show it.

Sol, however, had nothing but reservations. Her disagreement was loud, physically, and mentally.

"Why? Why did you keep this secret from me?" She asked again, as if somehow the right answer would be spoken, one that would ease the sting of betrayal.

Lora pursed her lips and sighed. "Your mother asked me to. I—I didn't want to intervene with her plans for you. Not until I had no other choice, which now I don't."

Through her desire to run, to flee and melt into the grasslands if it meant not dealing with this, Sol said, "I'm not going anywhere without you, Aunt Lora."

Lora smiled at her, sweet and tender, as she brushed a golden strand behind Sol's ear. "I will be close behind. I have some things to take care of here. I must make sure these people are protected."

Sol straightened. "You have magic too?"

Lora eased them from the floor to stand, her hands still grasping Sol's. "No, dove. But there are things other than a god's magic at our disposal."

Before Sol could inquire further, her aunt gently pushed her toward her room, the patter of rain echoing inside the cottage. "Sleep, Sol. We will regroup in the morning."

Solemnly, mechanically, Sol slid into her room. She didn't think or change into a nightgown before flopping onto the mattress and closing her eyes, praying to whatever god would listen that she would wake up and the day would have been all been a cruel, insane nightmare.

Irene's voice wavered, as if muffled by water. Words eased in and out of focus, taunting Sol. *"What are you so afraid of, Soleil?"*

Sol looked around, trying to locate where the achingly familiar voice came from, but her vision was clouded by shadows and mist. There was nothing but darkness beyond her, but she swore the air shimmered with specks of gold.

"Soleil, don't be afraid."

She swirled, the voice mere inches from her now. But there was nothing. There was no one.

"Mom?" Sol whispered. She shivered as a blast of cold wrapped around her.

"You've always been destined for this. You can't outsmart destiny, Soleil. Trust me, I tried."

The voice came from above her now, and when she looked up, she froze.

She recognized her mother's glacier-blue eyes, her black hair cascading over her face and toward Sol as her figure hovered in the air. But the closer Sol looked, the more Irene distorted into a stranger, something with blue skin and rotting bones. With milky, soulless eyes and sharp, eager teeth.

The thing smiled and the voice that came out of it was no longer her mother's, *"We can't wait for the Yarrows to finish what they started."*

Sol jolted awake.

She sat up and wrapped her arms around herself to soothe the shivers, then ran a hand over her sweaty forehead. Nightmares were common. She had always been plagued by them, especially when she slept alone. But that…

"It's going to be a long day," she whispered to the air, turning to look out her window. The sun barely peeked from behind the horizon, casting the hills and grasslands in a light pink.

To steady herself, she studied the tangible things around her. To her left, was a small washroom with a wooden tub she had spent nearly two months' worth of tips to purchase, and a delicately carved armoire, the decorative indentations courtesy of her mother. In front of her were her personal bookshelves littered with romance novels she swapped regularly with Mina. She also kept all the notes and parchments Leo handed down to her in small boxes there.

She placed her palm on her chest to calm her breaths, flinching when she felt the cold, metal chain resting there.

That encounter on the docks had been almost as bizarre as being told magic was real. Sol threw the necklace on without much interest after, but now, as she zipped the pendant back and forth on the chain, she thought perhaps she should have at least had a mage bless it.

The fragrant smell of carrots, onion, and garlic from the front yard greeted her beyond the closed door, and she sighed at the promise of stew waiting. She showered and got ready quickly, throwing on a casual pair of khaki trousers and a black blouse before walking to stand in front of her closed bedroom door.

With a heavy sigh and a knot in her throat, she pushed it open.

Lora leaned over a steaming pot of stew in the kitchen, the morning sunlight streaming in through the window beside her. Jars of herbs were open and out of order, showing she had truly tried to craft Sol's favorite food to perfection.

Her aunt gave her a small smile and pushed a bowl forward.

Sol tried her hardest to seem angry still, despite all of it subsiding after seeing Lora's regretful expression.

Lora said, "I'm sorry for not telling you, Sol. Truce?"

After a beat of silence, Sol sighed and pinched the bridge of her nose. "Just— no more secrets, right?"

Lora shook her head. "Whatever you don't know, I don't either, dove."

They each ate two bowls of stew and a whole loaf of bread, the sounds of the awakening town lively beyond the walls of the cottage.

Their cottage was small, but comfortable compared to their previous home. When Irene was alive, the three of them had lived by the Old Square in a two-story home made of stone and wood. The house had been enormous for Sol as a child, but it only became bigger when the murder tainted it.

Lora and Sol moved to the outskirts of town, sealing their old life and home with a heavy metal lock they only removed for monthly maintenance.

Sol ate quickly, adrenaline and anticipation making her nauseous. After thirty minutes of forced bites, they made their way back to the Hound Inn.

They hadn't spoken about it. About Sol's impending departure. Its promise hung thick between them during their walk. So thick, in fact, Sol decided to finally address it as they neared the town's main streets.

"I'm still not going with them," she declared. "No matter how much stew you bribe me with."

Lora chuckled. "That obvious, huh?"

"I don't know them, Aunt Lora. I can't leave everything behind and trust some strangers."

"They're strangers to you, I suppose. But your mother and I were very close to their parents. I knew Nina and Casimir as children as well. Briefly, but they haven't changed."

Sol peered sideways at her to urge her on, but she didn't have to as her aunt continued, "Nina Amana is the daughter of Clarisse Amana. She was your mother's primary handmaiden. Clarisse was a talented Earth Caller, much like her daughter is now. One of the few servants with magic, too. Her family was condemned to servitude for past treasons.

"But your mother loved Clarisse, and Clarisse loved her. So, Irene formally swore her into her court as her Royal Hand." Lora smiled at the memory. "They were quite the duo when I met them in Rimemere."

"So, where is Clarisse?" Perhaps she would have stories of Irene for Sol. Stories about her time as Queen, something to help Sol connect the new identity with who her mother was to her. Who else to do so than a close friend?

They neared the Hound now, the other shops around bristling awake.

Lora pursed her lips, sadness coating her features. "She— she sacrificed herself. When Irene left Rimemere, it was chaos. She and I waited for Clarisse and Axel, your uncle, at the gates. We were all meant to flee together." Sol stopped at the beginning of the cobblestone path directly in front of the inn, her aunt doing the same as she faced her. "Only Irene and I made it."

Sol's heart shattered, even though she didn't personally know them. She looked toward the Hound, where within it was the daughter of the woman who saved her mother's life. "Why? Why did my mother leave?"

Her aunt shrugged. "She never told us. Only that it was life or death, and we three were the only ones able to separate from the civil war within the castle."

Sol exhaled. "Who would even question her? Wasn't she the Queen?"

"By that time, she was undergoing trial. Her reign was taken by Semmena."

"And that is?"

Lora opened her mouth to respond but was interrupted by a creak of hinges and a scoff.

"My useless father."

Sol looked up to the second floor of the Inn where a window was now open and a woman with a single black braid looked down at them. Sawyer's dark eyes shone. "Your uncle-in-law, technically. Also, current King regent of Rimemere."

Lora smiled up at her. "I do hope Arnold is well, Sawyer."

Sawyer laughed. "I sure don't." Without another word, she disappeared beyond the wavering curtains.

Sol sighed, her attention lingering on the window. "There's no way we are related."

Lora arched her brow. "I kind of see it."

"Sunny!"

Sol swirled to find Leo jogging their way, relief flooding his eyes while he threw his arms around her.

"I didn't see you walk by last night on your way home, and I went to see if you were there just now, but you weren't and—"

He panted, holding her back by the shoulders to look at her. "I thought something happened."

She smiled. "I'm fine, Leo." A moment of silence, then she added, "Well, sort of."

"Let's talk inside, children." Lora gestured to the Inn. "We have much to say."

Chapter Six

Barmaids Don't Make Good Tea

The four Wielders were already in the tavern area, Sawyer being the last to enter. She gave Sol a smirk as she made her way down the stairs to join them.

They all wore similar armor, thin enough to keep their agility but reinforced with something like scales, the type of thing Sol had seen merchants marketing for hundreds of coins.

The tavern wasn't open to the public yet, available only to guests before noon. But besides them, no other guests were in sight.

Sol would have walked herself right back into her room if she had seen the people before her too.

"Who…" Leo stepped closer, gently tugging Sol behind him as he surveyed the Wielders.

Nina was the first to stand from her seat, her hands clasped in front of her, and a small smile pulling at her lips. "Hello," she said. "We are…"

"Friends," Lora interjected, saving Nina from coming up with anything.

Sol scoffed.

She would not call these people her friends. Perhaps not enemies...but definitely not friends either.

Leo sensed the word was too casual and gave Sol a side glance. "Friends?"

Sol shuddered. "Let's talk in the kitchen."

Without waiting for permission, she tugged Leo to the right toward the kitchen, painfully aware of the eyes that followed.

And as soon as they were behind the swinging door, Sol told him. Everything Lora had said, everything she had pieced together, she told him. Every single, life-shattering bit. By the end of it, he was silent. Sol wasn't even sure he was breathing. He gazed ahead, eyes glazed. But his breathing eventually evened out.

Sol was messing with a cluster of tea leaves on the counter when she finally whispered, "Please say something."

He cleared his throat and inhaled deeply. "I don't have much to say, Sunny."

"I should run, right? Get on a ship and sail far, far away?"

Leo huffed a small laugh and leaned over the counter, scooping Sol's hand into his. "I—I think you should go with them."

She cut her gaze to him, dropping the leaves. "What?"

"I think you should go with them," he repeated.

"You believe all this?"

"You don't?"

Sol blinked at him. At the question. Did she? It was something she couldn't quite answer to herself, much less to someone else. Perhaps she was just afraid to say what she truly thought—that a great part of her *did* believe it, despite the other wanting so hard not to.

"What's stopping you, Sunny?" Leo ran a thumb over her palm. "What's making you afraid?"

"I don't know these people, Leo. I don't know them or where they're from or what they do, I—" Sol took a deep breath, daring a second of vulnerability. "I don't know my own mother."

Instantly, she was in Leo's embrace, his strong arms wrapping around her tenderly. Sol hugged him back, her eyes burning with tears. "I don't want to leave all I know. I don't want to leave you or Mina."

Gently, Leo pulled back and brushed a stray tear from her cheek. "Growing pains hurt, Sol. There's a reason why they came to find you. Staying comfortable doesn't change the world."

You're needed to restore balance in Rimemere.

"I'll be no good as Queen. That's not me, Leo. I know nothing of that life. I don't want that life."

He tucked a strand of hair behind her ear. "You can't know that if you don't see what it offers first."

"Why are you being so uncharacteristically calm about this?"

Leo shrugged. "Because my best friend being the heir to a magical kingdom sounds really fucking cool."

"You're insane." Sol rolled her eyes, but the knot in her chest had eased slightly.

"Sol!" Lora's voice sang through the closed doors, then her head peaked through an open sliver. "Will you fix us some tea, dear?"

"They can get tea themselves."

"Great, herbal if you can!" She shut the door, completely ignoring Sol's defiance, and going back to chattering in the foyer.

Leo patted her shoulder and motioned behind to the door behind them, one that led to the back alley of the Hound. "I'm going to get something from home for you. Don't leave without saying goodbye."

Sol nodded meekly, then turned to the pantries to search for tea as Leo slipped into the back roads.

NINA

"She hates us," Nina sobbed, slumping into a wobbling wooden chair. "I knew we should have approached things differently."

"I think any way we would've done this would have resulted in her feeling betrayed, Nins." Alix slid an arm over her shoulders, warming her chilled skin.

The Inn was cold and humid, nothing like the castle in Rimemere. Nina sighed at the thought of a warm bath, of her bed after years of traveling and searching for the Yarrow heir who was finally here in front of them.

And she hated them.

"Maybe if we give her a gift…" Nina frowned.

Sawyer laughed, leaning back to lie on a dusty, crimson loveseat. "Like what, Nina? What gift could possibly convey the sentiment of 'sorry we're about to kidnap you and make you leave your life behind?'"

Tapping the table, Nina offered, "Flowers?"

She would have brought the stars down for their Princess if it meant having her trust them.

Nina had heard stories—rumors of her mother's friendship with Irene Yarrow. The Rimemere castle libraries still had portraits Irene painted of them strung around the shelves, portraits Nina admired any time she could. She had dreamed of having that same sort of friendship with Irene's child. Up until a month ago, the existence of that child had been a mere rumor.

But then that note found them in Graniela, leading them to Lady Lora and Yavenharrow. Whoever had sent them that letter with the Princess' location had been right indeed.

"It will take time for her to trust you," Lora said, walking toward them.

The woman radiated poise and knowledge, reflective of her previous position in Irene's court. The Royal Advisor, responsible for political relations and second to her mother Clarisse, Irene's Royal Hand. Lora Yarrow had been the only human to ever hold a position of power in Rimemere. She and Axel Yarrow had taken the Southern Continent by storm with their unprecedented union.

Nina read their history as a bedtime story through the years, praying to Flora she would one day have a love as great and unabridged as theirs.

Lora smiled at her. "I promise my niece is a kind soul. She is just..."

"Distrustful?" Sawyer scoffed. "Family trait, I guess."

"She might warm up to you first, Sawyer," Lora said, taking a seat on a chair beside Cas, who gave her a polite nod. "Family...it's important to her."

"You truly will not travel with us, Lady Lora?" Alix asked from beside Sawyer. "Yavenharrow is not safe any longer."

Lora shook her head. "I must reinforce the spells, to protect the people. I cannot leave while Irene's spells here deteriorate."

"Will you be able to do those alone?" Nina asked. "Dark Magic is...unforgiving, I've heard."

Looking out toward the window, Lora seemed lost in thought for a moment before responding. "I'll be fine. You all take care of her."

"King Semmena will want her to follow Rimemere traditions," Alix said, standing. "*All* of them."

Anger flickered through Lora's features. "Let Arnold do what he wants while he still can."

"Please boot him off the throne soon," Sawyer pleaded with a whine. "My father has become insufferable."

"He always has been," Cas muttered, breaking his silence.

Nina angled her head at him. "What happened last night?"

He looked over at her. "Which part?"

"How did you two end up in the Helian Ocean?"

Amusement danced in his eyes. "She took me off guard and threw us in."

"The great Cas Xanthos, Prince of Eswin and Royal Guard, bested by a girl with zero combat training." Sawyer gestured in front of her with each word, exaggerating them with the motions. "When the cadets get wind of that, they'll never let you live it down."

Lora chuckled. "Someone go back there to check on them. I'm afraid Sol will persuade the boy to jump on a ship with her to avoid this."

As soon as Leo was out of sight, Sol regretted not dragging him to the docks with her and onto a ship. When they were seventeen, Leo had traveled to the Scholar Towers to receive his formal diploma for finishing the fourteen levels of school. Sol always dreamed of doing the same, of studying and one day receiving her recognition as Scholar. Leo tried to persuade her to go with him, using the excuse she deserved celebration too since she always stole and studied his notes. But Sol stayed behind, taking care of Mina, counting down the twelve days it would take him to come back.

It had actually taken him twenty days to return, and when Sol had spotted him walking toward her after her shift at the Hound, she sobbed and clung to him the whole way home. They had made a pact that day to only sail together from then on.

Sol poured steaming water into a mug, sighing as the herbal scents caressed her.

Where would they go if she fled right now? Graniela?

The town was rich in exports, primarily woods and jewels. Or perhaps Hillarcliff, where Lora was born.

She threw a leaf of mint into the mix.

Maybe Rimemere wouldn't be terrible. Sol cursed the small spark of excitement that brewed within her. She had to get Lora to go with her. It was either travel with her, or not at all.

The worn hinges of the kitchen door creaked, prompting Sol to look up. She didn't think she would ever get used to the man's eyes. The kitchen suddenly felt too small as he stepped closer, those tendrils of shadows swirling around his ankles. Sol's eyes flickered to them as they spread toward her.

"They don't bite," he said, stopping in front of the counter where she lazily prepared a pot of tea.

She eyed the dark clouds. "They clearly do something."

Cas laughed, bracing an elbow on the countertop. "Well, they won't do anything to you."

"Why are you back here?" Sol tapped a foot on the floor, still eyeing the dancing smoke.

"Is it employees only?"

"You can stay if you answer more of my questions."

He bit on his lip, as if pondering it. "Depends on the questions."

Sol dropped the spoon on the table and thought through the billions of things she needed to know.

Lora had told her some of Nina's history, but she hadn't been able to say anything of anyone else. And if Sol would eventually have to travel with them, she would need to know *who* she traveled with.

"Who are you?" She locked her gaze on him, unwilling to seem small.

A smile pulled at the corner of his lip. "Cas."

"Cas what?"

"Cas Xanthos. Or Morozov, depending on who you ask."

"And what is your...position in this group?"

He arched a brow and pulled the empty cup toward him, then the mug of hot tea. "That also depends on who you ask."

Peeking from the sleeves of his scaled suit, what looked like a tattoo snaked around his right wrist, all the way down to his fingertips. And as he stretched his arm to grab the spoon from the table, the suit revealed his forearm, where a fresh, circular wound swelled with —

"Did...was that me?" Sol stammered, reaching to grab his arm out of instinct. Lora had always instructed her to inspect wounds to better determine what remedies would soothe them.

Cas pulled his arm back, and Sol instantly withdrew her hands. "Sorry."

"Yes, this was you. You have quite a bite." He held his arm between them and pulled his sleeve to his elbow, revealing the teeth marks already bruising.

Her face heated. "I...It was a reaction."

Cas served the tea into the cup, gently stirring the leaves aside. His black, wavy hair shielded his face as he took a sip.

"I'm not going back with all of you, you know," Sol said, crossing her arms across her chest. "Especially with your incredibly vague answers."

He looked at her over the rim of his cup, his brows scrunching as he set it down. "That...is terrible tea."

Sol scoffed and walked toward the kitchen door, deciding this man was not the one to have this conversation with. She was just about to push it open, when Cas said, "You are. You have to."

Slowly, she looked back at him. "I don't."

"It's already been decided, Princess."

"Not by me, it hasn't."

He gave her a slow smile, crossing his ankles as he leaned his back on the counter. Those silver eyes shining, he said, "Your aunt did warn us you were stubborn."

Without another word, Sol stomped back into the tavern.

CHAPTER SEVEN

LOVE IS TO BURN

After several minutes of Sol staring at the Wielders in silence and Nina looking like she might hurl, Lora pulled her aside. They went outside to the front yards where the sun was beginning to shine overhead, drying the left-over nighttime rain. People filtered in and out of the shops around them, some familiar faces sending them smiles and waves.

A pang of sadness hit Sol as she smiled back.

She wouldn't see her townsfolk again, wouldn't feel the saltwater breeze on her walk at the beach. She wouldn't be able to visit her mother's grave, and as her death anniversary approached, that last realization hit her the hardest.

Sol stopped on the street and faced Lora, "I'm not leaving. I don't care who they think I am or who my mother was, this is my home."

Her aunt reached into the pocket of her sweater. "Okay, Sol. Read this." She handed the worn piece of parchment to Sol. "If you still don't want to go after, I will respect it."

The parchment crinkled in her hands, and the slight smell of lavender made her memories stir. "What is this?"

"Your mother left it for you. In case this exact scenario happened, and she was no longer...around."

Sol blinked at the letter, holding it a little tighter. "I—"

"Read it, dove." Lora urged her forward, toward the docks. "Go. Then make your decision."

And although she should've feared the ocean after the night before, Sol clutched the letter to her chest and held her tears all the way to the shore.

SAWYER

Sawyer didn't particularly like Yavenharrow. It was humid and reeked slightly of fish, two things she disliked. They had always avoided this port town in their search for Irene's child, choosing to take the Rimemere docks out to the Northern islands instead.

But the gods did indeed have a sense of humor since they ended up finding her here.

She didn't know what she had expected of Sol. The stories of her Aunt Irene became rather dark toward the end of her reign, and stories were all she had since she was born after the Queen had abandoned her throne. Irene left her people to die and suffer the Jinn's brutal slaughters, instead of staying to kill them off like she was meant to.

Sawyer groaned, falling back into the love seat to stare at the Inn's ceiling.

Everyone thought she would be the savior, the only Yarrow left in Rimemere after her mother decided she too had enough and jumped to her death in the Melisandre Villa. With Irene gone, her Mother dead, and her Uncle Axel killed during his attempt to flee with Irene, Sawyer was the only one left. But she had been useless, as her Father so lovingly reminded her every time he saw her.

Her Semmena blood had taken to her instead of her Yarrow blood.

And it haunted her every single day.

"You seem oddly deep in thought," Alix said, sinking to a crouch in front of her. "I've never seen you so quiet."

"I can be quiet."

"But you usually aren't."

Sawyer sighed. "She's not what I expected."

Alix angled his head, his curls drifting with the motion. "What did you expect?"

"I don't know. Not a stubborn brat."

"Watch it, Sawyer," Nina called from behind the loveseat. Sawyer sat up slightly to peer at her best friend, the only person she had never threatened to incinerate. "You will respect the Princess."

"Yeah, yeah." Sawyer waved her off. "I'm only saying she could at least try to see our perspective."

"Her entire world changed overnight," Cas reminded from his place by a window. He looked out toward the beach. "Give her a break."

The front doors opened, and Lora Yarrow strode in, her honeysuckle eyes instantly finding Sawyer. The woman silently gestured her aside, and she followed her to the empty side of the tavern.

"Sawyer," she whispered. "I have something for you."

Sawyer watched her reach into her pocket to retrieve a thin, worn note.

"Irene left this for you—for her niece." Lora outstretched the folded paper, small specs of dust falling from it. "In case she was unable to return to Rimemere and the burden fell to Sol…" Lora met her gaze. "Because she was going to return, Sawyer. I don't know if you knew that."

She hadn't.

Her mother, Mel, had filled her head with all kinds of stories about Irene, mostly all negative, but with an expression that gave away the longing and pain their strained relationship had caused. Mel had only ever praised Irene's skills in Warding and Dark Magic, while at the same time blaming those skills for Rimemere's burdens.

What those burdens were, Sawyer never figured out, and her mother killed herself before she could ask.

Sawyer sighed and took the parchment from Lora. "What are we to do with Sol? She clearly won't come with us."

Lora just smiled. "She will." She gestured to the letter. "Read it. Alone."

Sawyer made to walk outside, briefly meeting each of her companion's curious gazes. The sun instantly greeted her, prompting her to walk to a small shop with a cloth roof.

The shop owner gave her a glare as she ripped open the crimson seal.

Dearest niece,

IF YOU ARE READING THIS, THEN I HAVE FAILED. I AM SO SORRY. IT'S UP TO YOU AND SOL NOW.

I LOVE YOUR MOTHER SO MUCH, SAWYERLYN. MEL IS EVERYTHING TO ME, BUT SHE DOESN'T SEE. SHE IS BLINDED BY HIM.

YOU HAVE TO MAKE HER SEE, IF SHE IS SPARED BY OUR TERRIBLE FATE.

PLEASE TAKE CARE OF SOL, SAWYER. KEEP HER COURT—YOUR COURT—CLOSE.

AND PLEASE....

BURN THEM DOWN.

-I. YARROW

SOL

Sol had never noticed how blue the ocean in Yavenharrow was. It was the blue of sapphires and butterfly pea flowers.

It was the blue of her mother's eyes and the moment right before sunrise.

She traced the lapping waves with her gaze, welcoming the sprinkles of salt water that landed on her cheek.

At least they camouflaged the tears.

Sol wondered which god her family had offended to be condemned to such a fate. Well, she supposed it was the god of Wards.

She gripped her mother's note tighter, then brought out the book she had grabbed from the Archives. One last time. One last reading.

Sol opened the book to a random page, then read aloud,

"In the beginning of time, four gods wandered Erriadin. Bored, they forged four items from their respective elements and then hid them amongst the land.

"They dared each other to find them all, and the winner would inherit all elements into their magical arsenal. After centuries of searching, Aquarene had found Emberdon's Relic, and Flora found both Aquarene and Winderlyn's. However, Winderlyn grew tired of the search. And from water and clay, Winderlyn constructed humans, convincing Emberdon to grant them life with his all-mighty flames."

Sol wiped a tear with her sleeve, then turned the page.

"And thus, humans were placed on Erriadin, and each god chose their favorites to bless with their elements, forever abandoning the search for their Relics. Centuries after their creation, the Wielders discovered within all Light, Dark dwindled. That darkness took shape and grew teeth, birthing Dark Magic to rival the Light Magic their gods had gifted them. Then, after Warren's emergence into a deity, it is rumored he constructed his own Relic, though kept hidden for himself instead of joining the forgotten game."

Sol stopped reading. Would the basic knowledge from these books and stories Irene told her throughout the years grant her any advantage in Rimemere? Surely her mother had her reasons for not giving her more, including Awakening her magic.

An overwhelming sense of betrayal settled into her chest, a soft promise she would get the answers she was owed. And somehow outsmart destiny.

"How did I know I would find you here?"

Sol wiped her face with her sleeve and gave Leo a small smile as he sat beside her. "Not many other places I like to go," she said.

He scanned her face, then looked down at the note. "Everything alright?"

She tucked it into her pocket, pulling her hair behind her ears. "No."

"Do you want to talk about it?"

"Also no."

He exhaled through his nose and turned to rummage through his satchel. "Now, don't get mad."

Sol raised a brow and leaned forward. "No promises."

A soft clang sounded as Leo retrieved a beautifully crafted iron dagger from the depths of his bag. The steel shone in the sunlight, the hilt adorned by silver vines with a small green jewel at its tip.

He held it out to her. "I was going to give it to you for your birthday in a few months, but—"

"Leo, no." Sol pushed the dagger back. "It must have cost a fortune."

He chuckled, rolling his eyes as he dropped it into her lap. "Take it. You'll need it."

Sol stared at the winking metal. "I can't do this. I have to, but I can't."

Leo wrapped an arm around her shoulders and pulled her close, his warmth easing her nerves. "I have no advice on how to rule a kingdom, Sunny, but I know if anyone would be good at it, it's you."

Sol let Leo brace her up while they walked back to the docks. Although she felt Irene was a stranger at the moment, it was obvious her mother knew her well by leaving the note. She wouldn't have agreed to leave Yavenharrow without it.

I need you to listen. Don't question—only listen.

With knots in her chest, Sol stopped at various merchant carts to look at her town's exports and beauties a final time. She would visit, she would have to. But when that would be, she didn't know.

Especially if what the note her mother left proved true.

The Hound was silent when she pushed its doors open, but a few of the upstairs guests had made their way down to search for food. And as Sol had been absent, she could only assume one of them summoned Keelin, who stood fuming behind the bar.

As soon as he spotted Sol, he marched her way. "Leaving the place unattended, Sol? One would think you're new here."

Keelin might have gotten closer, had Cas not stepped out from the shadows beside her and extended an arm to stop him. "That's close enough."

"And who the fuck are you?" Keelin surveyed him, then the rest of Sol's newfound companions as they walked up around her.

"Friends," Sawyer said. "With bad tempers."

Sol searched around for Lora, though her aunt was nowhere to be seen. She cast a glance to Leo, who motioned outside. "She said she'd see you at home."

Sol nodded and turned back to Keelin. "I quit. Sorry for the short notice."

The man's cyan eyes blazed. "You can't just quit!"

"I can. Sorry." Sol swirled on a heel and made to exit the Hound Inn, thinking she'd feel at least some remorse but felt something like hope instead.

CHAPTER EIGHT

No Rest for the Dead

Sol went straight home. Leo insisted on going into the town to scout for necessities she might need on her voyage, but accepting such an offer made it too real.

Nina also insisted on following Sol around like a puppy, mostly because the Jinn's magical signature—whatever that was—still lingered nearby. Sol protested initially, but eventually decided the woman wasn't terrible. Instead of the town, Sol veered to the farmlands, unable to bring herself to return to the beach, even for a final farewell.

They walked in silence through the tall, yellowing grass, focusing on the way it swayed as they took the long way to her cottage.

Sawyer and Cas kept a fair distance, both spreading into the land somewhere, scouting or doing whatever it was they did. She walked beside Nina and Alix, and Sol concluded she didn't mind Alix either. He was mostly quiet, offering only small kernels of information about the plant life they passed, or the small critters that ran across the roads. Nina, with her earth magic, made the small flowers bud into gorgeous blooms, and even went as far as to pick a Tigerlily for her.

And who isn't swayed by flowers?

The Wielders returned to the Hound by twilight, this time having to pay the regular guest fare. Lora packed some herbs and salves in Sol's satchel for her to take, though Sol stared at the things begrudgingly and tried to unpack instead.

She ate the seafood stew her aunt crafted, then retreated to her room before Lora could try to speak of Rimemere or magic or anything else Sol wanted to put on hold.

As she stared at her cracking ceiling, she zipped her necklace back and forth on its chain and sighed.

Surely there was a way out. Surely her mother's letter couldn't be true. Surely there were alternatives. Because the reality of there not being any was almost as overbearing as her succeeding.

Sol didn't realize she had fallen asleep until she awoke engulfed in winter. Sitting up from the comfort of her duvet, she slowly shifted her legs over the edge of the bed. Her breaths pooled in a mist in front of her face and her room was dark, illuminated only by the moonlight that seeped through her window. A harsh series of rumbles sounded beyond her room's closed door, the vibrations thrumming across the walls like a heartbeat.

Instantly, Sol was on her feet and reaching for her satchel where her knives and Leo's gifted dagger were. She tore through it and armed herself, then secured the bag around her chest.

The banging continued, making her books and things clatter to the ground with the force. Tears burned behind her eyes as she whispered, "Aunt Lora?"

"*Yaaaarooow,*" a voice called, one that instantly made Sol's blood ice over with fear. Slowly, she turned in the direction of it, toward her window.

If it wasn't for the pair of arms that grabbed her by the shoulders and pulled her away, Sol might have fainted at the horrible sight beyond the glass.

The Jinn peered into her room, its gray skin decrepit beneath the silver light of the moon. Round eyes were wholly black and focused on her, and when she slammed back into the hard body behind her, the Jinn grinned its wicked smile.

Sol fought against the assailant, sure her luck had run out and she would be Jinn food. But they released her, giving her the opportunity to raise her dagger at them.

"Careful." Cas jumped back, his armored forearm colliding with her knife. "First you bite me and now you want to stab me?"

Sol tried to steady her breathing as she said, "Maybe you should stop grabbing me without my permission then."

Behind her, a tap sounded on her window. Sol recoiled as she looked over her shoulder to watch the Jinn's talons scrape against the glass.

"They can smell you more than they can see you," he remarked in a hushed voice. "You were too close to the window."

Slowly, Sol turned back to face the man. "Where's my Aunt? Why are you here?"

He gestured to the door. "Living room. As soon as you left that Inn, we felt the Jinn around. We came over here to make sure you both are—"

Sol didn't care to let him finish as she eased past him and threw her room door open. It was the sort of chill that penetrated all the way down to the bones, the kind that produced shivers instantly. As soon as she stepped into the dark living space, she knew her life was about to change.

Maybe it was the way Lora lifted her head from her hands as she stood in the center of the room. Maybe it was the way Nina had her hand draped over her aunt's shoulders in comfort. Or maybe it was the fact the only thing Sol could see beyond the windows, was Jinn.

Cas closed the door behind them, forcing her to step further into the freeze.

Tears stained Lora's face, and she instantly pulled Sol into a desperate embrace. Sol let herself cry as well, knowing within her what came next.

Softly, her Aunt whispered, "I thought we had more time."

The horrible banging began once again, and Sol could now see it was something pushing against the front door, causing it to shake.

At that moment, Sol wondered why her mother had left these things alive. Why had she chosen to flee from her purpose and leave those creatures to roam Erriadin if she was the one charged with extinguishing them?

"I'll hold them off," Cas said, turning to the door. Sawyer and Alix flanked it, both with equally tense expressions.

"It's no use, child." Lora stopped him by his arm. "They won't stop. You can kill these, and new ones will sprout out of the Void itself to get to Sol." Lora turned to face her. "Now they know you live, they won't stop until they kill you. All of you must leave."

Panic rose in Sol's chest as she gripped Lora harder. "I'm not going anywhere."

"You must."

"I will not—"

A rattle resonated from Sol's room, tearing the words from her mind. Instantly, a gentle hand eased her closer to the Wielders. Nina smiled sadly at her as she positioned herself between Sol and her room, then Sawyer stepped to guard their backs.

Everything was wrong.

Too many people were putting themselves in the way of danger for her, and she felt herself begin to unravel at the thought of her being at fault for any negative outcomes.

She couldn't process that again.

"Listen to me, Sol. If you die, if you get hurt, everyone pays. Everyone. It's not the time to be selfless and try to help or ease people's pain, it's time for the opposite." Lora reached into her pocket and gathered materials she proceeded to drop into Sol's satchel.

"I give it maybe five minutes before they start gnawing at the walls," Sawyer muttered, her fingertips sparkling. "Then maybe thirty seconds until they start charging."

"Sawyer don't invoke them," Nina chastised. "They can hear you."

In response, a lanky Jinn with a gaping hole in its cheek tapped on the window, smiling from rotting ear to ear.

Sol shuddered. "I'm not leaving you here with these things, Aunt Lora. And Leo—"

Leo. Mina.

Sol couldn't leave her town and everything she loved in the claws of those demons. The people were innocent.

"No offense, dove, but you won't be much use here without your magic." Lora gave her a long look, as if memorizing her, then retrieved a small dagger from her skirt pocket. It was delicate, but stunning, the kind of craftsmanship that had to be from overseas. The steel shone with the stray moonlight and the emerald jewels encrusted along its handle winked as Lora sliced the blade along her palm.

Blood dripped onto the wooden floors, and with each drop, the pounding on the door increased.

"*Yarrroooow,*" the things hissed in unison. "*Let us innnn.*"

"I don't think the seals will last much longer, Lady Lora," Nina warned, pointing to the foot of the front door, where Alix knelt and inspected what seemed like glyphs.

He shook his head. "They're deteriorating."

"You will leave. You will finish what Irene started." Lora clasped Sol's hand and sliced her palm without warning.

Sol winced and watched in wonder as Lora joined their wounded hands together and closed her eyes. She didn't know what to say, only knew she felt everything all at once in a debilitating wave as a golden mist illuminated the darkness. The mist wrapped around their wrists and slid up their arms until Sol felt it melt within her chest with a warm sigh.

It felt as if she was in a dream, floating along muted streams of consciousness.

"What is this," Sol asked slightly breathless. "What did you do?"

Nina's face paled as she beheld their still joined hands. She looked at Lora. "A blood bond."

Her Aunt nodded. "A very simple bit of Dark Magic so we can be connected while you're gone." Lora placed her forehead on Sol's. "I will not leave the people here unprotected. And I cannot focus on both them and you, dove."

The front door splintered open with a piercing boom, the sound so violent it pushed Sol back into Nina and Cas.

"Take her. Now!" Lora spun to face the entrance.

Someone grabbed Sol by the waist and ran, taking her away from her family and friends and everything that mattered. She stared at the Jinn as they poured into her cottage. Lora stretched her hands in front of her and bellowed a fierce series of chants before she was engulfed in a blinding violet light.

As Sol yearned to see more, to make sure her Aunt was alive and okay and this wasn't history repeating itself, her kidnappers dragged her out the back door and took her away from her home.

CHAPTER NINE

THE JOURNEY AHEAD

It took Sol a whole hour of traveling on foot to stop trying to escape. Between attempted escapades, she took in the moon's place in the sky. Sawyer dragged her along at first, when the moon had been near the horizon, then after Sol stomped on her foot in an attempt to flee, she was passed over to Cas.

Sol immediately protested, she wasn't a rabid dog that needed containment, so she was eventually left in the center of their circle with a bit less restraint as the moon settled a quarter higher.

Apparently, the Wielders' horses were left on the outskirts of Yavenharrow, tied to a post near a trough of water by a small, abandoned farm. They were to ride through the rest of the night and hopefully, most of the next day since Rimemere was a week's ride away.

Sol couldn't help but constantly look back to Yavenharrow the further away they went as if waiting for a sign or signal or omen. But the town was silent.

Eerily so.

She didn't notice when they finally came before the horses until the Wielders broke their circle to reveal them.

Instantly, Sol shook her head. "There is no way I'm mounting one of those."

The creatures were massive, daunting things, all staring her down as if she was a plump, juicy apple.

They huffed at her.

"They look scarier than they are," Sawyer said, stepping up to release one from the wooden fence it was anchored to. "Unless it's Kahaida. She is just as terrible as she looks."

In response, a horse separated from the others, the color of ashy sand.

"Not true!" Nina whined and strode to it, the horse instantly trying to nibble at her auburn hair. "She is just selective."

Sol's head buzzed with a cocktail of feelings. Everything was unfamiliar. She had never felt like running backward but also trudging forward at once, battling the taut string of destiny tugging her onto her mother's homeland while simultaneously feeling tethered to Yavenharrow.

For a few hours, she remained silent, defeated atop Kahaida with Nina a soft presence behind her. She went back and forth between nostalgia and excitement, finally settling on indifference.

The homesickness would fade—it had to.

Right?

"We will stop for the night soon, Princess."

Sol flinched at Nina's voice as it sliced through the night.

"Please don't call me that." Sol shifted in the saddle. It was too soon and too unnerving to so willingly sink into that identity.

"What should we call you, then?"

"Just Sol."

"Typically, royalty is addressed with titles—names are sacred."

The sentence echoed within Sol, reminding her of the similar things her mother would say. The longer she was with the strangers, the uncanny similarities between them and her mother gave her an odd sense of familiarity.

She fought against it.

"Why is that?" Sol stared at the trees ahead, tugging at her braid. "My mother used to say the same."

"Our magic comes from our names—our bloodlines. When a Wielder Awakens, they offer their name to the gods, hoping one of them will bless them with their magic." Nina gently eased Kahaida to a stop. "After one picks you, your name belongs to them. No one else but you and them are allowed to utter it fully."

"Seems like a rule easy to break," remarked Sol.

Nina laughed. "It is, often other Wielders say names out of spite. But the gods who own the uttered name deal with them."

"The good old days when the ones who broke that rule would just explode were so fun," Sawyer said beside them as she dismounted her horse. "The gods aren't as brutal anymore."

They stopped at the beginning of a patch of hills. The moonlight vaguely illuminated the compact line of trees ahead, which seemed to spiral into tendrils of darkness. They stood in an open clearing surrounded only by those hills and rows of evergreens.

"Here, Nins? It's kind of out in the open." Alix frowned as he inspected the surroundings.

"We need to rest. The next mountain that can provide coverage is hours away." Nina eased off Kahaida then held out her hand to Sol.

Sol didn't take it and instead clumsily slid off the beast.

"We take turns, then," Cas said. "I will take first watch."

Unsurprisingly, Sol didn't sleep. She lay in the tent Sawyer materialized out of her pack, staring at the fraying seams. The sound of nature was soothing, reminiscent of Yavenharrow, but the murmurs and outline of the fire reminded her she was far, far from home.

The Wielders grew silent over the course of a few hours, so much so that Sol peeked her head out with hopes they had left.

They had not.

She resisted the nagging urge to mount the kindest-looking horse and gallop back the way they came. The night had grown cold enough Sol saw her breath in small puffs as she eased from the tent. Nina and Sawyer lay side by side near the fire, then Alix sat behind them, resting his head on a tree. They looked peaceful, almost human-like while they slept—no signs of those brutally trained individuals from the day before. Sol didn't think she would ever be able to replace that first impression.

"I thought you promised not to run away."

Sol nearly fell back into the tent. "Gods."

Cas leaned on a tree opposite his court mates, sharpening what looked like a branch into a stake. He wiped the wisps of wood away from the tip. "I told them not to trust you."

"I'm not running away," she said. "Although I thought about it."

"Out of curiosity," he glanced at her, "which horse would you have taken?"

"Not Kahaida—she tried to eat my braid earlier."

A small smile pulled at the corners of his lips. "She is probably the only one who would have listened to you. The others are trained not to let other riders that aren't theirs on them alone."

"Shouldn't you sleep?" She crossed her arms over her chest. "I swear I won't run."

"I'm not tired. And I don't trust you."

Silence fell.

"So, what's your deal?" Sol walked around the campfire. "You refused to tell me back at the Hound. And you've made an awful first impression by chasing me into the ocean."

Cas paused his carving. "Now, *I* didn't do that, Princess. *You* did."

She shrugged, "Semantics."

Resuming his weapon crafting, he said, "Officially, I'm your royal guard."

"And unofficially?"

He tapped the blade on the stake. "Just along for Sawyer's commentary."

"I heard that," Sawyer said, her eyes still closed.

Beside her, Nina giggled. "Aren't we all?"

The burning was stronger this time.

Sol didn't think she would ever get used to her birthmark flaring, but at that particular moment, it caught her too off-guard. It was a spear in the center of her back then a thick, pulsing oil spreading across the star's peaks. Her body wasn't her own as she fell to her knees and suppressed a yell.

"What's wrong?" Instantly, Nina was beside her.

But Sol couldn't speak, she clawed at her shirt and skin, feeling too tight in them both.

"*Off*," she said through tight teeth, nails digging into the ground.

One of them pulled her shirt off, leaving her in her breeches and camisole. Sol didn't care, she wanted to beg to take that off too if it meant the burning subsided.

"Sol, how do you make it stop?" Nina shook her at the shoulders. "Has it ever done this before?"

"The Yarrow mark. It's magic in itself," Alix knelt beside her. "Here, let me see."

Sol vaguely saw Sawyer and Cas standing over them, both with their blades out.

"If it burns, perhaps I can soothe it." Alix pulled Sol into his arms, carefully placing his palms over her mark. Slowly, the fire dwindled, and it was as if she had been doused with cold water.

Sol inhaled and exhaled, dropping her head on his shoulder in defeat.

Her mother had never truly explained the mark's purpose or origins, only that most of her ancestors had one as well. She said it was a family mark and joked that it only condemned them to the occasional discomfort. But Sol had never had to deal with it as often as she had in the last few days. It made her wish she would have taken Lora up on her offers to construct a salve for it when she was younger.

Sawyer crouched, meeting Sol at eye level. "Better?"

Sol struggled to keep her eyes open as relief flooded through her. "Better."

"Does that happen often?" Alix asked, patting her back, sending more waves of cool.

Sol shook her head. "Not usually, but it has lately."

"Last time was at the docks, right?" Cas asked.

Sol thought about it, her head pounding with leftover pain, then gave him a small nod.

Nina didn't wait for a response as she shot to her feet. "The docks had Jinn. Alix, stay with her. The rest of us will do a land sweep."

For once, Sol swallowed her protests and savored the sweet, cool magic.

They stayed like that for a long while. Sol hadn't realized how much she truly just needed to be held by a person. Her racing thoughts slowed, and her anxiety drifted. She was almost disappointed when she finally peeled herself from him, her face heating at the realization that she clung to the man for nearly twenty minutes.

She smiled meekly. "Sorry."

"Don't apologize. At your service." He juggled a stream of water along his fingertips.

Sol folded her legs beneath her, then crossed her arms over her torso. "Is my shirt anywhere?"

With a chuckle, Alix tossed it to her. "Has it ever felt like that before?"

Sol shook her head. "No. I'm not even sure what it means."

"There isn't much recorded on Yarrow marks, your mother and all the ones marked before her were rather secretive about it." Alix outstretched his legs and ran a hand over his tousled hair. "But we do know it's connected to your magic somehow."

"I don't have any."

"*Yet*. You will."

The idea she might have any sort of magic refused to register within her. She, in absolutely no corner of her imagination, could see herself handling the gifts these people so elegantly carried. Even though she had only found out her mother was a Wielder days ago, she could clearly picture Irene being great at it. Her mother had always had that gleam of mystery as if she always had something to say but couldn't. Her head was always held high and smile casually fierce, even when Sol tried her very best to get her angry just to see what it would look like.

Sol leaned back on her palms, releasing the memories into the wind. "I'm so lost."

"I know you must have a lot of questions." Alix gave her a small side smile. "After the official meeting with the Semmena Court, we will work to answer them."

Sol sighed. "I don't believe I've had the opportunity to ask what your duties are here within the group."

"I'm your Royal Scribe." He smiled, though a shadow passed through his features. "My father was High Scribe, then later demoted after Irene's departure." Sol couldn't help but notice the way he referred to his father in past tense, a spark of sympathy growing in her chest. "I'm sorry."

He looked her way. "Politics are brutal. It's something we all know when we choose our sides."

"There's sides?"

He nodded. "You'll see soon enough. It's something best experienced."

A shiver snaked through her, steering the change of subject. "And what of the others?" She cast a glance around them and toward the trees where the other three had disappeared. "I know basic stuff, but..."

"We all have different duties. Both as Rimemere soldiers and part of your Court." He stood and held out a hand to her.

"I, as a Water Dancer, oversee the ports at least twice a week, or used to at least...not sure if we will return to our old duties. Anyway, and as your Scribe, provide information and knowledge."

"Sawyer," Alix continued as Sol stood, "Is your Combat Leader. She will be the line holder and commander were we ever to go to war. As a Fire Wielder, and part of the Yarrow lineage, she is also Royal General of the Rimemere troops."

"It's still bizarre to think she's my cousin," said Sol, brushing the dirt off her breeches. "I didn't even know I had an aunt aside from maybe a vague mention of her."

"I'm sure Irene had her reasons for keeping everything so guarded. I wouldn't let it get to you."

The ruffle of trees prompted her to look up, ready to bolt if those beady black eyes emerged from the foliage. But instead of black and soulless, they were silver and steel.

Sol released a breath and all her anxiety with it when Cas appeared in the clearing. "All seems well," he said. "We didn't see anything."

"I really don't think my birthmark has anything to do with those things." Sol bounced on her feet. "It probably just flared with the weather."

"Well, no harm in checking, Princess," Nina said, coming through the trees with Sawyer close behind. The Earth Caller cast an apologetic smile her way. "Sorry—Sol."

And although she fought it, Sol returned the gesture before settling herself back into her tent with the zipper open, sure to keep in sight of the Wielders for the rest of the night.

The next two and a half days passed by in similar ways. They traveled, rested, ate, and repeated. During their breaks, Sol took advantage of the stillness and asked questions, most answered by Nina and Alix, while Sawyer and Cas dozed off. Sol learned Rimemere had been deemed a myth only because ancient enchantments kept it hazy in human minds, while Wielders all had an unspoken, collective agreement to keep the birthplace of their magic a secret. The more who it did not pertain to learned of it, the more risk of developing tension within Erriadin that wasn't needed—according to Alix, civil unrest amongst the Wielders was enough without adding humans with no connections to them into the mix.

It was during the final night that Sol's birthmark flared again, and Nina was not having it. The occurrence was bizarre enough, even though no Jinn were spotted this time either, she was condemned to ride with Cas the rest of the way in order to be Warded.

She had seen his Wards once briefly at the Hound before Sawyer tried to incinerate her face with a fireball. At least that's what she thought it had been. But seeing the magic up close in a less chaotic headspace was—breathtaking. Almost more distracting than his arms around her waist.

Almost.

His horse, Lilah, was gentle, much more so than Nina's, but still required occasional guidance with the reins. So, she was confined to a very limited range of motion, unless she wanted to melt to the ground with embarrassment.

If she leaned back, she would be pressed into Cas's chest. Either side and his forearms dug into her hips. Forward and her lower back would—

To busy herself, Sol quickly learned that Lilah responded to pats and gentle caresses, so she spent a long while doing so in silence while looking at the shimmering violet orb of lightning rods around them.

"So, you have Shadows and Wards?" she asked, lacing her fingers through Lilah's mane. "Is it common to have two?"

Cas adjusted his grip on the reins. "Yes, I'm a Dual Wielder. And no, it's not common."

"Is it difficult to have both?"

"Sometimes."

She blinked at the sparks of lightning "And what happens if I touch the—the Ward?" She itched to reach out and trace the sparks with her fingertips.

Behind her, Cas shrugged. "Depends on my mood."

"Does that go for your Shadows?"

"Mhm."

"Is all magic...responsive like that?"

The Ward flared slightly. "To an extent. The difference between Shadows and Wards is they can both harm or soothe, depending on what the wielder wants. Fire will always burn, water will always douse. It's difficult to explain." He nudged the back of her shoulder slightly. "You can touch it."

Sol peered back at him. "Touch what?"

"The Ward," he smirked. "It won't hurt you."

Sol turned back to face Lilah and the wider portion of the Ward. "Are you sure?"

"Pretty sure."

It might have been stupid, but the static was entrancing. As she reached to it, she wondered if that was part of the magic's play, to entrance the victim into its grasp.

Hesitantly, her fingers swept the violet haze and she flinched—but nothing happened. The static spread around her palm, tingling, and fizzy, but nothing as severe as she thought.

The sensation was almost…familiar.

She continued playing with the Ward. "So, what's Rimemere like? Is it really like the stories?"

"What do your stories say?"

"You know, the usual. A castle. Pretty things. Magic."

"A castle, yes. Mostly for Nobles and the current ruling parties. Students also frequent there to train with the royal guards. Pretty things? Subjective. Magic? Sometimes."

Sol rolled her eyes. "Your answers are always quite underwhelming."

"You'll have to judge it for yourself, Princess. Though, I'm sure it's all a step up from what you're used to."

Sol shifted in the saddle, purposely digging her elbow into his abdomen. "What makes you think just because there's a castle and pretty things it's a step up?"

He switched the reins to one hand, using the other to reinforce his ward with a wave. "A guess."

A guess.

Anger flared within Sol as she turned to face away, Lilah protesting beneath them. "Of course, someone like you would think castles and riches are all there is." Tears burned in her throat. They didn't understand. Why would they? "But being with people you love will always mean more than that."

And now she was alone, in a foreign place, struggling to hold on to her sense of identity as best she could.

"Are you crying?" Cas scoffed. "Is getting whisked away from a tiny town to a giant castle with everything you can possibly want really so bad?" His words were laced with judgment. She clenched her jaw. "Again, I don't expect the likes of you to understand."

"The likes of you?" his voice lowered.

"You know, spoiled, rich, probably had everything handed to him and his family on silver platters."

She slammed back into his chest as he yanked the reins, pulling Lilah to a sudden stop. "Hey!"

His silver eyes simmered. "You'll be surprised to know, because our families chose yours, we grew up with the exact opposite treatment."

She peered up at him. "I truly doubt life in a luxurious castle could be any kind of inconvenience."

Cas grabbed her by the shoulders and pushed her off the saddle. Sol barely had time to land on her feet before he trotted ahead, calling back to the others, "Someone else take her."

Sol coughed as dirt from Lilah's hooves flew into her eyes.

"Well, that's a record," Sawyer laughed. "Haven't seen someone piss him off so quickly."

"He started it," Sol mumbled.

"Come on, Princess. I will take you the rest of the way." Nina outstretched her hand. "We are past the part that needed Warding anyway."

Sawyer might have been the Fire Wielder, but smoke seemed to follow Cas the rest of the way.

CHAPTER TEN

Leon

Leon hadn't seen so many Jinn since—well, ever. Irene had told him stories, stories he always thought she exaggerated. But the day Sol left Yavenharrow, he realized they might have been *under* exaggerated.

The demons came from everywhere. From every crack in the land and pocket of the sea, they flooded into town with their waxy skin and rancid smiles. It took him and Lora two full days to contain the invasion and a whole heap of Dark Magic.

The townsfolk who hadn't been slaughtered, fled. The ones who remained were Wielders on travels, most committed to helping Lora when her identity was revealed. It was hard to abandon the only human on Erriadin that could wield Dark Magic.

"How are you?" Leo knelt beside her, the town around them a silent snapshot of pure massacre. Even the air itself seemed to hum with unease.

Lora inhaled calculated, careful breaths. "Fine."

"You used a lot of magic."

"Had to."

"We could have fled."

Lora shook her head. "Irene had a reason to protect Yavenharrow, one she wouldn't share even with me. But I trust her judgment."

Leo sighed and looked out to the town square. Buildings stood broken with roofs tilted from the fights. Typically, Air Singers could avoid landmarks with their winds, but Leo was untrained. The little he knew about his magic had come from Irene, who hadn't been an Air Singer.

He kicked pebbles away from Lora and cursed his father silently for being a coward and choosing not to train him. He gritted his teeth at the realization the invasion was probably his doing.

"Do you think this is my fault?" Leo asked softly, sinking to the ground. "Because I told them she was here?"

Lora's gaze turned distant, hazed, the whites of her eyes stained red. "I think they were close to finding her anyway."

"Her Court?"

"The Jinn."

Leo swallowed. "How do you think she is doing? I—feel guilty not telling her I knew."

Lora stood, brushing dust from her skirts. Her fair, worn face was stained with mud. "Fine. Probably pissed at one of those four by now, but she's alive. I'd know otherwise." She absentmindedly caressed the scar on her palm. "And don't feel guilty, Leon. We were all told not to tell her anything."

Leo sighed, knowing she was right. When Irene pulled him aside at fifteen and asked him what he would do for Sol, he meant it when he said *"anything."* But he could never have imagined what he agreed to.

"That was dumb, Lora. A blood bond?" He eyed the scar. "Sol shouldn't be near that at all."

"It was my only way to know she's okay, Leon. I was in a time crunch."

Blood bonds were born from the pits of Dark Magic. A sliver of the mage's blood spilled into the receiving person, then took hold of their skin in the form of a raised, red scar. Not only could one tell if the other person died, but —as was its main purpose—the caster could control and siphon their own magic to the receiver.

At a price, of course.

"I won't be lending her Dark Magic if that's what you're thinking." Lora raised a brow. "Don't need Arnold getting a whiff I'm alive, though I'm sure word of this mess will reach him soon."

Leo angled his head. "Are you really okay?"

The mage's eyes were sunken, shadows and veins all over her skin. Wordlessly, she nodded and made back into the Hound Inn, a tattered mess in the aftermath of war. "I feel okay—but if I start looking blue and smiling cynically, please do kill me, boy."

CHAPTER ELEVEN
Sand and Stone Walls Don't Mix

By the time they crossed the Dunes of San'ann, Sol wished the sun would disappear. The beige sands reflected the rays so intensely she was sure to be cherry red by the time they crossed the basin. The horses were hot. Everyone was hot. Just when she was about to ask to ride with Alix and his icy mists, she saw it.

It was a dark splotch on the horizon at first, then slowly progressed to a bigger, taller spec until it finally consumed the entire plane of her vision. The wall erupted from the sands and rose to the skies, clouds covering where it finished to make it seem endless. It was made of dark sandstone, such a contrast to the tawny sand surrounding it that Sol couldn't help but stare.

Nina seemed to have a knack for deciphering Sol's questions, or the confusion was so clearly strung across her face. The Earth Caller said, "The wall is relatively new I heard. It is guarded and meant to keep Jinn out, but I argue it actually keeps the stragglers in."

Sol tightened her hands around Kahaida's reigns. "Who guards it?"

A screeching sounded from behind the wall, a part of it booming open to allow a group of eight soldiers through.

Beside Sol, Sawyer rolled her eyes, her horse seeming to mirror the gesture. "They do." She trotted ahead slightly and added, "Or at least they claim to."

Nina pulled Kahaida to a swift stop and dismounted, holding out her elbow for Sol. "Sawyer has a particularly strained relationship with the Kingsmen. They're perpetually disagreeable."

Alix dismounted his horse, followed by Cas, who Sol was sure almost landed on the heel of her boots on purpose. She pursed her lips at him in warning to which he responded with a wink.

Well, at least it seemed he was over the previous day's disagreement.

"Aside from the wall being enchanted to confuse, it also requires brands from the soldiers to cross. The only bloodline that doesn't require their brand—"

Nina was interrupted by Sawyer sauntering by, Fey trotting beside her. She didn't bother greeting the soldiers who watched her pass, but she did peer over her shoulder and give them a fiery wave before disappearing across the open wall.

Literally disappeared. Sol supposed nothing else could surprise her at this point, but she still shook her head and blinked at the spot where her cousin was—then wasn't.

Nina sighed. "Only Yarrows can enter without a brand."

"Sawyer loves to remind them of that," said Alix with a smirk. He flanked Sol's other side. "Pisses them off."

"Looks like all those years of travel didn't teach that bitch any manners," a soldier clad in full armor and a scruffy beard remarked, prompting a laugh from the other men behind him.

Any sort of fear Sol felt was quickly replaced with annoyance as she cut her eyes to him. Sure, Sawyer had a temper, but a rather unwelcome sense of protectiveness struck her at the disrespect.

The comment affected the others similarly, it seemed, as Cas stepped behind Sol, the motion only decipherable by the warmth he radiated. She tried not to shiver as he said, "She's your General."

The man shrugged, amusement flickering in his eyes. "That role has been vacant for years as you four partied and fucked around all the corners of Erriadin while we actually did something useful."

"I'd be careful what you say, Finigan," Alix warned. "Especially after the journey we've had."

A warm breeze shifted through their group, blowing the sand in wisps around them. Sol covered her eyes with her forearm, unfortunately calling the main soldier's attention to her.

His beady eyes narrowed beneath ginger brows. "And what have you all brought back? A whore?"

Another soldier stepped up, leaning against Finigan's shoulders. "Xanthos's whore, if I had to guess."

It was Nina who snapped first. With a swift wave of her arm, sand compacted into a limb and slammed into the men, thrusting them aside. Her eyes shone as she stomped over to them, and all Sol could do was watch, astonished at the rare display of anger from the Earth Caller.

Sol didn't ever want to have that anger directed at her.

"You will respect Prince Xanthos and the rest of the Royal court. I don't know what's happened while we have been gone, but it's best you all resolve the attitude quickly and let us through."

"We don't let whores through the wall, Amana." Finigan stood, shaking off the sand. "And your 'Royal court' status means nothing without a Royal to rule."

"Luckily, we have her with us, don't you think?" Alix strode to join Nina's side, leaving Sol and Cas alone.

Sol glanced over her shoulder at him.

He was uncharacteristically silent, his eyes focused on the open wall ahead. He met her gaze briefly and shrugged.

Sol didn't particularly have any words to say. She wanted to ask if he was alright, although she was the one called a whore. She figured being called *his* whore held a bigger insult somehow.

The small glimmer of emotion in the brief second their eyes met made her dwell. It was foreign on him. She recognized it only because she had spotted it occasionally on herself whenever she would pass mirrors or spot her reflection in the quiet Yavenharrow ponds.

The ache of confinement.

Of not belonging.

Of longing to, but not knowing how.

So, Sol decided she hated those men. And she would let them know it, even if it meant playing a part she didn't know the lines for because screw anyone who made someone feel that way.

She gave Cas a small smile and grabbed his arm, gently leading him toward the rest of his court. He tensed beneath her touch but followed.

Finigan watched them, his attention shifting from her face to Cas's. "There is no way this girl is Irene Yarrow's daughter."

"I've been told that my whole life, actually," Sol replied. "We look quite different."

The other man, still sitting on the ground with wide eyes, stood as well. He cleared his throat and stepped back into formation with the rest of the soldiers, who watched them with unyielding expressions.

To his credit, he at least seemed regretful.

Finigan crossed his arms. "I'm not buying it. Where is Irene then?"

"My mother is dead," Sol said mechanically, the curated result of all the times she had to say the same to the townsfolk back home. It had been a horror and taken hours and hours for her to let all the tears out so she could talk about it without breaking into sobs.

He surely knew Irene was dead—Nina told her all of the South knew during their ride together. How the wind cried with her passing. How everyone's magic seemed to mute for days after.

Finigan was only digging himself deeper into Sol's bad side.

"I also don't care if you believe it or not," Sol continued. "You've been quite rude to my friends. Let us through, they deserve to rest."

Behind him, the soldiers gripped the hilt of their swords.

The man smirked. "If you're truly a Yarrow, you don't need my permission." He stepped aside. "Go on."

Beats of silence passed as Sol looked from the wall to the small man. She released Cas — after realizing she still held him—and pondered her options. Sol could walk inside, like Sawyer did and rid herself of the headache. But that meant leaving her…travel companions alone.

Surely, they can take care of themselves.

Finigan's expression turned smug as Sol took a step forward as if she had taken the bait. As if he expected for her to leave them behind.

Sol stopped, refusing to give him any satisfaction. With a false meekness, she said, "I think I'll wait here until you give my companions whatever they need to cross with me."

"Afraid of walking alone, Princess Yarrow? They can go with you. If you truly are Irene's daughter, who is the mother of the enchantment, then if they remain within reach of you, they'll pass unscathed as well." He mimicked her tone. "Unless of course, you aren't."

Sol dropped her façade. "And if I am and you've disrespected us like this? Surely speaking to me like this has consequences." As she finished, she looked the man up and down, making sure to exaggerate her displeasure.

She saw it then, the flicker of caution in his gaze. The realization that if she truly was who she said she was, he was more than likely in trouble.

Another aggravating breeze full of sand scraped Sol's face. Finally, Finigan jerked his head toward the open wall. "The brands are at the entrance."

"Come on." Nina grabbed Sol by the forearm, coaxing her to where the horses waited.

"I'll take her," Cas announced, swirling her over to Lilah instead. Sol didn't protest as she mounted the mare, even felt some relief at the gentle huff in greeting. Cas shifted on and wrapped his arms around her waist to grab the reins before easing Lilah on with a squeeze to her belly.

"Why are you suddenly wanting me to ride with you?" Sol asked, trying to shrink away from his arms.

Cas gestured up, to the towering wall. Sol followed his directive, barely able to see through the sunlight and haze. But she made out the figures stretched along the top edge of the wall, all angling something down at them.

Bows.

Taut and ready.

Anxiety gripped her throat. "They want to kill me?"

"Us, I think. But everyone wants to kill me beyond these walls."

He brought his arm overhead, shielding them from the threats above with his Ward. Sol traced the violet veins with her gaze and sank deeper into the saddle.

The soldiers watched them with razor focus as they trotted by, some stoic, but mostly with scowls. They had almost cleared them, almost at the front of the gate, when one of them said, "Maybe she's not his whore, but he's hers...Like his father was to Irene."

Sol shut her eyes and dug her fingers into Lilah's mane.

Cas pulled them to a stop.

She didn't have to know the full story to know that the sentence was likely that soldier's last.

"You might want to keep facing forward, Princess."

Sol clenched her jaw, recognizing the threat in his tone. "And miss the show?"

Cas dropped the Ward.

Instantly, they were surrounded by Shadows, wild and angry, flipping through her hair, leaving her in shivers as they spiraled into the air. They lingered for a moment before thrusting left where the soldier didn't have so much as a second to scream before the tendrils wrapped around him and lifted him in the air.

"Cas!" Nina jumped off Kahaida and ran to his side. She shook him by the leg, her expression mortified. "Cas, the King will kill you."

The soldier yelled and struggled while the men around him gaped, some scattering without hesitation.

"He can get in line."

Sol really should have listened to him when he advised her not to look.

A blood-chilling crack resonated throughout the Dunes as the Shadows coiled around the soldier like snakes, his body falling limp and swelling with blood. The darkness released him, only for a Ward to catch the body halfway. It fell on it, then sliced through it—in pieces.

"Gods damn it, Casimir," Nina breathed, holding a hand to her forehead.

Without another word, Cas hauled Lilah forward, making Sol jolt with the sudden force. She tried to keep herself together, tried not to hurl her entire insides as the image of the splattering body parts replayed in her mind.

A Ward enveloped them both as Lilah gained speed.

"I do hope you really are who we think you are, Princess," Cas said from behind her. He tightened the hand that held the reins around her, bringing them closer. "Because if not, both you and I are dead."

CHAPTER TWELVE

THE UNSETTLED

It was the strangest feeling. Like separating into billions of particles then slamming back together or a jolt of lightning bouncing through every nerve and inch of skin. It left Sol dizzy and covered with the sensation of crawling static.

They stumbled into cold air, and not the cold she was used to during the Spring. It was a dry cold, one that immediately had her teeth chattering. She swayed with Lilah's gallop, almost toppling over with nausea. As if sensing it, Lilah halted with a stomp, and Sol instantly hopped off, vomiting into a cluster of bushes.

"Took you long enough." Sawyer stood a few paces in front of her, leaning on Fey. She buckled a heavy-looking fur coat over her leathers. "A few more minutes and I would've left you all for a hot bath."

Sol coughed and braced her hands on her knees with a groan.

"The enchantments have that effect the first few times," Sawyer offered.

Sol turned to find Nina and Alix galloping through the open wall, materializing from thin air, both engulfed in a wind of fury.

"*You idiot.*" Nina stopped right next to Cas and slapped him. "We are in Rimemere for five minutes and you've already murdered someone."

Sawyer glanced between them. "What happened out there?"

Sol tried not to hurl again as another wave of nausea hit her.

"They struck a nerve." Cas shrugged. "He was useless anyway."

"That's not the point! He was alive. He had a family, Cas!" Nina shoved Kahaida into Lilah, the two mares now in a stare down like their masters. "You cannot just prance around and use violence when someone pisses you off."

"Like you didn't slam Finigan and the other fool to the ground with your magic?" Cas's voice lowered, laced with agitation.

"Gods, shut up, both of you!" Sawyer walked over to them, pushing the mares away from each other while banging and yells sounded beyond the wall. "I'm usually the one who needs an intervention. Disappointed in you both." Sawyer sent a spark of fire their way, then walked back to Sol.

"Come on, cousin. Let Cassie cool off."

Sol climbed onto Fey behind Sawyer, hoping after this mess she never had to ride another horse again. They took off down the road, and as Sol finally gathered her head and stomach, awe spread through her at the sight.

The dirt road stretched directly into what seemed like a town made of stone. Houses and stores and courtyards spread on either side of them, all made of the grayest and loveliest rock. As they continued down the path, people of all ages and origins crowded around their windows. They all dressed in a similar fashion to what she used to wear at the Hound, beige skirts or pants and ivory shirts. The women even donned bandanas to keep their long hair from their faces.

Like her mother used to wear.

A small smile pulled at her lips, for the wary onlookers, and at the connection she saw between this foreign place and her mother. It made it seem...not as scary.

Even as they continued, she watched the shops and their small flower gardens at their doorsteps, the familiar scent of mint and thyme making her sigh.

"These are the human sections," Nina whispered from beside her, all anger from before seeming to have disappeared. She kept a steady pace next to Fey, even as Kahaida stopped every other block to sniff the gardens and try to take a bite of nearby people. "Only those without magic but with connections to the Wielder bloodlines reside here," she finished.

"It's also a cease fire zone," Sawyer added. "Thanks to Queen Irene, no one may start conflicts here. Well, not legally."

Maybe Cas should stay here then, Sol thought. She didn't dare glance behind them at where he trailed silently.

The townsfolk seemed somewhere between terrified and cautiously curious. Sol met some of their gazes, and some smiled shyly while others grimaced.

"Up there," Nina waved her hand forward and Sol's breath caught, "Is the castle."

No number of stories could have captured the grandiose beauty of it. The building before her was an incredible work of art.

It was also made of stone with all sorts of dark grays and blues reflecting the hazy sky. Stone cylinders erupted from the ground holding delicate arches. Mezzanines extended every few spaces from the lateral walls, some occupied by silhouettes. The top of the castle bent into perfect cones, then flattened out into what looked like a massive flat rooftop. What was on that rooftop made Sol swallow a lump in her throat.

Fire. And water. And stones and earth all flying around with lethal precision. Spears of them shot from left to right in a dance.

Tracing her line of vision, Nina smiled. "It seems the students are training," she said. "They're learning different ways to manipulate their magic."

Sol hadn't realized the feeling of incompleteness she carried until it vanished as she watched magic dance. That nagging sense she was meant to be doing something other than living a blissful silence in Yavenharrow had been perpetual, but she always just figured it meant she wanted something a *little* bigger. Like going to the Scholar Towers and finding something she had a fire for doing, like her Aunt Lora with healing.

But she could never fully identify the source of the feeling, left only with awkward longing and no instructions of how to fulfill it.

It killed her slightly how right it felt to be in Rimemere. Angered her at how long she had been deprived from it.

Still, Sol whispered, "I—I can't see myself doing any of that."

At least not well.

"It's...bizarre at first. There are lots of things that go into it, but we are here to make sure you do it all safely." Nina leaned closer in a reassuring gesture. "Well, I can't guarantee Sawyer won't try to throw you off the rooftop training rink, but I can guarantee one of us will catch you."

Sawyer laughed. "My days of throwing people off roofs are long over, Nins."

"Are they?"

"I hope so."

They continued through the human sections slowly. Nina spoke to some of the citizens, engaged in laughter and gentle smiles. The people loved her. They loved the four of them, even Cas smiled and dismounted Lilah to help carry trunks of equipment into a lonely shop.

It wasn't until they were almost out of the sections that a girl, no older than fifteen with beautiful curls like a halo around her bronzed head and the most peculiar violet eyes, stepped in front of them, blocking their way down the singular road leading to the castle.

The girl crossed her arms over her chest and frowned. "And where are you all going without even saying hello?"

Beside them, Lilah cantered ahead and halted directly in front of the girl. For a terrible moment, Sol thought Cas was about to pulverize another person, though after the thought invaded, she knew he wouldn't hurt someone unprompted, especially not a young girl.

Well, Sol hoped.

The girl didn't seem afraid, though. In fact, she gave Cas a distasteful glare. "Gone three years and not a single letter, Uncle Cas? Really?"

Cas dismounted and embraced the girl in a tender hug, enveloping her completely, and lifting her from the ground.

The girl laughed and wrapped herself around him, the sound melting all the tension from Sol's shoulders.

Sawyer huffed a breath behind her. "Penny Xanthos. Quite far from your mother's claws, aren't we?"

Penny continued giggling, then finally trotted over to them after Cas set her down. Sol marveled at the expression of unfiltered emotion on his face. She had only been allowed glimpses of his gentle side, and her insides fluttered as he smiled after his niece.

"The castle is stifling," Penny said, patting Fey. "I escaped for the day."

"So, nothing has changed then," Alix said, also dismounting his mare and giving Penny a pat on her head. "Depressing."

"You're so big now, beautiful girl." Nina held her hand out to her, then pulled her up on Kahaida. "You look so much like Samara."

Penny made a face. "What an insult."

Sol smiled despite herself at the casual conversation. It was nice to see the familiarity among them, made her feel almost safer in their care to see their gentler sides.

Finally, Penny settled her gaze on her, gasping, "Is this—"

"Shhh, it's a secret until it's verified," Nina whispered, easing Kahaida to a walk. Everyone followed along. "It'll cause an uproar here."

Penny's gaze roved all over Sol as if she looked at a ghost.

"H...Hello," Sol croaked, not knowing what else to say, feeling too vulnerable beneath her attention.

"I can't believe they found you," Penny breathed, unable to tear her gaze from Sol.

"Neither can we," Sawyer added. "I was starting to think my father was going to rule forever. I was already writing my eulogy."

"He's gotten so bad, Sawyer," Penny said. "He's...cruel."

"More than before? Can't wait."

Behind them, the faint sound of yells carried through the streets, making some of the citizens bolt into their shops.

"Your uncle might be in trouble," Nina said. "We are hoping King Semmena won't mind much."

Penny looked at Cas, who led them on wordlessly. "What did you do, Uncle Cas?" When he responded only with a shrug, the girl sighed. "He finally got rid of Finigan, didn't he?"

"I wish," Sawyer laughed. "It was some other soldier."

"Bad day to have a temper, Uncle Cas. It's Flora's Day."

Penny looked over at Sol again. "Quite poetic the rightful Queen has arrived on the original goddess' bloom day."

Sol sighed. "I—would rather not be called that yet."

Penny smiled. "It must be weird. To be here."

"Very."

"The Unsettled are going to be so very happy to have a Yarrow here again." Penny looked up to the sky, her violet eyes sparkling. "We are finally going to be treated like living beings again."

"The Unsettled?" Sol glanced at Nina, knowing she would soothe her confusion.

And she did. The Earth Caller smiled, "A term for those of Wielder bloodlines who never materialize magic."

It didn't occur to Sol such was a probability until that very moment. Nina's answer only fueled more questions, but she decided to keep them for another day, especially as Penny gave her a small smile. "They say we are bad luck to have around, so they usually keep us at arm's length. I think they only tolerate me because of my mother's status."

"You are not bad luck, Penny," Cas chimed from behind them. "Don't let those idiots get to you."

"You're more talented than most of my prior students, Pen," Sawyer added. "A shame your mother isn't more like you."

Alix, who had been mostly quiet, hummed his agreement.

They continued to the castle, Penny sharing updates on Rimemere for the Royal court, most of them things Sol didn't understand. Apparently, nothing new except a handful of cruel laws and regulations no one was surprised had passed.

Sol became lost in the scenery, her companion's conversation soft in the background. As they exited the human sections, the small shops and homes slowly dwindled away, replaced by green and lively trees rooted in swaying grasses and bunches of yellow flowers. Sol admired the nature thinking how wonderful Earth Callers must be for the plant life. Indeed, there wasn't a single wilted flower or shrub, and any that looked sad, Nina made sure to caress on the way to revive them.

Behind her, Sawyer radiated a comfortable warmth, either by magic or just her presence. Her cousin shared stories of their voyages with Penny, the girl as intrigued with everything beyond the wall as Sol was with everything within it.

When Sawyer got to Yavenharrow though, they paused. A silent conversation passed among the Wielders, one Sol couldn't decipher until they collectively told Penny Sol was found in Graniela. She was confused at first, then figured they likely wanted to protect her town from this place as long as they could. Sol was thankful for that.

Penny looked over at Sol. "What was it like, Princess? Living such a different life?"

Sol's lips twitched in a small smile. "Unnervingly calm at times."

"And why did you choose not to come until now?"

It occurred to her that perhaps no one knew the truth. Maybe they thought Sol knew who she was all along and simply chose to hide, to live an uninteresting life instead. "I didn't know any of this existed until a week ago."

Penny angled her head in a gesture of contemplation. "I don't blame Queen Irene for choosing to forget about us."

"I do," Sawyer added. "She abandoned the kingdom when we needed her most."

"Sawyer!" Nina chastised. "We don't know what truly happened."

Sawyer shrugged. "She chose to flee. That's what happened."

As they neared the castle's steel gates, Sol wanted to argue. To defend her mother's choices and explain her innocence. But as she tried to formulate an argument, her fingers twirling in Fey's mane, she came up utterly, and sadly empty.

Truthfully, Sol didn't know. She loved her mother and knew she was good, but couldn't provide a defense for her actions, especially when everything pointed to the fact that Irene truly up and left.

Her mind drifted to her mother's note, wrinkled within her satchel.

The people are in your hands now, and for that I am so sorry, Soleil.

She wouldn't think of the rest. Not now. Not ever. Maybe someday, but not soon.

"I don't know what I'm doing here," she whispered.

It was meant to be more to herself, but Nina responded as she idled beside them. "For now, we rest. And eat."

Sawyer added, "and bathe."

"Then we will deal with the 'supposed to be's'," Alix finished.

They trotted along silently through the streets, and as they finally neared the castle gates, Sol tugged on the reins. Fey stopped without protest, as if she, too, was nervous.

Sol stared at the massive gates before her and the stone archways beyond them. The courtyards were alive, people dashing from one place to the other, seemingly uninterested in the people who were to enter. They all wore black or brown leathers, their hair braided tightly around their heads, men, and women alike. Some carried weapons, but Sol had the sense most didn't need them.

"Princess?" Nina lifted her brows in question.

Without taking her eyes from the monstrosity of a building, Sol said, "If you all don't stop calling me that, I will run."

"Don't get cold feet now." Sawyer looked up at the sky, sighing, "We are so close to finally having a decent bath."

Nina gave Sol an encouraging smile. "We are with you."

Sol closed her eyes and took a deep breath, a cold breeze caressing her. It cooled her warm skin, her racing blood.

She didn't try to stop Fey as she resumed her trot toward the gates.

CHAPTER THIRTEEN

Semmena v. Yarrow

Not a kind look awaited them beyond the gates. As the six of them made their way to the stables to turn in their mares, Penny groaning about returning to the castle so soon, only glares followed. Water and sparks of fire passed unnervingly close to Sol, enough so she was placed beside Cas who Warded them through the gardens and courtyards.

Sol focused on those lovely gardens instead of the obvious contempt the dwellers watched them with, trying to name the herbs she recognized and catalog the ones she didn't to learn about later. She fidgeted with her braid and picked at her nails as they strode up the black marble steps.

Beyond the massive iron doors, they were welcomed by another set of steps, towering up to twin hallways that stretched into dimly lit corridors. The floors were a shiny pearl and blue pattern, embellished with silver vines that wrapped around scattered pearl pillars. Vases with all sorts of flowers were placed atop exquisite wooden furniture.

The luxury unnerved her slightly.

Sawyer immediately stretched her arms over her head and yawned. "Home sweet home."

There weren't many people around them, only some who looked like servants or couriers, their status given away by the different, less pretentious fashion.

Nina looped her arm through Sol's and led her down the far hall. Before they got too far, a voice called to her.

"Miss Amana!"

As Nina turned back to see who it was, Sawyer rolled her eyes. "We were so close," her cousin grumbled.

A panting, short man dressed in an outrageous silver tunic stopped by their side, hands on his knees as he skidded to a stop. Cas and Alix halted next to Sawyer, and Penny gave them a quick bow before exiting back into the front gardens.

The man gave them all a polite nod, his eyes widening slightly as he took Sol in.

No one around her smiled at him, so she didn't either.

Sawyer tapped a foot on the floor. "On with it, Caleib," she said, already beginning to unbraid her hair, surely for the bath she had been describing their whole voyage.

Caleib straightened, smothering the front of his silk attire. He gave Sawyer a small smile. "Miss Semmena, lovely as always."

"Do *not* call me by that surname."

"His Majesty insisted on addressing you properly now, since—" his eyes flashed to Sol, "there might be a true Yarrow on premises."

"Word got here quite fast." Sawyer looked at Sol. "Great. Let the man torture you now, *Princess*." She walked away with no further comment and turned a sharp corner into the depths of the hallway.

Caleib turned his attention back to them. "His Majesty requests the Yarrow Court in the throne room. Along with your...prospect. Immediately."

This time, Nina blinked at him, and even Cas clicked his tongue.

"Why now?" he asked, folding his arms across his chest.

Caleib flinched slightly. "Not sure, Prince."

Sol glanced at Cas sidelong. It wasn't the first time he was referred to as "Prince."

"Can't this wait until tomorrow?" Nina whined. "We all need rest. And healers."

Caleib fidgeted nervously. "I'm afraid not, Miss Amana. The King seems...in a foul mood today. He wishes to meet who you've brought."

Sol was not prepared for this so quickly. She did not want to meet perhaps the few people she should care to impress covered with mud, horse fur, sand, and gods knew what else. Her conviction began to waver, and she wondered if she would be successful in fleeing back to the stables, stealing a mare, and riding back to Yavenharrow.

"Fine. We will be there in a bit," Nina said. "Will you be so kind as to fetch the Royal General for us?"

Caleib blanched slightly but nodded erratically and hurried Sawyer.

Sol was a nervous mess as they walked down the foreign hallway and into the heart of the castle, even more so as she beheld the heavy activity within it. The hallways were blurs and specks of white and red and black cloaks, all hurrying wherever they went with purpose. Noticing her curiosity, Alix explained the White Cloaks were castle officials and workers, such as couriers or low-level scribes. The Reds were students who had yet to graduate, and the Black Cloaks were either high-level students, alumni, or distinguished Magic Wielders. The people without any cloaks were human.

Not surprisingly, those without magic manned the labor, the cooking, or the personal attention of the Wielders. Servants. Also not surprisingly, they ignored her, aside from polite smiles and bows.

After the initial shock of the crowds, Sol grew even more nervous at the thought of standing before this King. Nina assured her, technically, he was only the temporary overseer of Rimemere, so King Regent, until she claimed the role. Sawyer's mother never had the chance to step in as Regent.

Sol was learning the Yarrows seemed to have unfortunate endings.

She was too busy cataloging the information she didn't notice when they finally stopped in front of a massive set of wicker doors.

Before pulling them open, Nina leaned, and whispered, "Just try to nod, look nice, and do what they say."

Sawyer, though, waltzing up from behind them with Caleib a mess of nerves by her side, told Sol, "Don't. Make them hate you."

Cas laughed softly behind them. Sol didn't know what to expect when they walked through the doors, but it certainly hadn't been what sat before her.

Or who sat before her, more like it.

The room wasn't a throne room like she expected, but instead seemed like an ancient conference room. Rows and endless rows of bookshelves on either side of them, spread into wings, spiraling into dark corners. That familiar smell of parchment, ink, and candlewax hung thickly in the air, and a massive chandelier hung in the center of the room, illuminating the five people sitting in a semicircle, directly facing the door.

They all smiled slowly when Sol and her Court entered, except for the man in the middle.

Sawyer looked exactly like her father. The man was tanned, chiseled, and had the most arrogant smirk, one Sol instantly preferred on Sawyer. While it was taunting on her, the way the man carried it was...unnerving. Like he knew something they didn't.

He also had onyx eyes, which seemed to go on forever, even under the direct light from the chandelier.

To his right was a stoic woman with brown hair in intricate braids and violet eyes spearing daggers into Sol. The young woman next to her was similar, violet eyes, and ashy hair tied in a knot on her head. She, however, didn't have the raw elegance the older woman did. They gave her an echo of Penny's peculiar gaze, but the young girl was not nearly as cold in demeanor.

To the King's left was an older man, hunched over a dusty tome. He barely looked up as they entered.

Alix cleared his throat slightly, then fell into a polite bow, which Nina followed flawlessly.

"Your Majesty," he said as he leaned.

Sawyer and Cas remained like statues, both looking distant and bored as they took their place against the closest bookshelf.

Sol gave everyone a small curtsy.

That seemed appropriate.

"The Yarrow Court," The King said, adjusting his golden crown. He motioned them forward. "It's been a long time."

Nina placed a gentle hand on Sol's back, leading her forward.

Sawyer and Cas sat, then Alix next to them. Nina skipped a seat for Sol then sat as well. As Sol reached the edge of the table, everyone's gaze burned and weighed heavily on her. And as she leaned to pull out the heavy stone chair, she paused.

A figure behind the King shifted, one Sol hadn't noticed upon arriving. He was tall, maybe as tall as Cas, and donned traditional silver armor. His face was partially shielded by a metal helmet, a slight beard peeking from it.

Sol wanted to shrink to the floor and live with the vermin amongst the bookshelves as the King let out a hearty laugh. "Though you don't look like Irene, you sure have her demeanor. Sit, girl. We won't bite."

Slowly, cautiously, Sol sat.

"A pleasure to finally meet you," the older woman said from beside the King. "What is your name, darling?"

"Sol."

"Your full name, Sol?" King Semmena braced his elbows on his knees, his eyes lifting to meet hers.

Nina tensed beside her. She might've said something, but Sol interrupted, "I don't use my full name."

The King angled his head. "Oh?"

"Uttering your name is safe within these walls, child." The older man gave her a tired smile, clasping his hands together across his chest. He wore long brown robes, like the older woman who now tapped her slender fingers on her forearm.

Sol didn't like these people. Didn't like their smirks, didn't like the King's snaking gaze. Especially didn't appreciate the younger woman's scowl.

Nina said to be nice. So, she should smile, maybe give them her name. Bat her eyelashes bashfully.

But she didn't want to.

Sol returned the King's smile. "You tell me yours, and I'll tell you mine, *Majesty*."

They all stilled. Everyone except Sawyer, who shamelessly let a smile creep over her lips as she looked at her father.

"Watch yourself, girl," the older woman snapped, slamming her hands on the table.

King Semmena merely grinned. "Ah, it's fine Gina," he said. "It's been quite a while since I've had someone unafraid to speak to me in such a way."

"What, Sawyer's profanity isn't enough?" The younger woman rolled her eyes.

This time Cas cut his attention to the woman and sneered, "Watch it, Samara."

Samara winked at him. "Good to see you too, brother."

Sol's brows rose.

Samara...Penny's mother?

"Enough." The King's command boomed through the room and Sol swore the lights flickered. Everyone obeyed. Even Sawyer had the good sense to avert her gaze.

"We shall focus on the task at hand. Banter on your own time." He resumed his casual tone and stood, striding over to the man behind him. He leaned close, whispering something to which the man gave a curt nod.

King Semmena turned back to Sol, his face calm, and once again pleasant. "I assume they have told you what you are here for. And introduced themselves."

Sol nodded.

"Well, let me tell you again, with some added details." As the King spoke, the man behind him emerged toward the table holding a silver chalice. "The four people around you are children of Queen Irene's trusted circle and Court," the King started. "They are appointed to her successor, then their children to their successor, and so on. I've kept Gina and Samara, though." He gave her a small, forced smile. "I do hope you don't mind."

The armored man set the chalice down in front of the King, then extended an arm toward Sol.

"The reason you are here now, Sol, is because you have claimed to be the late Queen's daughter, therefore Heiress to the throne of our glorious kingdom."

Sol didn't move. Nina gestured to the King, then to the man with his arm extended. Alix too, gave her a small smile and jerked his head to motion her their way. There was no way Sol was nearing those people. The ridiculous table between them was barely enough distance. Sol met Sawyer's gaze to her left, then Cas's. And although Sawyer made a move to near her first, Cas put a hand on her shoulder and extended his hand past her and Alix to Sol.

That hand, she took.

She might not trust the people around her, but she sure felt more protected with them than alone.

Cas led her along the side of the table, his hand warm and tender around her own. They walked in direct vision of Samara, who, to Sol's delight, seethed with anger. They stopped in front of the armored man, who slipped past Gina and Samara to meet them by the edge of the table. His hand was still extended. Cas raised their joined hands and gently slid hers into the man's grasp. The man's grip was smaller and colder, but firm.

Still, Cas only stepped a few steps behind her instead of returning to his spot.

Gina smirked. "Xanthos and their Yarrows."

Sol did her best to keep composed as the armored man hovered their hands over the chalice.

"Gaven here is my personal guard. He is going to do what's called a Lineage Trace." The King held up his right hand, a thin red band shining on his ring finger.

"This here." He wiggled his finger, signaling to the ring. "Is a Wielder ring. It contains a small blade we use to draw blood when offerings are needed."

The armored man—Gaven—picked up his free hand where he also had a Wielder ring. The slice was quick. Sol didn't even feel the sting until after her blood began to drip rhythmically into the chalice.

Drip.

Drip.

Drip.

She averted her eyes.

After a few painfully long seconds, Gaven pulled a square cloth from the side of his armor and wrapped her hand before releasing it.

She cradled it to her chest and took a healthy step back. She felt the nerves resume, their relentless tug a dull ache in her chest as Gaven swirled her blood in the chalice. If she didn't pass this test, would she be allowed to return home? Would all this just become a nightmare as she resumed her life? And if she did pass...

It's in your hands now...

Sol wanted the day to be over.

"This silver chalice is an original Yarrow artifact." King Semmena leaned back in his chair, his expression bored, as if he was explaining trivial things to a bothersome child.

"In theory, if Yarrow blood comes into contact with it." He looked at his daughter. "True Yarrow blood, the one belonging to a marked one, then the gods will take the offering."

"And if it's not the blood they want, it simply remains there," the older man next to the king finished, startling Sol with his sudden speech. She had forgotten he was there.

They all watched the cup in silence. Only the soft hum of the torches filled the space.

"Well, seems like you're not—" As soon as the words spilled from Samara's red-stained lips, the chalice shook.

Gaven took a step back from the table, and everyone else seemed to blanch while the King's jaw twitched. Smoke swirled from inside the chalice, twirling up and away around it. The haze turned ruby red as tiny particles and droplets of blood circled into the atmosphere until it all vanished.

The torches extinguished. One by one, they went out, then the chandelier above them rattled. The air itself seemed to chill, to hang, and still.

Nina gasped softly and even the brown-robed elder gestured a silent prayer.

"Sol."

Sol flinched.

"Soool."

Again, she flinched, the sound of her name surrounding her entirely. She looked at the King and his Court, their eyes fixed on the chalice with faces pallid.

"*Soool.*"

She looked back at Nina and the others. They had their eyes fixed on her.

A hand on her shoulder made her nearly jump out of her skin, but Cas leaned near and said, "The gods will call you. Now that they know who you are, they're going to prompt your Awakening, they're going to ask for your name."

"*Sol, Sol, Sol of the Yarrow clan, tell us your complete name.*" A multitude of tones and voices pierced her skull. They were old and young and male and female and the most awful sound she had ever heard. She held her temples.

"*Tell us your name, your full name, beloved.*"

She shook her head, and Cas lightly squeezed her shoulder.

"Samara, fix that." Sol barely heard King Semmena through the chorus in her mind. The woman groaned, but gracefully walked to her.

As Samara closed the distance between them, she shut her lilac eyes and hovered her ivory hand over Sol's forehead. She chanted in a tongue Sol didn't understand, whispering sounds over and over until the voices halted.

Sol willed her breaths to even out and her heart to remain in her chest. After a few seconds of swollen silence, she relaxed.

"The gods are quite stingy," the King said. "Once you give them a taste, they only want more."

A headache bloomed behind her eyes and the cut on her hand began to throb. Both her palms had slashes now, one from her aunt and the other from this day that might have been the beginning of her life sentence. She could feel her Court's attention on her, as one by one, the torches revived, and the atmosphere seemed to settle once again.

Sol exhaled a shaky breath.

"Well." King Semmena stood, eyes meeting Sol's. "Welcome home, Crown Princess Yarrow."

CHAPTER FOURTEEN

Prince of Nothing

Sol was to begin her training immediately. After she mentioned her lack of magic and Samara remarked she was useless without it, the King ordered her court to at least grace her with basic history since she couldn't start her Wielder training.

Without palpable magic, she couldn't claim her birthright. Not that she was in too much of a hurry, the Semmena Court also didn't seem to care. The only thing that mattered to them was for her to seal the Jinn gate. That, and her attendance at a Royal dinner in five days to formally announce her arrival in the South.

As Sol and her court stood in the great hall after an uninteresting dismissal, she couldn't quite focus on what anyone was saying. She focused on a spec on the wall, tracing the edges of the dirt spot with a lazy gaze.

The people are in your hands now, and for that, I am so sorry, Soleil.

"Sol?" A hand on her shoulder made her return to her body.

"Hmm?" Sol looked at Nina who peered at her with a furrowed brow.

"Are you alright?" she asked. "You've been staring at the wall in silence for a while now."

"Sorry," Sol said, blinking away the haze.

Sawyer began to lead Sol down the hall as the rest of them fell in line, but a voice halted them. "Princess!"

Sol turned back toward the doors with a stifled eye roll at the title. She was going to have to get used to that.

Gaven, Semmena's kingsguard, emerged into the hall followed by Samara.

"What is it?" Sawyer asked, returning Samara's nasty stare. Alix mumbled something that might've been a prayer to the gods.

"His Majesty has requested for me to take over the Princess' personal protection," Gaven said, removing his iron helmet. He had deep, golden skin, the kind of tone painted by evenings in the sun.

"That's Cas's role. You're not needed." Nina crossed her arms, stepping between Sol and Gaven.

The man shrugged. "He has requested Prince Xanthos and yourself, Miss Amana, in the throne room. He is on his way there."

Nina stiffened.

Sol tugged at the sleeve of her blouse as Cas stepped forward, a trail of Shadows in his wake. She had to arch her head to look up at him, but as his jaw tensed and his eyes were shone, she averted her gaze and wished to never be on the receiving end of that expression.

"Why?" was all he said.

Gaven had the good sense to back up a step.

"I— I was not given the details." He shifted his helmet to his other hand. "I'm just following orders, Prince."

"Please don't scare her," Sawyer huffed. "She's finally become tolerable."

Samara scoffed and walked forward, placing a hand on Cas's forearm. "I sure hope you haven't already gotten into trouble, brother. You've just barely returned."

Behind them, Alix cleared his throat. "I must return to the libraries." He gave them a small bow. "I'm sure I have a lot of unopened correspondence. I will check on you during dinner, Sol."

Nina looked at Sol, then gave her a small hug. "We will be back as soon as we can, Sol."

"I'm not going anywhere," Cas said, continuing to stare at Gaven.

The idea of all of them leaving her alone, with no familiar faces, made her want to break into a sprint to the stables. Or at least tag along with one of them, but she wasn't about to ask.

Nina squeezed her arm, then pulled Cas along with her. "We will not piss off anyone else today, Cas. Let's go."

Sawyer frowned. "Gaven will show you to your room, cousin. I have a small thing to take care of." She stepped into a walk with Nina.

Sol rubbed the scar along her palm, wishing more than ever to have Lora nearby. She must be fine since Sol hadn't felt anything amiss. But still, Sol yearned to know the state of her home.

"You don't leave the castle grounds without one of us," Cas said, looking down at her. "We won't be gone long."

Sol gave him a simple nod, then watched him catch up to Nina and Sawyer.

Gaven smiled, a true gesture of goodwill. "I promise I won't bite, Princess. I will show you to your room."

Sol stepped past him and pretended to know where she was going. As he fell into step behind her, she just said, "Don't call me that," and stalked up the giant staircase.

Gaven wasn't terrible. Sol judged him harshly. He trailed silently after her for nearly an hour, even as she walked in circles around the castle. At first, she hovered around the second floor. But after realizing it was filled with mostly black cloaks, she fled back to the first floor where the glares weren't as threatening.

She gave up trying to pretend like she knew where she was going soon thereafter and settled to learning her surroundings instead. She discovered a staircase that led to lower levels which she concluded were the kitchens after a flood of people emerged carrying trays and pitchers.

There were other uninteresting rooms, meeting spaces, and areas with expensive couches and furniture. The most notable part of the first floor was the enormous, golden doors past the bottom of the staircase, engraved with a three-tier crown. The edges were embellished with carvings and glyphs which she took a few minutes to observe in silence before a servant carrying a tray of roasted pork nearly smacked into her.

She went upstairs after that.

The second floor had sleeping quarters, presumably for the students. She quickly found another set of stairs that took her to the third floor. Gaven shared her room was there, along with the rest of her Court's. He also shared that until she took the official title of Queen, they were to remain in this main area. The Semmena Court resided in a separate wing entirely.

At least she didn't have to worry about running into them too often then.

The fourth and final floor had the interesting stuff. Sol saw three libraries, two with students concentrated on their studies, and one with mainly white cloaks that had to be scribes. The smell of old books and sounds of turning pages made her sigh with nostalgia. She wanted to stop and search the bookshelves but opted to return at a time when it was less populated. Especially since every single head turned her way when she stepped onto the first one.

Sol began to make her way back down to her room when Gaven fell into step beside her.

"If I may, Princess."

She glared at him.

"My apologies—Sol—" he corrected as they turned a corner. "If you'd like, I can show you around the castle gardens and courtyards? They're quite lovely."

Sol thought about it. If she needed to escape at one point, examining the outside layout was perhaps smart.

She nodded.

On the way, Gaven offered her extravagant portions of foods she had never seen, but all she could think about was Lora's stew.

"There are establishments in the town that specialize in foods like that," Gaven said. "But someone from your Court will have to accompany you. I don't feel like being executed by Prince Xanthos."

Sol had snagged a handful of almonds from a bowl in the kitchens which she plopped in her mouth as they walked along the outside gardens. There weren't many people outside, whether it be due to the hazy day or because most students were in classes, Sol didn't care. With each step away from the castle and into the foliage, she felt herself lighten.

"Prince," Sol mumbled. "What makes him a Prince?"

Gaven removed a stray piece of branch from their path.

"He is technically the Crown Prince of Eswin, a territory Southeast of us." He plucked another branch free. "But due to his sentence, he is bound to Rimemere for another seventeen years."

Sol halted, the hedges around them caressing the side of her head. "What do you mean by his sentence?"

Gaven stopped a few feet in front of her, his expression unreadable.

The sky above them was a misty blue, and the wind began to push against the walls of vines around them. It sent a whiff of roses adrift as Sol anxiously waited for a response.

"He hasn't told you?"

Sol shook her head. "He hasn't told me much."

Gaven huffed a laugh and began walking again, motioning for her to follow. "I suppose that's typical."

Sol fidgeted with her nails as they emerged from the hedges, diving into what seemed like was meant to be a garden of some sort but held only bare pots and dirt. There was a stone fountain in the middle with carvings of the Original Creators, and like the statues in Yavenharrow, Sol swore their eyes followed.

"His father, Draven Xanthos, was your mother's Guard," he started, lowering his voice to a near whisper. "Rumors said he was in love with her, but Queen Irene never quite returned the sentiment. When the Queen's Coronation Vows came to pass, Xanthos participated. He was desperate to be with her, even if it meant bound by law."

"I'm sorry, Coronation Vows?"

Gaven led her down to another courtyard. "The South has a tradition that calls for a sort of tournament prior to a ruler's official coronation." He looked at her sidelong. "Though it has been almost three decades since Rimemere needed to host such a feat—I'm not sure if Semmena will call for one, especially after how the last one ended."

Sol shivered as they passed a fountain.

"Anyway, Draven was one of the prospects—but so was Arnold."

"The King?"

Gaven nodded. "It was down to them both at the end. The survivor would marry Irene. But Lady Mel, Sawyer's mother, begged Irene to find a way to not only save Arnold, but also let him marry her. No one really knows how, but your mother found a loophole and saved both Draven and Arnold. She agreed to marry Draven, letting Arnold be with Mel."

"Why don't I know any of this?" Sol's blood boiled with fresh betrayal. There was so much about her own mother she hadn't even heard whispers of. Lora hadn't said any of this, neither had the others. The small meter of trust she had begun to feel for them plummeted.

Sensing this, Gaven sighed. "It's a difficult part of our history. I only know it because my father was the main kingsman at the time and told me the story. It's not typically recounted."

Sol bit the inside of her cheek. "So how is Cas related to any of this?"

They continued to a labyrinth of rose bushes.

"A month before Irene and Draven's holy union, she became pregnant—by someone else. She never told anyone who sired the child. There wasn't a single speculation, except that it wasn't Draven. He was so furious when he found out that he threatened the child if your mother didn't reveal who the father was." Gaven glanced at her. "Because of the threat made to you, he was executed."

Sol stared at a single red rose, willing herself to process the words. "So, guards executed his father...because he threatened my mother?"

"The Queen personally oversaw executions," Gaven said. "She executed him in front of the Counsel." A pause, then, "and the Prince. He was eight years old at the time."

Sol was going to be sick. She was glad she hadn't eaten much because her stomach swirled with nausea. She spotted a lone bench near a gaggle of blackbirds and quickly leaned against it.

"Oh Gods," she muttered. "I—why is he in my Court then? How—"

Gaven sighed and leaned against the side of the castle. "Your mother gave him a choice. Swear loyalty to her and her Clan or die. He chose the former."

"At eight years old?"

"Yes."

They were silent for a long time after that.

CHAPTER FIFTEEN
NINA

Hate is a strong word, but Nina hated the King. Anyone other than a Yarrow ruling over Rimemere was an insult to the land's origin. Initially, everyone looked at Sawyer to rule. As soon as she Settled as a Warden and the mark of the Heir appeared on her back, she was to step up.

But the girl was wild. Unchained. All the things Nina fiercely loved about her court mate made her an unsuitable ruler as she grew. Then she Settled as a Fire Wielder instead and bore no Yarrow mark.

So, her father took the throne when Sawyer was thirteen, a month after her Awakening, after years of it being bare and broken, and overseen by a group of useless councilmen. Sawyer and her father journeyed to Rimemere, where he was meant to rule only until Irene returned, or if another of Yarrow blood claimed it. But Irene died, and no one else stepped forward.

So, Arnold stayed.

And no one had been able to make him step down since.

Wars brewed, alliances once blossomed during Irene's rule burned, and with them any help from other Southern continents.

Later, alliances once again were formed, but by blood, bargains and at a wall's length.

Thus, Rimemere continued under Semmena's rule. Nina and her court had set out to search for Sol after whispers of her existence reached them then soon after their departure the man commanded the wall to be built.

"To keep the uprise of Jinn out", he had said.

But it also kept all the citizens seeking help out, and all the ones who wanted to flee in. It kept exports difficult and alliances scarce.

It was a nightmare.

Now, as Nina and Cas stood in the throne room where they had declared they were leaving three years ago, similar nerves bubbled inside her, though instead of them being laced with excitement, they were mixed with dread. They awaited the King and his court, standing beside each other as if they had been summoned to the headmaster's quarters. Caleib stood at the end of the room against a wall, a mess of nerves like always.

When she had been smaller and more naive, Nina liked to play here. She met Cas here, in fact, after the whole fiasco with his father happened. They had stood next to each other, much like they did now, holding hands and holding back tears.

Smiling sadly, Nina did the same now, grasping her friend's hand. He glanced sidelong at her and returned the smile.

"We're never here for a good reason, huh?" he said.

Nina shook her head. "Nope."

The doors behind them boomed open and multiple sets of steps neared, sending chills over Nina's skin. This had to be about the wall. She had scolded Cas, but he was right—she also used her magic against them.

The idiots deserved it, though.

"What a way to make your return known, Yarrow Court." King Semmena's voice was grating. Nina had pleasantly forgotten it during her years away.

He strode past them and turned, his dark eyes full of smoke and embers. "I'm especially disappointed in you, Miss Amana. Violence was not ever your thing."

Nina cleared her throat, dropping Cas's hand. "They disrespected the Princess, Majesty."

"And that should be reported to me, then dealt with by *me*."

Gina and Samara flanked Arnold, the women near mirrors of each other in everything but poise. Samara's fingertips crackled with Shadows as she angled her head, a small smirk on her lips.

Nina bowed her head slightly in silent acquiescence. "Our apologies."

She knew she had to apologize for them both because Cas wouldn't. Cas had been looking for ways for the King to finally kill him and end his misery, release him from his sentence of servitude to Rimemere and the Yarrows. Which is exactly why Arnold hadn't done so. He loved keeping Cas within his leash and miserable and knew the memory of his past tortured him more than the mercy of death.

"Unfortunately, that means nothing to me, Miss Amana." Arnold turned toward his throne, taking long, unhurried steps toward it. "But before we deal with all that—How did you all find this girl?"

Arnold sat down, bracing his clasped hands on his knees as Samara and Gina followed to sit beside him in their own seats.

Nina swallowed the urge to run from the question. She didn't trust these people, most of the Yarrow followers and protectors didn't. She herself wasn't even sure of the answer to that question. When the note had originally found them, they had been in Graniela, quite literally about to abandon their search. Then, that wrinkled piece of paper had landed on their Inn's doorstep, as if carried by Winderlyn himself.

"Luck," she said finally.

Clearly, Arnold was not satisfied with the response. "No such thing."

"We ran into—"

"She lived in Graniela. Alone. The birthmark on her back gave her away."

Nina cooled her features into disinterest, inhaling a bored breath as if she wasn't caught off guard by Cas's blatant lie.

"I don't believe I asked you, Casimir." Fire pooled in the King's eyes. "I also don't trust a single thing you Xanthos say about Yarrows."

"He tells the truth, Majesty," Nina assured. "We found no other kin, or anything left behind by the late Queen."

The lies burned like sand in her mouth, but she understood. Cas was protecting not only Sol, but lady Yarrow as well. Nina wouldn't put it past the King to seek the healer out of spite if they told him the truth.

"Word reached this morning that a port town called Yavenharrow is under Jinn siege." He observed them with calculated calmness, provoking Nina's very soul into a tremble. "Anything to report from there?"

Nina bit the inside of her cheek.

Think. Fast.

"We traveled through there on our way back to Rimemere, Majesty. During our journey, we only saw some stragglers, but nothing more."

"You didn't encounter Yavenharrow under total chaos, near rubble beneath fire and blood?" Gina angled her head, as if the woman could see right through her. "Quite the luck you all had by avoiding it."

After some beats of silence and the realization Nina and Cas weren't divulging any more information, Arnold sighed. "We shall begin the Coronation Vows in a week. I must send out formal invitations to the continent."

Her breath hitched. "The—Is that still a practice?"

"Of course. Rimemere tradition," Samara added, studying her silver nails. "One of the more fun ones, if I do say so myself."

Beside Nina, Shadows rose from the ground, swirling around Cas's feet. "I believe the Princess' situation calls for an exception."

"Are you still speaking?" The King stood. "And no. Her situation does nothing for her except make her a weakness."

Blood heating, Nina squeezed her hands into fists, but before she could counter with something, anything to get Sol out of the gods' awful ritual, Arnold clapped his hands in a summon. "Finigan."

As if from thin air itself, Finigan Cale stepped into the room, sword in one hand—and whip in the other.

"Punishment for unprovoked assault is ten lashes, Miss Amana."

Hands gripped her arms, kingsmen she hadn't noticed dragging her forward. Nina struggled not to trip as her bones turned to ice and vision blurred at the sight of the whip up close, the image of the last time she had seen it used burning through her eyelids. Panic squeezed at her throat as they pushed her to her knees.

"It was provoked. Your kingsguard called the Princess a whore!" Cas's tone was fierce, but the edge of desperation tugged at Nina's chest. "I will take Amana's lashings. Let her go, Semmena."

Arnold peered at Cas, a tight smile pulling at the edge of his lips while his golden eyes shone with anticipation. "You are due for something way worse than lashes, Casimir Xanthos Morozov."

Instantly, the room fell dark.

The chandelier flickered, and then extinguished, the hall firelights exploding at the mention of the Prince of Shadow's gods-given name.

Nina hadn't seen a Draining in years.

Unfortunately, the gods weren't fond of punishing their connection to the terrestrial plane—the Rimemere ruler. So, the Draining would be for Cas and not the one who uttered his name.

Nina twisted out of the kingsmen's grasp, crawling her way back to Cas.

With an awful groan, he fell to his knees, illuminated by his violet Ward in a halo around him.

"Cas..." Nina breathed as she reached him. She grabbed his arm and slashed it open with her wielder ring.

His blood fell in streams, and where it met the marble ground, it evaporated into golden stars. Cas's face relaxed, his breathing trembling, as he glared at the King with the promise of vengeance.

Around them, the tension dissipated, and the chandelier stuttered back to life as he gave his blood to the gods, the consequence of having his full name uttered by anyone other than himself.

Tears burned in Nina's eyes as she took him into a hug.

If she hadn't let his blood flow, he would have burned out quickly. Without another entity to punish, he would have received it tenfold.

"It always stuns me just how quickly Warren demands your blood, Casimir," Arnold said. "So peculiar."

"Quit the fucking shows, Semmena." Samara said, the sound of her footsteps storming forward. "Piss off the Yarrows all you want, but leave my brother alone."

Her mother laughed. "So honorable of you to protect your half-brother, Samara," Gina said.

"Ten lashes for Amana." Arnold tapped the throne's armrest with lanky fingers. "Now."

Nina clung to Cas, her tears flowing. He pressed a small, gentle kiss to her forehead and whispered, "You won't be hurt, Nins."

"I will supervise her lashings outside." Samara grabbed Nina's arm, her nails digging into her already sore skin. "Don't need to get blood on the floors again."

Arnold waved a hand. "Fine. Gives me more room to deal with the rest of the problem."

As Nina was dragged away, the King's eyes shone with storms, and she feared Cas's lightning would be no match for them.

Samara's grip was rough.

Not rough with anticipation like that of the kingsmen—rough with desperation.

She dragged Nina through hallways, everyone parting for the Semmena Advisor and the Yarrow Hand. No one dared meet either of their gazes, and Nina didn't blame them. A wrong look at Samara and she was even less restrained than Cas when it came to using her magic.

Though *she* never got punished for it.

Finally, they exited the castle and Nina felt like she could breathe, inhaling gasps of the outdoor air to replace the filthy one from inside.

Samara continued to pull her through the gardens, passing the courtyards and rose bushes and lilies, all which Nina yearned to stop and touch. The scent of flowers and mud followed them all the way to the stables, but before they made it inside, she was called to stop.

"Miss Samara," a breathless kingsman said, jogging up to their side. "The King said to do the lashes publicly."

Nina's breath hitched at the statement, but Samara laughed and threw the stable door open. "Fuck off, Kelvin. The punishment I am to give her for her insolence isn't for the public."

Kelvin blanched. "His—His majesty said lashings."

Samara smirked and removed her dagger from a hidden pocket on the side of her baby blue dress. "I say blades."

Leaving the man stunned, Samara shoved Nina into the stable rooms and shut the door behind them.

Nina wouldn't deny she missed the smell of the stables. As she landed on a pile of hay, horse huffs and startled whinnies in the background, a soft sense of nostalgia spilled through her. If anyone else other than Samara was before her, Nina would have begged for mercy.

Instead, she crossed her legs beneath her and looked up at the woman. "I don't need your help."

Samara tossed the dagger aside, the blade glinting in the dim orange light. "You're an idiot. Really, Nanette? Messing with the kingsguard as soon as you come back?" She shook her head. "Not the way I wanted to find out you were returning."

"Surprise."

"You could have written."

"You never answer."

Samara sighed and sat beside her. "I've missed you."

The heat between them grew, sending Nina's heart into a staccato. She curled her fingers into fists to resist reaching for her. But failed as she did every time.

She raised one hand to Samara's neck, cradling her gently as she slid the other to her waist to pull her close. Samara obliged, melting into the touch, and shifting to sit on Nina's lap, her violet eyes beacons in the swirl of her Shadows.

As their lips met, Nina had no other thoughts except the woman before her. The chaos of the throne room melted with each kiss and her anxiety drifted into the air, carried along by the tender caress of Samara's Shadows. Nina savored the sweet, rich scent of berries and pine, tracing the delicate slopes of her lips with her own. Samara's neck was smooth under Nina's fingertips, the Shadow Wielder exhaling a shaky breath as she leaned into the touch. Pressing their bodies together, Nina sighed against her lover's shoulder.

"What's wrong?" Samara protested as Nina broke their kiss.

"This," she motioned. "This is wrong."

"Don't act like you don't like it, Nanette," Samara whispered, trailing a finger along the neckline of Nina's blouse.

"And what will your court say when I don't have lash marks on my back?"

"The healers here work wonders."

Nina sighed. "I don't need this, Samara. What about Cas? Your brother is likely to get thrown in the dungeons."

Samara looked up at the ceiling. "He's a brute, he deserves some time in there."

It had been years. Years of the same thing, of sneaking around and late-night meetings. Of Nina having to look at Samara with disgust in public instead of what she truly felt. Nina didn't know when exactly it happened. It had started as subtle glances, then accidental touches. Nina never dared anything more, for fear Cas would slay her. Then, one night, Nina accidentally walked in on her and her mother having a heated disagreement, one that ended with Gina throwing Samara off the rooftop training rink.

From the entrance to the area, Nina had Earth Called the ground below into the thickest flower beds she could conjure, then ran all the way down to the side of the castle with a box of healing gear in hand.

Samara had landed on a mattress of interwoven tulips, so distraught and embarrassed that Nina had tended to her small cuts in silence. Nina never learned what happened that night between her and her mother, but she had also never asked. They spent the night on the bed of tulips before resuming their lives without explanation. Samara started sneaking into Nina's room at night, using her Shadows to open her window and slide through. Nina didn't complain—she also learned that Shadows can be used for way more than just destruction.

"Sol will not easily agree to the Coronation Vows, you know," Nina whispered, stroking Samara's loose hair. "I may have just met her, but I know her enough to know she doesn't like being told what to do."

"Too bad. Ruling a kingdom has plenty of that."

Nina peered at her. "You can't truly agree with it."

"It's fun. Rimemere needs alliances, what better way than with a marriage?"

The Coronation Vows were an abomination, to say the least. By Southern law, a Royal must rule beside a political partner, be it man or woman, but never alone. Semmena ruled beside Mel until—well until he didn't.

There was no stipulation about having to remarry if the first one fell through. And the citizens didn't care. All they knew was it was a time to drink and dance and watch the prospects tear themselves apart for a chance to wed into Royal bloodlines.

The Rimemere Coronation Vows had always proved most heated, since marrying into a Yarrow line was the closest thing to the divine one could get.

"Irene hated it, too," Nina commented. "Almost got herself exiled by breaking the rules at the end."

"Which is exactly why your little Princess should just deal with it. I'll be sure to select suitable prospects from the other territories for her."

"She won't agree to it."

"She has to."

"She doesn't."

"The king will find out she was in Yavenharrow, you know," said Samara. "Jinn talk. It's kind of one of their main skills."

Nina scoffed, easing Samara off her. "Your point?"

"That you should've told the truth back there. Tell me, did you find her or were you just following Jinn and got lucky?" Her violet eyes flared. "Because it's quite a blow to think you all searched for, what, three years with no luck, but a single Mind Slayer and finds her in a month."

The words buzzed in her ears. "What?"

"You think you three were the only ones trying to find her? The entire South has been praying for their shot at her." Samara leaned back, her gaze roving over Nina's. "You're being quite uncharacteristically defiant for this girl." She reached a finger to Nina's lips, tracing them with her thumb. "Do I have to worry about competition now?"

Nina stood. "What are you talking about, Samara?"

"Lots has changed, Nanette. People are starting to see Rimemere's weaknesses, despite Semmena trying to show the opposite. Sol won't be a good ruler. You're better off killing her and letting Arnold be."

Nina turned to look at her slowly, the ground beneath her shaking. "Let me make one thing clear, Samara." She lowered her voice. "You so much as breathe the wrong way at Sol, and I swear to the gods the number of years we have known each other will not matter. I will protect her. She is the rightful Queen. And you better understand your place."

CHAPTER SIXTEEN

MASK OF FURY

The days went by incredibly quickly.

Sol was tossed from meeting to meeting, greeting professors, students, and all the officials in between with forced smiles and laughs. She wore painfully tight corsets and ridiculous shoes, mostly accompanied by Nina and Sawyer everywhere she went. Cas was nowhere to be seen, which proved to worry her more than anticipated.

Since the day of the Lineage Trace, no one had seen him. Nina mentioned the last time she saw him was in the throne room and hadn't heard of him since—but the darkness that flickered through her gaze every time it was brought up made Sol think Cas had not just gone out for a stroll.

Alix swam in occasionally, but was mostly occupied in the libraries, scribe duties ticking with the need for invitations to be distributed to the rest of the continent. Because Rimemere was isolated by the wall, courtiers had to cross it before being able to send the invitation by transport.

The royal dinner approached quickly, and though Sol had initially chosen to ignore her blatant lack of preparedness, the closer it loomed, the more her inexperience stared her right in the face.

She had grown keen at pretending to at least be poised in front of the castle-dwellers but didn't think she'd have the confidence to keep up such a neat façade with the nobles.

The day of the dinner, Nina finally agreed to let Sol sleep in. She didn't take it for granted. Sol woke only to shut the curtain to her room once the sun began to bleed in, then buried herself back into the cover of the extravagant quilts and duvets.

The first few nights, Sol mostly spent exploring her assigned quarters. Never in her life had she seen such a luxurious space. It was a little unnerving. To a degree, it made her feel guilty she was assigned such a space when Leo and Mina lived in a one-bedroom cottage. While Lora remained in their cottage—if the Jinn had left it standing.

Aside from the agitating silence and foreign surroundings making it difficult to focus, the fate of her town and family left her restless. There hadn't been a single night since she left that she wasn't plagued by nightmares of beady eyes and her Aunt's expression right as they were torn apart.

Although Lora told Sol to go, to survive, the guilt made it difficult.

Sol watched the ceiling with a lazy gaze when a series of knocks at her door made her flinch.

"Princess Yarrow!" a ragged, but feminine, voice called.

Sol veered sideways and looked at the front door, past her bedroom door and the living area. The wooden frame shook again as more knocks sounded.

"I'm coming in!" the voice declared as the door eased open to reveal a small woman with silvering hair tied in a knot atop her head and beige skin wrinkled with age.

Sol shimmied deeper into the covers, only letting her eyes peek at the stranger.

"Please don't call me that," she mumbled. It still sounded foreign.

The woman waddled in, a tray in one hand, and clothes on the other. "Yes, yes, I've heard you dislike formalities, Princess." She set the tray down on the mahogany desk, her brown skirts swaying with each step. "However, you must get used to it, especially as there will be lots of them tonight."

She swirled toward the bedroom and met Sol's gaze. Her eyes were brown, kind, and crafted with wisdom. Still, Sol recoiled further into the bed. The woman narrowed her eyes at her and wrinkled her nose. "Are you truly still in bed? It's almost noon."

Sol blinked at her. "It's been a long few days."

"And the long days are just beginning, *Princess*."

Sol angled her head toward the hallway, still only exposing her eyes. She glared at Sawyer. "Nina said I could sleep in today."

Her cousin leaned against the doorway and shrugged. "Yeah, sleep in. Not sleep all day. You must get ready for the dinner. It's noon." Sawyer stepped into her room and sighed. "And it might take the entire time to fix you up."

Sol had only worn casual gowns since their arrival, and the rest of them kept mostly to their tactical uniforms. However, it seemed even her Court was to dress up tonight.

Sawyer wore a deep red gown, resplendent against her tanned skin and soft curves. Her toned arms were adorned by carefully embroidered lace sleeves, and she wore her hair in a casual knot around her head. It was an easy sort of beauty, one Sol couldn't help but admire. The Fire Wielder frowned. "What?"

"I've only seen you in dirty leather suits," Sol said, sitting up. "Are you all finally to suffer with me and wear ridiculous gowns?"

"Nope, still just you." Sawyer grabbed an apple from the tray the woman brought in.

The woman swatted her hand away. "Sawyerlyn, I will be sure to get you a more uncomfortable gown if you don't shoo. I need to get started."

Waltzing into Sol's bedroom, the woman yanked her comforter to the floor. Sol only heard Sawyer's protest and what might have been a mocking, "Good luck."

The woman's name was Francis. She introduced herself as she dragged Sol to the washroom, then said she would be her assigned handmaid as she tore her nightgown off.

Sol tried to evade the large, circular mirror that hung across the bathtub, but as Francis practically pushed her into the steaming, oil-infused water, she caught a glimpse of her dusty blonde hair, pulled into pin curls Nina had hastily pinned before their first meetings. Her skin was still flushed from the journey in the sun, and even the recent night's rest hadn't erased the purple shadows under her eyes. Her gaze snagged on her abdomen, and she flinched at the thin, raised scar that trailed across it.

She looked away as quickly as she could and sank into the tub.

It was horrifying to have the woman scrub her down. Sol suddenly felt like the goats at Leo's who they hosed down and washed once every few weeks to get rid of their grime. The goats would scream relentlessly the whole time, and Sol was a scented lotion away from doing the same herself.

"When was the last time you brushed your hair, child?" Francis pulled the wooden brush through Sol's hair, the rickety thing nearly snapping in half.

She bit back tears. "I fell asleep before I could work through it."

Francis scratched her head with her free hand, ultimately deciding to leave the brush in the depths of the mess and grabbed a vial of oil instead. She worked it into the locks. "Some of the more traditional styles are a pain to remove, that's for sure."

Finally, her blonde hair began smoothing into its natural waves, the oil making it shimmer with the sunlight that peaked through the room windows, opened at Francis's orders. "Haven't seen hair so golden in a long, long while. It'd be a shame for it to damage."

They sat at a vanity near the bed, white and embellished with navy blue specs. A simple mirror faced them, making it easy for Sol to study her without being too obvious.

Unlike the people who wandered the halls, Francis was simple. Normal, if you will. Didn't agitate Sol's nerves. Sol met her gaze through the mirror and gave her a small smile. With a soft shake of her head, she smiled back.

"You look just like your mother, you know."

It wasn't what she had expected to hear, and it immediately pulled at her chest. "I'm the exact opposite of her," Sol said a bit sadly. Even having her mother's eyes would've been a comfort, since at least she could see that small piece of her through reflections.

Francis shook her head slightly, softly parting Sol's hair down the middle. "Your smile is the same. The way you both despised brushing your hair is the same."

"You knew her?"

A nod. "I did indeed. I was one of her handmaids."

Nina flashed through her mind. Her mother had been Irene's handmaiden too, from what Lora told her, before being sworn into her Royal Court. Sol wondered if Francis knew Clarisse as well.

"How... how was she? My mother?" Sol fidgeted with her nails. She didn't want to admit to this stranger the topic weighed on her. That she was nervous and alone and homesick and needed words of comfort.

Francis pursed her lips, grabbing a pallet of cosmetics from the desk. She was silent for a while, long enough that Sol doubted she would answer. But with a click of her tongue, she said, "Your mother was kind. And fair. She made some harsh decisions, but with her people's well-being in mind. She was one of the fiercest women to have ever sat on the stone throne."

Francis wove delicate green gemstones into the crown of Sol's head. "The Wielders are going to tell you one thing. Us without magic will tell you another. At the end of the day, you judge for yourself, child."

A knot in Sol's chest loosened ever so slightly. Only for it to immediately tightened again as Francis retrieved a gown from the armoire to the left. Through the mirror, Sol watched as she laid it atop the lilac sheets.

The dress was surely a Northern import. It was a rich, long, and elegant pine green, but with a risqué essence she hadn't seen in the typical Rimemere fashion. The satin neckline plunged in a delicate V and the seams were a laced gold, same to the trail of gemstones that wrapped around its middle. The golden flecks spread all the way from the bodice to the skirt, and the sleeves were a delicate, beige mesh. An emerald corset rested beside it with golden strings, all held together by golden strings that would secure down her back.

It reminded Sol of a sunrise over the Yavenharrow forests.

"It was your mother's," Francis said, gazing at the dress. She ran a delicate hand over the fabric. "It was the dress she wore for her Awakening." The woman placed a gentle grip on Sol's shoulders. "I hope it brings you similar luck today too, Princess."

Sol released an anxious breath. "I don't know if I can confidently wear that."

Francis tapped her shoulder gently in a small gesture of encouragement. "No one knows you don't know what you're doing unless you tell them, Princess."

By the time Sol finished donning the full costume of Heiress, it was fifteen minutes until the dinner was set to begin.

Not only did Francis help her with her appearance, but she also gave her a basic lesson on the Southern territories—the magical version.

Sol knew the ten Isophele territories. Each space had its own coveted export, each unique in culture and custom. She had studied them through Leo's notes, though to the regular citizens, only nine Isophele territories were known. Rimemere was absent from all records outside of Wielder lands.

Romalia was ruled by two nobles, their bloodline so pure it was said they were somehow related. The territory hugged the southernmost coast, and a thin mountain range bisected it and their neighbor Polimende.

Romalia lands were rich with animals and always had bountiful harvest, courtesy of it mostly housing Earth Callers. Not many foreigners were allowed in, but the ones who were and made it out shared the city was made of pure stone and lion furs. The nobility was said to live in a cottage by the hill and were often gone for months at a time.

Polimende was the central territory, flanked by five others, making it the most diverse of them all. They got the meats and vegetables from Romalia, the weapons from Melisandre, the exotics from Dianese, and the occult from Niome.

Sol looked over at Francis to where she smoothed the sheets of the bed. "What is 'occult'? Should I be...scared?"

Francis laughed. "Niome is special. Their nobility are one of the only gods'-called Wielders left on Erriadin. It makes the whole place rather.... otherworldly."

Sol paced around her room, trying her best not to sweat through her gown or cosmetics the woman had so neatly painted on her. "I'm never going to remember all this, Francis."

"Something will stick. Let's continue."

Ventry was separated by a strip of the Seas of Leona at the tip of the continent, making harsh weather and storms common there. Their export was seafood and beauties of the sea, from shells and sands to clothes made of anglea thread. Sol never missed a Ventry export in Yavenharrow—their sea mallows were divine in Lora's stews, though goods from anywhere beyond the Dunes of San'ann were usually scarce.

Now she knew it was likely due to the Rimemere wall.

"Teriopa and Stone Ledge capitalize on travel. They both have some of the largest ports on Erriadin, right next to Yavenharrow." Francis glanced over at her, as if she had noticed Sol's heart skip a beat at the mention of her hometown. The woman smiled kindly, walking over to Sol with a mug of tea. "We are only going through this, so you are not completely lost out there."

Sol nodded. "Thank you."

A soft knock at her door made her jump and nearly drop the cup of tea.

"Sol?"

Her shoulders eased at the sound of Nina's voice. She hadn't realized how much she had grown attached to the woman until she began to notice her absence. Sol supposed her entire Court was the one familiar thing in the sea of uncertainty.

Brutally ironic, truly, since they were the opposite only a few weeks ago.

Nina eased the door open slowly, her face peeking around the edge. A smile instantly bloomed as she took Sol in. "You look stunning, Princess!"

Sol was about to protest at the title, but with a wave of her hand, Nina cut her off. "I get to call you that today, as you truly do look like one."

The Earth Caller stepped into her room, and like Sawyer, she wore a figure-hugging silk dress. Nina's was green, a deep emerald, with silver vines around the neckline. She held out her hand. "Ready?"

Sol shook her head. "No."

"We will all be with you, Sol." Alix appeared beside Nina, clad in elegant, all black attire. "You have nothing to fear."

"Unless Nina gets her hands on the Ventry wine," Sawyer chimed in from behind them. "Then we have *much* to fear."

Nina rolled her eyes and made to playfully push her.

The interaction caused Sol's chest to sigh with a newfound calmness. Sure, she may be in a foreign place, but at least there seemed to be people in her corner.

But as she fell into step between them into the hallway, that empty spot at her back was a worry she couldn't quite keep concealed.

CHAPTER SEVENTEEN

The Southerners

The Southern nobles slowly arrived through the days but had remained hidden in the guest quarters and other landmarks within Rimemere. The Polimende nobles spent their stay by the Winderlyn temple, honoring their god in his original grounds while they could, same with Romalia as they lodged by Flora's.

Melisandre, Sawyer's home territory, mostly remained around her, choosing the quarters directly beside her. They—and Eswin—were the only two territories who didn't send anyone of noble status, sending instead higher-level generals.

This delighted her cousin, as Melisandre soldiers were apparently the most visually appealing. She pointed them out with a shameless smirk as they neared the staircase that would lead them into the castle foyer where they were to gather before the dinner.

The whole thing felt like a death march.

Alix informed Sol through subtle whispers that it was customary for everyone to gather together, then filter into the assigned room where they were to host the gathering by rank.

Beside her, Nina squeezed her hand. "It'll be over quickly."

"I have a weird feeling." On Sol's other side, Sawyer looked around. "Something is off."

"Let's not speak that into existence," Alix pleaded, peering over his shoulder at them.

Sawyer shrugged. "I'm only saying."

Sol sighed as anxiety gripped her chest. She wouldn't admit it, but she felt it too. The scar on her hand thrummed with caution.

"I don't like how we don't know where Cas is," Sawyer continued. "This isn't like him."

"Well," Nina said quietly. "He sometimes goes to visit Eswin without telling us, though. Maybe—"

"No." Sawyer's tone was firm, and Sol swore the space around them heated. "My father did something."

Nina remained silent, as if afraid to agree.

Sol said, "Would he be punished for killing that kingsman?"

"More than likely," Alix called back. "But I also searched the dungeons. He isn't in the castle."

They reached the staircase. "After this dinner, we split up. I'm not ok with one of our own being gone for so long." Sawyer looked at Sol. "It's *not* like him."

Sol held her gaze, not failing to notice the panic. It made her wonder the dynamic between them, between them all. To have a group so interwoven together...would she ever fit in with them?

She nodded, deciding it was a thought for another time.

Sol's blood raced as she peered over the railing to the floor below. A sea of people, all dressed in different fashion and luxuries, awaited at the foot of the stairs, their conversations halting as they spotted her. She recognized the Dianese staple attire, skin-tight dresses and outfits made from iridescent fish scales. And the Romalia furs wrapping around a plump woman with purple lips and amber hair.

Sol didn't know who to focus on if she should smile or frown, or just jump off the balcony and end her misery.

Beside her, Nina looped an arm, beginning the gentle descent. "You look like you've seen a Jinn."

Sol's stomach twisted. "I'm going to throw up."

"I told you not to eat," Sawyer remarked, her shoes clicking against the stairs. "But no one listens to Sawyer."

"They are just people, Princess," Alix said as he shifted to the spot behind her, letting her lead the way instead. "They are merely curious about you."

Sol wondered if telling the nobles she didn't have any of the answers they sought would make them leave her alone. Surely, they wanted to know about her mother—or compare them. Inquire about Sol's magic or lack thereof.

Again, Sol knew none of that, so they would be just as disappointed as she was.

They made it to the bottom of the steps. The entire castle seemed mute. Not a single sound resonated, nobody moved as Sol stepped into the foyer. Crowds parted for her and her court, leaving them in a semi-circle of glares.

Sol inhaled and focused on the outside, beyond the open doors behind the guests, pretending like the evergreen trees were birches and the stone was the sand of home.

When she finally felt like she wouldn't faint, she met some gazes.Faces from all edges of Erriadin glanced back at her, some with curiosity, others with disinterest.Just as Sol was about to speak, to say anything to break the palpable tension, the room warmed.

"Welcome to Rimemere, my dear Wielders," Arnold Semmena's voice boomed from the floors above as he and his own court began their descent to meet them.

He wore a deep, navy-blue attire, his golden crown resplendent against the silver décor. Samara and Gina wore similar gowns, gray and simple, though Sol had to admit the dress was stunning against Samara's darker features.

"We appreciate your company on such short notice," the King continued, reaching the final block of stairs, smoke trailing in his wake.

Sol turned to face him as her court took spots beside her.

"We will be having a small dinner in the ballroom," Gina continued as they stepped onto the foyer, directly in front of Sol. She didn't have to look around to know everyone watched their interaction—the Crown Princess and the man she had to dethrone.

With a flick of her wrist, Samara's Shadows led the way to the ballroom at the end of the right hallway, snaking between the guests to carve a path. "After that, we shall dance."

Nina pulled her closer by her skirt, easing her out of the way from Semmena's walk behind the Shadows.

But Sawyer stopped him.

Her cousin's eyes simmered like embers as she crossed her arms over her chest, blocking the open path to the ballroom. Whispers erupted through the spectators like an uncontrolled fire, forcing Sol to clench her fists to keep from intervening.

Sawyer gave him a small smile, one full of challenge and defiance. "It is customary to enter Royal dinners by rank," she said. "Which means Sol goes first."

Sol felt the blood leave her face as all eyes cut to her. "Sawyer—"

"Very glad to see you remember your traditions, daughter." Semmena eased her aside. "So, you should also remember that the King surpasses a Crown Princess."

"For now," someone in the crowd added.

Semmena stopped.

Beside her, Nina tensed as she scanned the people to see who dared the outburst, but everyone remained neutral. Sol couldn't decipher who it was either, as if the wind itself had uttered the warning.

"Of course." Semmena regained his composure, resuming his casual stride forward. "For now."

Sol exhaled a shaky sigh of relief when the Semmena Court disappeared around the corner and down the ballroom hall.

In front of her, Sawyer shook her head. "It should have still been you."

Nina motioned her forward, but the commotion behind them made the Earth Caller halt, her magic flaring green. But as she looked over Sol's shoulder, Nina relaxed, and melted into a radiant smile.

As two women walked through the crowd, the noblemen and women parted. Time seemed to slow until the couple finally stood before Sol.

For some moments, they just watched her.

The first thing that came to mind when Sol studied the woman on the right was winter's first snow fall. The woman wore her short, silver hair cropped to her chin with eyes so pale blue they seemed to glow. Her skin was the softest brown, a mirror to her companion's own. The duo seemed opposite each other in every way physically, but the one thing appearing eerily similar was their demeanor.

Simultaneously, they curtseyed. "Princess Yarrow," said the silver-haired woman. "What an incredible pleasure."

Sol nearly screamed when Nina yelped beside her. "I never thought I'd see the day the Ladies of Niome graced a dinner with their presence."

The women laughed as Nina pulled them into a hug. Such a casual interaction seemed to do the trick, the tension fading as the others dispersed around them, some waiting for Sol to lead the way into the ballroom, while others returned to the outside.

"We could never miss the return of the Yarrow court," said the woman with darker hair. She frowned as she studied them. "You do seem to be missing a member."

"Casimir is currently out of the castle," Alix shared, taking the women's hands into a bow. "Though I am sure he will join us at some point."

Sol tensed, knowing Alix was trying to avoid rumors or panic, but the latter snaked through her anyway.

"Great Irene Yarrow's daughter," the silver haired woman crooned. "Do grace us with your common name."

Sol looked from Nina to Sawyer, who merely tapped her fingers against her side with impatience.

"My name is Sol," she said finally.

"Poppy." The silver-haired woman bowed. "My wife here goes by Sonia."

Sol smiled at them both, an easy, genuine smile at perhaps the first Wielders beside her court that seemed kind. Odd, but kind.

"Well..." Sawyer swirled on her foot and started toward the dreaded ballroom. "Let's get this over with, shall we?"

The room was washed with blues and silvers, reminding Sol of a winter dream. It was reminiscent of the rest of the castle décor, though this room held more artwork and Wielder memorabilia, some captivating enough that Sol yearned to stop and admire them. There was a single, long rectangular table, perfectly set and ready in the center of the room.

She had never seen so much food at once. Rows of vegetables and exquisite greens spread over it surrounding platters of meats and things she had never seen before. Despite the desire to not be there at all, her mouth watered.

Semmena, Gina, and Samara stood at one of the ends with the King on the head of the table and the women flanking him. It struck Sol then that Jeriyah was absent.

She made a note to ask Alix—another unexplained absence did not sit well with her at all, even if she didn't know the old man too well.

The Southern nobles who remained gathered behind Sol, waiting. Assessing.

"Let us enjoy this feast, to welcome the great Yarrow heir home." Semmena grabbed a chalice of what looked like wine and raised it. "Please, all. Sit."

Slowly, the guests strode to the seats. If there was any confusion over who went where, no one showed it.

"You are to sit directly across from him," Nina whispered. "We will sit beside you."

Sol felt like a pawn. Like a measly pawn on a chess board, the kind she and Lora would play with when she was a child. Cheap and always missing pieces, like she lacked everything to make this meeting worth it.

What did she have to offer these people? Was she truly to sit and stuff her face with roasted duck, laugh, and chat about…politics?

Politics she knew nothing about.

It has always been a burden we carry—our bloodline is cursed.

She thought back to the note, folded and worn in her satchel.

Right.

Right.

Sol stepped forward, not breaking Semmena's stare as she placed her hand on the back of the mahogany chair.

"What an honor to share a meal with a Yarrow," Semmena said, tapping the chalice. His eyes shone. "I can already feel Rimemere humming with happiness at the matron bloodline being here once again."

Nervous laughs fluttered through the room as people sat.

Sol glanced to her right, where Nina bowed her head slightly in encouragement, Poppy and Sonia settling into the chairs beside her.

She glanced left, to Sawyer and Alix. Then back at Semmena. Who amongst these people were her allies?

Sol might not know much about royal politics, but she knew people.

So, she pulled out her chair and sat.

Immediately, her Court did as well, followed by the Ladies of Niome and the fur-clad Romalia couple. At Alix's other side, two men gave her courteous nods as they sat, both dressed in beige, extravagant tunics.

Nine guests remained standing. Six sat with her.

She supposed it could have been worse.

Semmena gave her a slow, knowing smile as he slid into his own seat, everyone else following suit. "A toast. To the Yarrow reign." His Court and his people grabbed their chalices. Slowly, she met the gaze of each of her own people around her table. Her mother's people.

Her bloodline's people.

She didn't know how to convey what she felt, not with her gaze alone. But she tried. She met Poppy's and Sonia's curious eyes, the couple beside them, and the men next to Alix. She tried saying she was sorry this was what they had—but was going to fight for them.

Sol raised her chalice.

And so did they.

CHAPTER EIGHTEEN
Chained to Destiny

The dinner was as uncomfortable as she expected. Besides casual conversations, everyone spent most of the time sizing the others up. When Alix said it was better for her to see the political pains firsthand while on the road, he meant it.

The Ladies of Niome chatted with Nina and Sawyer effortlessly, and Sol enjoyed listening to the adventures of their younger selves. The Southern nobles attended Rimemere Wielder Academy during the final year of their studies, to be taught with ancient texts only the libraries in the castle held. Also, Rimemere was the only place in the South with temples, so they used that final year of studies to dedicate themselves to their gods.

According to Sawyer, regular offerings to the gods were generally better, but as long as it was done at least once a year, the Wielder would remain with their magic.

"And if no offerings are made?" Sol asked in between bites of an overly salted roast. "What happens then?"

"The Wielder dies," Poppy said. "Happens quite often, actually. Especially now that Rimemere has a wall, and we cannot come pay our respects without getting brands and verbal threats from the kingsmen—"

"Poppy!" Sonia whispered, lightly nudging her wife. "Quiet."

"It's true, is it not?" Poppy crossed her arms. "The wall was uncalled for."

Sol flicked her gaze to Semmena who watched her over the rim of his chalice.

Shivers skidded through her. "It's meant to protect from these Jinn?"

The man directly beside Alix, with sun kissed skin and a long, ebony braid laughed. "I suppose that is what the official reports say."

"Those demons get through anything," the Romalian woman — Kenia, Sol had learned—chimed. "They dwell in water. And there is no wall along the coast."

Memories from the Yavenharrow disaster flashed through her mind. It had truly been incredible the creatures hadn't found her before the Wielders did.

Sonia seemed to have the same thought, as she leaned on a hand casually, her lashes grazing her cheeks. "Do tell us, Sol. How was life in Graniela? Did you truly live as a commoner?"

It wasn't lost on Sol how all conversations halted. Of course everyone was interested in that response.

"I—"

Don't say something stupid. What would your mother say? What would Lora say?

She took a steadying breath. "I can't really say it was a 'commoner's' life, as I had nothing grander to compare it to. But, I loved the simplicity and the town."

"Did you never feel the pull to us?" Poppy asked. "Didn't Warren call to you?"

"My dear cousin has yet to do her Awakening, as you all know," Sawyer added, drinking directly from a pitcher of wine. "A reason why she didn't need our dear, dear temples."

They all blanched simultaneously, similar versions of horror on their faces. Semmena's people, though, laughed.

"So, it is true?" A woman with a scaled dress that might as well have been her skin, cackled, shaking the plate before her with a slap of her hand on the table. "The Yarrow Heir is human?" She let out another deafening caw.

"Unsettled, technically, since she is past fifteen summers," another person said. "What a disgrace."

Semmena watched with amusement as Sol tried to suppress an embarrassed flush.

They didn't know.

"We thought this knowledge was distributed," Nina said, looking to the end of the table.

Samara shrugged. "Oops."

Hushed murmurs erupted, the nobles leaning to whisper to each other, casting glances her way.

Penny's words about the Unsettled echoed in her memory from their first meeting.

They say we are bad luck to have around.

"I think it's a strength, actually." Sol's voice was stern. "I've lived my whole life without magic as a crutch."

Sawyer smiled, a small laugh echoing from within her raised pitcher.

Sol continued, ignoring the onlookers, and donning that casual mask, giving her uncle a sweet smile. "I believe my set of expertise will only aid us once I do Awaken."

"And what are those, Princess?" Gina set her sharp chin on her hand. "Do tell us."

"Not placing worth on someone's name or power and seeing them for who they are instead." Sol stood. "Seeing people not as assets and additions, but as human beings with lives and rights. Supporting those who aren't heard. Using knowledge to heal and not harm."

Even her Court watched her with tentative surprise at the blatant display of courage, one Sol had to admit was likely fueled by adrenaline. Poppy's face gleamed with pride, as did her wife's.

But Sol didn't stay to see any other reactions as she set down her chalice and stepped away from the table. "I also have a pretty good aim with daggers." She bowed. "Lovely feast, Majesty."

As she left the feast without waiting for a dismissal, Gaven held the doors open then offered to walk with her to a mezzanine overlooking the throne room before the next part of the celebration, which was the dance.

Her court trailed behind her silently the whole way, and Sol wanted to run back to them and apologize for acting like an offended child.

After arriving at the ballroom, musicians playing lazily, she expressed the sentiment to Nina, who only gave her a small hug. "Don't be sorry, that was amazing."

Sawyer, albeit a tad tipsy, nodded in agreement and said, "Screw the hierarchy," before stumbling away to a table of what Sol had to guess were Melisandre soldiers. Which led way to the next concern.

Not only was Cas absent, but his territory, Eswin, was also. Sol noted the table with their label looming in a corner, empty and bleak compared to the energy of the others.

Nina cursed at the realization, sending Alix into the bustling crowd to see if he could subtlety gather intel on why they were the only territory who declined the offer to visit Rimemere. As Nina took her arm and dismissed Gaven with a wave, she explained Eswin was originally ruled by the Morozov clan, Cas's maternal line and notorious Shadow Guiders. They were a relatively secretive family, but after Draven had left Lady Alyana, Cas's mother, for Irene, the territory only secluded itself further into isolation. Sol rubbed at the spot between her thumb and index finger, a holistic point of pressure Lora had taught her could relieve unwanted tension.

For the first time, it didn't work.

She and Nina leaned on the mezzanine railing, watching the couples sway to the bright strings and deep notes of some wooden instrument Sol had never seen. The nobles had apparently been allowed to bring guests, one per house. The guests now mingled, tripling the size of the original crowd.

Like the ballroom, the throne room was painted with silvers and blues, something she came to realize were the Mornett colors—Samara and Gina's maternal bloodline. Gina was tasked with the castle decor, and she obviously tried to erase any trace of Irene whenever she could. Melisandre colors were scattered in between, mostly in the quieter, dimmer rooms, where they could dwell in the shadows and not gain much attention.

Most bizarre of all though, and a new addition to the decor according to Nina, was a large, seemingly useless cube settled on the far wall next to the golden double doors. It was an eyesore with the rest of the elegant things. It seemed like a crate of sorts, with a crimson curtain draped over it to directly conceal whatever was beneath it.

Alix mentioned Semmena enjoyed bringing exotic animals from Polimende as entertainment. The thought of a lion or some other beast in the room with them made Sol's headache insufferable.

She smiled softly through the pain as the Dianese guest, a boy with large, puffy brown sleeves and sleeked hair, spoke with Penny in a corner, both exchanging pieces of food for the other to try.

Sol traced the wallpaper with her eyes. She supposed she should be downstairs, mingling with the nobility. But she was tired. Tired of pretending like she was put together. Of pretending like she no longer resented her mother for making the transition into this world so much harder.

My dear girl, I am so sorry.

She grabbed her necklace, zipping it back and forth on its chain as Nina sighed.

"Awkward, huh?" The Earth Caller caressed a lonely plant beside her. "I didn't think it would be this bad."

Sol shrugged. "I didn't expect a welcome party."

They watched the people below in silence. Poppy and Sonia laughed together in an intimate dance, making Sol sigh.

She had never truly craved that sort of relationship with anyone, nothing apart from the occasional distraction. But seeing them, the attention they regarded each other with, the way they seemed to be suspended in their own world— it pulled at her chest.

"They're a rarity," Nina said, following her line of vision. "The last gods' called union still alive."

Sol tore her gaze from them. "Gods'-called?"

"Poppy's god, Aquarene, called her and Sonia's union." Nina smiled down at them, also seemingly enchanted. "Sonia was a Fire Wielder, but resigned her fire and took some of Poppy's magic during their union. As a reward for accepting the bond, Aquarene granted Sonia Duality, letting her keep Emberdon's flames while also able to Water Dance."

Sol looked back at them. "That's possible?"

"The gods are odd. They occasionally call two individuals together, whether for power or strength," she shrugged. "We will never know the gods' motives."

The couple laughed in unison, Sonia grabbing a mug of wine from a servant. She caught Sol's gaze and gave her a polite nod, followed by Poppy peering back to do the same.

Sol returned the gesture. "So, they're like soulmates?"

Nina laughed. "I guess that's comparable. But gods' bonds can be accepted or rejected. Though rejecting it is apparently painful, physically, and emotionally. The bonds are so rare, not much is truly known of them except that accepting them grants the couple great, unique power. And well, unmatched love, it seems."

"Please tell me we can leave soon." Alix strode up behind them, placing his arm around Nina's shoulder.

She smiled up at him. "Bored already? Go mingle."

He frowned. "Not really anything worth mingling with."

Sol shook her head and smiled. "I vote we leave soon Alix."

"Ah, what the Princess says, the Princess gets." He laughed and bowed in fake reverence.

Nina opened her mouth to speak, but the music below came to a sudden standstill.

Alix peered over the railing.

"My dear Wielders," Semmena's voice carried through the room. "It is time for the main event of the night."

Exchanging a wary glance, Sol and Nina joined Alix at the railing.

The guests parted to let Semmena and his Court through to the dais that held his throne. The nobles remained in a sort of semi-circle before it as the King settled into the stone throne, Gina and Samara standing beside him. Jeriyah seemed to finally decide to appear, as he stood behind the seats beside Gaven, both their expressions wholly serious.

"As you all know, the gods have finally blessed us with my niece's presence after many years of searching for her." Semmena's usual, playful demeanor was muted, replaced by that fierce, terrifying ruler Sol heard rumors about. Until now, although he had been slightly hostile, he hadn't shown the side of him Sawyer warned them about. The side that built a wall to fight against "Jinn," when in reality it blocked civilians and those seeking their temples.

The way his eyes shone now, as if they could conjure Emberdon's flames themselves, made Sol shiver.

As if sensing her attention, he looked at her. "Following Rimemere tradition, my niece will have to Awaken her magic before being sworn into her reign." He motioned in front of him with a wave of his hand. "Of course, after her Coronation Vows."

The crowd cheered.

"No," Nina said breathlessly. She gripped the metal rails, her knuckles turning an icy white. "He wouldn't."

Semmena continued, "We have selected a total of nine prospects from all over the South to compete for godly blessings, to join the Yarrow line in their rule."

Breathing became difficult as Sol watched the guests separate, most stepping back to leave a neat line of individuals facing the throne.

Coronation Vows.

Where—Where have I heard that before?

"Of course he would." Alix's jaw tensed, glaring at the people below.

"On this day, we present the prospects for the 53rd Rimemere Coronation Vows." Semmena rose, motioning to the line of people. "Please, introduce yourselves."

"What is this?" Sol said, not knowing if to focus on the people or the guests or the way the King smirked her way—

The first person, a man, stepped out of the line, turning his face up to Sol.

"Princess Yarrow," the man crooned, lowering into a bow. "Ezra Sonte, eldest son of Polimende Lord Elias." His hazel eyes shone. "A pleasure to be considered for your hand."

Before Sol could voice her confusion, a woman stepped forward. She had to be younger than Sol, hidden behind a heavy curtain of wavy brown hair. "Zeri Zoar from Ventry, Princess," she curtsied. "An honor."

"Are you fucking serious?" Sawyer stepped forward from directly beneath the mezzanine, side stepping the line of people now facing Sol. "She isn't a Rimemere native, she doesn't have to perform the Vows."

"Sol Yarrow is the direct heiress of the Rimemere throne, and she will adhere to the traditions that accompany that title." Gina released a string of Shadows from her place beside the King.

Sawyer met them with a wall of smoke. "So, you're delaying her coronation another two weeks?"

"I am merely following traditions, daughter." Semmena strode down the dais, stopping foot to foot with Sawyer. "The true delay is Irene not Awakening her."

"Good gods," whispered Alix, stalking to the staircase. Nina looked after him with furrowed brows and an expression that made Sol's anxiety spike.

"What's happening?" Sol repeated, this time grabbing Nina's forearm.

The Earth Caller turned to her, expression was distant. "Sol... I'm so sorry."

The next person separated from the line. "Cade Lane," the man said, voice smooth as the sea. "Next in line for Teriopa reign."

Then the next.

"Cattya Zelaya." The woman spun in place, winking at Sol with burning, baby blue eyes. "Lady of Stone Ledge."

And the next.

"Jonah Ketar, Princess." He inched his chin down. "Eldest son of Dianese Nobility."

There were more left, more introductions and announcements of places she didn't know. But when the next individual stepped forward, half the size of any of the others, Sol's head spun.

The boy bowed, low and full. He had to be no older than twelve, his clothes loose around long, lanky limbs. "P—Phil Ketar." His voice wavered. "Youngest son of Dianese Nobility."

A thread snapped. The mask of poise she tried to keep well fastened at least for the night melted.

Evaporated.

Sol swirled on her heel, fists clenched and chest hot with fury as she followed Alix to the chaos below.

CHAPTER NINETEEN
Coronation Vows

Sol stared at the prospects.

By the foot of the stairs, all eyes shifted from her to Semmena, the silence so thick, it felt as if Sol struggled against it as she stalked forward.

The eight of them immediately bowed and parted for her, which made Sol's blood roar in her ears. Semmena wore a careless smirk. Beside him, Hand Gina batted her lashes calmly, waving at a nearby servant to bring her another pitcher of wine.

Samara seemed impatient, her nails tapping on the throne's armrest. When she met Sol's gaze, she rolled her eyes. It was perhaps a combination of all those little things that made Sol continue walking until she was at the foot of the dais. A combination of all those mundane gestures, of the disinterest the Rimemere officials regarded the occasion with.

Behind her, Nina's soft gait followed, the only sound other than the howling of the wind against the castle walls. Sol looked up at Semmena, tears of pure rage burning in her eyelids. It struck her then, Gaven had mentioned this tradition briefly when they spoke about Cas and his sentence.

Rimemere tradition has a sort of tournament to see who the Queens marry.

Screw this man.

And screw traditions.

She knew she needed to be here, to continue her mother's work, but gods be damned if she was going down without a fight.

"I'm not marrying any of those people," she breathed, halting in front of the King. "I don't agree to this."

He shrugged, his crown—her crown—shifting atop his black curls. "It's mandatory for rulers to take a partner through the Coronation Vows. You cannot Awaken, therefore take the throne, without it."

"Where is your partner, *Majesty*?" Sol crossed her arms over her chest. "You rule alone."

Gasps fluttered through the room. Clearly, the crowd was appalled at her outburst, but she didn't care. Even Hand Gina gave her a stern glare, but as soon as Sawyer stepped up next to Sol, even Samara seemed to tense.

"I can argue that was the plan all along," her cousin said.

"Keep your theories out of facts, Sawyerlyn," Gina sneered. "Your mother befell a great tragedy."

Sawyer scoffed. "Yeah, she *befell*, alright."

"If you aren't in agreement with the way we do things here, Princess, you are free to return to your life in Graniela and let us continue to prosper." Semmena raised a brow. "You have my blessing to relinquish your right to rule."

Sol let a small smile spread across her lips, fueled by the challenge. "Convenient."

"We are wasting time. Leave or be fine with this, Yarrow," Samara said, waving a hand. "If we don't have to host the Vows, it gives us more time to do what actually matters, like kill the Jinn and all. Something your mother should've done."

"Watch it, Samara." Nina warned, stepping to her other side.

The whispers and gasps dwindled into silence again, but this time even the soft sounds of the birds and the wind from beyond the walls seemed to halt.

As if the gods themselves were listening.

Nina cleared her throat. "If we may, your Majesty? Alix or I will join the Vows."

Sol snapped her gaze to her. "You will not—"

"You can't anyway," Gina said. "None of you are noble. Amana, your mother was a servant. Alix, your family is made of commoners. Incredibly intelligent, but not noble."

Sol narrowed her eyes at them. Semmena had planned this. Although he didn't truly know her, his gamble was well organized. He gave her a way out, which for a second, she contemplated.

A way out. Back to Yavenharrow without needing to worry about any of this anymore.

If you don't succeed, Sol, nothing will matter. There will be nothing left to love if you don't continue what I started.

Sol sighed. And all logic left her as she said, "I'll join then. If I win, I don't marry."

There was a beat of silence then Samara laughed. "You're out of your gods-damned mind."

Smoke curled on Semmena's shoulders as he raked his gaze over Sol. He angled his head.

"If I win, this tradition is done. Southern rulers won't be shackled to people they don't know," Sol continued.

Murmurs sounded from around them, and she briefly registered the Ladies of Niome smile from the corner of her vision. Beside them, another couple looked at each other, then back to Sol with furrowed brows. Then gave her a small nod.

It made her wonder how many of the nobles were together under free will, or if they had also been thrown into lives they had no control over.

She hadn't spoken for anyone else other than herself, but a shimmer of pride settled in her chest. She held her chin high, even more so as Nina grasped her forearm. "Sol, no. These people are—"

"You realize you'd have to kill all prospects to win?" Semmena said. "Have you ever held a sword?"

Sol peered over her shoulder at the prospects.

Five men. Three women. Well, four men and a *child*.

She'd find a way to spare them. She—she'd go into the Vows and somehow have them survive. There had to be something she could do, what else was she good for if she couldn't save the lives she left everything to fight for?

Sol looked back at Semmena. "I'll join."

Her uncle grinned. "What an interesting turn of events."

"You can't be serious," Sawyer spat at her father. "You cry about traditions then make *this* exception?"

Semmena stood from his throne, making the audience fall to their knees in a bow. "I'll allow it."

I'll allow it. Okay.

Panic swirled in Sol's stomach, but she kept her jaw shut, unwilling to change her mind. She had to Awaken her magic. She had to get through this.

And she wasn't going to do it with a stranger shackling her down, observing her every move. She *couldn't* have anyone beside her, not for what she was meant to do.

Sol turned to walk back to the shadows of the ballroom, painfully aware of everyone's attention. The prospects eyed her, most with surprise. Some with fear. Some with a mix of both, laced with a curiosity she had no intention of satisfying.

The room seemed suspended in time. Everyone whispered amongst themselves in between coy glances, and the crowd of Rimemere students that gathered by the open doors dissipated back into the castle hallways as Sol neared the exit.

That was about all she could take for the day.

Sol knew if she focused too much on what she had just done, she would melt with nerves. Run back and beg to rethink her decision.

Arnold hummed pensively, making her stop her escape and look back his way. He crossed an ankle over a knee. "You know, I feel like I am missing something. What could it be?"

Beside him, Gina's violet eyes sparkled with mischief. "The gift!" She signaled to the mysterious, red draped crate by the wall, almost directly beside Sol. She took a healthy step away from it.

"The gift!" King Semmena echoed, clapping. "I suppose I should've unveiled it prior to your little announcement, niece. My mind wanders lately."

Nina shifted, grabbing hold of Sawyer and Alix as King Semmena strode down his dais and onto the floor. Smoke seemed to trail him as he walked toward Sol, toward the eyesore of a decoration.

The crowds that gathered around it parted for him.

Nina met Sol's gaze from the other side of the room, and Sol dipped her chin, a silent request for them to come to her side.

Perhaps it was a bear. A lion, like Alix had suggested. Something Semmena could unleash, and it would take care of the problem Sol posed to him.

"Before you graced us with your very brave display of defiance, Sol Yarrow," Semmena said, running his hand across the crimson fabric. "I was actually going to announce one more prospect."

As the curtain slid to the ground, Sol didn't know what to focus on first. On the fact that beneath the cloth was a cage made of steel bars and stone. Or on the fact who resided within.

Cas.

"What the fuck." Sawyer voiced Sol's thoughts as she raced forward.

Sol was frozen as her cousin ran past, trying to keep her breathing normal, willing her mind to settle. Cas lay against the far bars, his head limp against them, as if they were the only thing offering support.

Slowly, Sol walked closer.

His skin was smeared with dust and sweat, his hair pressed to his forehead and cheeks. His chest rose and fell in hollow pants, and when he met her gaze, those sterling eyes were as dim as the rusted bars around him.

"What the fuck is this?" Sawyer repeated, pulling at the bars frantically. Her palms flared. "Let him out!"

Beside Sol, Nina fell forward with a sob, pressing her face to the cage while her knees collided with the marble floors. "Cas," she pleaded. "Cas, are you okay?"

Cas didn't move, instead giving the Earth Caller a small, gentle smile.

"Casimir Xanthos is hereby sentenced to his participation in the Yarrow Coronation Vows as punishment for the murder of Gerson Xamthee." Semmena rubbed his palms together, as if the motion would cleanse the filth from them. "His immediate execution would have been a mercy compared to the terror my kingsmen experienced upon his return."

Sawyer narrowed her eyes at her father, tears pooling at the edge of her eyes. "Your kingsmen disrespected the Heiress Apparent."

"Can you blame them for assuming she wasn't Irene's daughter?" Gina eyed Sol. "Not to mention insults should not result in death."

Fury coated Sol's throat. She could feel it heat her face, her chest, her closed fists as she surveyed Cas, as his wrists bled beneath solid cuffs and his exposed skin flecked with bruises.

She turned to her uncle. "Release him."

Amusement danced in the man's eyes. He surveyed her with a calculating ferocity, then just shrugged. "He will go to the dungeons until all the prospects depart to the Gods' Villa tomorrow. Yourself included."

Sol remained welded to her spot, all too aware of the wandering eyes, whispers, and the gods-awful sight of the warrior inside the cage. Again, she said, "open the cage."

"You don't order the King—" Semmena held a hand up, interrupting Gina mid-chastise. But Sol didn't look at the woman.

She remained with her attention on the King, on the man she knew was going to be an absolute nightmare to remove from the throne.

Her mother's throne.

Her family's throne.

Seconds ticked by, but neither of them budged. Finally, the King motioned a kingsman forward. "Take him to the dungeons. His blood is making the place reek."

The guards stepped forward, one of them holding a ring of keys.

Sol sidestepped him, outstretching her hand. "Keys."

"The King ordered us to do it."

"I heard. *Keys*."

The guard swallowed and looked from Semmena to Sol, then surely at Sawyer who stood behind her with the heat of an inferno radiating from her.

As the King turned to walk back into the ballroom, his Court in tow, the guard dropped the keys into Sol's open hand.

She merely tossed them back to Sawyer.

"Let us gather outdoors, Noblemen and Noblewomen!" King Semmena continued his walk into the crowd, stopping only briefly at the entrance to motion them forward. "We have fantastic antiquities and things to showcase outside."

"We will come inside for beverages and dancing once the room is cleared." Gina clipped the last of the words with a glare at Sol.

The clatter of the lock and keys resounded through the room as Sawyer pulled the door of the cage open.

"Cas," her cousin whispered, followed by a sob from Nina.

Both the women crowded into the cage, Alix full of stone, primal fury beside them.

"Why," was all the Water Dancer said.

Sol flicked her gaze to him, pursing her lips and shaking her head. She didn't have an answer for him.

The kingsmen remained in the room as the rest of the people filed out. Penny looked back at her uncle with a tear-stained face, ushered forward by Poppy Niomoe and the boy she spoke to before—the boy Sol now realized was one of her marriage prospects.

Oh gods.

She willingly signed up to participate in what seemed like a death sentence. Did her rash decision gain her allies? Or enemies?

She traced the scar on her palm, wishing with all of her will that her aunt Lora would walk through the throne room doors and embrace her, tell her all was okay, and she would get them out of this.

No.

No, that didn't seem likely to happen.

Sol turned around.

Aside from the blood and bruises, Cas seemed slightly better now that Nina and Sawyer were beside him. Sawyer ran her hands gently over his face, presumably to warm him. Nina materialized plants—Sol recognized the aloe vera leaf the Earth Caller harvested salve from. She smoothed it over Cas's face.

He met Sol's gaze and gave her a weak smile. "The one joy of being beaten almost to death is the way it brings out their nurturing side."

Sol shook her head as Sawyer and Nina protested.

"Is that why you pick fights so often, Cassie?" Sawyer snickered. "To feel the touch of a woman?"

Despite her tears, Nina laughed. "We will hug you more, Cas. I swear it."

"Why didn't you call for help?" Alix knelt beside the cage, wrapping a palm around a rusted bar. "Why just lay here?"

Cas shrugged. "I'm tired. Plus, I was very entertained by the Princess's speech."

Sol knelt in front of him, her dress spilling around the rusted cage.

She searched his face for a hint of sincerity, or emotion. But it was cold. Vacant.

And she understood. So, she only said, "He will pay."

The three of them looked at her, the two women cautiously surprised. But Cas grinned. "Welcome to the Yarrow court, Princess."

ACT TWO

Once upon a time, a girl forged her own path....
but realized too late that sticks, stones, and bones were all she had.

Myths, Tales, and Truths of the Southern Continent: Laws and Orders

Est. 1897 A.Y

On this 37th day of Winter, it is written into law that all royalty settling into their reign must first take part in gods-mandated vows of honor to rule beside another of royal blood.

Thus keeping each other true and honest, to faithfully serve the gods that bless us.

<u>Amendment 1, as per Romalia:</u>

Prospects must present themselves before the territory's counsel.

<u>Amendment 2, as per Ventry:</u>

Must take place before 23 winters, or before the Wielder's Awakening.

<u>Amendment 3, as per Rimemere:</u>

Prospects shall show their devotion to the gods by participating in a series of tests to put themselves at their mercy. The survivor may wed into the sacred Yarrow line.

Updated Rules for the 53rd Vows

 Due to the unprecedented permission granted by King Arnold Semmena, Fire Wielder, Melisandere Lord and King Reagent of Rimemere, for the Crown Princess's participation in her own Coronation Vows, the rules in place will be as follows:

 In the case of Sol Yarrow as the sole victor: Permission to reign as the sole Royal. The dissolution of the Coronation Vow law throughout the Southern territories. Those next in line for their reign may choose to remain alone.

 In the case of a prospect as the sole victor: Said prospect may join the Semmena Court, as per King Arnold Semmena, Fire Wielder, Melisandere Lord and King Reagent of Rimemere. All benefits gifted to the Semmena court will be indefinitely transferred to the prospects' home territory and bloodline.

 In the case of a draw: Remaining parties may yield. Yielding will keep their lives but will force the party who chooses to do so to relinquish their noble status.

Prospects of the 53rd Rimemere Coronation Vows

Ezra Sonte: (Ez-rah Son-teh)
Eldest son of the Polimende Lord Elias. *Earth Caller.*

Zeri Zoar: (Zeh-ree Zor)
Youngest daughter of Ventry's Nobility. *Wind Dancer.*

Phil Ketar: (Fil Ke-tahr)
Youngest son of Dianese Lady. Half sibling to Jonah Ketar, Eldest son of Dianese Lady.

Sent by stepfather to maximize chances. *Wind Dancer.*

Jonah Ketar: (Joe-na Ke-tahr)
Eldest son of Dianese Lord and Lady. Heir to Dianese lands. Half sibling to Phil Ketar. *Earth Caller.*

Cattya Zelaya: (Kat-yah Ze-lay-yah)
Youngest Lady of Stone Ledge. *Fire Wielder.*

Cade Lane: (K-aid Lein)
Heir of Teriopa. *Water Dancer.*

Felice Mintz: (Fe-Liz Meen-ts)
Eldest daughter or Romlian Nobility. *Earth Caller.*

Lucas Mintz: (Loo-kahz Meen-ts)
Romalian Nobility, brother of Felice. *Earth Caller.*

Casimir Xanthos:
~~Prince of Eswin~~. *Shadow Guider, Warden.*

Sol Yarrow:
Heiress apparent of the Rimemere throne. *Unsettled.*

CHAPTER TWENTY

SAWYER

Sawyer followed the guards all the way down to the dungeons.

After Sol seemed to be possessed by Loumallet himself and officially joined their hate-the-King club, the kingsmen ordered them out so they could escort Cas back into the depths of the castle.

Sol and Nina only moved aside when Sawyer declared she would go along with them.

The kingsmen warned the King would not like that.

Sawyer told them to go fuck themselves.

She trailed behind the four kingsmen all the way to the other end of the castle, utterly annoyed when Finigan joined them somewhere on the journey. The rosewood door that led to the lower levels loomed in a hidden corner, easy to miss unless one knew what they looked for.

And oh, did she.

The tepid air hit her immediately as the door opened, forcing a cough and a flood of unwelcomed memories.

Cas ambled between the kingsmen, his wrists shackled in copper cuffs to suppress his magic. The four men strategically placed themselves at his every angle, as if afraid the Prince would flee, even as constricted as he was.

Uncharacteristically smart of them.

They circled down and down the groaning staircase for what seemed like forever. It spiraled into the ground below the castle and Warren's Temple, which hovered beneath Irene's old throne room. The cylindrical structure made Sawyer yearn for the freedom of the outdoors, and she wouldn't say she was afraid of small spaces. But the moldy walls, the dim atmosphere that seemed to only thicken the further they descended, would make anyone uneasy—even a Fire Wielder.

She let a spark of fire free at her fingertips. The kingsmen didn't protest, surely thankful for the speck of light. But Fin scowled. "You disgrace Emberdon using your fire to light a place like this."

"You disgrace Winderlyn with your existence, yet here you are." Sawyer didn't balk when his expression filled with hate.

Finally arriving at the bottom, Fin pushed the towering dungeon doors open with a shove of his shoulders.

Everything beneath the castle was interconnected through the kingdom's ancient tunnels. The rulers before Irene, all bloodthirsty bastards, needed a place to dump their prisoners. Greta Yarrow, Irene's great-grandmother, decided what better place to have slaves and criminals await their death than right beneath their castle?

When they were smaller, Sawyer and Nina tried to implode the place—then quickly realized the castle would tumble to the ground as a result.

Perhaps that was the reason for the morbid placement.

They walked silently into the cellar hall. Cells expanded along the entire right wall. Last time Sawyer had been down here there had only been twelve cells, albeit several people crammed into them. Now, Sawyer counted fifteen, then the kingsmen finally stopped at the sixteenth.

"In, Xanthos." One of the men shoved him into the cell.

Or at least tried to.

"Watch it, asshole, he's still part of the Royal court." Sawyer stepped forward, fire sparking at her fingertips. But Cas didn't need the back up. A single glare from him had the men stepped back with only Fin standing his ground.

"That means absolutely nothing, Sawyerlyn." Fin gave her a once over, dangerously slow. "You're looking better than ever, you know. If you ever need some company—"

Sawyer laughed. "I would rather kill myself."

"You're more like your mother than you know, then."

Cas lunged at Fin. In a smooth, calculated motion, he wrapped the dangling chain between his shackles around the lead kingsman's neck, slamming him back to his chest into an effortless hold.

Fin struggled against Cas, but the Prince showed no signs of pain or intention to release him. "Apologize," Cas said, voice slow and low. "I'm already serving punishment for killing your comrade, I have nothing more to lose if I kill you too."

The kingsmen had their swords out in a flash, the metal singing through the silence. Cheers erupted from the other cells.

"Kill them!" someone called. "Kill the kingsmen!"

Sawyer exhaled, releasing Fin's words with the breath.

You're more like your mother than you know, then.

"One day, Finigan. One day I'll kill you, and it will bring me so much joy to finally never have to see you again." Sawyer tapped Cas's arm. "But that day is not today."

Cas released him, then pushed him forward.

Fin glared at them both, rubbing at his neck between labored breaths. "You have five minutes before I tell your father you're down here."

"Just go do it now, asshole. We both know you need to kiss his ass daily."

The man clenched his jaw, his eyes narrowing on her. "You were a good commander, you know." He strode past her, sure to shove her aside. "Too bad it got to your head."

Sawyer waited until the dungeon's door clicked shut and the kingsmen beyond it scattered before she slammed a fiery fist into the wall. "*Pricks.*"

A sigh resounded through the dimness as Cas slumped against the cell's far wall.

Sawyer was too busy imagining all the ways she could pummel Fin that she didn't notice the kingsmen locked the cell door before they left.

She sank to the ground in front of it and looked at Cas. "You look like shit."

"So do you."

Sawyer frowned at her gown. "This dress comes straight from Ventry, you jerk. It's pure feather silk."

Cas inched sideways then slid himself to the ground. "Exactly."

This wasn't the Prince of Eswin's first time in the dungeons. In fact, it was that very fact that made Sawyer follow him down here, to make sure the memories didn't implode the little grip on himself he regained through years of careful healing.

His mother and sister had been down here after his father's execution. Had been down here for months, all of which Cas had spent mostly where Sawyer sat, reaching, yearning to be reunited with his only remaining family. When they disappeared, that thread of humanity Cas held on to vanished with them.

Sawyer looked around at the neighboring cell. It was empty save for a tray of rotting food, presumably from its previous dweller. The firelight along the hall shone amber but seemed cold, not an ounce of warmth emanating from a single corner of the subterranean space.

She traced circles on the dirt beneath her. "What's your sentence?"

Cas's head lolled toward her. "Hmm?"

"What did my father tell you?"

He slid his hand behind his head. "After his kingsmen beat me with barbed whips? Nothing. Just threw me in that cage. I learned about my participation in the Vows at the same time everyone else did."

Sawyer couldn't hide the grimace, anger permeating through her features. "Cas, I'm so fucking sorry."

"Don't be. It's not your fault."

"He's my father. I—"

"Sawyer, it was always like this." Cas sighed. "Before we left, it was like this. He cycles through us like seasons. We all suffer." He looked at her, all the times she had been in his position hanging thickly in the damp air. "Including you."

Clenching her jaw, she shook her head. "He will only get worse now there's an heir."

Cas managed a dry laugh. "Obviously."

Although the cover of darkness helped, the man wasn't as good at hiding his emotions as he thought.

Sawyer tapped the cell bars. "So, you and Sol—"

"Don't."

"You know that's not going to end well, right?"

A muscle in his jaw ticked. "Does it look like I have a choice, Sawyer?"

She pressed her forehead against the bars.

Irene's own Coronation Vows had been similar. The Rimemere history books say Draven joined the Vows willingly, out of his love for her and despair she wouldn't have him in that way.

Sawyer, though, knew better than to trust those books. She knew from firsthand accounts that Draven joined to spare her from Arnold, who was the prospect from Melisandre. The entire South knew of her father's reputation as a fighter, as a killer, and Draven joined knowing he might pose a challenge for him the other prospects did not.

Cas sat up, and that's when Sawyer noticed it.

He was a fool. Even after them being almost inseparable for eighteen years, he still refused to alert her when the blood was low.

Sawyer thought maybe the man had a death wish.

She shook her head and signaled him forward. "You need to tell me when it starts to get low, Cas."

He eyed her for a moment, hesitating. The tattoo seemed to lighten with each passing second, and Sawyer had to tap the bars again for him to admit defeat. "I was able to go almost four weeks without it this time." He stood, shaky but strong.

"And how long was the maximum before?"

"Three and a half weeks."

She grabbed his arm through the bars as he lowered himself beside her. His skin was cold and covered in bruises. The anger festered in her chest, burning hotter than her flames as she eyed the wounds. "I'll kill him," she whispered.

"Leave it, Sawyer."

She let his arm hang through the cell bars as she sliced a thin, precise cut along her palm. "Never. It's my life mission to make him pay."

Sawyer inhaled a heavy breath and brought her bloody palm down on his forearm.

Her blood sizzled against the markings, spreading into the scarred edges, filling the tattoo. Cas relaxed against the bars.

Irene's magic had truly been one of a kind. Not only was she able to fully master her Wards, but she had studied the ancient, god-written scriptures of the Western Stones before the island and contents were incinerated in battle. From those coveted texts, she learned binds and spells—Dark Magic—that only the most powerful Wielders possessed knowledge of, the sort of magic the Immortal Relics were rumored to channel. Those Relics were legends, artifacts crafted by the gods themselves that scattered with time.

"I hate this."

Sawyer looked up at Cas, a distant expression on his face as he trailed the stone's engravings with his gaze.

"I know," she whispered. "It's not fair."

Queen Irene was brutal with Draven's punishment. She not only executed him, but she forced Cas to resign his title as Prince of Eswin and his freedom. The punishment for his father conspiring against the crown was for Cas to be bound to Yarrow blood for half a century. Stray too far from the Yarrow bloodline, and the tattoo ink would kill him, crafted from Irene's blood itself. No one besides them both knew of this. Everyone simply thought he was bound to Rimemere, as he was exiled from Eswin.

Brutally ironic.

They had discovered her blood resealed the volatile Dark Magic within the tattoo by accident during a sparring drill a month after she had arrived in Rimemere, after her father's coronation. She had been eight years old. He had been thirteen.

It hadn't always been that way. The tattoo was fine and full since it was branded when he was eight, but once Irene died and the Jinn attacks became more frequent, the magic that held his tattoo began morphing too.

Sawyer helped him every two weeks ever since.

"You know, Sol might be able to —"

"No," he cut her off.

"But her blood might be more useful—"

"I said no."

The tattoo filled completely, and Cas wiggled from her grasp, turning away to look at the inside of his cell.

She knew the pain remained. He had let the detail spill a few years ago. His forearm ached perpetually, a reminder that the blood used wasn't from the original spell caster. But Irene was dead. Her siblings were dead.

Sol was the next best thing.

"She might be able to make it stop hurting," Sawyer whispered.

Footsteps sounded outside the dungeon entrance. "I'm not telling her about this." He cut a glance to her. "And neither are you."

She stood, her temper rising. "She owes you that much, you know. Her mother did this."

"Exactly, Sawyer. Her mother. Not her. Not you," Cas told her as he settled into a solid metal cot by the side stone wall.

Sawyer peered at him. "You know only one of you can survive the Vows, right?" She tapped her fingers on her thigh. "Unless we find out how Irene made that exception years ago."

He was silent for a moment as if truly thinking about it. But then he closed his eyes. "I don't really care."

Sawyer sighed and shut her own eyes.

Fool.

CHAPTER TWENTY-ONE
The Prospects

The rules were simple: If Sol won, she could rule alone. If she didn't, it meant she was dead.

This wouldn't have been too terrible if Cas wasn't one of the people she was now meant to "eliminate". She also hoped she wouldn't have to "eliminate" anyone at all and would somehow find a way to end the whole thing before it had a chance to begin. It didn't seem likely.

The whole night, Sol tossed and turned haunted by one of the stupidest decisions of her life. How was she to save people she needed out of the way? It was an impulsive decision, propelled by anger and disgust, and the desire to be right.

At least her court was just as baffled.

Nina chastised her to no end the rest of the celebration, sobbing and begging Alix to find a way to get Sol and Cas out of the Vows. Alix had obliged and left to the libraries if only to calm Nina for a while. Sawyer merely told Sol she succeeded in showing her inexperience at ruling to the entire South, then stalked to the dungeons after Cas. Which was fine–she wasn't wrong.

When her cousin returned, she slept on the sofa while Nina spent hours pacing the room, muttering what could have been either curses or prayers.

Between self-deprecating thoughts, Sol stared at the ceiling beneath her duvet. Cas's face was imprinted in her eyelids every time she closed them, followed by Semmena's vile smile at the reveal.

Although it wasn't her fault, Sol couldn't deny she had gotten them both into irrevocable trouble.

"You need to learn to sit the fuck down and let others win sometimes. You've only shown the South your rashness."

Sol flicked her gaze to her cousin. She played with a string of fire around her fingertips, her braid hanging from the side of the sofa. She had not said a word since returning from the dungeons.

"Perhaps if one of us takes *her* place—" Nina started, rubbing her temples. "Maybe—"

"You're going to think yourself into a panic," Sawyer sighed. "Sit down for a second."

"How are you so calm about this? Cas alone would have survived, but now with Sol too—"

"It was her choice."

"She didn't know—"

Sol sat up. "I can hear you both."

The women looked at her, both washed in amber hues from the fireplace. "That's the point." Sawyer said, standing. "Listen to the aftermath of the worst decision of your life."

"It's not the worst decision of my life, in case it matters." Sol jumped off the bed. She knew her cousin was trying to make her angry, to get her to regret her outburst. And Sol did. She felt shame and guilt all on her own—she didn't need anyone else's help with it.

"It's about to be," Sawyer assured. "You might have just doomed the South."

Sol walked to her, squeezing her hands into fists. For a moment, she considered telling her what the true worst decision of her life was, but it wouldn't matter. Not now, not ever, not to Sawyer. So instead, Sol said, "I wasn't about to sit back and watch people die for me."

Sawyer glared, onyx eyes unyielding. "You'll do a lot of that when you rule a territory, *Princess*. Get used to sitting back and assessing instead of placing yourself in situations we can't protect you from."

"I don't need protection."

"Get over yourself," Sawyer scoffed. "It's not even about you. It's about the Jinn gate."

"Sawyerlyn!" Nina placed herself between them. "Stop it. Now."

The words rang through Sol, gripping her bones. Her cousin wasn't wrong. Again.

Sol's survival was vital, if not for herself, for the sake of closing the Jinn gate eventually. She herself had nothing of value.

Well, except her blood.

Nina peered at Sol over her shoulder. "Don't," the Earth Caller warned. "Don't let that sink in. She's angry. You matter as a person, not just what your destiny holds for you."

Sawyer looked away from them, a flash of regret on her face as she crossed her arms.

"We aren't children. We don't insult each other like that." Nina grabbed Sawyer's arm. "We are all we have. You understand?"

The Fire Wielder nodded but refused to look at them. "I understand."

Sawyer turned to the front door instead, just as a set of knocks pounded through it. "Think that's for you, cousin."

Sol sighed. "Any advice?"

Sawyer narrowed her eyes at her, suddenly serious. "Cas has gone through a lot, Sol. Remember that."

"I—I will. Anything else?"

Nina pressed her lips together in contemplation. "Don't die."

When Sol was nine, she and Irene had been at the town marketplace during a raid. Soldiers surrounded the wooden carts, sending the townsfolk into a terrified frenzy. Sol didn't learn until she was much older that the soldiers were contracted by some Northern territory to seek out a mercenary who fled their shores without paying for his goods.

At the time though, Sol only knew the cold terror she felt as her mother held her against her chest, turning her away from the chaos, from the song of swords and screams as the soldiers dragged the middle-aged mercenary from his post. They took him away in shackles while his family sobbed on the sidelines as the soldiers shed not a single tear or showed a mere shred of emotion.

Sol cried along with the stranger's family, and Irene carried her all the way home, whispering sweet things and tales of a land where families wouldn't be torn apart, where death wouldn't be the only option for crimes committed out of necessity.

As Sol stood at the entrance of the Rimemere castle, Cas in copper cuffs beside her, the memory was bitter in her mind.

"A land where families wouldn't be torn apart."

The day in the gardens with Gaven was a particular weight in that moment as she watched Cas sidelong. He seemed better than the day before, not as weak, or dirty. But hollow. Defeated.

Sol was about to say something, anything to the man, but a girl maybe two feet shorter than her, with pin straight hair and scarlet lips, sauntered over from her place at the end of the line. Sol vaguely recognized the woman from the dinner. She didn't remember much of last night.

The woman looked at Sol. "Cattya of Stone Ledge, Princess." She curtsied. "I do hope you don't mind if we switch spots?"

Sol looked from Cattya to Cas, then leaned forward to locate where she had appeared from. There was an empty space almost at the end of the horizontal line the prospects stood in, awaiting the carriages that would take them to wherever the Vows would take place.

"Get back in line, Cattya," Cas said, mercifully taking Sol's need to respond. "The guards will be suspicious if they see us talking."

"Why? They know our history." Cattya reached out to touch Cas on the shoulder, but before she could, a sway of his copper chains made her flinch back. "Rude."

"Bye, Cattya."

Sol suppressed a smile as the woman scoffed and stomped back to her spot. "Interesting choice in women," she muttered.

Cas only sighed through his nose.

The carriages came into view moments later, four of them pulled by pairs of majestically massive horses, bigger than the ones they had traveled to Rimemere on. For a slight second, Sol missed the beasts.

"I didn't take you to be this reckless, Princess," Cas whispered, a gust of wind rusting his hair.

She peered up at him. "What made you realize I am?"

"This. You shouldn't have joined this mess. You only made things more difficult."

"In my defense, I didn't know you would be a part of this."

He huffed a harsh laugh, "Neither did I." He leaned down slightly, so his whisper would reach only her. "We must stick together. It's the only way for you to survive."

Sol suppressed the urge to back away. "I can take care of myself," she countered. "I'm not some helpless maiden."

Cas gave her an exasperated look, a muscle in his jaw ticking. "These people will kill you if given the chance."

"Again, I can take care of myself."

"How, exactly? You have no magic. Do you have some hidden ability you haven't shared."

Shrugging, Sol returned her attention to the gate and the carriages emerging through it. "Now why would I tell you such a valuable secret?"

The rattle of his chains gave away his growing impatience. "Well, weapons are banned at the Gods' Villa. So, if that was your plan, you might as well find a new one. Only magic is allowed, which you *don't* have yet."

The prospects around them feigned ignorance, suddenly examining the walls behind them, or listening intently to the pounding of hooves against cobblestone.

Cas pulled Sol to the side, his shackles clanking against each other. "We must kill them before they have the opportunity to kill us."

Sol glared at him. Was that his plan? The exact opposite of hers? She held her chin high. "I am not killing anyone, and neither are you."

"Sol—"

"Not a single soul, Cas." She pointed a finger at him. "I joined this to make a difference. We will not feed into the brutality."

He narrowed his eyes. "If it's you and me in the end, you won't kill me?"

Sol stared at him for a long moment. No, she had not thought of logistics. She joined the Vows prior to Cas's big reveal. She had not anticipated having to—remove someone she might not want *permanently* removed.

"We will figure that out at the end."

For a painful second, he stared at her, a cocktail of emotions swirling on his face. Then, slowly, they all melted into a mask of indifference. He shrugged. "Fine."

The carriages came to a stop in front of the castle. Fin stepped off the one in the front, his boots sending dust adrift around them. "Three prospects per carriage." He jerked his head at them. "Move."

Kingsmen filed out of the crimson and black carriages, each ushering the prospects forward. Finigan made to grab Sol, but Cas pulled her behind him. "Remove my shackles."

Finigan laughed. "Not until we get to the Gods' Villa, Xanthos."

"No one else is shackled. It puts me at a disadvantage."

Cas and Finigan glared at each other, neither man willing to move. Around them, the prospects filed into the transports, leaving only Sol, Cas, and another man who stood protectively in front of the small boy who tore Sol's heart to pieces when everything was announced the day before.

The boy gave her a small smile then hid behind the man.

"There's an uneven amount left, Sir." A kingsman strode to Finigan, signaling from the carriages back to them. "Two carriages and four prospects."

"The Princess can ride alone," Finnigan said, looking over at her. A slow smile spread across his lips. "In the one I'm directing at the front."

Again, Finigan reached to grab Sol, but this time she sidestepped Cas, crossing her arms over her chest, and away from the man's reach. "Don't touch me," she warned.

"So, you can veer off the path and likely kill her or whatever else your *King* ordered from you? She will not be riding alone with you," Cas added. "Come on Finigan, you have to try harder than that."

Sol tried to hide her surprise. She hadn't thought of that. She supposed she was an open target now as well since her participation made her both a prize and a threat. Eliminating her meant rewards in a caliber similar to marriage into her bloodline. As Alix had explained the night before, prior to his exit to the libraries, Sol's elimination from the Vows was second best to dragging her to the end, then having the other person yield.

Although that would cause them to lose their noble status, if they were to convince Sol to marry them anyway after, that lost title wouldn't matter.

Too bad she wasn't granting mercy to anybody if that became the situation.

"Then all four of you ride together and we return one carriage to the stables." Fin shrugged. "However, will you defend yourself if the others decide the ride over there is the perfect place to get rid of you both?"

That was another thing—there was no penalty for killing other prospects. The only thing they needed to refrain from was cheating during whatever the "tests" were. Cheating would anger the gods, and the whole point was to gain their blessing.

Sawyer had ripped the rules from Alix's grasp after that, incinerating them out of spite with an exasperated groan.

"We mean no harm to you, Princess," the boy whispered from behind the man's leg.

The man hushed him. "Quiet, Phil."

Call it intuition or overall exhaustion, but Sol said, "We will all ride together," then pulled Cas forward, not failing to notice Finigan looking her over until she tucked herself into the depths of the carriage seat.

The man's name was Jonah. He was the eldest son of the Dianese Nobility, an Earth Caller, and older brother to Phil who very eagerly shared all the information despite his brother's annoyance.

"Jonah and I are only half siblings," he continued, hands tapping his knees with excitement. "His father thought it would be smart to have us both here, to have double the chances to be with you, Princess."

Sol looked away and watched the trees zip by instead. "This shouldn't be happening at all."

"It's been tradition for centuries," Jonah said, the first thing he shared aside from soft chastises at his brother. "We have all made peace with it."

Still, Sol shook her head.

"You must get to the end, Princess," Phil chimed. "We will help you."

"I need to find a way to save you all." Sol ran her hands through her hair. "I—I cannot just watch the slaughter."

"If you would've just *not* joined, you wouldn't have to see anything." Cas pulled at his chains. "You can't expect to save people in a tradition requiring the exact opposite."

Sol rolled her eyes and shifted sideways, further away from the Shadow Guider. He obviously wasn't dropping the subject any time soon, and she supposed she could've rebutted with something smart. But the image of him beaten, bruised, and broken inside the cage made her clamp down on the words.

From the edge of her vision, she watched Cas smirk. "What? Say it."

"I have nothing to say."

"Just say what it is you're holding back."

Sol sighed, shutting her eyes. "Just...I know this is stupid, okay? But it's done. Deal with it."

Jonah blinked at her, looking back and forth between them both. Phil nibbled at his nails, but maintained a pleasant smile as if the bickering was entertaining.

No one said anything else the rest of the way.

CHAPTER TWENTY-TWO

Gods' Villa

The Villa was cozy—would have even been homey was it not for the unfortunate circumstances.

The architecture was simpler than the rest of Rimemere, but deep green shrubs, vines and trees covered the area surrounding it, making nature the luxury. It also successfully concealed the building's true greatness until their carriage crawled closer.

The way to the Villa consisted of withering labyrinths through the forest making Sol lose her sense of direction every time she tried to regain it.

Defeated, she perched an elbow on the carriage window most of the way and watched the branches zoom by the endless expanse of foliage somewhat comforting. It reminded Sol slightly of home. With each bump on the road, Sol felt increasingly helpless. Her first, bold move as the Heiress and it was the wrong one.

She peered at Cas.

Although he tried to hide it, he drifted in and out of sleep, same as Jonah. Phil fell completely asleep maybe ten minutes into the journey, leaving Sol alone with her thoughts. All three of them finally slept, letting Sol truly look at them.

Jonah was handsome, in a boyish sort of way that reminded her of Leo. Phil's presence had awakened instincts she didn't even know she had, of needing him to be safe and cared for.

Maternal instincts, she supposed.

Cas wore his usual black tactical suit, though the sleeves were pushed to his forearms and the usual high neckline was slightly open. His head rested against the side of the carriage door, his dark hair falling in waves to his chin. Sol frowned at the remnants of cuts and bruises along his neck, lesions still lingering on his forearms. Even his tattoo, vibrant as the night sky, had dark shadows around it from where the bruises struggled to heal.

She didn't know much about the effects of copper on the Wielder, only that it suppressed magic, from what she was able to gather through snips of conversations. She wondered if Wielders had other abilities, such as faster healing or those other things species from folklore possessed.

By the look of his wounds, it was unlikely.

Sol wished she had brought her satchel, packed with salves from Yavenharrow, and Leo's dagger, but none of them were allowed any additional belongings.

When she looked up, she found Cas watching her. Clearing her throat and trying to downplay the blush washing over her face, she gestured to his arms. "Do they hurt?"

Do they hurt? Really?

She held her breath, wanting to toss herself out of the carriage window from embarrassment.

Cas merely shrugged. "Not really. I'm used to it."

"What happened, Cas? After we were separated that day?" Sol couldn't help the curiosity over his absence. He had only been gone three days, and it had apparently not been out of the ordinary for him.

He faced forward, silent for so long Sol figured he wouldn't answer. He eventually sighed. "Semmena wondered what to do with me. Kept me in the throne room while he and his kingsmen went over punishments out loud."

"For killing that man at the wall?"

Cas nodded. "After hours of that, and the occasional punch if I would speak, they sent me to the dungeons. I lost track of time for a while until they took me out to whip me. Then I woke up in that cage and, well, you know the rest."

Somewhere along the story, Jonah and Phil woke up, both watching Cas with furrowed brows.

Softly, Phil said, "Semmena is a coward."

The Shadow Guider smiled. "I knew you looked smart, Phil."

Sol hadn't gone through many instances that required comforting strangers, or at least anyone else but those within her immediate circle. For them, she typically remained by their side until they felt better or held them while providing words of comfort. But both of those seemed too intimate for Cas, especially since they had been back and forth and was unsure where they stood.

So, she gave him a small smile. "I'm glad it's over."

He turned back to look out the window. "It's never over."

It hadn't been too cold in the center of Rimemere, but here on the outskirts, closer to the water, the air was jarring.

They were dropped off at the foot of a mansion, a rustic and beige sandstone with domed, glass tipped roofs. The other prospects had arrived first, likely already inside the Villa to avoid the threat of rain that loomed on the horizon.

The four of them trudged up the steps, stopping on a large, marble half circle with a fountain in its middle.

Sol made to follow Cas forward, then stopped.

Sounds of waves, gentle and melodic, beckoned her, lapping at what sounded like clusters of stones. Her chest swelled with nostalgia as she darted to their song, not caring to wait for permission.

Taking the steps in clusters, she jogged across the ground and to a small brick fence. She stood on her toes to peer over it, the sound of the sea pulling her from within.

And there it was.

The ocean was wild, crisp, and violent, nothing like the sapphire waters of Yavenharrow. Nevertheless, it was igniting to be so close to it. Like how there was only one moon, the oceans connected, and in a way it meant they all held her soul.

Her mother's ashes floated in them all.

Sol sighed and sank back to her heels. She had to survive. She and Cas would make it to the end then figure it out. For now, she just had to avoid being killed—and find a way to get some of these people out, or pardoned, or *something*.

"Quite beautiful, isn't it, Princess?"

Sol jumped then smiled down at Phil.

Up close, she could see his tanned skin was peppered with freckles and a youthful naiveness that made her want to shove him in a carriage and send him back to his home.

At the lack of response, he angled his head at her, a slight blush creeping across his cheeks. "Apologies...my brother said I should leave you be, but I was coming to be closer to the sea and felt you here."

Sol looked back out, right as a wave crashed into a million shining droplets on a wall of stone. "No bother at all, Phil. I also came to be closer to it. Do you wish to see it?"

The boy was short, maybe to Sol's midriff—he couldn't simply stand on his toes as she had.

He smiled and shook his head. "I cannot see at all, Princess. I lost my eyesight as an infant from an illness my step-father felt was best to leave untreated. But by the sound, I can tell it's ferocious. Is it?"

Sol stared at him stupidly. Carefully, she sank to her knees to investigate his face. She was hyper aware of the proximity, a small voice in her mind warning perhaps this was a trick to impale her with a dagger.

But Phil's eyes...They were muted, glacier blue, distant, and unfocused.

"I—I hadn't noticed."

He kicked the ground with a foot. "Not many do."

"Then how—"

The boy held up a hand and the air around them shifted into tendrils, slapping her hair aggressively around her face. Sol stood and stared in awe as leaves and flowers swirled to her, twirling around her arms and legs. She dared a small smile.

"I'm an Air Dancer. I can see by feeling around with it. Negative space, my brother calls it."

Through the awe, Sol looked over his shoulder to Jonah who leaned near the front doors, his jaw set, and arms crossed while watching them.

"Why were you both sent here? Truly just for better chances?"

"I think his father wanted to get rid of me," he said. "His father is the current ruler. I posed a threat since I came from an older, stronger bloodline."

The more Sol heard of Wielder politics, the more she hated them. All of them, for allowing such brutality. She shook her head. "I'm sorry."

"Don't be. Like my brother said, we prepare for this our whole lives. It's an honor to even speak to you." The boy cleared his throat, the air returning to its usual calmness. "You should hurry inside. From the stories the survivors tell, which isn't many, you pick your own room." As he skipped away, he called back, "Pick one on the higher floors!"

"Wait!" Sol called. "How did you know I stood here? That it was me and not someone else?"

Phil reached Jonah, who held out a stern hand. The boy smiled sheepishly. "The air dances around you," he said. "It did at the dinner, too. It seems to really like you."

Sol took the boy's advice. After several minutes of awe-struck wandering around the Villa's foyer, she followed a spiral staircase to the upper floors, no other prospect in sight. Cas had vanished, though she didn't doubt he lurked in the shadows somewhere.

The rooms were in the cylindrical tower of the Villa, wrapped around the staircase in a disorienting spiral. As the stairs seemed to wrap around and around with no end in sight, she regretted taking Phil's advice so literally. Once she finally reached the top floor, she found herself in a small circular space.

There was only one door not flanked by other rooms or halls or anything other than two paintings, one of a serene night sky flecked with multicolored stars, and the other a portrait of a lightning storm mid strike.

Examining the lock, she eased the door open, surprised to find the room before her mostly empty. It had only a cot on the far wall with a cream-colored duvet and various vines on the wall behind it. There was a small, rectangular table with two benches, then a stove with a kettle ready to be used on the countertop beside it.

A door hung slightly open on the wall opposite the cot, revealing a modest washroom and bathtub. The simplicity of it was soothing. Maybe, if she tried hard enough, Sol could forget she was in a villa fighting to the death for her freedom so she could rule the kingdom her mother abandoned. If she stood in the center of the room and closed her eyes, it was almost as if she stood at the Hound, with the soundtrack of the waves and even the mild scent of mildew.

But then knocks sounded at her door. Illusion shattered, she faced it and frowned. Slowly, she grabbed a tea kettle from the stove. Better than no weapon.

"Who...Who is it?"

Unsurprisingly, no answer came, but a thin, crimson envelope slid beneath the door, landing with a phantom gust by her feet.

CHAPTER TWENTY-THREE

Cas

Cas didn't have any idea what room Sol would pick, but he didn't think she would pick the highest, smallest one. In a way, such a bizarre choice was fitting for such a bizarre girl.

He leaned against one of the walls facing the libraries on the first floor satisfied Sol would likely not leave the room any time soon. He figured he would give her space to sort out whatever brewed in that head of hers.

"Prince of Eswin."

Cattya's voice hadn't changed at all throughout the years. Still as slightly jarring as it had been when they met at the Rimemere academy. She slid over the wall's corner, tracing one hand against it, and the other down his chest. Her boldness hadn't changed either, it seemed.

"Cattya," he said, eyeing some lingering kingsmen on their way out. "Surprised to see you dragged into this instead of your sister."

Stone Ledge was a brutal place. Cas had gone only twice, one for the crowning of their Lord, and the other for his burial.

Cattya was now heiress of Stone Ledge, with her older sister Serene as Lady—with a nobleman beside her, though Cas couldn't remember who. Serene had been the one trained to eventually take a try at Rimemere, whenever, if ever, an heir appeared. But with her as the ruling party, the task seemed to be tossed to her younger sister.

Cattya shrugged. "Sister dearest is busy sucking cock and starting wars."

Cas smiled despite himself. Checked out with his own memories of Serene. The woman had different partners each time he saw her. She was likely despising married life.

"Oh, come on." She leaned closer, so close her breath sliced across his neck. "There used to be a time when you loved my vulgar mouth."

He slid his gaze to her. "What do you want, Cattya?"

"Only one of us is getting out of this alive to share the glorious throne with perfect, little, Princess Sol." She traced the angles of his jaw with a nail. "Might as well have fun for now, no?"

It was true, they had fun before. Before he and the Court had left the kingdom, back when he had trivial preoccupations like which one of the noblewomen would keep their affairs quiet. Cattya was the one who sought the same at the right time.

"Because that's your plan, right?" she continued. "Help her to the end, then you yield, having her win and you save your own ass."

Cas clenched his jaw, annoyed she figured it out so quickly. "I'm still not sure what I will be doing," he lied.

"Bullshit. You have no noble status to surrender if you yield, you're already exiled."

Changing the subject, Cas said, "I hear you have sources."

She arched her brow, visibly annoyed at his refusal to bite her bait. "Sources?"

"To know what the trials are."

Cattya laughed. "Does it matter? We are all part of Semmena's little game. We all know it'll be you and Sol at the end. I'm just trying to figure out which one of you will have the balls to kill me." She sighed and melodramatically placed a palm on her chest. "Meanwhile, we are all just pawns for entertainment."

"It might not be me at the end." He shrugged. "Maybe someone will best me."

Cattya snorted. "Please, Cas. The moment Semmena revealed you—very dramatic, by the way—we all knew we were fucked."

He traced the stone along the wall with his gaze, the enormous villa suddenly stifling. A movement in the corner of his vision had his attention sliding left, where a kingsmen emerged from the villa's front doors. He wore Semmena's sigil, a golden brooch engulfed in crimson flames, probably the only show of Melisandre colors the king dared display so boldly.

Cattya seemed about to speak, but she turned toward the kingsman instead, frowning as he stopped before them.

"A letter from the King," the man said mechanically as he outstretched a folded note their way.

"Beat it, you. Guards aren't allowed in here." Cattya made a show of wrapping her hand around Cas's bicep, and he was one more uninvited touch away from blasting her with a Ward now that his shackles were off. "You're interrupting something."

His Shadows rebelled against her, forcing her to take back a step.

When neither of them took the note from the man, he simply placed it atop a decorative table beside him. "Be punctual."

Without further explanation, the kingsman continued walking, surely to deliver the notice to the rest of the prospects.

Cattya sighed, striding to retrieve the paper. She cleared her throat, then in a mocking tone read, "Dear Prospects of the 53rd Coronation Vows, a welcome feast will be held in the dining room promptly at twilight. Attendance required." She finished the sentence with a scoff. "Why the fuck does it not say an actual time?"

"Let me know what your sources say about the upcoming trials." Cas pushed off the wall, rubbing his forearm. Sawyer's blood calmed his tattoo, but it always left him with a relentless itch, as if it knew the blood was diluted.

Not from its creator.

"I don't do things for free, you know." Cattya smiled wickedly, burning the note in a flicker of flames. "From what I remember, though, you don't mind my prices." She inched closer and traced a hand across his chest, leaving a trail of sparks.

Enough.

He let his chest flare a flash of violet light, willing it to merely shock her. "Ask your people, Cat."

"Don't tell me you actually think she will make a good Queen," she called after him, rubbing her hand. "Semmena is just looking for a way to kill her without starting a war."

"Ask your people."

"But—"

"Or don't." He walked back into the hallway, the Shadows along the wall taking him into an embrace. "Sol and I will survive either way."

CHAPTER TWENTY-FOUR
The Thing About Sitting Still

The note didn't say where the feast was to take place, but Sol had no trouble finding everyone else. She spotted a cluster of prospects on their way, obvious by the red envelopes in their hands. She recognized Felice and Lucas Mintz, siblings from the Romalian Nobility.

As Sol trailed behind them, she wondered what the 'Vows' actually were. From what she had gathered, they were tests of some sort, and Finigan mentioned something about possible sabotage amongst prospects. Were they allowed to just grab her and slit her throat, or were there certain times slaughter was allowed?

Perhaps she was being paranoid, but the promise of bloodshed was the one thing that seemed definite. Not that she was excited for it, she wasn't. But the lack of it made her more nervous for when it began, as if it would start all at once then never stop.

It would be fine.

It had to be.

She just had to avoid being killed.

The dining room was grand, as was everything in Rimemere. A sparkling, cascading chandelier lit with firelight winked at the golden wallpaper, and extravagant, silky red curtains hung over paintings of mountains and catacombs. In the center was an oblong table covered with foods even more foreign than the ones from the castle feast.

The savory scent of meat made her mouth water and her stomach clench, reminding her the last time she ate was the day before. Steam danced from the pots of soups and cremes, bowls of fruits glimmered with beckoning sweetness.

The prospects filtered into the chairs and a few immediately reached for the food not caring to serve themselves. Others simply looked around, scouting for danger or the most logical person to sit beside. Sol categorized herself with the latter crowd though she truly had the feral desire to behave like the former. She spotted Cas toward the end of the table, alone and leaning back on his chair with a bored expression.

Sensing her, he glanced over and winked, to which Sol responded with an eye roll and a sharp turn in the direction away from him. She didn't want to sit with these strangers and had half a mind to pluck a slab of meat and bolt back to her room, but a small hand tugged at her own.

Phil sniffed toward the table. "It smells amazing in here," he breathed, feeling for the chairs. Beside him, his brother pulled one back for him.

"Don't eat too quickly, Phil," Jonah said. Before Phil could sit, the boy stopped and turned to Sol.

"I—Something is strange."

The people behind them continued feasting, but Sol felt it then. More than felt, smelled. She inched closer to the food, instinctively gliding in front of Phil. His brother did the same.

When Sol was young, Lora had taught her basic healing. Her aunt hoped to inspire a passion for it, but Sol was stubborn, distracted by the colorful flowers and petals and earthy smells. The one lesson she never forgot, however, was the one on poisons. Primarily due to the fact she couldn't even touch those plants, so she had spent the entire lesson sulking. Secondly, due to the rancid smell. The entire cottage reeked of ammonia for days, a smell Sol grew to associate with the back alleys of the Yavenharrow taverns.

Here, though, it was only a small whiff that lingered. But it was enough.

Sol glanced at Cas who watched her with a small smile. He glanced from her to the food in silent question.

"Poison Savit," she whispered. "It's native to the Driodell forest."

Phil sneezed and grabbed his brother's hand. "The smell..."

Sol roved over the prospects. Most had caught on. But two, to be precise, had not.

Felice slowed her chewing, dropping the piece of meat she had in her hands. She looked to her left, to her brother, with an expression of pure terror.

At the end of the table, Cattya smiled. She turned to Cas, who sat to her right. "Here I thought the Romalian lands would know most poisons."

Cas didn't respond, but his silence might as well have been a slap to the face. He had known, and let the siblings eat anyway.

Returning to herself, Sol shook her head. "The food is poisoned." The prospects turned to her. She kept her attention on Felice and Lucas who instantly turned ashen. "It smells like Savit."

"The Princess has some knowledge, after all." Cattya tossed her hair over her shoulder. "How very lovely."

"I—-The trials don't start until the second day," Felice stammered, her chair screeching as she pushed away from the table. "We—we should have received a warning."

Sol's hands shook as she retreated a step. Her instincts told her to run, paranoia squeezing at her as Phil grabbed her hand.

"What's happening, Jonah?" the boy whispered.

Jonah clenched his jaw but said nothing.

"While we wait for the Savit to kill these fools, I will ask the questions we all wonder." Cattya glared at Sol.

Felice and Lucas fell to their knees, interlocked in an embrace. Taking a moment to breathe, Sol looked away, willing the tightening in her chest to loosen. She couldn't bear she was the reason they were here, that now a whole continent was looking so closely at her, and she had no clue what to do.

She closed her hands into fist and clenched her jaw before meeting Cattya's challenging gaze. "What is your problem?"

With a smirk, Cattya braced her chin atop her hands. "I only think it's fair, Princess. We are all forced to be here for your hand in marriage, yet your little show of defiance screwed that up completely."

"Being here is a privilege, Cattyiana," the prospect warned, standing from his seat. He wore his auburn hair in a low bun and gripped the edge of the table as he inched toward her. "You should be grateful of the opportunity."

"Grateful?" Cattya spat. "Fuck you, Cade. Grateful we were all shipped away from our lives to kill ourselves so we could rule with someone who clearly has no idea what she is doing?"

Sol bit the inside of her cheek to keep from yelling and fought to keep composure as she replied, "I am new at this. Of course, I can't be excellent at it."

From the edge of her vision, she saw Cas angle his head toward her.

"Tell us, Princess, what have you been doing all these years? And your mother? There's so many rumors." The woman neared her.

"Careful, Cattya," Cas warned.

"And you, Xanthos? How do you feel about being in this mess, after your father went through the exact same—"

Cattya was fast in her defense. But Cas was faster.

He stood and slammed his arm over the woman's chest so quickly, Sol blinked and Cattya was against the table, food and silverware clattering to the ground. Everyone stepped back.

"I said *careful*."

Sol leaned their way, but the horrid sound of bubbling goo made her stop cold. Her breath hitched in her throat as Felice toppled over onto the sea foam carpet. Lucas wailed a scream of pain as he followed. From their mouths spilled yellow and white foam. They jerked and seized, clawed, and screamed as the Savit took hold. In that moment, Sol didn't see enemies or people in her way of success. She saw people who were dying a horrible death.

No one moved.

But Sol did.

Slowly, she made her way to them, then faster as their consciousness began to fade. Savit wouldn't be poisonous after digestion, but Sol was still careful to avoid the fluids as she knelt beside them.

"Please-" Felice croaked, reaching for her. Her baby blue eyes welled with tears. "Please."

"I'm sorry." Sol clasped the woman's hand and held it over her lap as she reached and placed her other hand on the man's chest. "I'm so sorry," she whispered again.

Jonah knelt beside her silently, giving her a small nod of support. Felice looked up at the ceiling, her tears flowing in streams down her cheeks. Sol vaguely heard voices around her, but her attention was on those she held.

"In my hometown, we have a prayer we say," Sol said softly, "When someone passes."

For a second, Felice seemed to regain a glimmer of awareness as she looked at Sol. "Tell me."

Gently, Sol recited the parting prayers she would watch at the Yavenharrow sermons, mostly from afar, with Leo as a shoulder to lay on when the atmosphere grew heavy.

As she spoke, Lucas's breathing slowed and slowed, until it came to a stop as she finished the broken prayer. When Sol looked down, Felice had also stopped moving, and a small sense of relief fluttered through her at the fact the woman at least looked peaceful.

Sol shook slightly, suddenly feeling the heaviest weight on her shoulders. She could almost physically feel the girl from Yavenharrow slip away the moment she looked at Felice. Mourned her, even. Phil stood behind his brother, and though he couldn't see, his small face was solemn, too painfully aware of what happened.

The mourning for her leftover innocence transformed into anger as everything slammed into her all at once.

These people were here to die.

And by placing herself in the Vows, it might all be in vain. All because she was too stubborn to marry someone she didn't love, eager to defy a tradition she didn't agree with.

Cas's chastise replayed in her mind.

No.

Sol wouldn't let his cynical ideas grab her. She was here with a purpose, to dissolve a tradition that was poison to not only Rimemere but all of the Southern continent.

"Princess..."

Sol wiped her face with her sleeve and turned to Jonah. Wordlessly, the living prospects filed out of the dining room, but Cattya stopped before her, her shirt wrinkled and hair unruly from Cas's threat.

She glared at Sol, but this time, Sol glared right back. "Ask your questions, then," Sol said.

Cattya looked from her to the bodies around her then turned to Cas. The Prince of Eswin watched her with eyes like daggers, his fingers thrumming the table.

"I believe I have my answers," Cattya said, stepping over the bodies before stomping out of the room with the prospects following suit.

Sol was left with Jonah, Phil, and she assumed Cas as she could see his Shadows around them. Stroking Felice's hair, Sol whispered "This is wrong. People shouldn't die because of me."

"If not for you, it would've been for another Southern noble," Jonah offered.

Sol shook her head. "It's Barbaric."

"It's our normal," Phil said softly. "But it's an honor to be fighting for you."

Sol met the boy's eyes. "How old are you, Phil?"

Phil tugged at the sleeves of his blouse. "Ten summers."

Determination spilled into her like scalding steel at the revelation. "I will figure out how to end this. I will not stand here and let all of you die without at least trying."

"Princess—"

Sol cut Jonah off, "That's a promise. And I don't break those."

CHAPTER TWENTY-FIVE

At The Castle

SAWYER

Sawyer was called to the throne room that same night. Sol and Cas's departure resulted in the castle dwellers being more on edge than usual, especially as the last of the nobles returned to their lands or respective dwellings within Rimemere. Some would stay until the end of the Coronation Vows, though others left and would return only to see the crowned victor.

The two weeks the Vows would likely take were far too long to be in Rimemere for most of the other Southerners. Sawyer didn't blame them. She had been back for a week and was already aching to burst out.

Alix and Nina dedicated the rest of the afternoon to the libraries, attempting to find any sort of loophole to get both Sol and Cas out before the end of the trials. The most obvious solution was for them both to make it until the end, then Cas yield. However, whatever happened in between was far too open-ended for Nina, and she was determined to get them out sooner.

Sawyer was on her way to the stables for a much-needed ride around the Human sections with Fey when Caleib delivered the summoning. She didn't bother to read it. Only looked at the man and led the way to the throne room.

Sawyer tried not to meet the stare of the black-cloaked students who hovered in the halls. They were old enough to remember her from before the expedition and were surely either curious about the rest of Erriadin, or about Sol.

Sawyer had no desire to speak of either.

The throne room was bleak with stray rays of sunlight dispersing across the white, marble floors from the scattered, tall windows. She focused on the courtyard beyond instead of the man on the throne.

"You're dismissed, Caleib," her father said, his voice low and harsh.

Sawyer dared a glance his way, surprised to find the rest of the Semmena court absent. That could only mean whatever she was summoned for was not good.

As soon as Caleib clicked the door shut behind them, her father stood. "Have you located what I required from you?"

Ok. No greetings today.

Fine. Sawyer placed her hands behind her back.

There were five Immortal Relics known to be scattered around Erriadin. Originally, they had been gathered in the depths of Rimemere, somewhere within the underground tunnels, during Ivet Yarrow's reign.

Somehow, they became scattered throughout the centuries, and her father was now taking the personal task of reuniting them. At first, she thought it was some sort of joke— The Relics were a myth. They were rumored to be palm-sized spheres that could conjure any and all Wielding Magic at once, as well as assist the holder in channeling Dark Magic from the Void itself without the need to sacrifice the soul.

Irene Yarrow had been the last known Wielder to learn the Dark Spells—then passed them to the only known human to practice them, Lora Yarrow.

Aside from them, the only way to wield Dark Magic was with a Relic.

In theory.

Her father thrummed his fingers on his throne, sending sparks flying. "Well?"

Sawyer cleared her throat. "I have not sensed anything amiss."

"In your four years of travel, daughter, you did not sense a Relic at all?"

Her exterior faltered. She tried with exhausting effort to keep a cool demeanor in front of her father, to seem unbothered and bratty as most people already labeled her.

But gods did he terrify her.

To keep her voice from shaking, she only said, "No."

The King stood. "You never fail to remind me of how useless you truly are."

Sometimes, when she saw the fire coming, she would shield herself with a small burst of her own flames. Her skin would still be left aching and swollen but not burned as if she hadn't shielded herself at all.

This time, she was caught off guard.

Sawyer fell to the ground with shriek, her father's fire wrapping around her arms, her back, her lungs—

Sawyer inhaled, holding the breath in her core, and letting it simmer with her boiling blood. She slid her gaze to him, clenching her jaw as her skin screamed with agony. "Learned from the best."

"Find them, Sawyerlyn."

She watched him leave the room then, leaving her alone in a pile of ash, smoke, and flickering fire.

NINA

Nina hadn't read through so much Rimemere history since her second year in the Wielder academy. That year had been full of books and the smell of dried ink, all while Sawyer and Cas decided to use it as their last attempt to rebel before royal duties became their life. Nina and Alix had aced their tests, received honors, and graduated without penalties—the other two were shipped off to the Jinn den that summer as punishment for failing.

"There has to be something," Nina whispered to herself, scanning the ancient pages of a dusty tome called *Rimemere Traditions and Their Origins*.

Ironically, the tradition she sought loopholes for was missing from the reports.

There had to be a way to get both Sol and Cas out of there quickly. Sawyer hadn't been too concerned, saying Cas just had to yield at the end, and Sol would prove victorious.

Still, there was no harm in having a failsafe.

A knock at her door prompted her to shut the book of Rimemere Laws, sending dust afloat. "Come in."

Sawyer was always covered in something—mud, dirt, alcohol.... but never blood. She never failed to bathe before coming home from the battle stations, at least tried to clean her face before addressing anyone. It was a personal thing, something about not being able to bear other's blood while hers remained inside her.

So, when she stood in Nina's doorway, face, hands, and neck covered in blood and smelling like fire, Nina felt the ground itself shake in response.

"What happened." Nina pulled her into the room and closed the door, reinforcing it shut with ivy and branches she kept nearby.

Sawyer's eyes were hard, distant.

Nina grabbed her hands. The blood was warm.

"Sawyer."

"It's my blood—just in case it grossed you out."

Instantly, Nina removed her cloak and wiped her friend's face. Small cuts revealed along her cheeks and forehead, then gashes around the sides of her neck. Peeking from beneath the neckline of her battle leathers, scarred, red skin bubbled.

Nina's jaw clenched, icy hot rage awakening in her chest. "Who?"

"Who do you think?"

Nina hadn't missed being away from Semmena's cruelty. Sawyer's father wasn't only a blood thirsty, cruel ruler, but he was the same as a father. If he could even be called that.

"Why?"

"Because I'm useless."

Nina continued working away the sticky, thick blood from her face and neck, then gently guided her to the bathing room. They had no shame or reservations around each other, not anymore. They had seen all of the intimate parts from an early age, physical and emotional, and everything in between. So much so that Nina often felt like Sawyer was an extension of herself. Not a friend, or a sister, but a piece of her soul.

Nina made sure the bath was cold, but smoke still curled from Sawyer's shoulders when she stepped into it.

"He wasn't so bad before," Sawyer said, her voice small and absent of emotion. "He didn't even ask how our travels were."

Nina sighed, a wave of sadness pooling within her at that eternal youthful side of her friend that relentlessly searched for her father's care. She grabbed the softest rag she found and lathered it with aloe vera salve.

"You never deserved his cruelty, Sawyer," Nina said, fury lining her voice as she pressed the mixture over Sawyer's wounds. "None of us did."

"I'll kill him." Smoke lined the tub, the water suddenly scorching. "I swear to Emberdon I will."

Nina heard the unspoken reasons in Sawyer's waver. *For my Mother. For my Lands. For Cas. For Sol.*

She hugged her friend's shoulders gently, withstanding the heat that made Sawyer so incredibly special. "And we will be by your side, S."

A knock at the door made them both jump.

Nina had no positive ideas of who it could be, half expecting Alix to come in with a bloody nose after he too received the King's wrath for whatever reason.

But when she pulled the door open a sliver, it was Caleib who stood in the hallway, his hands holding a folded piece of parchment with the Semmena sigil.

"Miss Amana," he bowed. "Word from the Gods' Villa."

A massive shiver snaked down Nina's spine as she snatched the paper, slamming the door in the courtier's face after a breathless dismissal.

"Sawyer!" Nina yelled, prying open the wax seal. "News on the prospects!"

Within a matter of seconds Sawyer was in the room, the splash of the water still spilled in the background as she hurried to Nina's side wrapped in a towel.

Once Sawyer was beside her, Nina flipped it open, and prayed to Flora the names of her friends would not be on the Death List.

CHAPTER TWENTY-SIX

To Grieve

After the dinner—if it could even be called that—Sol went to her small room and sobbed. She buried herself beneath the duvets and mourned the easy life she had taken for granted. She let herself wallow in self-pity for twenty minutes exactly.

Just twenty.

Then, she sat up in her bed, wiped her tears, and sank herself into a freezing bath while she formulated a plan. She couldn't let the prospects die. Their death would be on her hands, even if it was by proxy. There had to be a way, a loophole.

Nina assured her they would search for one, and Sol believed her. But she also knew she and Cas had a good possibility of making it to the end, and their lives were her court's only true concerns.

Sol shuddered at the thought.

If she and Cas survived, the options were for one of them to yield, or fight. She wanted to think he would yield, but she also had a sense the man was unpredictable.

The day after the feast fiasco was calm. Sol spent it isolated, only coming out of her room for nuts and berries Phil assured her were safe. She thanked the boy and begged him and Jonah to stay safe, only catching glimpses of the other prospects between escapades.

It was on the third day, in the middle of wondering if she should go hunt for squirrels instead of settling for eating rabbit food, something tapped on her window.

Her hand gripped the side of the table where she sat. The window was behind her—dodging whatever it was seemed futile.

Grabbing a vase in front of her, she threw it back at the window before diving to the ground. If a Jinn had found her, if somehow they had the ability to fly now—

She reached for another makeshift weapon then actually looked at the window. She shivered with relief.

"Penny! Oh gods." Sol crawled and pushed it open. "How are you—"

Penny grinned at her. "Fantastic aim, Princess!" She glanced over at the shattered vase. "Shame the vase had to suffer though."

"How are you here?" Sol looked around frantically. The girl was floating.

"My air dancer friend is helping." Penny grinned, pointing to the ground below.

Sol looked over the window's edge to find Phil sitting on the grass with his hands above his head. Sensing her, he waved.

"Penny, you need to leave. If anyone finds out you're here, I'm sure it won't end well."

"They won't. There are no guards, the King is dumb, and I was stealthy. The tunnels run directly beneath this Villa," She reached into her pocket and revealed a folded parchment. "From Ninanette. She is truly a ball of nerves without you."

Sol smiled slightly and took the letter. "Tell her we are alright."

"We saw the names of those who passed a few days ago," Penny said softly. "The next trial should come soon."

Sol sighed, "I'm so stupid. I shouldn't have interfered in this."

Penny shrugged, swaying with the gust of wind beneath her. "A lot of people think the opposite. They are just too afraid to say it."

"I don't know what I'm meant to be doing here. I know what I *want* to do, but I have no way to execute it."

Penny sighed, "Survive. Tell us your plan once you formulate one and we will help from the shadows."

Sol smirked at the girl's simple suggestion. "I thought your uncle was the Shadow Guider."

She laughed, "Us Unsettled have to learn our own tricks—magic free."

"You need to return home, Penny," Sol said, glancing below and eyeing the dangerous distance to the ground. "You'll force me to tell on you to your Uncle."

"Oh, please don't!" Penny whined with a palm to her forehead. "He is worse than my mother sometimes. He'd never forgive me for using the tunnels."

By the sound of it, Sol could bargain she wouldn't. She pursed her lips, bracing herself for the girl's response. "Tunnels?"

Penny blinked her lilac eyes at her. "Have you not seen them?"

Sol had to see the things for herself. Before Penny agreed to return to the Castle, she gave Sol a brief explanation of Rimemere's subterranean connections. The land had always been uniquely curious. Aside from it harboring the temples and therefore greatly concentrated magic, it had a naturally occurring web of caves and corridors beneath it. Alix had mentioned Nina was in charge of charting the tunnels during their journey, but Sol hadn't stopped to process what it meant.

As they lived their lives above ground, an entirely different one could be unfolding beneath it.

Penny had assured the tunnels are regularly monitored for this reason, and Jeriyah, as High Scribe, protected them with simple enchantments. For now, the only legal activity within them was merchandise transport.

As Penny had descended into the overgrown grass beside Phil, Sol asked where they were located within the God's Villa. The girl only laughed and disappeared into the trees.

So, Sol acquired her task for the afternoon: find them.

Perhaps they could be useful in her quest to get the prospects to safety. And if they were deserted, who would know, right?

Connecting the different sections of the Villa was a daunting spiral staircase, one that had almost driven her into madness when she had first scouted for her room. As she began her descent, it again gave her that unsteady feeling, each step calculated, the repetitive motion calming.

First, she stopped on the fourth floor.

Was it likely the entrance to subterranean tunnels was on the fourth floor?

No.

But she had seen more surprising things during the last few weeks that caused a sigh to slip and her feet to step onto the level anyway with tentative expectations.

The floor beneath hers was lovely. It was decorated in vibrant greens with mustard yellows and vines draping from golden chandeliers. The carpet was a mossy green, but in an appealing way that blended with the decorative foliage around the hollow, circular loft. Across where she stood, on the other side of the staircase, Sol made out small fountains.

She wandered toward them, gently running her hands over the cool water once she reached the first one.

"Princess Yarrow."

Sol jumped, instantly reaching for a knife in her belt she did not have. She swore to herself she would find some sort of weapon in this wretched place since she was devoid of magic. But not even a blunt fork was able to be unaccounted for after meals. She pushed herself against the wall beside the fountain, earning a low laugh from the man before her.

She could instantly tell he was an Earth Caller. His green eyes, a mirror to Nina's, fit in with the decor around him as if he had walked out of the wallpaper itself. His brown ringlets fell around his cheekbones, and a hint of a beard softened the angles of his jaw.

What he wore made Sol do a subtle double take. A leather bodysuit reinforced with what looked eerily like reptilian scales.

The man smiled. "I don't believe we've had the chance to formally meet." He outstretched a hand. "It has been an eventful couple of days."

Sol returned a small smile to seem polite, and loosely grasped his hand in what she figured would be a handshake. But he flipped her grip and planted a kiss to her knuckles instead.

It was likely customary to greet a woman of status this way, but gods did it make Sol want to bolt from the interaction. "I—uh. Nice to meet you," she said, withdrawing her hand to her side.

"My name is Ezra. I am the heir of the Polimande lands." Ezra leaned against the railing behind him, the only thing preventing a tumble from the level to the foyer below.. "I've done nothing but prepare for this opportunity since I Settled."

"You—you've done nothing but wait for the opportunity to marry into Rimemere royalty?"

"To rule beside a glorious Yarrow." He traced her with glowing eyes.

Instead of listening to every fiber of her being that warned her to run, she gave herself a mental shove.

Queenly. Act Queenly.

Raising her chin slightly, she dipped her fingers into the water. "I thought I was no more than a myth until recently."

"Ah, but the South never lost hope that Queen Irene left us an Heir." Again, his gaze roved her from head to toe. "And such a beautiful one, too."

Yeah, no.

"Well, Ezra, lovely to meet you." Sol gave him the sweetest smile she could muster, the kind she would give the Yavenharrow sailors after they had too much liquor and she needed them to pay their tab and leave. "But I must leave. I have a…someone waiting for me."

Not waiting for a response, she began her way back to the stairs. Mercifully, Ezra stayed where he was, examining her from a distance. "Prince Xanthos, I presume?"

Sol paused at the beginning of the steps and met his gaze. Although it was a lie, she would rather the man think she was in fact going to meet the one person they all seemed to fear. "Yes."

"I'd be careful, Princess." Ezra pushed off the railing. "Xanthos and Yarrows tend to attract chaos when together."

As Sol continued her descent, she said, "I'll keep that in mind."

She tried to shake the bizarre encounter as she explored the other floors but was ultimately too distracted to truly take in the Villa's raw beauty. It seemed like each floor corresponded to a god, the notion finally clicking as Sol reached the bottom.

Hers seemed to be the one mostly absent of elemental memorabilia. The fourth floor appeared to represent Flora, with its greens and plant life. The third was loudly Emberdon with crimson walls, black furniture, and golden accents reminiscent of a flame. The second floor was serene and bright, with lovely baby blue hues and a large fountain with mementos of Aquarene carved into its stone. Finally, the main floor where Sol now stood was constructed of muted beiges, down to the sandstone pillars that stretched all the way to the very top of the place. Although there was no clear indication the floor belonged to Winderlyn's memory, the paintings of clouds and symbols for air etched around the walls were enough for Sol to make the assumption.

She craned her head all the way up. That left the fifth floor to be Warren's.

Of course it did.

Sol scowled at the door to her room, tiny in the distance, and continued her way around the main floor. The dining area where the spiral of despair had started was empty, the large rectangular table bare aside from a bowl of fruit. The eating schedule was consistent and hopelessly out of line with Sol's own appetite, so she snagged an apple as she continued into the depths of the Villa. She hadn't truly ventured around the area, mostly out of defiance for the reason she was there to begin with.

Just as she made a turn into the next hallway, she paused. It would have been easy to miss had the engraving not been a personal beacon to her. A few steps before the corner to the next room, the corridor forked to her left, into what seemed like a pointless, rectangular extension that only had a mirror at eye level and an unremarkable plant beneath it. Sol stepped into the peculiar space, only an arm's length in all directions, then looked down at what had called her to it.

The main floor of the Villa was constructed of a muted, beige tile, the ones beneath her feet no different. However, carved on a singular one, as if with liquid gold itself, was a six-pointed star.

Sol plopped down on the floor beside it, touching her necklace which bore the same shape.

"What are you?" She traced the peaks of the stars along the tile with her fingers—the tile clicked.

It sank into the ground slightly with a soft sound, then an echo had Sol turn to the wall behind her.

The outline of a door etched into the wallpaper.

She smiled.

Found you.

A slick coat of adrenaline tugged at her chest as she crawled to it and pushed, covering her face with a forearm when the moment awoke a film of dust. As if pulled by phantom hands, a large panel of the wall fell away into itself, sliding out of view to reveal darkness.

And stairs.

"Oh, I don't think so," she muttered.

It was unwise to explore the nook. In all those books she and Mina enjoyed so much, the characters who pursued unwise decisions never survived.

Sol frowned at the looming stairs, dropping into the depths of the Villa without a single shred of light in sight. If only she had a weapon.

She peered up at the mirror.

It shattered quite easily. Clamping her mouth shut to keep from groaning, she held her elbow as the pieces clattered to the ground. She remained frozen for a moment, listening for footsteps or anyone that may want to come investigate the noise.

Luckily, the Villa remained silent.

Sol picked the most menacing and dynamic looking shard before entering the hole in the wall.

CHAPTER TWENTY-SEVEN

Shadows of the Past

Sol didn't have a single idea where she was going. The only light was the one from the hallway behind her, though it slowly disappeared the further underground she went. For a good stretch, she was in total darkness.

She gripped the shard of glass as tightly as she could without drawing blood and guided herself with her other hand until she finally reached the end of the stairs. A glimmer of relief settled at the solidness beneath her where the anxiety had been. It was only then flickers of flames shone in the distance, likely from torches that lined the tunnel's interior.

She had set out to find them without much expectation or hope she would, but now that she was here, she didn't have a clue what to do. Was she going to march upstairs and usher the prospects into a hole in the wall? Then tell them to go on, and be free?

Sol examined the damp stone around her, suddenly feeling like perhaps the idea would not work.

Penny was traveling through these?

If the girl ever returned, Sol would beg her to stay well out of them—there was something eerie about the way a breeze still flowed when, in theory, there should be none.

"*Sol.*" It was a mere whisper, carried past with an unnatural gust. It pulled her forward with the gentlest tug. *"Come closer, Sol."*

As if in a daze, she followed the beacon, the crunch of dirt beneath her boots bouncing in a loop around her. She neared the first torch, then the second, before the straight path cut into a vestibule with no way forward, but with paths on both sides. To her right, the path was dark. The left was lined with more torches, all bright, and illuminating just how complex the system was.

Sol angled her head inquisitively.

Wouldn't someone have to light these?

Before the realization could fully settle, the world tilted, and the torches disappeared as something pulled her back and against the stone. The impact left her breathless, but she still brought up the shard of glass instinctively while she willed her vision to settle.

If someone had found her, followed her down there, it would be an easy end. She should have known a piece of glass wouldn't be enough to—

Cas brought a hand to his lips. A silent gesture for her to be quiet.

Through the shock, her exhales trembled between them, before shuddering completely as voices reached their way from beyond the corner. As if someone walked their way while engaged in casual conversation.

"I'm telling you, patrolling these things is pointless," said a male voice, his volume increasing with each word. "The old fool has them enchanted anyway."

Sol's eyes widened as she looked into Cas's in a wordless plea.

He leaned closer, pressing her against the cave's interior while he braced his arms on either side of her head. He was taller than her in this position, enough so he had to dip his chin to be at eye level. It took willpower she didn't realize she had to remain still as the footsteps continued their approach.

"Stay still," Cas whispered, their closeness making her comply without a fight. Shadows swirled from his forearms, engulfing their faces in their darkness before cloaking them both entirely.

The sensation of his shadows against her skin never got easier to absorb. Just as the first time, her skin cooled and prickled in all the places they touched; her face, to her neck, to the tips of her fingers.

And she knew her expression gave away her intrigue as Cas only smirked and pressed himself closer.

"At least it's an excuse to leave the castle." The voice was as close as Sol was to Cas. She shut her eyes.

"Everything's been so annoying since that bitch got here," the other voice replied. Stone groaned as Cas closed his open hands into fists. "Hopefully the Vows get rid of her. Or the Jinn—that might be more fun."

The two kingsmen laughed, their status given away by their crimson uniform and cloaks. They strode past without a glance in their direction, continuing to the lightless path. Clenching her jaw, she studied their silhouettes as they lit the torches on that side as well.

A soft groan from Cas broke the budding desire to march to the men and scare them senseless. She glanced at him, then down at his chest—where the shard of glass was digging into his shirt.

Sol released it.

It landed on the ground noiselessly, muted by Cas's skilled shift of his boot to ease its landing.

Her palm burned where the glass had nicked, but her focus was on the steady stain of blood pooling into the fabric of his tunic.

She pressed her palm against him in a panic, the one that bore Lora's blood bond and was clean of her own.

They remained like that for what seemed like long, swollen minutes, the sounds of their hushed breathing the only thing around as the kingsmen's vulgar complaints faded into the depths of Rimemere.

As soon as Cas leaned back, Sol pushed him. "What do you think you're doing?"

"Did you leave the entrance open?" He motioned to their left where she had so bravely marched down from only to be almost caught by Kingsmen.

Sol braced her hands on her hips. "Well, I didn't know there was a way to close the wall behind me."

Cas dug through a small leather satchel secured to his waist. "The fact you went into it at all is foolish—though somehow not surprising." He extended a hand to her. "Come here."

"I will not."

He met her gaze, silver eyes flaring as he stepped forward instead.

Defeated with only the cave wall behind her, she didn't evade him. Although it wasn't a conscious reaction, Sol knew she was upset about the dinner. She could tell by the heat that rose to her face when he reached for her hand, and she refused the touch. Could tell he knew it too by the way he glanced away and sighed through pursed lips.

He held a piece of cloth between them. "Here, then."

She eyed it, shaking her head. "You use it. I stabbed you."

He chuckled lightly. "Take it, Princess."

Sol sighed. She wasn't used to feeling betrayed, at least not until recently. It wasn't something she wanted to get used to either. "I'll bandage my hand in the Villa." Without a glance his way, she braced herself for the dark way back to the nook where she came from.

"Oh, I closed it," he said. "It doesn't open from this side."

Any sentimental emotion she had felt a mere second ago fizzled into irritation. "You what?"

Cas shrugged as if he hadn't a care in the world nor the creeping panic that speared through her at being locked underground. "If anyone else would've caught you on this little quest they would have reported you." He dabbed at his chest wound with a frown. "Impressive ingenuity."

"So, now what?" She looked down the length of the tunnel. "We are stuck here?"

"No, the tunnels have multiple ways out." He smirked her way and pointed to where the kingsmen had emerged from, away from where they went into. "We just have to avoid the kingsmen."

Cas's way of getting back was by engulfing them in Shadows as they walked. To Sol's annoyance, it meant being very close to him as they scouted for another exit. He'd given her several options: be carried, to carry him, or for him to walk directly behind her pressed together and she'd have to lead the way. She might be prideful at times, but she was no fool—Sol chose to be carried.

But not like she had been in Yavenharrow when they first met. Instead, she clung to his back, legs wrapped over his waist and arms, hugging him tight enough to make him uncomfortable. Each time he tripped over a stray rock, Sol squeezed them tighter.

"You know, if you make me pass out, you'll have to find your way out alone," he muttered, rolling his neck, and pressing his hands into her thighs where he held her.

In response, she squeezed his waist. "Tragic."

They walked for long enough Sol lost count of the passing minutes and instead twirled the Shadows between her fingers. They would linger over her wound as if pointing it out to her before continuing to snake over her wrist. After she grew tired of that, she sank her chin to Cas's shoulder and peered at him. "Why didn't you do anything to help Felice and Lucas?"

She hadn't meant to ask so boldly, but as soon as the words were out, she realized she needed an answer. He was meant to be the one person she could trust, but could she? What did she really know about the Shadow Guider?

That my mother killed his father.

Cas glanced at her. "Is that why you're upset?"

"Why, Cas?"

"Because the whole point of this, Princess, is to get rid of prospects, not to save them."

Sol bit the inside of her cheek to keep from arguing further. Instead, she just said, "We have to try."

They'd been going in exasperating circles over the topic since they'd arrived, and it seemed he wasn't yielding. But neither was she.

"It just doesn't work like that, Sol." The edge of frustration in his voice was obvious, making Sol feel like a small child being chastised. "The faster you accept the way things are, the faster we can move on."

She unwrapped herself from his hold, jumping to the ground and stepping back from the cloak of his darkness. "I will not accept things the way they are. In fact, I will be doing the opposite."

Cas looked past her and behind him, ensuring no one else followed before turning back to face her, his jaw tight and hands sparking with violet lightning. Sol eyed them, yearning to touch them as intensely as she had on their ride to Rimemere. A small smile pulled against her lips at the memory. She had been so scared and lost back then. Although it was only weeks ago, it seemed like years. Granted, she still felt a bit of both, but in a different way.

She moved past him, continuing their walk away from his cover of safety. His Shadows seemed to reach for her as he wordlessly followed behind her.

"I think this lack of understanding between us comes from us being raised very differently," Sol back to him. "Perhaps if we got to know each other some more, we would be willing to find a compromise."

And I would feel less inclined to still keep you in my peripherals when you walk behind me.

"Is there a compromise to you wanting to save people I want to kill?" Instead of dwindling behind her, he side stepped to walk beside her, but still maintained the distance she had placed between them. He messed with a ball of lightning on his fingertips. "Seems like the kind of thing that requires one of the two parties to give in."

Sol tapped a hand at her side. "Well, let's shelve that and start with other things, then."

They came to a fork in the tunnels, all three paths illuminated by torches and the soft scent of wet mud. Cas looked at each path, then finally chose the one to their right. "Alright," he said as he motioned her that way.

Okay. This was her chance to pry. But where should she start?

"You're from Eswin," she started, trying to come up with exactly what she needed answered to decipher him. He was like a puzzle she didn't have all the pieces to and having unfinished art unsettled her. Art was meant to be admired, afterall—but how could it be if it was lacking the whole story?

He nodded. "That is correct."

"Tell me more."

It was clear Cas was not used to this. Sol was. She would often pry personal anecdotes from sailors at the Hound since building trust helped with the tips. It had only been a handful of times she'd purposefully wanted to know of someone's past for the mere purpose of knowing them. She was almost giddy to know—because there was something. Something about him.

Cas ran a hand through his hair. "My maternal line, the Morozovs, have ruled there forever."

"That's the Shadow Guider line, right?"

He peered over at her. "That's right."

The tunnel they traveled was getting smaller, forcing them to travel closer together. Sol couldn't see an end to it, but the torches became more scarce as they continued. "And do you miss it?" Sol asked. "Eswin?"

Cas stopped walking.

He looked past her in a way that made her wonder if he had seen something, but she didn't see anything when she followed his line of vision. "Cas?"

"Do you miss Yavenharrow?" he asked softly.

The question took her off guard. "Well, yes. But I lived there my whole life."

He shrugged, the cloud that dimmed his expression passing. "I don't think the amount of time you spend in a place is indicative of how much you're allowed to miss it." He pointed up to the cave's roof. "The next exit is up there."

"Cas–" Sol grabbed his arm. "I know about the history between our families." He tensed. That was what bothered her. Why in the world should she trust him if he had all the motivation to hate her?

"I'm not talking about this." His voice was harsh, rough in a way she hadn't heard from him before. He outstretched an arm above their heads, a snake of Shadows swimming to the roof. The only thing that told the exit apart was a nearly invisible rectangular outline, painted with a red so bright it looked like fresh blood. The Shadows pressed into it, and the stone popped open, revealing a rush of sunlight, and falling leaves. Sol covered her eyes at the jarring difference.

"Wait, Cas. I just need you to know I'm sorry." The rush of the breeze killed the torches surrounding them. "I know being exposed to cruelty like that can make it seem like that's all there is—"

"I'm going to help you up first," he said, ignoring her.

Sol looked up at the opening. It wasn't too far, she would likely only need a small boost. If she would be able to pull herself out, though, she didn't know.

"Are you literally trying to toss me out of your way instead of responding?"

"I said I am not discussing this with you. Up." Not giving her time to protest, he pulled her closer, kneeling before her, and tapping her foot with his clasped hands. "Up, Sol. Unless you want to be left here when the enchantments come back up."

Sol released an exasperated breath. Her technique wasn't working. All she needed was a small crack in his exterior, a small display of a soul. She braced her hands on his shoulders and accepted his boost. The effortless lift made her lose balance for a second before throwing her arms over the opening, clawing at the grass and vines to keep from falling back into the tunnel. Cas didn't help her with the second part, so she squirmed and pushed herself away from the grassy land until her upper half was well enough over the edge of the opening that she could crawl over the rest of it.

Once her entire body was back above ground, she collapsed, her arms burning with the effort.

The first thing she was doing if she managed to survive this, was training.

Sol tried to steady her harsh breathing as she flopped onto her back, relishing the sweet warmth of the sun. She could lay there all day. She never wanted to be underground ever again.

She waited for Cas to call her. Surely, he would need to be pulled up.

The ground beneath her rattled and shook, and for a horrible moment Sol thought maybe the ancient tunnels beneath her couldn't stand the sudden change in their architecture, and it was preparing to collapse.

She sat up in a panic. She wouldn't die because of the Vows—it was the tunnels that would take her out. "Cas?" She crawled to the fracture in the ground and peered into it. He wasn't there.

"There are things you will never understand about me, Princess."

Sol jumped, nearly falling back into the tunnel had it not been for Cas's hand gripping her bicep. He drew her back and away from the hole. On his other arm, he carried a slab of stone with fuzzy, green foliage on one side and black-gray rock on the other. He tossed it into the hole. It secured perfectly into it, erasing any trace of the mysteries below.

Sol peered up at him, then behind him. There was a similar opening by a pine tree a few paces away from them, except the outline of something peeking from it and into the forest ground.

"There were stairs?" she groaned. "There was a way out with stairs, and you made me pull myself up?"

Cas crouched across from her, meeting her at eye level. His gaze moved from her face to her chest still heaving with effort and adrenaline, then finally landed on her hand, still bloody and now covered in mulch. Again, he reached into his satchel. "You want to know what being shown cruelty since you've been born is like, Princess?" He retrieved a bandage this time along with a small jar of what looked like water.

"It's like everyone around you taking the goddamned stairs when you have to pull yourself up to meet them." He grabbed her hand, not asking for permission this time.

"Except there isn't someone below to help you up." He pulled the cork from the jar with his free hand and gently poured the liquid over her wound.

The water was cool against her skin, the slight sting of where it washed the splinters and dirt away making her flinch. Sol remained silent, watching him as he focused on her.

"Then, when you're tired and sore after finally catching up to the others, there isn't someone there to tend to your wounds either." He placed the empty jar on the side and worked the bandage over her palm, wrapping it over itself and over her wrist to secure it.

When he was finished, he stood. "I'm not going to apologize for believing extreme measures are safest when it comes to dealing with people who don't deserve mercy."

Sol couldn't move or bring herself to stand. She simply stared at him, clumsily trying to process the last few minutes. His black, wavy hair curled over his forehead with the wind, exposing his eyes. Eyes Sol wanted to look and get lost in every time she was graced with a glimpse.

Breathless for reasons she couldn't quite place, Sol said, "Everyone deserves mercy." Even as she said it, the once truthful words rang dull in her ears, laughing at her for still trying to keep grasp of the silly notion of her youth.

She stifled the feeling away, tucking it deep behind walls she had many memories locked behind. Mercy was good. Balance, justice, understanding was good.

Cas gave her a sad smile. "No, Princess. Not everyone does."

"What happened, Cas? To make you feel that way?"

He was silent for a while, looking over at the Gods' Villa to their right. Sol hadn't noticed they'd traveled so far from it underground.

Finally, he looked back at her. "Your mother killed my reason to feel any other way."

CHAPTER TWENTY-EIGHT

Flora's Trial

Sol still hadn't shaken free of her conversation with Cas by the time they all arrived at Flora's Temple the next morning.

She refused to make eye contact with him during breakfast and was relieved when the guards forced her to take her own carriage. His words resonated with something buried and frozen within her, something she tried for years to forget.

And she hated it.

Although Sol preferred peace, as Fin stood before them at the entrance of the Temple, she wished Cas would have ended *him* when they first arrived at Rimemere instead of the other kingsman.

Finigan wore a smug smile as he stepped out of formation, sure to glare at her seconds longer than the rest of the prospects. "Two prospects fell to the first test," he announced. "In order to be part of a Royal Court, one must be sure to know how to detect all sorts of poisons, especially those hidden." He came closer, his cloak grazing Sol's boots as he walked down their line. "In order to keep the Queen safe, of course."

Several scoffs sounded to her left, but it was Phil who said, "Doesn't seem like she needs help there."

Sol smiled sweetly at Fin as he shot her a glare.

"Did your time in the farms teach you how to sniff out Savit, Princess? Or did someone help you through the first test?"

Sol shrugged. "I'm sure one of the many spies you have within the Villa wouldn't mind recalling the event for you."

He narrowed his eyes at her and stepped closer, forcing Sol to lift her chin to keep from him colliding with her. "There are no spies in the Villa—the gods wouldn't forgive it."

"Better pray harder, then."

Before Finigan countered with something smart another soldier stepped forward. "The first official trial is the walk of Flora, Goddess of Land and Blood." The soldier met every prospect's gaze with lethal fierceness, so much so that even Sol had the good sense to remain silent as he continued. "To pass it, you must know the tale of our first Goddess."

A carriage pulled up to their left and the noble sigil made Sol tense. While she surveyed it, she caught Cas's eye from his place at the end of the line. He gave her a slight nod. She pursed her lips and looked away, annoyed. She wasn't through being mad.

"Hand Gina will be today's spectator," Fin declared, leaves crunching beneath his heavy steps as he made his way to open the navy-blue carriage, casting a final scowl her way before lending his hand to the person inside it.

The Semmena Hand was dressed in blue robes, much like the ones she had worn at the castle. Her sandy hair was pulled back in a perfect knot, and her violet eyes were lined with a thin flick of kohl. Sol didn't know if she would ever get used to the uncanny resemblance the woman shared with Samara, or how Penny also shared their peculiar gaze.

"Hello, Southern prospects." Gina stepped out of the carriage, holding Fin's outstretched hand. "I do hope the Villa has been to everyone's liking."

Sol stifled an eye roll, and beside her, Jonah scoffed.

Unbothered, Gina continued, "To fully honor Flora's glory, we will be issuing Kerproot. A way to mimic her descent into madness."

Kerproot.

They're not serious.

"It will also mute your magic for a few hours." Gina retrieved a small, silver box from within her robes. "To mimic the way Flora's own became scarce during her journey on Erriadin."

Instantly, Sol looked over at Phil beside her.

The boy seemed unphased by the announcement, his glacier blue eyes not wavering a single beat. If Kerproot stifled magic…

"My brother needs his air magic to see," Jonah said from her other side, chin held high. "He cannot see with his eyes. He sees with the wind; it helps him map out the locations of things around him."

Sol's palms began to sweat, and her heartbeat boomed in her ears as she awaited Gina's response.

Finally, with an expression that yielded no kindness, Gina said, "All must be treated equally."

"You can't be serious," Sol blurted, stepping forward and out of their line. "He will have an incredible disadvantage if he cannot see. That's not equality. Equality would be blinding us all."

Gina smirked at her. "I'm sure I can arrange that if you'd like, Princess."

"Princess." A small hand wrapped around her own, gently pulling her back. Phil shook his head. "It's okay."

Sol's chest ached.

When she turned back to Gina, she let some of that anger slip voice. "You will not give this child Kerproot."

"I will."

"You will *not*."

The tension was palpable as Sol and Semmena's Hand glared at each other. She already started off on shaky ground by joining these things, might as well continue the pattern of defiance.

She would be labeled impulsive, but at least consistent.

She was the one meant to be Queen, after all. Perhaps it was time to act like one.

"Sol," Cas warned from the end of the line. "Let it go."

"I'm afraid we have different views on this, *Prince*." She cut her gaze to his own. "Considering your lack of action during the Savit mess."

"We are wasting time." Gina flicked the box open, the smell of the Kerproot immediately wrapping its earthy, acid scent around Sol's temples.

She did not have a good experience with the herb. She and Leo had come close to being thrown into the Yavenharrow pits, a place for law breakers to sit and rot into repentance. And it had been her fault for nearly burning half the ships down in her unhinged search for fresh seafood, a promise the Kerproot hallucinations had whispered to her until the effects wore off the morning after.

She eyed the herbs with trepidation but remained solid in her conviction. Sol met Gina's violet gaze again, deciding to give it another approach. "I will take his dose, then."

Gasps resounded behind her.

Cas stomped forward, grabbing her forearm. "You will *not*—"

"Let me go," Sol ordered, her tone letting him know just how she felt about him currently. "I will. End of discussion."

His gaze roved all over her face, his brows furrowing slightly, and lips pressing into a tight line. But he released her. "As you wish."

"Again, Hand Gina said it must all be equal," Fin countered with a scowl. "Now stop being difficult and—"

"I'll allow it," Gina said. "Let's move on."

The woman walked over to the end of the line where Cas returned, offering him the first thread of the vibrant, green plant.

Sol stepped back in line, her heart hammering in her chest.

"Princess, I—" Phil twirled his hands, his breath quickening. "You will struggle. I will be okay with a dose of Kerproot."

Sol simply said, "No."

"I will take my brother's dose, Princess," Jonah said urgently. "You must be well to travel the length of the Temple labyrinth."

"I will be fine."

She would not be fine. But she wouldn't let Gina win, and handing off the dose to another was cowardly after her bold acceptance.

So, when Gina stepped in front of her, two stems of the plant in her palms, Sol placed them in her mouth before she could truly think of the consequences.

The prospects were taken to individual threads of the forest, all interconnected to Flora's Temple at their ends. They were each to travel into the rows of seemingly endless trees and make the correct turns based on Flora's legend.

A legend Sol could not for the life of her recall as the blades of grass began to twist into bows and ribbons.

At first, the hallucinations were small. Little flickers of light in her peripheral, or stones that seemed to ebb and shrink in her path. The first fork in the road was easy. To her right was a dimly lit path lined by broken, dry trees, while to her left was a path with resplendent golden flowers, mimicking the sunlight Flora was born from.

That part of the legend she remembered, primarily because she had thought it so unbelievable when she had first heard it from mother.

The second fork, though…that's when the second dose of the herb truly hit her. Sol glanced from one pathway to the other, her eyelids unbearably heavy. The right path shimmered as if showered in emeralds. The left shone red, the ground that led to it a mess of weeds.

Emeralds. Sol liked Emeralds.

She turned to the right, pointing a lazy finger at the opening between the trees. "This way—"

"It's not that way, you know." A small, bright voice whispered. "That way leads you to a pit of serpents."

Sol halted. At least, tried to. But the forest shifted slowly sideways, as if melting like wax from a lit candle. She angled her head the opposite direction and the world dripped that way as well, strings of rainbow shimmers wrapping around the edges.

Fuck.

"Kerproot from Rimemere is quite strong, Queen of Wielders," the small voice said again, this time with a hollow timbre.

Sol looked around. Aside from the melting trees, there was nothing that seemed able to speak. Beneath her, the dirt turned to tea.

She giggled. "It's chamomile tea."

"You must go left, Queen of Wielders." The voice wrapped around her in a warm hug, softly smelling of lilies and begeroot. "You must hurry."

The branches waved, and the leaves reached out their hands to guide her, grasping her by the hair and sleeves. "Are you talking, leaves?" Sol's throat was mush as she focused on her speech. "You aren't meant to talk, I think."

"The Kerproot is too strong, Queen of Wielders. We must help you." Beady eyes bloomed on the evergreen leaves, and Sol gasped.

All around her the dim forest was ablaze with ruby light and life before it shifted into an amber, warm hue. The tea on the ground fed blooms of orchids, and the branches guided her forward toward the left side of the fork.

"Wow," she breathed.

"Our Mother has been closely watching you, Queen of Wielders," the forest sang in unison. "Our Mother has a warning."

The path to the next fork seemed endless, but Sol didn't mind. She traced the lovely plants with her fingertips and sang with them, lost in the lull of the Kerproot. She couldn't remember why she was so bewildered by it before—it was fantastic.

Her limbs were feathers and the world was gold, alive and brutal and gentle all at once.

"Why is—" Sol's words trailed into incoherent babbles as an orb of iridescent glow hovered at the center of the next fork.

It was the glow of the moon on the darkest of nights and falling stars. Green tendrils swirled around, and Sol walked to it, entranced. As she neared it, a curious figure appeared within its center.

"Yarrow," the figure said. "Daughter of Wards, come closer."

Sol obeyed. She floated closer to the green essence. "What are you?" she whispered.

"I have come to issue guidance, Daughter of Wards." The figure's voice was clear as bells and all around her, as if Sol was encapsulated within it. "You must close the Jinn gate before the moon shields the sun, Yarrow. After that there will be no hope."

Sol watched the sparks of gold dance around her face as she said, "I will."

"You will not do it in time, Yarrow."

Sol pulled a deep inhale, saving it at the pit of her belly. "I must—I must do what my mother said."

The figure within the orb pulsed sapphire. "Your mother failed. She did not heed our warnings; she sought another way." The figure grew and morphed into a body. Faceless, featureless, but daunting. "There is no other way. Close the Jinn gate as dictated in the skies."

Sol's hands burned. They dripped. Her skin, her bones—they melted.

Her words were sandpaper against her mouth as she said, "Her note, it said—"

"There is *NO* other way," the figure boomed. Around her, the temperature flamed. "Your humanity will doom you, just like those before."

The golden light of the forest dimmed, turning into a muted violet. The humming leaves hushed in a gasp, and the tea beneath her feet turned to mud.

Through the haze, Sol looked up. She met the figure fully. "I will not fail."

"Why are you here, Daughter of Wards?" The figure ebbed and flowed an emerald tone, circling around Sol. "Your mother had a duty. She was on the throne since she could Wield. She then fled to save you. And now you return, after all that trouble. Why?" Electricity sizzled as it leaned closer. "Why are *youuuu* here?"

That's when Sol lost it.

The sky muted and the air stilled as the words echoed, digging into the corners of her mind, and burrowing.

"Why are you here?"

Why are you here?

Why?

The words pulsed like a heartbeat as Sol sank to her knees. "I—I'm here to finish what my mother started."

"Wrong answer," the voice thundered, and the orb faded into nothing, dispersing into gray mist. As the figure faded, it whispered, "The gods don't need someone like you on the Rimemere throne."

Sol sank further into the mud and sobbed. Because the voice, whether real or Kerproot induced, was right.

What *was* she there for? Because a note from her mother told her to be?

Her mother's wish and instructions had gotten her this far, but would they take her far enough?

She was no Queen.

She had no magic.

She played the facade well, but gods knew she grew tired of trying to fit into their molds, clear by her defiance toward Gina. Her kingdom hated her, and the people that didn't were weeks away, abandoned when they needed her the most.

Like she had done with her mother on the day she was murdered. She had left her to die then, too. Left everyone she loved to die, while she played pretend in a role she was doomed to fail.

Fail.

Failure.

Her sobs broke through her chest as if her heart itself begged to be let out of a body that couldn't bear it. Sol threaded her hands through her hair and pressed her forehead to the ground, heaving heavy breaths while begging herself to get up. Falling apart wasn't an option. Even if that was all she had wanted to do since the day she left Lora and her town behind.

"Sol," the wind whispered her name. *"Sol, come on. You can't let the Kerproot win."*

Branches—no, fingers wrapped around her arms, forcing her to look up.

She knew this man. This man with midnight hair and eyes of moonlight. Still, she sank further into the mud, her face burning with tears.

"What am I doing here? Who—who am I," she shook with each sob. "I don't know who I am."

The man knelt in front of her. He shimmered like fog at midnight and smelled of sage.

His name...his *name*.

"We need to keep going, Princess. We are almost at the end of the path."

She pulled out of his grasp. "Who am I? If I don't even know, then the floating orb is right, I'm useless."

The man sighed. "You really shouldn't have taken a double dose."

Failure.

Failure.

Your mother failed, why would you succeed?

Everything around her shifted and swirled. The leaves that once sang instead hissed, the sky that was gold instead a mossy green. And inside her everything bled, everything cried.

"Sol? Sol." Hands, warm and soft, grasped her face, and she was met with silver eyes. "You need to get it together."

Her tears were acid as she whispered, "Who am I?"

The man pursed his lips, his brows furrowing. "You're Sol Yarrow. You're a barmaid who makes terrible tea. You're stubborn, but fiercely loyal."

Sol exhaled.

"The rest will come with time, Princess. For now, know we are all glad you're here," he continued. "And those who aren't are the exact people who shouldn't be."

She angled her head.

Cas. The man's name was Cas.

The memory of him spread like a sigh.

"Have you always been so handsome?'" She lifted her hand, tracing the soft edges of his jaw.

Cas laughed, but his eyes drifted closed as he leaned slightly to her touch. Sol wished she would remember the sight forever. "You're going to be very embarrassed when the Kerproot dwindles off."

"Because, I remember thinking you are kind of a little ugly." Sol hiccupped as her limbs tingled with feeling and the skies bled back to blue. "Or maybe I think that because you're a little mean?" She leaned against his chest. "Will you carry me the rest of the way?"

For a moment, he didn't answer. To Sol's surprise, he laid his own head on top of hers. "I'm sorry, Sol. For what I said yesterday. For not even trying to help Phil back there, or Felice and her brother..." He sighed against her, his breath sending a wave of shivers through her. "I—I can't risk making a mistake to help others and in turn losing you."

She peered up at him. He was so close she could make out strings of cobalt in his gray eyes, and the slight sadness that swam within. Despite the pull of the Kerproot, she whispered, "I can't let the bad people win again."

Cas clenched his jaw, as if he might have said something more. But the flash of contemplation left as fast as it came.

"Come on." Cas pulled her up. "Let's get out of here."

To Sol's dismay, he did not carry her the rest of the way.

CHAPTER TWENTY-NINE

ENEMIES AND ALLIES

Mercifully, everyone survived Flora's Trail. The good news placated Sol and gave her at least a little more emotional room to let the Kerproot dwindle out of her system.

Sol watched the forest through the carriage's window fighting against the Kerproot's sweet lullaby. She was condemned to ride back with Cattya, Cas, and Zeri, while Jonah, Phil, Ezra, and Cade took another. The names swirled in Sol's brain, oily and thick, as they slammed into a pounding headache. She couldn't deny the forest dwellers—real or not—had shaken her. They weren't wrong. What was she doing here?

"You must close the Jinn gate before the moon shields the sun, Yarrow. After that, there will be no hope."

"There is no other way."

Sol closed her eyes and let her forehead press against the cool glass. Screw the talking leaves. Sol would be fine. Everything would be *fine*.

"First time the oh-so-innocent-Princess has done Kerproot?" Cattya snickered, twirling her loose hair around a finger. "I've heard it makes some people sick. Not me, though. I've always had a great tolerance for it."

"She took two doses," Cas reminded, inching away from the flick of her hair. "That would make anyone sick."

Cattya waved a hand in dismissal. "When I Awakened, I smoked Kerproot for days straight. Felt fine afterward."

Sol cut her gaze to her. "Weird way to say you had no one to celebrate with so you resorted to hallucinations."

Zeri, Lady of Ventry and a surprisingly easy presence to be around, giggled from the seat next to Sol, but said nothing as Cattya narrowed her ruby-red lips into a smirk, her shoulders simmering with smoke. "I actually wasn't alone in my celebratory adventures that week."

"Cattya—" Cas pushed her smoke away with a push of his Shadows.

"Prince Xanthos here was *very* much in my company." She lowered voice, placing the hand closest to him on his thigh. Although Sol tried to hide her annoyance, it was obvious her face twisted with it when the woman laughed. "No hallucinations there—all we did was *very* real."

A wave of nausea tore Sol's attention from them, from Cattya's hand on Cas, and the way he just *left* it—

"Must have been so lovely, Cattya. He is quite affectionate when he wants to be." The words were out before Sol could stop them. She thought the wretched herb was out of her system already, but then from Cattya's head bloomed a branch of thorns and tiger lilies, forming horns around her forehead.

Cattya turned to Cas. "Is he now? What a marvelous change to his personality."

He shrugged, removing the woman's hand from his leg with a zap of electricity.

Sol sighed, placing a hand over her chest melodramatically. "I don't know much about you, Cattya of Stone Ledge," Sol said. "Only that you're quite obsessed with my Royal guard."

"Well, we were meant to marry before he very boldly decided to go search for you instead."

That caught Sol off guard.

Cattya's horns vanished in a plume of smoke, the Kerproot making the carriage walls shimmer instead with each bump of the dirt road. The woman leaned forward. "I'd be careful if I were you, Princess. You've managed to tally up quite the number of enemies here so far."

"Careful," Cas warned, his voice low. "Tread carefully, Cattya."

"Whatever would the other prospects do if they learned the Prince was helping the Princess? That's how you managed to survive that Trial, and everyone knows it." Sol couldn't tell if the spark of fire the woman flicked her way was another hallucination until Zeri quite literally dissolved it with a wall of air.

"Leave her alone, Cat. We are all here for an opportunity to serve her, to become her partner," Zeri said.

Cattya huffed and leaned back in her seat as the carriage drew to a stop. "I'm not." She motioned to Cas. "He's not."

The carriage lurched into a hasty stop, reviving Sol's nausea.

Sol sat up and watched Cattya kick the door open and jump out. The woman peered over her shoulder, blue eyes wavering with an intensity that had Sol's blood race in alarm.

"Gods know why the rest of them are here. But I promise you, *Princess*, not everyone is here to help you to the end."

Sol swore those horns broke through Cattya's skull again as she stepped toward the Gods' Villa.

The Death List was strung up by the entrance. So far, only two names were on it. With three trials remaining—and whatever else Semmena decided to throw in between—it was only looking like the bloodshed outside of them would begin at any second.

Still embraced by the Kerproot's effects, Zeri shyly introduced herself formally and asked Sol if she'd like to see the Villa's libraries. The mention of them alone was enough to peak Sol's interest, so she agreed. Perhaps it was a trap to lure her away with the promise of books, and then ambush her—then again, Zeri seemed kind.

Maybe that's the point.

Sol shook the paranoid thoughts away, and for once decided to trust her judgment.

They walked in casual silence past the foyer and the kitchens, then past the secret wall entrance to the tunnels. Sol had to clamp her hands together to keep from becoming a fidgeting wreck as they walked right past the six-pointed star on the tile, but as soon as they stepped into the library, the subterranean world beneath them was forgotten.

It was like the Yavenharrow Archives in one room.

Rows and rows of wooden bookshelves spread on each wall, then when that space ran out, came out into the room in sections. Sol marveled at the way the shelves were filled with books. Not a single space was vacant.

Candelabras hung from the ceiling to illuminate the area in a comfortable golden light.

Although Sol hated to admit it, she could picture herself spending hours here, lounging in an armchair with whatever book piqued her interest.

Zeri ambled to one of the shelves and plucked out a book. She gave Sol a small smile. "They have things here I cannot find in Ventry."

Sol examined the bookshelves deciding to start her exploring on a particularly dusty one. "What does Ventry primarily produce?" she asked, swatting at the flying dust. "I'm afraid I am still familiarizing myself with the South."

Zeri sat on a sofa, plopping her book open beside her. "Seafood, Princess."

At that, Sol grinned. "Oh, would I love to visit there."

Zeri's eyes gleamed. "You are welcome any time Prin—Sol."

It didn't take any effort for Sol to become comfortable with Zeri. They spoke for hours, sharing details about each other's homes. Although Sol had been told to say she was found in Graniela, she tried to lace as much truth as she could into her stories, still bringing Yavenharrow to life.

Zeri was fascinated by the idea of seasons and beaches with tender waves, unlike her own that were always chaotic. The girl shared she was told since childhood that were the opportunity to marry into Rimemere's royalty came, she would be the one to participate for the chance.

Sol grew nauseous at the disclosure, then even more so at the fact that apparently most of the prospects here had gone through the same.

"We are all here because that's what our role within our territory is," Zeri said, lazily turning the pages of her book hours later. "Southern relations."

Sol shook her head from where she lay on the carpeted floor, a pile of books beside her. "That isn't right. I—It's brutal."

Zeri shrugged. "Perhaps for you who grew up away from the brutality of Wielder life. To us, things like these are normal."

Sol shook her head. "I will get you out, Zeri."

Zeri smiled at her a bit sadly. "It's you who must survive. Not us."

They only left the libraries to eat dinner, then returned with Jonah and Phil when they suggested they all go over the other god's stories prior to the next Trial. They didn't know when it would be but based on the unpredictability of the Vows thus far, Sol agreed they should prepare. That, and she had no desire to lay alone in a cloud of her thoughts.

Zeri suggested the Trials might be going in order of the birth of the original creators, so she suggested Aquarene's Trial may be next. Luckily, she was well versed in the god, talking Sol through not only Aquarene's history, but also shared Winderlyn's, her assigned deity as a Wind Dancer.

"So, Winderlyn came from Aquarene and Flora's prayers?" Sol tapped the feather pen to her temple, dipping it into a vase of ink before sprawling notes on her paper. "Are they...do they have tangible bodies?"

Zeri shrugged. "At one point. Once they left the terrestrial plane, their power was so great, unable to be fully extinguished, they ascended to the skies to forever watch over their people."

Sol blew air out her nose. "I never paid much attention when it came to them, I'll admit. I was more interested in the things we can see."

"We can see their existence through us," Zeri offered, wiggling her Wielder ring, the only thing close to a weapon allowed on the premises. "Every time we give an offering, we see it before our eyes."

"Well, I just recently found that out." Sol laughed, drinking a tea Jonah prepared for her to chase away the aches.

From the other side of the library, Phil sighed. "I usually don't mind not being able to see until I am quite literally surrounded by books."

Jonah laughed softly from beside Sol. "You are not missing much, little brother."

Phil shrugged. "Still, I want to read the stories."

Sol's chest ached as the boy plopped on the ground.

She nodded to Jonah and stood, making her way to the boy. The scar on her back ached, the pain radiating to her palm as she sat beside him. Ever since Flora's Temple, both things had been pestering her.

Phil angled his head her way. "Princess? Are you alright?"

Sol nodded but rubbed at a spot on her shoulder in hopes of some relief. "My birthmark." She decided to not mention the blood bond, especially since Dark Magic seemed to be a strained topic.

Zeri looked up from her book from her spot on a rosewood table beside them. "All Yarrow Wardens have it, did you know that? That's how it's almost certain Warren will choose you."

"Any idea what it does?" Sol grimaced, leaning forward slightly as she plucked a book from the shelf behind her.

"From what I know, not much is recorded about them," Jonah chimed from his spot on a couch.

Nodding, Zeri closed her book, throwing her hair into a knot. "That's correct. It's quite a mystery."

"Did you all know," Phil started, leaning against Sol's arm, "that Winderlyn prefers offerings directly from the neck?" The boy giggled. "Fascinating."

Sol smiled and tapped the book in her hands. "Want to find out what else he likes?"

Zeri and Jonah conversed softly in the background as she opened it and began to read out loud. Phil listened intently, urging Sol to continue every time she would stop to catch a breath. It was endearing.

Time passed and with it the sun settled beneath the horizon, casting the library in purples and blues as the four of them finally exhausted their attention spans and just talked instead.

Between thoughts, Sol tried to formulate a plan to get them out, refusing to forget the reason she was there to begin with. Surely, no one before her had this opportunity to see the Vows from the inside. She had to be able to do something they could not. Still, she had nothing.

She rolled her head to Phil, tapping at his shoulder as he lay calmly on the carpet beside her, seeming to be on the brink of sleep. "Hey" she whispered, glancing toward the others. "I need to ask you something."

Phil nodded, his eyes closed. "Mhm?"

"Penny...has she been back?"

She needed to speak to her, to inquire about the underground tunnels. Perhaps she would be able to take the prospects back with her somehow and guide them back—the girl had to know how to avoid the patrols down there. The rest of the plan, she was still working on.

"The tunnels below us have enchantments," Phil whispered. "Sort of like Wards, but not Light Magic."

Sol nodded. "Cas mentioned that."

"The enchantments are only lowered twice a day, I think–I don't know though, Rimemere procedures are always changing." He yawned. "Penny can only come when they are down–maybe they haven't been."

Sol tugged at her braid. "Maybe."

Without a sure timeframe for Penny's return or knowledge of when the Wards may fall, Sol's plan faltered.

Exhaustion pulled at her eyelids, making her yawn as well.

She was about to suggest they all return to their rooms to rest when a couple of kingsmen marched through the door of the library.

Conversations halted as they approached Zeri and Jonah, Jonah immediately standing to block their path. Zeri stood behind him.

"Tomorrow is the next Trial," one of the kingsmen said, tossing an envelope his way. "You are all expected outside by dawn for travel."

CHAPTER THIRTY

Sawyer

After Nina tended to Sawyer's physical wounds in that way that made her emotional wounds flare with neglect, she just stayed in her rooms.

Letters came and sentries knocked for her assistance with training or strategies to better protect their borders. She didn't care. In all the years she had taken her father's beatings, this last time was perhaps the worst.

Not the pain, she was used to that. But maybe because she was gone for so long with her friends, finally experiencing a semblance of normalcy and happiness, that having him remind her the illusion was dead and gone tore through her body more severely than any slash of his whip.

After two days of sleeping, picking at roasted potatoes and carrots that appeared at her door, and showering with scalding water, Sawyer got the fuck up and headed to the stables. Fey was in the middle of indulging herself with a stack of hay when Sawyer got there.

"The run will do you good," she told the mare, scratching the back of her ear before mounting her.

The guards knew better than to ask questions when she approached and signaled for them to let her through the gates. They only gave her a bleak nod and a respectful salute as she dug her heel into Fey's side and was off into the evergreen land.

She decided to avoid the human sections and the outskirts of the city, opting to gallop straight into the forests instead. It was half an hour on horseback to Emberdon's Temple, which would be empty by the time she arrived, save maybe for stray acolytes.

She and Fey moved in unison with lethal precision, the mare already knowing when to evade trees or jump over fallen branches without much direction from Sawyer.

And she was thankful.

It meant she could focus on the wind and how it played in her hair and kissed her skin. The sky had taken on the most beautiful orange and pink hues as the sun set on the horizon to the left. She took in the freedom with all her senses, wishing with everything she had that it could be forever. That they had never returned.

Sawyer enjoyed being the Royal General. She cared for her legions, thrived under pressure, and excelled at producing valuable statistical plays during battles.

But she was tired.

Her father had drained her. The desire to burn Samara and the kingsmen to a crisp had exhausted her. The outlets to relieve the piling frustrations were limited to training, riding, or distracting herself with whatever she could find—and none of her usual guilty pleasures did the trick anymore.

Twilight approached as she dismounted Fey and took in the sight before her.

Indeed, the temple was utterly empty. Not many of the new students came to pay their offerings regularly anymore unless it was during the Awakening or a ceremonial ritual.

Throughout the generations, the devotion to the gods had become more of a chore for the students. They were more preoccupied with the strength of their magic, training for hours, or reading as much history as possible so they could learn from it. What they didn't realize was that the strength of their magic was directly connected to how much their god liked them. And the gods only liked those who gave regular offerings.

Fools.

Sawyer gave Fey an affectionate pat and left her with a few apples before striding into the stone and marble chapel.

It was similar to the material the castle was made of, however, also had obsidian interwoven into its walls. The whole interior radiated as the setting sun bounced off the polished stones, sending multicolored rays all over the black floor. The room was open to the elements, only large archways holding up the roof and ever-lit torches. There were pews along both sides of the space, then a simple, square table at the end of the rows with a chalice on top. The chalice was carved into the stone table itself to not risk it being lost or stolen. Because it had apparently happened before.

Sawyer walked to it, leaves crunching beneath her boots.

Her god stared down at her as she reached the offering stand. He, too, was carved of obsidian and depicted as a large, chiseled man with flowing hair and soul-piercing green eyes. Next to him, carved into the walls and glowing a fiery red, were the surnames of the most famous and ancient Fire Wielder bloodlines.

Sawyer climbed up to the dais and ran a hand across them.

Jestaller, Kolden, Viotto, and Semmena.

She paused over her own surname.

The union between her parents had been arranged. Her mother, Mel Yarrow, was the younger sister of the Rimemere Queen and a Wardress of the infamous Yarrow line. Her father, Arnold Semmena, was Lord of Melisandre, and Fire Wielder of the third most feared bloodlines, behind Kolder and Viotto. Originally, her father had been a prospect in Irene's Coronation vows—but for whatever reason she let him live, along with Draven, who became her betrothed. A few weeks later, Arnold was engaged to Mel. Either way, the union was celebrated, despite her father bringing in an older daughter from a previous affair with a Water Wielder, Rebekah Semmena.

Sawyer was not particularly close with her half-sister, as she was an absolute bitch and currently ruled over Melisandre. She sighed, cursing the day for taking such a solemn turn.

In the distance, beyond the mess of trees and shrubs, was the Northern guard post. It was a small, square building with Royal green flags swaying atop its roof. It was one of the only posts near the coast, and although it was also the one closest to the Jinn Gate, it actually had minimal activity. She knew her third legion would be within, readying for the day's end to begin night patrols.

As she carefully sliced a small cut on her forearm with her Wielder ring, she could almost hear her men in the guard post singing and laughing the way they always had while they changed shifts so many years ago.

Sawyer let her blood drip into the stone chalice and watched as it immediately evaporated into a crimson mist. She narrowed her eyes and looked back at the building.

It was completely silent.

Something along her neck prickled, like an invisible hand begging her to pay attention. She shook off the excess blood from her hand and unsheathed her sword.

Beyond the post were only hills and the ocean. The waves roared as they crashed into them as Sawyer approached it, stepping off the temple grounds and into the lingering tree line.

Once arrived, she pushed the doors to the post open, only to be greeted by an empty, swollen silence within.

That wasn't good.

Sawyer released a long breath as she stepped onto the tiled floor and gave the area an attentive assessment. There wasn't much furniture for entertainment within the fort. Only couches and the occasional cot, and sometimes Sawyer would sneak in the castle blankets and leftover food.

A movement to her right had her sword and hands up in flames as she shifted toward it.

Sawyer would have recognized the Mind Slayer anywhere. Unlike the others, this one was a deep blue, and was absent of decrepit, rotting holes. Its face was slightly more humanoid than the rest, slightly more...sentient. It had no hair, no clothes, no grin.

Only its flashing, white eyes. Watching her.

Sawyer's sword shook in her hand. "You."

From where it sat in the center of the room, it clicked its talons on the floor. "It's been a long time, Sawyerlyn. You've grown into quite a woman."

"What the fuck do you want?" Sawyer spat. "Where is my third legion?"

The creature shrugged. "Place was empty when I got here."

Somehow, that revelation made Sawyer even more uneasy than seeing the Jinn.

She sheathed her sword. "How did you get into Rimemere land?"

"How did it take you all so long to figure out I was here?"

The thing was just as annoying as Sawyer remembered.

Morna, the name the Mind Slayer goes by, had been the only reason Sawyer made it out of Melisandre alive the night her mother died. Sawyer had been in their backyard, dragging back a pitcher of water from their well when it happened.

Her mother stepped into the window of their room, dressed in a white nightgown and expression utterly empty, visible even from the distance. Sawyer didn't have time to scream before she jumped.

She didn't let herself recall the rest of the memory, knowing herself enough to save it for when she could break down and spiral alone.

Morna stood, the full length of her almost twice the size of a typical human. "Still raw, is it?"

"Why don't you things wear clothes?" Sawyer turned to the wall. "Or at least keep a skin regime."

"I have a warning for you, Fire Wielder." It inched closer. "It requires your immediate attention."

Sawyer told the thing during their meeting in Melisandre never to approach her again—and to never blab to anyone she had taken help from a Jinn.

With a calculated step back, she motioned for it to continue. "I believe I told you last time I would not let you leave alive again."

The Jinn laughed, the sound jarring enough to make Sawyer flinch. "Afraid to say a threat from a small, seven-year-old with anger issues was not very scary, Sawyerlyn."

"What do you want?" Sawyer clenched her jaw. "I want to forget about this meeting as quickly as possible."

"Someone within your castle is lying." Morna's eyes flashed white. "They pose a threat to us."

"So? I don't care about your kind."

"*Us* as in those on the Yarrow's side." Morna scraped the walls with her talons, getting closer. "So rude."

Sawyer scoffed.

The Jinn had told her the same thing in Melisandre—that Sawyer's survival was vital for the Yarrow destiny. Sawyer knew not to believe words from a Mind Slayer, especially kind ones. They were usually tactics to manipulate the victim later on.

Still a youthful, stupid side of her thought perhaps it meant she was special, that she would Settle as a Warden like the rest of her maternal line.

Then she hadn't, and she had been angry ever since.

"I don't believe anything you say for a single second, thing." Sawyer let a wave of fire ripple over her arms. "So, if that's all you have to say, I guess we can fight now."

"I saved your life, is that not enough to trust me?"

"Fuck no."

From beyond the stone walls, the wind howled.

"Fine. I will provide you with a peace offering, Fire Wielder." Morna continued forward, and it took everything within Sawyer to remain in place. The creature may be docile compared to other Mind Slayers, but the reek remained the same.

"Aren't you curious to know how to get the Yarrow heiress and the Prince of Shadows out of their predicament?" Morna angled her head, a motion more animal than human. "I hear they've gotten themselves into quite a problem over at the Gods' Villa."

Sawyer crossed her arms over her chest, narrowing her eyes. "They'll get to the end, and he will yield—not really a predicament."

Morna's pupil-less eyes flashed. "Do you truly think it'll be that easy?" She waved a hand. "Well, alright then."

"Wait." Sawyer pursed her lips. "Why wouldn't it be?"

"Have you ever known anything to be that easy, Fire Wielder?"

Morna was right. In theory, it was a simple solution for Sol and Cas. Which made it all that much more unlikely to work out, especially if her father had any say. "What about Sol and Cas?"

"Go into your father's study," Morna said. "Their way out will be there. The trip may also prove of other value."

"Well, that's vague."

Morna shrugged, her lanky limbs making the motion awkward. "You want more details, it will cost you—nothing is free, Fire Wielder. Especially from us."

Sawyer rolled her eyes and turned on her heel, toward the open door. "Beat it. I am in no mood to kill you tonight."

"Sawyerlyn, you must remember your castle has traitors," Morna called after her. "Nothing we do will matter if they succeed."

She peered over her shoulder. "Who?"

Morna smirked, that trademark Jinn grin that made a shiver skitter through her. "That sort of information will cost you your soul, Fire Wielder."

CHAPTER THIRTY-ONE

Friendships Like Flames

The whole way back to the castle, Sawyer fought the urge to incinerate the forest. Flora would hate her endlessly, but gods did she need a way to calm herself and the fire bubbled in her blood with a relentless intensity that made her very skin itch.

Go into your father's study, their way out will be there. The trip may also prove of other value.

Sawyer decided against offering her soul for the full explanation of Morna's warning. The second one seemed more informative and more attainable. Still, was she truly contemplating listening to a Jinn? One of Loumallet's children? The bloodthirsty demons who kill innocents and children?

Grant it, this particular one was nice, which truly added more to the confusion.

She and her Court had seen countless slaughters during their travels through Erriadin, significantly worse the past few months. The Jinn were, beyond a reasonable doubt, evil vermin who sought only to feed on the weak and mess with the minds, from the Lower, animalistic kinds to the Mind Slayers. If they had kept to their island within the Helian Ocean exclusively, perhaps they could have co-existed. At a point in time, it was said they did.

But the Jinn got bored, as most evil does.

Someone within your castle is lying.

Running a hand through her hair, Sawyer decided she would deal with that warning later.

By the time she rode back through the gates, it was nearly midnight. Still, the courtyards were lively with Earth Caller students tending to the gardens, some also in their excavating gear, surely going into the tunnels for nighttime lessons. If they were making their descent into the land, it likely meant Jeriyah had taken repose from holding his enchantments within the kingdom. As High Scribe, it was the one duty the old fool couldn't slack on.

Sawyer left Fey in her stall after some minutes of quiet mane brushing, a habit that served to placate them both. Students, servants, and officials all gave her small bows as she passed. Sawyer always wondered which of her birthrights they bowed to.

The chances of her making it to her father's study unconfronted were slim. It was deep within the castle, behind labyrinths of hallways, doors, and eyes.

Sawyer stomped past the throne room, past the dark corner she knew would lead her into the first of the path of hallways, ultimately converging into the one that would lead to her father's study. She took a moment—just a moment to think it through. Was this really what it had come to?

With a tight sigh and heat in her bones, she backtracked her steps and turned into the hallway.

Thankfully, the castle staff were preoccupied elsewhere. Sawyer was met with no resistance as she rounded the final corner, the severe silence only adding to her unease. She passed a few servants when she crossed into the next corridor, but they paid her little attention besides a disinterested glance. After minutes of her moving through corners, cracks in walls, and avoiding guards, she reached the final turn, that single red and gold door looming alone at the end.

She had only been allowed near it a handful of times, and each of them left her plagued by nightmares. Her boots scraped lightly against the carpet as she stopped before it.

Reaching her hand to the doorknob, she sighed.

Not even Emberdon's fire could calm the chill that ran through her.

For Cas.

For Sol.

For Erriadin, damn it.

She pushed on it with her shoulder, then let out a sigh of momentary relief as it didn't budge.

It was locked.

The relief turned into horror as she realized who would likely have the keys.

It took Sawyer twenty minutes to find Samara. First, she tried the throne room, figuring the wench might be accompanying the King or kissing his ass.

The throne room, mercifully, was empty.

Next, Sawyer tried her room. The Semmena side of the castle was confusing, cold, and unwelcoming in several degrees. She moved through it quickly, knocking on the woman's door three times, then made her way back into the light of the Yarrow side, both relieved and disappointed at her failure.

She turned the corner of the staircase to go to her rooms when she decided to try one final place.

The second library was used for many tasks. The first consisted of mostly Scribe duties, the third for mostly reads of leisure. She hadn't expected Alix to be in the second one but found herself pleasantly surprised as her friend greeted her with a radiant smile. He wore beige robes and was exiting a main meeting room with a stack of books in his arms. He silently motioned her over to a table by the main entrance, surrounded by circular bookshelves.

He set the books down before pulling her into a hug. "I'm afraid I've gotten used to spending every waking minute with you all," he whispered, planting a kiss on her cheek. "I miss you."

"Is the old man really so possessive of you?" Sawyer eyed the room he had emerged from. She could vaguely see Jeriyah within it, sitting with his hands clasped before him.

Alix sighed. "I'm one of the only other scribes who knows the Enchantments. He is needing more breaks than usual."

"Dark Magic is outlawed." Sawyer braced her hands on her hips. "Just because that one spell benefits my father doesn't mean it should be the exception."

"It's barely Dark Magic, Sawyer," Alix said. "It hardly uses any."

Sawyer rolled her eyes. "If it comes from Loumallet, it's Dark Magic."

The enchantments the High Scribes were still allowed to practice were only used to keep things and people out of places they shouldn't be, like the Jinn Den or sometimes reinforcements for the wall.

Of course, allowed by the mighty King.

"I'm looking for the noble bitch," Sawyer said, looking away from the High Scribe. "Any idea where she is?"

Alix chuckled. "You should show her some respect—she's quite good at her role."

"Sure."

With a shake of his head, he motioned to the second floor, to the mezzanine that loomed over them. "She was up there earlier. I have not seen her depart."

Sawyer patted his arm. "Great. If I don't come back in fifteen minutes, either I killed her and fled, or she managed to best me. The latter is unlikely, though."

"I'll be sure to keep a close look out." He gave her a small wink and pulled open one of his books as Sawyer climbed the thin staircase to her left.

The second floor didn't have many bookshelves, unlike the level below. It mostly consisted of sitting spaces and orbs of firelight. It didn't take long for her to spot Samara over a table by the center of the room, holding a softly lit lantern over what looked like maps of Erriadin and the South.

She didn't look up before saying, "I'm busy, Semmena."

"Please don't start this off wrong by calling me that." Sawyer flopped into an armchair nearby. "I've already had a shitty day."

The Semmena Advisor peered at her through lowered brows. "It's a privilege to share his Majesty's name."

"Yeah, yeah." Sawyer waved a hand in dismissal. "Let's talk about him as little as possible."

Samara continued her close surveillance of the maps, moving to the other side of the table.

With a flick of her wrist, Sawyer brought the chandelier above them to life, the candles concealed within crystal orbs providing a clear view of the maps. She had learned not to be in dark rooms with Shadow Guiders.

Samara only sighed, "What do you want?"

"I need the keys to my father's study."

"Go cause chaos somewhere else, Sawyerlyn," Samara said, extinguishing the lantern she held as it became useless. "I wish no part of your schemes. I am busy."

Sawyer scoffed. "You used to love scheming."

"And then we grew up. Get over it."

Sawyer and Samara had been friends at one point, perhaps just as close as she was now with Nina. She was closer to Sawyer's age both being five years Cas's junior. Their mothers had gotten pregnant at nearly the same time, ironically, and gave birth mere weeks from each other.

When Sawyer arrived to Rimemere at thirteen, Samara and Cas had been her only escape from her father. Nina had been ushered away to distant family in Romalia after her mother's death, then arrived to Rimemere when it was time for them to join the Wielding academy. Samara graduated into the Semmena Court and grew to hate the friendship Sawyer and Cas built, blaming Sawyer for Cas's desire to continue his devotion to the Yarrows instead of joining his sister, despite Irene being responsible for their father's demise.

It all became too complicated to heal.

"Regardless," Sawyer said, clearing her throat. "I am not scheming. I left something important in there."

"Like what?"

"A notebook. With notes."

"You didn't study in the academy, yet you expect me to believe you want to do so now?'

Sawyer sighed, her patience wavering. She jumped to her feet and walked to the table. Samara's violet eyes watched her every movement.

Sawyer studied the maps, tapping her fingertips along the wooden edge. "You're trying to ally with Northern territories."

After a few moments of hesitation, Samara Guided Shadows over her plans. "I don't have the keys. I'm afraid you are wasting your time."

Irritation made Sawyer incredibly tired. "Who has them?"

A small smirk bloomed on the Shadow Guider's lips. "Who do you think?"

Sawyer looked at her for a long time before turning on her heel. "Start with the Driodell territory if you want allies. You can at least bribe them with Earth Callers."

CHAPTER THIRTY-TWO

Winderlyn's Trial

Sol saw stars the second she set sights on what they were expected to do.

There was no way.

None.

Zero.

This was where she died, surely.

Cattya slid past her, a cocky smirk on her stupid face. "Scared, Princess?"

Sol bit her cheek to keep from screaming.

They stood near the edge of a cliff. Pure sandy stone floated beneath them, behind them the remnants of a patchy forest and their carriages. She could tell they were far up on a sort of mountain by the proximity of the clouds and the seas of green the horizon danced with far below the apex of the jagged, looming stone ledge.

On that ledge was a thin, wooden bridge connecting their edge to another about thirty paces away. As they walked closer, the bridge became thicker, maybe the length of both her feet pressed together. It swayed lightly, taunting them with its instability.

It was almost like a parapet, except nothing held it up other than luck and wind.

It wasn't Aquarene's turn, as Zeri had predicted. It was Winderlyn's.

Beside her, Phil angled his head. "Is it a...a rope of some kind?"

"Might as well be," Jonah said, frowning. "Might have better luck climbing across it instead of walking."

Sol felt like she might hurl. At least she had been allowed a dagger this time, as everyone was granted a blade for offerings—even if her blood meant nothing.

The fact there was no more Kerproot involved was at least a small relief. Not a great one, but with her sanity intact, she would at least have the opportunity to think herself out of this.

"The task is simple," Fin bellowed from behind them.

Sol resisted the urge to roll her eyes as she turned to face the kingsman, Jonah and Phil beside her. The rest of the prospects scattered nearby, Cas included. He had kept his distance, though Sol had as well. She flicked her gaze to Cattya to find her already watching, ruby-red lips pursed in a challenging smile.

Sol didn't smile back.

"You are all to walk across the bridge. If Winderlyn sees you worthy, he will allow you through." Fin crossed his arms. "Magic will be allowed," he added, briefly glancing at Sol. "We don't need anyone too incapacitated to walk this time around."

Sol's face heated at the wave of snickers that rose around her, but Phil tapped her hand. "They're meanies," he whispered.

Sol smiled at him. "Huge meanies."

"This trial is timed." Fin stepped forward, signaling to the cliff. "The eight of you have until sunset to cross."

Heads collectively turned to the sky. It was midday.

Surely plenty of time.

And they were allowed weapons this time—Sol still felt conflicted by that.

"Any other rules?" Cattya looped her arm around Cas's bicep. "Or can we get started?"

The Shadow Guider remained still, bored almost, while he removed himself from her claws.

Fin shrugged. "Drag each other over if you want. The goal is to get across and exit before sundown." The kingsmen began the retreat to their horses. Before Fin mounted his gray stallion, he said, "Winderlyn is quite picky with his subjects. Scribe Jeriyah awaits as spectator on the other side. Good luck to you all."

They rode away in a boom of hooves and dirt, leaving the eight of them standing in clouds of dust.

Winderlyn, God of Wind and War.

Sol recalled the notes from the night before, thankful they had decided to study after all.

She glanced at Zeri sidelong to where she stood by a lonely cluster of rocks. She looked nervous, small, in her worn leather breeches and blouse. Her light brown eyes flickered around with unease until they met Sol's. A slight blush creeped on her cheeks, and Sol smiled slightly back to her.

She had to keep her safe. Her, Jonah, and Phil—they were her priority. The rest of the prospects mattered as well, they were lives, after all. But they were wobbly and untrustworthy.

Sol might have a soft heart, but she wasn't totally stupid.

"Winderlyn likes offerings straight from the neck," Phil said. "Not even Emberdon is so brutal."

"Sick bastard," Jonah muttered, earning a shove from his younger brother.

Phil chastised, "Don't bad mouth a god!"

Sol chuckled despite herself as the kingsmen faded into the distance, plumes of dirt drifting into the air.

Cattya wasted no time. There was something rather comforting about the consistency in the woman's character, ironically.

She stepped up to the precipice and retrieved a long, silver dagger that shone in the sunlight. Stone Ledge colors adorned the hilt—brown and steel gray. Without hesitation, she brought it to her neck and in a quick, smooth motion, slicing her skin.

Although Cattya faced the peak of death, Sol could still see the blood seep with drips onto the ground beneath her. It only dripped for moments before the red trail was swooped into a mist of gold. Wind roared around them, a breath from the god himself as Cattya stepped onto the bridge—if it could even be called such.

Although the grassland and trees around them swayed, the bridge remained straight and solid, as if it existed within a bubble of stillness. Sol watched, entranced as the woman cleared half of it in moments.

"Now, we aren't going to let the Lady of Stone Ledge pass with no fun." Ezra marched forward from behind Sol, making her jump out of the way with surprise.

She had only spoken to him that time by the fountain, so she wasn't sure what to expect from him other than an uncanny ability to appear as if from the ground itself. Not surprising from an Earth Caller, Sol supposed.

"Leave her alone," Cas warned from his spot beside Zeri. "She's not one you want to mess with."

"What, afraid you'll lose the easy fuck?" Ezra glared at him, slowly crouching next to the cliff's edge in contemplation "I'm sure you'll survive, Xanthos."

Sol's anxiety morphed into annoyance. Sure, she and Cas were iffy right now. But that didn't mean anyone could just speak to him like that.

She was about to remark that if anyone wanted an easy fuck it was him and she would out him for the absolute creep he had been the first night when she wandered the halls of the Villa.

Cas seemed to sense it coming, because he glanced at her, then narrowed his eyes.

Don't.

Before Ezra had reached the edge of the cliff, Jonah had his hand on his dagger, surveying. Calculating to see who would follow, to see who else he needed to have on his radar. By the way Phil's small hands twitched, Sol knew he was identifying everyone and their locations as well.

As if sensing the challenge, Cattya stopped her walk. She turned and smiled at the man with a broad grin. "Come and get it, Ezra."

"I'm not stupid, Cattya." Ezra sliced a thin line on his own throat with his Wielder ring. Instantly, it evaporated into mist. "I know you're gods' blessed."

Cattya shrugged. "It's called being a devoted daughter of the Creators. You should try—"

A spear of stone shot from the deep abyss below, narrowly missing her. It flew over her, then exploded into a rain of pebbles.

As Cattya shielded herself with a forearm, eyes shone as if made of the hottest flame. "You coward."

Ezra laughed and made a mudra with his hands. "They didn't say we couldn't use our magic to sabotage. Only we shouldn't *kill* with it."

"Winderlyn doesn't like traitors," Phil stepped forward, crossing his arms. "The point of the Vows is to gain each god's favor."

"Go play with the rocks, kid," Cade chimed, moving into the circle. "Let the grown-ups talk."

Cade had been a nearly invisible presence the entire time at the Villa, Sol only remembering his face from the first dinner that had killed Felice and Lucas.

"Watch yourself," Sol seethed, looking the man straight in the face.

His amber eyes flickered, his gaze running down her body like talons scraping against her skin. She narrowed her eyes at him in challenge.

"Back up, Cade." Cas was between them in an instant.

A scream laced with terror made Sol spin back to the cliff. Cattya still stood on the bridge, but it now wobbled as the phantom wind protecting her disappeared. The woman was annoying, but she was smart. She took off into a sprint to clear the rest of the way as more spears of stone propelled toward her, shredding parts of the bridge in their wake.

Fuck.

"As long as we honor the rules of the trials, we will get through," Phil assured. "That has proven true since the beginning of the tradition."

Ezra laughed, standing from his crouch by the edge of the cliff. "Arnold Semmena made it to the end, boy, and he didn't follow that rule."

"He didn't win, though," Jonah smirked. "Draven did."

Cas's face tightened at the mention of his father, and Sol looked away. Every time she had the misfortune of hearing about her mother's trials, the story only got more unbearable. At first, she had wanted to know everything about her and who she was. But now, Sol wanted the opposite.

If she was eventually going to step into this role, like she had already decided she would, perhaps following in no one's footsteps was better.

She could make her own fuck ups and blame only herself for them.

"Draven only won because the Yarrow whore called it and had them draw," Cade drawled, striding up to the bridge and bracing to give his own offering while Cattya disappeared behind the mountain at the other side.

Her fuck ups began today, it seemed.

Hot anger coursed through her. "I'm getting rather tired of people referring to my mother and I as whores."

Ezra grinned, delighted Sol had finally took someone's bait.

"That's what she was." He strode forward, "It's exactly what started the civil war."

"Any closer and I'm afraid I'll have to throw you off the cliff, Ezra," Cas said coolly, not bothering to draw his weapon or call forth his magic.

Ezra rolled his hazel eyes and stopped, but it was Cade who said, "Don't you get tired of other people fighting your battles,

Princess?" He once again eyed her without reservation or restraint. "Perhaps it's time to grow up."

"Now, why would I do that when I can save my energy?" Sol made a show shrugging, stepping into the role these people surely assumed was true.

Dumb. Brash. Inexperienced. Impulsive.

She would admit she was three out of four of those—she was not dumb.

She almost added it to her arsenal as a figure in the distance made her attention snap back to the bridge. They were so busy engaging in childish insults that no one noticed Zeri, who was already halfway across the bridge, her arms outstretched to her sides for better balance.

A wave of relief washed over Sol. She planned to be last and let Zeri go before her, so she knew no one could sabotage the bridge while she crossed.

But her running to the other side worked too.

"I don't fucking think so, Zoar!" Ezra lunged toward the bridge.

And everyone lunged after him.

Jonah brought Cade down with a swift maneuver, pinning him to the ground with tightly coiled branches that erupted from beneath them. The Water Dancer tried calling to the water below, but Aquarene didn't seem to lend her help without an offering.

Cade spat at Jonah, "You're going to pay for that, Ketar!"

In response, Phil loomed over them, using his wind to send a wall of sand and dirt into Cade's face.

Cas had Ezra pinned down, the Earth Caller's face smushed into the ground. Shadows spun between tendrils of dirt and air, the sky dimming as clouds covered the sun.

The Sun.

Sol looked over at the horizon to the sun quickly approaching it.

"When it's just you and me at the end, Yarrow, I'm going to make sure our wedding night is extra special," Ezra said through mouthfuls of dirt.

Sol's chest heaved as Cas dug his knee into the man's back. "Tell me why I shouldn't kill you for that sentence, Sonte." He palmed the dagger at his hip.

Beneath him, Ezra laughed, half-mad. "Because the gods don't like cheaters in the trials, and you're apparently so keen to follow the rules all of a sudden."

Ezra brought his arm up at a speed only a soldier could muster, colliding his elbow with Cas's nose. Sol hurried to unsheathe her own dagger as Cas lost balance, but she was a second too late.

Like she always fucking was.

Ezra shot a hand to the bridge and the tip of the stone fell away as if slashed by a phantom knife, sending the bridge crumbling and Zeri along with it.

CHAPTER THIRTY-THREE

The Fire of Vengeance

Sol's scream was brutal as Zeri fell over the edge of the dangling bridge. The girl held on to the wood for a second, locking eyes with Sol. She gave her the smallest smile before the wooden bridge slammed into the rocks of the mountain base on the other side, propelled by a ghost wind.

The impact sent Zeri straight into the jagged edges, then without a sound, into the forest below.

Everyone was silent.

Even Ezra seemed slightly stunned, as if he only expected to make it harder, not impossible, for the girl to survive. The land itself was still for a moment. Until a bone crushing, soul shattering impact resounded below. The clouds covered the sun entirely then, dimming the landscape as the wind moved in circles around them all.

The roar was deafening, snapping Sol's senses back into herself. She could only stare at the spot where Zeri had been, then wasn't, even as the cold air strained to drag her attention away from the bridge.

A horrible numbness seeped from the base of her neck to her feet, leaving her in a breathless shiver when it snapped into a teeth-chattering rage.

Jonah and Phil ran to Sol's side, leaving Cade yelling in pain beneath their magic as the wind picked up speed.

Winderlyn was pissed.

And so was she.

Sol had never witnessed a god's wrath firsthand, and certainly never been stuck in the midst of it. The atmosphere itself seemed to change, becoming electric with every new gust. Pebbles and branches slammed into each other and everything in between, echoing the sound of the bridge as it slammed to the stone over and over and over. She wanted to move. She vaguely heard Jonah say something as he came to her side, but Sol was woven to her spot.

Zeri.

Zeri.

She cut her gaze to Ezra.

Cas stood over him now, his Shadows dark as nightmares unleashed completely. They pinned the Earth Caller to the ground. Cas's eyes sparked with lightning, his shoulders coated in the remains of a Ward. He turned his face to her slightly as she joined him.

"Your call, Princess."

Sol knew he would kill Ezra. Would damn the consequences of meddling with the trials and toss him over the side of the rock.

But it was only the second trial. And Sol had a sudden thirst for vengeance.

"Spare him," she said numbly, then turned to Cade. "Him too."

Cas's lips twitched at the corners, his Shadows spreading to Cade to pin him down as well.

"Winderlyn is angry," Phil whispered, pulling at Sol's hand. "The air feels—it's not responding to my call."

"And not to alarm anyone further, but," Ezra said, seemingly unaware he now had a bounty on his forehead, "the sun is setting."

Indeed, as Sol turned to the horizon once more, a small patch of lighter clouds was descending dangerously close toward it, almost reaching the tops of the pine trees.

Jonah gave Sol a small nod and grabbed Phil into his arms. "Quickly, then."

With a careful dance and sway of his hands, green magic flared from his palms. The land instantly responded, the place where the stone had crumbled to drop the bridge shaking. Sol gasped as the blunt peak began to stretch, the mountain itself seeming to reach an arm to replace with stone where the wooden bridge had once been.

"You'll get a penalty, Jonah!" Phil cried as Jonah slit a delicate wound on his brother's neck.

In response, Jonah did the same to himself. "I'll take the gamble, brother." He turned to Sol, outstretching his free arm. "Princess."

Lightning began in the distance. The sky continued to dim as if ink had been splattered upon it. Sol knew she needed to act quickly. But as she looked from Jonah, to Cade, to Cas, then to Ezra, she wanted nothing more than to melt into the ground. The deaths of Felice and Lucas had been ground shaking, melting something within Sol that first night in the Villa. Two people she failed. But seeing Zeri fall snapped something. It clicked in her ears, echoing and twinning with the fury that looking at Ezra ignited.

"Princess." Cas observed her with lethal focus. "Get across safely. I will hold them down."

Sol shook the fog, the nausea that had her hands shaking. Through the airborne dirt, she said, "I'm not leaving you here."

Ezra laughed, a caw. "Surely you would provide great reinforcements against me and Cade, Yarrow." He pouted in mockery. "What even are your skills? Besides the uncanny ability to boss Casimir around."

"I heard she was a barmaid when they found her in Graniela," Cade drawled. He seemed inclined to continue the thought, but Shadows wrapped over his mouth.

"Sol," Cas's voice lowered. "Go."

Sol knelt beside Ezra, tapping the edge of her dagger against his temple. She dragged it lightly down his cheek, creating a thin slit through Cas's Shadows. She willed her face into calmness. Her jaw tightened as she whispered, "You are going to pay for her death."

Ezra's eyes became wild, a grin spreading. "There's that Yarrow rage."

"Sol."

Cas's stern tone made her glance up, clearing the haze of fury. His silver eyes shone. "Go."

This time, she listened.

With a final glare at Ezra, Sol stood, and ran toward the makeshift bridge, relieved to see Jonah and Phil already on the other side.

Jonah wore an expression of pure anguish as he glanced below to where Zeri fell.

He will pay.

He *will* pay.

Tears pooled in her eyes as she sprinted, ignoring her limbs and their begging for solace. It wasn't until she was safely in Jonah and Phil's embrace that she shuddered with emotion. She peered over her shoulder to where Cas remained, his Shadows slowly unwrapping the men on the ground while he walked cautiously to the bridge. His sword was strung toward the men, and his back was to Sol as he walked the bridge backward. He wouldn't risk Cade and Ezra first—Ezra would tumble it as soon as he was across.

"I will hold it for him." Jonah stepped forward, gesturing to the passage behind them. "Phil, you must exit to the other side."

"But—"

"I've already messed with the rules. I might as well stay and make it worth it."

Phil admired his brother with simultaneous awe and sorrow, then turned to Sol. "Make him pay."

The song of swords sang in the background as she gave the boy a curt now. "I promise.". Cas tried to delay them, keeping them at a distance with his sword. He still walked backward, his Shadows interwoven with the violet lightning of his Wards lining the way. It was like watching the raw promise of destruction a brewing storm held–breathtaking.

With one arm, Ezra reached to the bridge, his hazel eyes flaring green. The rock shivered, sending pebbles and dirt flying.

Jonah groaned beside her, his entire body shining in an emerald light as he struggled against Ezra's own magic. Blood flowed from his neck, evaporating into golden shimmers resembling a halo, feeding Flora in exchange.

"Let it go, Ketar!" Ezra yelled, slashing a clear cut down the length of his arm. He smirked, wild with anticipation as the atmosphere instantly responded. "We both know Flora likes me better."

Cas continued backward, his steps slow and calculated and defensive.

They were maybe a fourth of the way across, already hovering over the gap between mountains. As Cade lunged forward, his sword slashing down against Cas's, Sol fell to her knees.

It was too risky.

Cas could easily send both the men to their deaths using his magic—but it would be a violation. And she wasn't willing to test the wrath of his gods.

Ezra ran forward, his sword slamming into Cas's side as Cade took the opportunity for a physical hit. Cas expertly dodged both, landing a kick against Cade, his blade dangerously close to Ezra.

"The Prince is good, but he has no time," Jonah ground out. "He must cross quickly."

Sol looked from the chaos on the bridge to Jonah, not knowing what to do.

There was nothing she *could* do.

Jonah's skin was drenched with effort, and his entire body shook as he sank to his knees beside her.

Cas's Shadows swirled along the length of the bridge, the mist lightly lapping her legs.

Sol shut her eyes as the wind slammed against them, the skies continuing to darken, and the sun bleeding in warning toward the horizon. "Cas!" she yelled. "Cas, *please!*"

He didn't so much as falter a step blocking Cade's attacks while Ezra continued his battle of wills against Jonah. Every time Cas tried advancing, the men would block him somehow, as if wanting to remain suspended over the air—because they likely didn't care about the consequences of killing a prospect during an active trial.

Ezra certainly hadn't.

Fuck. *Fuck.*

Perhaps if she went to him she would distract them somehow and buy him time to run—

"Don't fucking think about it, Yarrow."

Sol immediately raised her dagger toward Cattya.

The wind whipped the woman's hair all over her face in a frenzy as she stepped up beside her. She peered down at Sol. "Relax, I'm not in the mood to hurt you."

"What do you want?" Sol stood, angling the weapon at her.

Cattya shrugged, "I wanted to watch the show."

"Princess—" Jonah's voice was laced with pain. He was now on the ground, blouse completely drenched in blood. They were out of time.

Ezra still stalked forward, an evil grin sprouting on his face at Jonah's struggle.

Cattya braced her hands on her hips. "What a mess."

"Please." Sol lowered the dagger and turned to her. "Please help, Cas."

The woman looked from Cas to Jonah, a pout on her face. "Queens don't beg, Yarrow."

"Even for their people?"

They glared at each other for a precious second, Sol's desperation cooking into horror as the time continued to pass, the very land beneath them shaking with Jonah's effort.

Finally, Cattya sighed. "Jonah, beat it. Ezra won't collapse the bridge with himself on it."

Within moments, the sparks of green magic beside them shuddered and disappeared, leaving Jonah in a mess of breath and blood. He looked up at Sol, but before he could protest or speak, she gestured to the small opening along the back wall that would lead him to safety. "Go."

"I'm only giving him mere seconds." Cattya stepped forward onto the bridge as her chest winked with flames. "That is going to have to be enough."

Sol bounced on her heels behind her, feeling defeated and useless. She cursed her mother and everyone who kept this side of her life hidden, leaving her defenseless and unable to help her people.

The inadequacy she had felt at the beginning of everything, the fear of never fulfilling her mother's shoes, and of not being good enough for her birthright melted with each drop of sweat, transforming into a raw desire to prove her mind wrong. To prove everyone wrong.

She clenched her fists.

She would get out of these awful Vows and Settle, learn her magic, and hopefully never experience the total helplessness she did as she looked after Cattya.

The Fire Wielder stopped in the center of the bridge, almost directly behind Cas. She swayed her arms in a circle, materializing an incredible wall of flames. She pushed it forward as Cas Warded them with a swift wave of violet.

Then they ran.

Ezra and Cade disappeared behind the wall of fire, giving them time to flee uninterrupted. By the time they neared the end, rain began to pour. The flames extinguished with a sizzle and smoke, revealing Cade with his face toward the skies and a stream of blood along his neck. When he met Sol's gaze, his eyes glowed.

"Damn Water Dancers," Cattya mumbled as she stepped into the safety of the mountain, not sparing a single glance at Sol before continuing to the exit. Jonah slumped near the opening following behind Cattya only after assuring Cas cleared the bridge as well.

Sol grabbed Cas by the arms, utter relief washing through her. Although he said nothing, she could tell the sentiment was shared as he also grasped her arms with a gentle squeeze. His silver gaze roved all over her, searching for wounds or maybe just ensuring they had truly made it.

The rain drenched them both in a heartbeat, his hair falling over his eyes as her own swelled with tears.. "Let's get out of here," he whispered.

Sol nodded frantically and didn't protest as he pulled her toward the exit, his hand sliding to interlace with hers.

"I don't fucking think so."

Sol was ripped from Cas's grasp and slammed hard against Ezra's chest, the smell of smoke still strong. Before Sol could warn him, Cade tackled Cas into the exit, leaving her alone in Ezra's hold.

CHAPTER THIRTY-FOUR

To Survive

The first thing Sol could think to do was elbow Ezra in the stomach. She put her entire, adrenaline-fueled strength into the move, then let herself fall to the ground, hoping the sudden shift in weight would throw the man off balance.

As he released her, Sol made a mental note to give Leo the biggest hug whenever—if ever—she saw him again for teaching her basic self-defense skills during their childhood.

She crawled away from the Earth Caller and swirled to face him. Ezra's clothes were singed and smoke-stained, even after the quick but fierce deluge Cade had called.

Now, in the silence after the storm, Sol stared at the man, calculating her best chance for survival. The wind had slowed, rolling into soft caresses. Dirt swirled in tendrils around them, sending leaves adrift within it. She stood, unwilling to seem small before him.

The cliff they stood on wasn't wide enough for her to back away without the threat of falling, and Ezra cleverly positioned himself before the opening to the exit.

He angled his head, the motion mixed with the mess of blood and ash on him making him an utter terror. "I was planning on taking us to the end, you know." He chuckled humorlessly. He sheathed his sword. "But seeing your attitude, I think I'd rather just get rid of you and take the benefits of a Semmena court mate instead."

Sol shrugged, trying her best to seem calm between uncontrollable tremors. "You'll likely fit in better there anyway."

His eyes flashed. "Careful, Princess. There's no one to save you here."

"Good." A smile pulled at her lips, ignited by vengeance. "Because if anyone is going to put you in your place, it's going to be me."

Bold words, dove.

Sol flinched. She looked down at the palm that held her dagger. The scar there flared red, and she could feel the blood pumping beneath her skin.

"What the—"

The distraction cost her.

Ezra slammed into her, throwing her down to the ground with merciless force. All the air left her as her back collided with the rock, the distinct taste of copper filling her mouth.

Breathlessly, she spit it out. "Coward."

Ezra laughed. "You would've made a terrible Queen, just like Irene." He retrieved a dagger from his belt, pressing it against the center of her chest. "Such a shame." He pinned her with a straddle, pressing his inner thighs to her hips, making her unable to shift beneath him. "A waste of a pretty face."

Panic gripped her as she fought to breathe and escape him simultaneously, especially as his eyes glazed over in a way she knew all too well.

Ezra replaced his blade with his palm. "The only thing I regret is that Xanthos won't be here to watch."

Fight, Soleil.

Again, the disembodied voice echoed in her ears, as if it was both within her and around her all at once. Her hand burned. Realization struck that she still held her dagger and Ezra had underestimated her, so she crushed it into his exposed side.

Ezra fell from atop her with a yell, frantically pulling at the blade as Sol rolled sideways and away from his grasp.

"You *bitch*." The clatter of her blade on the ground was enough to tell her the injury was nothing crucial, and she was now without a weapon.

Still, she stood and faced him. She would fight, even with just her fists.

For Zeri, who had no chance to.

Let me in, dove, the voice sang. *Let me end him.*

This time, the voice was familiar. Slightly different, but clearly Lora.

Sol pressed her hand to her chest, not quite knowing if to respond or if she was in such a stressful situation she had merely gone insane.

She barely saw Ezra lunge again, this time bringing his dagger forward at a ferocious speed Sol couldn't completely avoid. The blade slashed her exposed chest in a diagonal gash across her collarbone. Biting her tongue to keep from screaming, she evaded his next maneuver, landing on her stomach nearly at the edge of the cliff.

"You fucking whore."

Before Sol could stand and flee from the precipice, he dug his sword into the side of her blouse, holding her in place just long enough for him to press his dagger to the back of her neck.

He knelt next to her face, and Sol could hurl from the sight of him being so near.

Killer.

Pervert.

"You're a disgrace to your goddess," Sol whispered through tight teeth. "I would've given you a fast death, you know. But you kill me, and I doubt my Court will be as kind."

Ezra gave her a vile smirk, running a hand along her thigh, then hip, then shoulders. Each squirm only made him go slower. "Once I'm part of Semmena's court, I'll ask for Sawyerlynn as my wife." He lowered his lips to her cheek. "And I'll be sure to remind Rimemere just how easy you were to kill."

End him, Sol. Let me in and end him.

Sol breathed heavily, the sting of the knife at the side of her throat was nothing compared to the ache over her body. Again, her aunt chanted in a haunting song, in, in, let me in, dove.

"But of course," Ezra flipped her over, not caring as his dagger fell over the edge. He held her in place with a forearm to the neck, then moved his mouth to hover over her own, the reek of the blood from his neck making her hold her breath. "I must first know how you taste."

Sol shut her eyes. Come in.

A ghastly laugh shook her very bones before a spear of cobalt light shot from her palm, penetrating Ezra directly in the chest and sending him flying over the edge of the cliff.

CAS

As soon as Cade Lane tackled him into the exit slit, Cas knew they were fucked. Not just him and Sol, but anyone and everyone else who got in his way on the other side.

They landed with a heavy crash at the beginning of a prairie, and Cas wasted no time.

He sprang to his feet, dragging Cade up by the collar of his leather battle suit. The asshole laughed, spitting in Cas's face.

"Your Princess is so fucking dead, Xanthos."

Cas punched him in the face. Again. And again,

Cade went down with unbelievable ease, his back colliding with the ground as Cas continued to pummel him, then after deciding it wasn't enough, unleashed his Shadows to pin him down, sure to tell them to burn.

To scorch.

To kill.

"Casimir and Cade." Vaguely, Cas heard Jeriyah call to them from a few yards away. The old man waved a paper at them. "Now, now, we are still on Winderlyn's premises—killing will result in a penalty."

Wards replaced Cas's fists, singeing Cade with each collision. "I don't give a—"

"Gods, Casimir." Arms wrapped around his chest pulling him off Cade. "He's not worth you getting on Winderlyn's bad side, you fool."

He shrugged out of Cattya's grasp. "Do not touch me."

She brought her hands up in mock surrender. "I'm not the bad guy today, love. Your Princess begging me to save you pulled at my cold, cold heart."

"Where is she?" Phil ran forward, his hands shifting frantically. "I—She's not here. I can't feel her."

"You left her?" Jonah's expression darkened, even through the exhaustion. "Your job is to protect her, and you left her?!"

Cas didn't need the Dianese Heir rubbing it in. Not knowing what was happening behind the sealed, towering wall was quite literally killing him, even his Shadows seemed to turn against him.

Where is she, where is she, where is she, they chanted.

"Lower your enchantment, Jeriyah," Cas demanded, marching to the old man. He watched the wall with a bored, blank look, whispering mumbles and oaths to keep his makeshift ward intact.

Cas hated the Dark Magic enchantments. They were an abomination to Warren's Wards, to the Light Magic that birthed the skill.

Rimemere would rather put souls in peril rather than ask for assistance from Wardens in other territories—though they were scarce nowadays a days. The wretched enchantments often glitched or caused tunnels to crumble since they were mostly used beneath land. Or, like today, when they seemed to be testing his morals and his patience. Because he could just knock Jeriyah out...that would drop the thing.

As if sensing the unspoken threat, Jeriyah took a step back. "Trust in her, boy." The Scribe gave him a long look. "Trust."

"Screw your trust, Jeriyah!" Cas yelled, stalking toward the stone, to the wall of thick, oily ripples that would tear him to pieces if he tried to cross. "Let me back in."

Cas's magic rebelled inside him, begging to be unleashed. He gritted his teeth and cut a small wound along the edge of his tattoo to relieve some of the charged, incessant surge of power. Having two gods call to him was madness, especially when mixed with adrenaline.

Take the blood, Warren, and let me breathe.

Cas knew Loumalett wouldn't take his blood offerings—he never had. He had no temple.

How he continued to grant him Shadows was a mystery he hadn't bothered to decipher.

"Please, Ezra is doing us a favor," Cade spat, still kneeling on the ground. His face oozed red. "I won't be yielding my status at the end for her—we will have more fun fighting amongst ourselves for the spot in the Semmena court."

Cas peered at him over a shoulder, slow and lethal. "You were never going to make it to the end, Lane."

The laugh the man exhaled gave Cas just the edge he needed to continue beating him. Until the crackle of the enchantment made him pause.

Sol looked devastating.

Her pants were torn, tattered at her knees and thighs. She dragged herself forward with pure will, her boots pulling the vines wrapped around her ankles. The sleeves of her blouse were ripped from her shoulders, her pale hair now completely out of the braid she usually wore. Every time she was near he saw the embodiment of the sea, lethally beautiful. Right now, though, she looked like a storm.

Cas stepped forward, unsure what to do.

Her skin was smeared with mud and soaked from the rain, blood, and cuts and—

"Sol," Cas breathed, reaching to the gash on her chest. She evaded his touch, her usually bright, emerald eyes muted.

She continued forward, slowly passing him, giving him only a light touch on the shoulder to signal it wasn't about him.

And Cas understood.

"Princess!" Phil sprinted forward, burying his face in Sol's waist. She placed a gentle hand on his head, but her expression remained ice cold.

Jonah strode forward as well, his attention shifting from her, to his brother, then finally to Cas.

Cas shook his head slightly. Don't talk about it yet.

"I assume you are the final prospect, Miss Yarrow?" Jeriyah lowered his hands, killing the enchantment.

Sol nodded bleakly.

"Great. I will send kingsmen to search for the bodies of the others."

Sol ambled forward, Phil still in her embrace. She stopped beside Jeriyah, but looked straight at Cade as she said, "You will only find Zeri's. There is no body left of the other to search for."

CHAPTER THIRTY-FIVE

The Jinn Den

To thank Flora for sparing Cas and Sol, Nina spent the day planting lilies in the Castle's bare gardens. She woke up at dawn to tend to the soil, releasing the hounds to keep her company. Gardening soothed her. The dirt beneath her nails instead of the blood of battle was a welcomed change, and the soft fragrance of the blooms wrapped her in a much-needed hug.

She tended to the dirt for hours, ensuring it was tender and rich enough to plant the seeds. She could've made the process faster with her magic, but there was a sort of magic in letting things happen naturally, too.

By noon, Nina planted lilies and roses all along the front courtyard, her skirt wonderfully filthy and hair full of mud. As she stood to admire her work, the sound of footsteps behind her made her reach for the concealed dagger.

"Are you so paranoid you carry a weapon on castle grounds, Miss Amana?"

Nina sighed in relief. "Many people dislike us, Gaven."

Gaven smiled down at the mess of holes and gardening tools by her feet. "Needed a distraction?"

"You can say that."

Although Gaven had graduated into the Semmena Court, he and the Yarrow Court had been good friends during their time as students. He was meant to join them in the Yarrow Court, his spot earned by exemplary performance and intricate Wind Dancer abilities. But Semmena claimed him for himself for no other reason than to separate them.

Still, Gaven found ways to interact with Nina and the others, though he was closer to Sawyer as they both were part of the tactical Rimemere team.

And because he was infatuated.

"Not that I don't want you here, Gaven, but your presence usually means something is needed," Nina said, shaking away the ache in her hands. "Surprised you didn't summon Sawyer."

Gaven chuckled. "I did. She didn't open her door."

Nina grimaced at the thought of her friend in her room, alone, and more than likely tending to both the physical and emotional wounds her father inflicted. But she knew her well enough to leave it alone for now, aside from the occasional check-in through the plants Nina left in her room. The only thing keeping her from trying to drag her out was the fact Sawyer went out on her own accord the day before, which meant she wasn't so far deep in her mind to need help.

"Yes, perhaps let her rest," Nina said. "What do you need?"

Gaven sighed, turning to look past the castle gates for a moment before looking back at her. "The King has instructed me to go to the Jinn Den. He said to take Sawyer as well."

Nina's heart skipped a beat.

The Jinn Den was the one place in Rimemere most Wielders avoided, and rightfully so. The place housed Jinn of every level, from the rabid lower levels to the ones right below the Mind Slayers. It was put in place before Nina's time, meant to house the creatures to better understand them and their weakness, to perhaps one day best them permanently with something other than Yarrow blood.

Before Nina and her court had left Rimemere, the four of them were tasked with rotating patrols along with several human guards, forced to choose between that and the dungeons for whatever it was they were under the King's radar for.

Whatever reason Arnold had for wanting Gaven out there with Sawyer…

"For what?" Nina demanded, crossing her arms.

Gaven looked around, his expression darkening. "Apparently a Mind Slayer was caught and taken in. He asked me to…question it."

Samara's statement eased back into Nina's mind.

Because it's quite a blow to think you all searched for, what three years with no luck, but a single Mind Slayer finds her in a month?

She picked at the dirt beneath her nails. "Now why would we keep one of those at all? Where was it found?"

The man shrugged. "I truly don't know why, or why he wanted me to take Sawyer. It was captured around Emberdon's temple late last night."

Nina smoothed her skirt. "Well, you're getting me instead."

Before they departed, Nina changed into something more equipped to handle a Mind Slayer. She donned a dark green tactical suit, one she found in her room from her days as a student. It was a few tugs too tight, but the reinforcement it offered against a Jinn bite was too enticing for her to give up. After squeezing into it, she threw on a black cape and her usual sword before tucking several daggers into her waist belt.

When Gaven spotted her from his spot by the castle gates, he let out a low whistle. "Miss Amana, I don't think I've seen you in this suit since before graduation."

Nina rolled her eyes, though still felt a tad embarrassed at how tightly it hugged her. "You are correct, Gaven. It's my second-year suit."

He gave her a small smile and motioned her forward to where Kahaida waited. "Smart choice."

Gaven rode on his own horse, a stunning white stallion, at a steady pace beside her as they galloped through the forest in comfortable silence. The day was warm, a sign summer began to approach. Nina enjoyed most seasons, especially in Rimemere where they were clearly distinguished. But out of them all she liked summer most.

The sun seemed to always make things better.

The Jinn Den was a half-hour ride from the castle, sometimes shorter depending on the route taken. This time, they decided to ride along the coast, with the beach and ocean beside them, the Jinn gate looming in the distance.

As they arrived at the Den, Nina couldn't help but look past it to the spec in the distance where the Gods' Villa and her friends were.

Before Nina went to garden that morning, the Death List was issued from yesterday's trial—Winderlyn's trial. Zeri and Ezra, both marked as penalty kills.

It was such news that prompted the immediate need to feel the dirt on her skin.

Nina gently pulled Kahaida to a stop a healthy distance from the gate, knowing the mare was more sensitive to Jinn presence than even she was. Gaven did the same with his stallion. He looked up at the building constructed of onyx and laced with violet streams.

"This place never gets easier to come to."

Nina eyed the wards—Jeriyah's enchantments—shimmering around the walls and knobless door. "It truly doesn't."

Even the trees and grassland around the place were dull and brittle, as if the very life was replaced with the Jinn's endless death. Usually, guards would greet them by the main door. The lack of any made Gaven and Nina glance at each other with heightened caution.

Wordlessly, Gaven retrieved his sword from his belt and took the lead, Nina behind him with a sense of unease in the pit of her stomach. It never made sense to her why the King harbored these creatures within the wall that's meant to keep them out, nor did it make sense why the wall did not extend along the coast when the Jinn mostly swam to land from their isle.

"Semmena didn't say what exactly to ask it," Gaven whispered. "Only to see what it said."

Nina tightened the grip on her daggers. Mind Slayers within Rimemere couldn't mean anything good.

As they reached the door, Gaven knocked a series of sounds on it with the hilt of his sword, a code that would signal the keepers to open.

Nina had a sudden wave of dread that perhaps they were also missing, but after a few moments, the door creaked open—no guards in sight.

It was a single hall they stepped inside, the door snapping shut behind them, and leaving them engulfed in total darkness. Slowly, a blue glow seeped from beneath the many doors flanking them, stretching into the abyss beyond. Nina looked from door to door and fidgeted with the hilt of her daggers.

Each door was solid, bolted, and warded with enchantments that predated Jeriyah's position. Nina didn't trust the ancient magic at all, but it seemed to be doing its job.

The doors were adorned with individual carvings, depicting different classes of Jinn. To her right was the portrait of a giant, bird-like creature with feathered wings and talons stretching from its lanky fingers. Where the beak should have been there was a gaping hole filled with long teeth and a pointed tongue. Its eyes were giant, bulging, and on either side of its head—A Middle-Level Jinn, more sentient than the Lowers.

"Where in the world are the guards," Nina whispered, pressing her back to Gaven's to keep a full range of surveillance. Her breath came in puffs of cool mist, the temperature within the place a permanent winter.

"I've never seen the place unguarded," Gaven responded. "I have a bad feeling about this."

"Your little soldiers were called away about an hour ago, Wind Dancer."

Nina knew the voice of a Mind Slayer. They had a distinct sort of timbre, one that made their victims drawn to them, all part of their manipulation. It came from the end of the lone corridor, highlighted by a soft, baby blue light.

She and Gaven exchanged glances.

He shrugged. "Your call. We can come back with reinforcements."

The Mind Slayer cackled. "Oh, no need to fear little old me. Come. Come here, Earth Caller—I can smell the land on you."

If they left now, Nina doubted she would get the opportunity again to see what made Semmena so interested in the creature. Maybe the King would somehow drag Sawyer here for whatever sick reason.

No, Nina wouldn't risk that.

She nodded in a silent order forward.

Gaven obliged.

The thing was...fatally mesmerizing. It sat on the floor, back against the wall and knees folded beneath it. Unlike the Lowers, Mind Slayers were typically more humanoid, making them even more unsettling. Its entire being was covered with radiant, blue skin. Its hands were casually draped over its knees. Where its fingers should be, there were only thin, needle-like rods. It had no hair, no semblance of humanity.

Their eyes met.

Its depthless, black eyes flashed white as it stood. It had no nose, only slits where one should be. Its eyes dimmed as it walked toward them, so slowly it could have been floating.

"Ninanette Amana Lochar," the thing hissed, its voice wrapping around her in a slither. "What a treat."

Nina blew a breath through her nose at the instant debt to Flora. Her very blood heated at the mere mention, demanding release to pay the tithe. With a hard squeeze of her fist, her Wielder ring pricked her palm. "How *dare* you speak my full name."

The creature grinned. "Just making sure it was really you, Yarrow Hand."

"State your business." Gaven stopped in front of the Mind Slayer's cell, his sword pointed at the bars. "Why are you within our lands?"

"Are we not allowed to wander around the planet?" The creature ran a long talon along the steel bars. "Your people are the ones who captured me while I was simply minding my own business."

"Your kind does not belong in Erriadin," Nina spat. "You will always be exterminated when found."

The thing watched her with unyielding attention, its smile widening. "Is that so, Amana?"

The locked doors surrounding the cell rattled with shrieks and growls.

"Pity to know you think so," it continued, its voice lowering while it ran its tongue over its teeth. "I have come to issue you a warning—as a peace offering, I suppose."

"We don't listen to the likes of you." Gaven eased Nina behind him. "We will ask one more time. State your business."

"My business is with the Yarrow Court, not with you, Semmena filth." The Mind Slayer lunged at the bars, its jaw snapping inches from Gaven. The man had the creature instantly disabled with a stab to its side. It shrieked. "If it wasn't for my oath your blood would already be gone, Wind Dancer."

"What do you want with the Yarrow court?" Nina side-stepped Gaven, taking the creature's attention.

It glared at her. "Like I said, I come to issue a warning."

"Issue it then."

The Mind Slayer smirked. "Someone within your castle is lying."

Nina blinked, any fear she felt quickly replaced by annoyance. "That means nothing to me."

"They are a threat to your Queen." It unrolled to its full height, black blood seeping from the wound Gaven carved. "You must rid Rimemere of them."

"Again, why would we listen to anything a Mind Slayer says?" Gaven sheathed his sword and stepped up beside Nina. "All you things do is spill lies."

"Ah, but we have similar goals, the Yarrow Court and us." The creature sat back on the floor. "It's the *others* you all shouldn't trust."

Mind Slayers were notorious liars. They were built to confuse and mock and spiral their victims into madness. *It made their blood tastier* is what several had told Wielders before attempting to make them a meal. So, naturally, there was no reason to continue the conversation.

But, still...

Nina crossed her arms over her chest, the blood in her palm continued evaporating in a golden mist. The Mind Slayer eyed it. "The *others*?"

It nodded, attention never leaving the dripping blood.

"How are we meant to care about this if you won't even be direct with your *warnings*?" Nina asked. "Even if we chose to believe you—which we don't—you've only said a whole lot of nothing."

"Nothing is free, Amana." It inched closer. "I will give you direct answers for a price."

Gaven easily retrieved his sword with a smooth motion, inching it through the bars in warning. "That's close enough."

Nina shook her head. "Typical." She motioned Gaven back the way they came with a wave of her hand. "We aren't taking your bait."

They began their way back, Gaven falling into step beside her.

For a second, Nina had a lapse of judgment. Perhaps the thing calling the Semmena Court filth resonated with her, called her attention. The Jinn usually didn't take sides like that, never having shown interest in their political dynamics.

"The day Sawyerlyn's mother jumped to her death in Melisandre," The Mind Slayer called after them. "Aren't you curious how your dear friend escaped? How her killer didn't get the Fire Wielder too?"

Nina stopped so quickly that Gaven slammed into her back. She narrowed her eyes at the creature, turning back to it.

It had its face pressed to the bars, teeth bared in a wide grin. "Because we all know Melanese Yarrow didn't truly jump from that tower."

Her breath quickened as she stomped back toward its cell, blood roaring in her ears. Sawyer had always suspected foul play with her mother's death. It was never confirmed, but she had also never said much about that day, not even to Nina who knew her almost down to her soul.

Nina pulled a dagger from her belt and held it directly to the creature's forehead. "Who the hell are you?"

Its eyes flashed, "My name is Morna. I am—an ally of the Yarrows."

"*Bullshit.*"

"You Wielders have us all labeled as evil. You aren't wrong. However, some of us share a common goal with you, Amana. It's the *others* you should be afraid of. Not us."

"Who are the others?"

"Nina," Gaven warned, placing a hand on her shoulder. "Be careful."

"Everything comes with a price." Morna ran their tongue over the edge of the blade.

Nina clenched her teeth. "What is your price?"

Gaven sighed and turned away, letting out a string of curses.

The thing turned, walking back to the far wall. Its body moved awkwardly, twitching with each step and breath. From the angle, Nina could barely make out a chain on its wrists, glowing a white-blue light.

"I will tell you one of the warnings fully," it turned to look at her, "for a helping of your blood."

"Oh, *fuck* you."

"We may have a common goal, but that doesn't mean I will help you Wielders without getting something out of it."

Nina raised her hand, blood still oozing from her palm. She closed it.

Instantly, the floor rumbled and shook, the dirt around them lifting slightly.

Gaven was beside her in an instant. The walls contorted, limbs of stone spearing from it, aiming directly at *Morna*. The thing laughed. "It's in your best interest to give in, Amana. The others already knew your Queen's location. It is only a matter of time before the rest of their plans fall into place."

"Who," Nina commanded. "Who knew her location?"

The Jinn put their hands up in defeat. "Only a few drops of blood. I swear it."

She watched the creature for a long moment. Nina squeezed her palm so fresh blood would flow and held it through the bars. Yes, it was crazy. But so was not taking an opportunity to keep her Court safe.

Morna was beneath her palm in an instant, mouth open like a starving animal.

Nina's blood dripped into it, and she had to look away at the pure delight the creature drank it with. She looked at Gaven instead, who looked back and forth between the Jinn and her. He gave her an incredulous look but said nothing.

"The Jinn have been long divided," Morna started, wiping the corner of their mouth with the back of their clawed hands. "Some want the Jinn gate closed, such as yourselves. Others want it torn totally open. Those *others* are the ones who pose a threat to the Yarrow heiress."

"Why would any of you want it closed?" Gaven said. "It gives you direct access to…food." He grimaced, eyeing the blood that dripped from Nina's hand now tucked to her side.

"Our Void Magic, or Dark Magic as you idiots call it, is being constantly stolen." Morna sighed, "We want it back, and in our dimension, only."

Nina and Gaven were silent. Although she didn't want to admit it...it wasn't too unbelievable.

"And these *others*...are they who found Sol in Yavenharrow?" Nina was too anxious to realize the slip-up, realizing the Semmena Court thought she was from Graniela. The Wind Dancer only gave her a small smile and nod.

The secret would be safe.

"Yes," Morna said. "We had been protecting her all this time. We slipped up."

"Let's say all this is true." Gaven arched his brow. "Why tell us?"

Morna walked back to the far wall, sitting cross-legged on the floor as they had first found them. Satisfied with the snack, evidently.

"Because for us to get what *we* want, we need the Yarrow heiress alive." The Mind Slayer glared at Nina. "So, keep her that way."

CHAPTER THIRTY-SIX

To Sacrifice

Cattya's bed was too warm. Even Cas's Shadows seemed stifled beneath her.

They had been a good team before, back when Cas had no real worries, or when he spent most of his time finding ways to defy the system out of spite.

When they had ended their partnership, before he and his court left Rimemere, it had been sad, but not debilitating. They had both known it was never meant to be a long-term thing...even if they had been engaged for reasons other than love.

He hadn't expected to see her ever again if he was honest. Cattya was meant to walk the castle of Stone Ledge, tasting the imported foods, and demanding her ladies give her the next worldly gossip.

Cattya was a familiar face at the beginning of the Vows. But now, as they neared the end, Cas couldn't for the love of Warren remember why he had ever tangled with her.

"I was thinking of changing the color of my hair," Cattya said, twirling her dark braid around a finger. She lowered her chin to

Cas's bare chest, blinking at him. "There's a new sort of plant that makes dark hair lighter."

He had almost said no this time. Sol hadn't left her room in days, and although he and the Ketar brothers left food by her door, none had been touched. Cas passed by her door so many times he lost count but couldn't bring himself to knock.

Watching her expression absolutely shatter after the last trial was almost as horrifying as watching Zeri fall off Winderlyn's bridge. She hadn't spoken to anyone about what transpired between her and Ezra. Not having a weapon when she emerged from behind Jeriyah's enchantment didn't go unnoticed. So, she either used the dagger she'd had or used something else entirely. The subtle scent of burnt flesh on her when she walked past him told him she likely wouldn't reveal how she did it.

The mystery of it gnawed at Cas's every waking thought. "Did you hear what I said?" Cattya whined. She sat up on her bed looking down at Cas. Slowly, she ran her hands over the lines of his tattoo which had been in a state of incessant itching since Flora's trial.

Whatever soothing Sawyer's blood had provided the Kerproot seemed to have deteriorated it.

"Your hair is fine," Cas said finally. He stretched an arm behind his head. "You always hated lighter hair."

"But you like it." She slid a leg over his hips, settling herself over him. "Surely it will look good on me."

"I have no preference." Cas gritted his teeth.

Cattya's price for the continuous supply of information on the trials was this. For him to lay with her. And although it was effortless entertainment, it felt wrong. Any sort of pleasure when so many things were at stake felt wrong.

Even Cas had the moral sense to know that.

Obviously, Cattya didn't.

"You used to be way better in bed, Casimir. Did the years of traveling make you boring?"

"People are dying, Cattya."

She scoffed. "People are always dying. Doesn't mean everyone needs to stop having fun." She lowered herself onto his chest, her now loose hair draping around them like spilled ink. She hovered her lips over his own, rose red and slightly parted.

And Cas couldn't help it as he looked down at them. "What's the next trial, Cattya?" he whispered. "I have other places to be."

She smiled slowly, nipping his bottom lip. "Better places than with me?"

You need to know what's next. You need to know what's next.

Cas recited the words in his mind like a prayer as he tangled his fingers in her hair and brought her down into a kiss like he knew she liked. The way it made him want to bolt from the room surprised even him.

There was no other way to know the next trial. The only way he had been able to evade the Kerproot during Flora's was due to Cattya's intel. He paid her price again, and again, reminding himself it was to help him, and Sol make it out of the damn Vows alive. And if he didn't make it, at least guard Sol as long as he could.

And though Cas had always been an expert at hiding his true feelings, feigning interest in a woman was one of those things he struggled to lie about.

Cattya's kiss was urgent, and unwelcome, forcing him to break it. "The trial details, Cat."

Cattya rolled her eyes and slid off him. She shrugged her robe on. "You'd think I was asking you to kill me instead of fuck me, Casimir." She leaned against the dresser, a hint of disappointment in her eyes. She looked him over. "If I told you I had a way to make it you and me at the end—would you agree?"

He blinked at her. "No."

She scoffed as if she hadn't expected another answer. "It's water. Aquarene's trial." She inspected her fingernails. "Don't know anything else."

Cas sat up, holding the sheet around his waist as he turned to face her. "You always know more."

Cattya shrugged. "Guess they're being extra secretive about this one."

CHAPTER THIRTY-SEVEN

The Xanthos Sentence

Two-hundred-fifty stains.

That's how many Sol was able to find all over her walls and ceiling, but she was sure there were more behind the small chandelier. So, on the second day of doing nothing but laying in her bed, she removed it.

There were in fact two more splotches behind it.

The imminent promise of the next trial loomed, but Sol didn't care. She didn't try to prepare or to worry about it. She just—existed.

Because taking that for granted seemed like a sin.

Zeri's terrified scream as she fell to her death was the only noise that rang through Sol's ears. That and the occasional soft clatter of what was likely food trays outside her closed door, but she didn't have the motivation to inspect it.

Zeri died.

Sol failed her.

She had killed Ezra after saying she would never take another life.

She pulled a pillow over her face and yelled.

The second they had gotten back to the Villa, Sol begged the guard to retrieve her body and give her a proper burial. They ignored her. Jeriyah was only to burn it.

She had stomped right up to her room and hadn't left since. Resorted to counting stains on her walls and letting the guilt fill her stomach instead of food. Sol promised herself that joining the trials had been for a reason, one of the main ones being to find a way to save these innocent people. Grant it, now she realized they weren't all inherently innocent—but still deserved to have a choice over who to be with.

Who to die with.

Who to die *for*.

At least, that's what she would continue to say to keep from throwing herself off the spiral staircase.

"Everyone deserves mercy."

"No, Princess. Not everyone does."

A knock at her door had her sliding her gaze toward it.

She remained silent.

The room was dark thanks to her disemboweling the flame-lit chandelier. Maybe they would think she was sleeping and leave her be.

The knock came again, louder this time.

Sol groaned and turned to face the wall, covering herself with her quilt.

"Sol? If you don't open the door, I will."

Sol peered at the door once more, bracing herself on her elbow. "I'm fine, Cas. You can leave."

"You haven't eaten." His voice was gentle, foreign enough to make Sol feel a little guilty for not wanting to see him.

After Winderlyn's trial, she didn't want to see anyone. She wanted to rot in bed until it was time for the next thing, then the next, then hopefully the end.

She fell back into bed.

Unless he tore the door down, he would eventually leave. Sol had bolted both locks, mostly for the false sense of security. Cattya could easily incinerate her way in if she felt like it.

The mere thought of the woman made Sol bite down on her jaw to keep from screaming.

"Unlock the door, Princess."

"Leave, Cas."

For a moment, the room was silent. Sol let her eyelids flutter closed for a second, thanking the gods he decided to listen for once. But then the lock mechanism clicked.

Sol bolted up.

Cas's Shadows still hovered over the locks, slowly dispersing into the room as the door creaked open.

He leaned on the door frame. "Sorry to defy your wishes, Princess."

"Neat trick," Sol sighed. "Or should I say scary?"

Cas shrugged. "You didn't leave me much of a choice."

He walked into the room slowly, surely surveying the unkept mess, herself included. He wore his usual black tactical suit, his black curls slicked into a loose updo that made Sol look away. From the corner of her eyes, she watched him put a cup down on her table. "The Ketar brothers sent you this."

Sol eyed the cup, exhaustion pulling at her eyelids. "What is it?"

"Vegetable stew." He sat in a chair, positioned to look straight at her. "They tried finding some sort of seafood for you, but settled on vegetable since that is Jonah's specialty."

Despite the gloom that pooled inside her, Sol let a small smile pull at her lips. "That's sweet of them."

"Come eat." Cas tapped the table. "You need to be well for the trial."

She shook her head, the motion sending spears through it. "I'm not hungry."

He frowned, his silver eyes flickering as he grabbed the mug and walked toward her. The room was still dim, even darker as his Shadows trailed him to the foot of her bed. "Can I sit with you?"

She looked up at him. "If I say no, will you *defy my wishes*?"

Holding out the mug to her, he smiled, "I do the opposite in a woman's bed."

A laugh tore from her, true and utterly unprompted. It instantly lightened the weight that pressed against her temples, and for a second made her feel something other than dread. Which had obviously been Cas's intention as he too laughed along with her.

Sol patted the spot beside her. "So many women's beds you've been in to have that line saved, huh?"

"None have ever openly laughed like that, though."

Sol took the mug of stew and her mouth instantly watered. It could've been made by Lora's own hand with the way the herbs all blended in familiarity, making her feel slightly nostalgic as she took a sip of it. It was warm and fragrant and exactly what she needed. The steam and heat caressed her, pulled her in a much-welcomed hug.

She took small sips in silence, Cas only a comforting presence beside her.

Slowly, with each mouthful of roasted carrots and broth, the darkness in her mind gently cleared. Even the room seemed to lighten slightly, as if the rays of sunlight were no longer afraid to graze it. Cas's shadows remained out but were thin and lazy across their feet.

After a while, Sol set the cup on her nightstand. "I failed her."

The words were almost jarring in the silence, but she kept her composure in check, biting on her cheeks to keep from crying.

Cas glanced sidelong at her. "You did not kill her. Ezra did."

"I've done nothing to help these people when that's what I swore I would do."

Cas sighed, bracing his hands behind him, but saying nothing.

Sol let herself fall back on the bed, her legs dangling over the edge. She inhaled slowly, "Ezra isn't the first person I've killed." She didn't let him answer or let herself take back the words. Instead, she let them all spill out. "When I was fifteen, my friend Leo and I snuck out after hours to a local tavern. We didn't drink or anything like that, we mostly went to dance and meet the students from his school." She closed her eyes. "That night, I decided to leave early, right before sundown. Leo told me to wait for him, but I didn't.

"By the time I got into the town square, it was dark. I don't really remember what the man looked like anymore—only how much everything hurt after it happened." Sol paused for a moment, shaking away the haze of the memory. "I only told my mom what happened. She begged me to report it, but the man let me go and I never wanted to see him again, so I refused. Five years later, that same man came into the Hound with some other sailors."

She dared a side glance at Cas. He watched her silently, jaw set, and eyes hard as steel. His hands gripped the quilt beneath them in fists.

Sol looked back up to the ceiling. "He didn't remember me. So, I made sure to make him cozy and left the Inn with him. I told him my cottage was closer. Took him down the same alley he took me, and I killed him."

Cas was silent for a long while, so long Sol had to look over to see if he was still there. Wards crackled around his shoulders. "Good."

"Not good, Cas. He had a family I later found out about, and I took a life out of pure vengeance and hoped that it would heal whatever he had broken inside me." Slowly, she sat up, wiping the sweat from her palms on her knees. "It didn't. It only made it worse."

"Not everyone deserves to live, Sol. Especially people like that."

"Everyone deserves to live."

"Not anyone that hurts you." His Ward winked out. "Ever."

She sighed, wanting to continue explaining how it wasn't about her. That it was about morals, about how they couldn't play gods as they had. But she didn't. She kept his gaze long enough for his expression to soften, despite the rising heat, the intimacy of it brewing in her chest.

Finally, Cas stood. "Let's take a walk."

They walked through the Villa silently. Sol was pleasantly distracted by the way it seemed to transform in the nighttime. The moonlight gave the spaces a sort of divine light that was missed during the day, and she wondered how many beautiful things she had missed from avoiding being out at night.

They went to the kitchens to pick at bowls of fruit left from breakfast and chocolate pastries that had a small card stating they were from the Semmena Court for the remaining prospects. Sol almost didn't eat them out of spite, but *chocolate*.

They ended up at the library. How Cas knew it was the one place within the Villa that didn't totally agitate her, she didn't know. But now as she looked at the couches in its center, all she saw was Zeri's ghost.

She turned into one of the bookshelves, inhaling and exhaling the soft scent of knowledge.

Cas followed suit. "I'm not a huge fan of libraries, but they always smell.... peaceful."

Sol pulled out a yellow-spined tome. "I used to love spending time in the Archives of —" A pointed look by Cas. "Graniela," she finished.

"Tell me more about your life there."

He leaned against the bookshelf to face her. His eyes beamed, the darkness around him curving in to caress him, reminding Sol of stars against a night sky.

She pursed her lips and grabbed another book. "Not much to say. I'd work at the Hound and hang out with Leo and his sister." She moved to the next shelf. "Definitely not as luxurious as life in Rimemere."

"Trust me, there is nothing luxurious about it." Cas followed behind her, also inspecting the shelves.

"What is your favorite thing about it? About Rimemere?"

Sol kept her attention on a book titled *Failed Pleasures*. She frowned and looked around. She hadn't seen these titles the first time around.

"I often visited the coast," he said, blowing a puff of dust off a particularly sad-looking journal. "With my mother and sister."

"With Samara?" she asked, grabbing another book.

A Body to Kill For, a memoir.

Huh?

Cas looked past her, as if in a daze for a moment. "No, my other sister, Maya."

Sol turned from the shelves to face him. She remembered Gaven mentioning another sister. How she and his mother had been condemned to the dungeons after Draven's execution, an order from Irene herself. And although it had nothing to do with her, a pang of guilt pulled at her chest.

"I'm so sorry, Cas. I never really got to tell you that."

For a moment, emotion swirled in his features. But the cool mask he usually wore hardened a second later. "It's in the past."

Sol decided to drop the subject, walking to a lone table to sit and inspect her findings.

Opening the first book, she was immediately greeted by an intensely graphic love scene. She scanned the pages, but when a "generously crafted member," neared a "velvety soft and moist entrance," she slammed it shut.

"What kind of books are in here?" She pushed the book away with a finger, feeling her face heat.

Cas pulled it toward him. "Books from all over the world, I think."

He let the book fall open, dust and dirt flying at his face. Coughing, he narrowed his eyes at whatever was on the pages, then lifted a brow at her. "Is this what the great Crown Princess of Rimemere is into?"

She cleared her throat and snatched it back. "Maybe." They spent a good hour roaming the place, Sol finally finding her specific type of novels somewhere along the far right bookshelves. She stayed away from history, or anything related to the Wielders this time. She wanted distractions.

Finally, as the moon beyond the open window loomed at its peak, they decided the walk had served its purpose of getting Sol out and agreed to call it a night.

They gathered their findings and made their way back the way they came when a series of figures in her peripheral made her freeze. The first time Sol had been here she had spent it in the center of the room, with the Ketar brothers and Zeri. Still, the fact she managed to miss what looked back at her was odd.

At the end of the row of shelves, was a tapestry. Enormous enough to take up the entire wall. It depicted seven individuals. On the right, a man, and a woman, both with black hair and sapphire eyes, almost twins were it not for the man's darker skin. Between them was a youthful looking woman, her auburn hair tied back and face lit with a resplendent smile. Next to her, was a smaller woman, with chestnut hair and golden eyes.

Immediately, Sol ran forward.

To the left was a massive, ebony-skinned man, holding a series of scrolls and wearing robes of deep ivory. In front of him, was a woman with violet eyes and hair tightened in a tense knot. Then, stark in the center, sitting on an all too familiar stone and gold throne, was her mother. Hair dark as night, eyes a piercing cobalt.

She looked younger, angrier than Sol remembered. Regardless, she felt tears burn her eyes as she looked from her mother to Lora, then to who had to be her Uncle Axel and Aunt Mel. Gina, the woman who now belonged to King Semmena, and to the woman who had to be Clarisse, Nina's mother was next. Finally, she admired the man behind them who would be Alix's father.

Her mother's Court before Lora had arrived to it.

Sol didn't have many portraits of Irene. She often painted Sol or Lora, or other strangers Sol didn't ask about, but self-portraits were scarce. She fought the urge to touch it.

"I'll never look like this," Sol whispered. "I'll never be able to fill this." Her birthmark pulsed slightly, either soothing her or in agreement.

Cas was beside her but watched a speck on the ground instead of the beauty before them. He shifted on his feet, his boot tracing the delicate patterns on the rug.

She looked at him. "What is it?"

His expression was distant, so much further away than she had recently seen it.

Sol turned back to the tapestry.

Lora. Axel, Mel, Clarisse, and Gina. Alix's father, whose name she couldn't quite recall.

She stiffened. There was one person missing.

"He was removed from all Royal portraits after it happened," he said, not looking up from the ground.

Sol felt conflicted. She felt bad his family had been subjected to such dishonor, and that it followed him despite it not being his fault. But at the same time, there wasn't much she could say or do to make it better. He had shown her he disliked talking about it, avoided the topic all together when she brought it up. She didn't think this time would be any different. "I'm sure what happened was a last resort," Sol said at last.

The room darkened ever-so-slightly.

"The consequence for demanding to know who his betrothed had sired a child with during his absence shouldn't have been execution." Cas's closed fists shook slightly the atmosphere charging with tension.

"Threatening a Queen is treason," she countered. "Surely there was another way for your father to handle it."

When they had first arrived at the Castle, Cas had given Gaven the deadliest look outside that meeting room where they had verified her lineage. Sol never forgot it, and as he slowly turned toward her and gave her that same look, she knew whatever trust they had created was cleaved in that very instant.

She struggled not to falter at the rawness of his gaze while he turned to fully face her, his fingertips sparking violet and his Shadows seeping from his shoulders.

"Did they tell you the full story, Princess?" He leaned toward her, his eyes welding her to her spot, beacons in the dimming light. "Or did whoever told you leave out the grueling details, as everyone always seems to?"

Sol's chest heated, her stomach churning with caution. "I don't see how any details would excuse your father for wanting my mother dead," she said tightly.

He scoffed, "Let's see."

The firelights went dark. One by one, the orb lights around them flickered until the only light was the sparkle of violet at Cas's fingertips.

She had never seen him this way. Although severe with others, Cas always remained rather gentle with her, even when she wasn't.

The stark difference made Sol step back, truly for the first time scared of him.

"Your mother was to wed my father," he said, his tone as cold as ever. "He was declared winner of her Coronation Vows. He discarded *my* mother, left her for yours in the name of power." His Shadows heated around them. "A Xanthos and a Yarrow, two of the greatest Warden lines. The power their children would hold drove the South feral with ambition. To remain on their good side, to be appointed to their Heir's court."

Sol's back pressed against the shelves, the furniture slightly swaying with the impact. Cas grabbed her wrist.

If to keep her from falling or from running, she didn't know.

"My father was in love with Irene. Blind with it," he continued. "Left me and my sister to rot in Eswin. Got Gina pregnant in hopes of moving on with her but could never quite shake off your mother. Left Eswin to my mother's reign, to a woman without a single clue how to lead."

Her birthmark burned.

Still, she held his gaze.

Still, he held her firmly to her spot.

"Your mother never cared. Never accepted his proclamations, his unrivaled devotion. She said she'd marry him for duty, nothing more." His breath was labored, seeming at the brink of whatever restraint he managed. "Seems like you both have that fucked up sense of duty in common, huh?"

"If you wanted to insult my morals, *Prince,* there was no need for these theatrics," she said, voice wavering. "You've told me plenty you disagree with me about."

He gave her a cold smile. "See, you don't get it, Sol. I don't disagree with you. I simply don't care about others as much as you claim to."

Sol glared at him, betrayal oozing with an icy ache into her chest. After everything. After he sat with her to make sure she ate, after she told him her biggest secret… "You lie to yourself, Casimir."

The Ward at his fingertips faltered, but he didn't. "My father left Rimemere to the borders of Romalia, to fight in a war your family started. He came back and… Well, I assume you know that part of the story."

Sol was never leaving her bed again. Screw this. Screw Cas. Every time she felt closer to besting his self-loathing it plummeted back into her with the weight of falling ceilings, of tombstones, of a kingdom. Trusting anyone other than Lora, Leo, and Mina was a mistake. None of these people cared about her. Didn't care about her mother, why would they—

"What I know they didn't tell you, Sol, is that after my father was executed, I chose death."

At the mention of her name, she met his eyes. They weren't angry. Despite the atmosphere hanging cold and daunting, despite the sparks of lightning around them and the shivering darkness, his face was calm. Stoic. Detached. "When Irene made me choose between being bound to her or death, I chose death."

"Cas—" she breathed, inching forward.

This time, he took a step back.

"And I think your mother knew I'd choose that." He tightened his grip on her arm as the memory consumed him, his Shadows becoming denser, almost obscuring him completely from view. "Because after she ordered everyone out of the execution room, except her Court and me, she brought out my mother and sister. My six-year-old sister. Maya."

Sol shivered.

No. She didn't know the full story.

"She then gave me another option," he continued, his eyes trailing her face, her tense shoulders. "Swear loyalty to her or she'd kill them, too."

Breathing became difficult. And as the sparks of the Ward shone and frayed, Sol wished he'd let her go, so she could fall to her knees and sob.

"I'm sure you can guess which one I chose," he continued.

"Cas—" she repeated, almost begging for him to stop. She didn't need to know this. She didn't *want* to know this.

"So, Irene threw them in the dungeons, to ensure I kept my allegiance and remained in Rimemere. Her Court was livid, upset she wouldn't kill us all and be done with it. A few were on our side, though I don't remember who at this point." He softened his grip. "Not that it matters."

Sol hated herself. She hadn't known this, and cursed Gaven for not telling her the entire story. Her chest ached for him, for what he had to choose at an age not much younger than his own niece was now. Guilt pooled inside her at all the clueless mentions of his family. She hadn't know the full story and made comments about it anyway.

With that ache, shame gnawed. Shame for the things her family had subjected other people to. It hadn't just been her mother, either. Sol was learning this long line of injustices had been facilitated since the beginning of the kingdom, gone unchecked and unquestioned by the people meant to protect it.

"And now?" Sol's voice was barely a whisper. As if anything louder would rupture the fragile bubble they both danced on. "Where are they now?"

Instantly, the Shadows dissipated from the room around them. His features, however, were as fierce as ever.

"I don't know," he shrugged. "After your mother left, the nobility here didn't care. I went to visit them one day, and they were gone." He outstretched his tattooed arm, the leather around it groaning.

"So, tell me, Princess," he said, running a thumb along her wrist, his grip now gentle. "Did those details change anything? Did that sound like a fair consequence for a man whose only sin was loving a woman too much?"

Sol's mouth was dry as she tried to come up with something, anything to defend her mother's honor.

She came up utterly empty.

Cas gave her a sad, but bleak smile.

She could almost count his lashes, almost feel the silken waves of his hair against her skin as he turned away and began to walk to the library entrance.

"Cas, wait—"

"Tomorrow's trial is water. Wear something light."

Sol watched the spot he disappeared from for a long time before making her way to her room. She was ready to throw herself on her bed as soon as she opened her door, maybe even cry herself to sleep out of pure frustration, when Penny swirled to face her from where she stood by a kettle of tea. "Princess—"

Sol threw her arms around the girl and sobbed. "Penny."

Penny didn't know why Sol cried, but the sweet, sweet girl just patted her back. "There, there."

They sat on the floor for a while, crying and talking and hating everything together, until Sol finally regained a sense of logic and told Penny she wasn't safe here.

But just as she opened the window, everything clicked. As if she had only needed to cry herself dry to see the obvious solution, one she had been toying with all along.

Sol had a plan to save the prospects.

CHAPTER THIRTY-EIGHT

Aquarene's Trial: Part I

When Sol felt her shift at the Hound Inn was bound to be terrible, she would sneak sips of ale throughout to bear it. It was perhaps the only way to maintain sanity. The habit often left her messy drunk by the end of the night, then begging for relief the day after.

But unlike those days, now she couldn't just take a tea, stew, and a hot bath to feel better. As soon as Sol tried to pry open her eyes, she knew Aquarene's Trial would be the most difficult thus far.

She inhaled with each attempt to pull them open, careful to let the sunlight in slowly.

When had she gone outside?

Last she remembered was being with Penny, formulating a plan together, then nothing.

Sol remembered nothing after that unless she wanted to hurl. When the nausea finally subsided and her sight adjusted to the blazing brightness, her stomach churned.

The salty scent of the ocean was the only familiar spark within her senses, calming and alarming her all at once. Every corner of her vision was blue. The ocean spread in all directions, meeting with the blue of the sky almost seamlessly. The waves and the clouds along the horizon almost mirrored the other's ferocity, making it seem like reflections of each other.

Sol looked beneath her. She sat on a wooden raft. It was more like a long, thick mass of plywood, really, but it was big enough that the oddity had to be intentional in its design. It was absent of edges and any semblance of functionality. She tried to move, to stand, or at least sway to the side, but nothing gave.

"Don't. Move."

Cattya's voice was directly behind her. Sol's breath hitched as she tried to pull herself forward–then couldn't.

Her wrists were bound behind her back and against what felt like a post. Beneath her, her ankles were also bound with—

"Copper shackles," Sol whispered.

Cattya scoffed. "Lucky time to be Unsettled."

Sol snapped her head to the side. Jonah and Phil rested against a post as well, bound and visibly weak.

She looked to her other side.

Cas and Cade were bound to each other similarly, but as Cas simply stared out at the sea, Cade seemed like he might flood continents if released. "This is fucking stupid. Who does Semmena think he is?" The man yelled, struggling against his shackles. "Drugging us and tossing us out to the middle of the Helian Ocean without magic? They didn't even give us any instructions."

Sol racked her brain for anything she ate that could have contained a sedative so strong, especially one she hadn't sensed.

She knew the chocolate pastries had been too good to be true.

"In my experience, pushing against the cuffs only makes it worse, Lane," Cas said. "It also is greatly testing my patience."

"If you had any common sense, Cade." Cattya shifted against the post, tugging the shackles tighter against Sol's wrists. "It's obvious the goal is to get the fuck away from the Jinn gate."

The evaporated any mental haze Sol fought with had been replaced with a severely calm sort of panic. "What did you say?"

Cattya moved sideways slightly, and Sol peered over her shoulder. "Take a look at what you should be guarding right now, Princess."

Sol didn't have to see the thing fully to know it was terrifying. The Jinn gate had been a story until now, a promise she would have to deal with in the future.

But there it was.

At first glance, it was only a lonely, bare island. It didn't seem too long to walk fully across it, didn't seem menacing at all, in fact. Sand covered on its shores, scattered trees the color of rotting wood spread along the edges of it. Sol lifted her chin slightly, letting her see inland as the wooden raft they sat on swayed with the waves.

Even from where she sat, she could see the wound in the land. It was as if the island imploded on itself, folding into the planet in a massive tear. From within the slash, blue smoke spread in a fog, a fog that still reached them from where they floated. No birds flew around the land. No sounds of animals. No jumping sea life.

It was all very...dead.

"They're going to come to us any second," Phil said, his voice almost calm. "And we won't be able to stop them."

In fact, everyone around Sol seemed eerily calm, aside from Cade. It likely meant they had no hope of escaping.

"Okay, so what do we do?" Sol cataloged their problems. Copper. No magic when it was perhaps the one trial they needed it in.

Cas hadn't so much as looked her way.

It was more an annoyance than a problem, she would admit—but the guilt of the night before was still something she needed to settle with him. Preferably before they died.

"Not much to do," Jonah said. "Any sharp move from us and the Copper will seep into our blood. That's a death sentence in itself."

Fuck.

"Okay, but it won't kill me." Sol pulled against the shackles, then stopped as Cattya wailed.

"You move, and it cuts me." For once the Fire Wielder sounded scared. "If the Jinn end up here, you'll need me alive."

Smart for the woman to remind Sol of that, since technically poisoning her with copper would get rid of a problem. But Sol had no intention of hurting the woman, not if she could help it. She wiggled her hands slightly. They weren't bound too tight. If she could just squeeze one hand out—

Slowly, and carefully, she straightened her hand, moving it side to side and hoping the sweat and humidity would help it slide out. Even Cade was silent as she worked, as she tugged without moving the chains to avoid hurting Cattya.

After twenty minutes of the same thing, just as she contemplated breaking her own wrist, her right hand slipped free. She laughed, gripping it to her chest for a moment before messing with the second one. When it finally came free, she lay on the raft, arms outstretched across almost the entire expanse of it.

The sun burned overhead, but even it couldn't clear the mist the Jinn Gate emitted.

They had swayed away from it slightly, mercifully. It was smaller in the distance.

Sol ran to Jonah and Phil first, deciding they were the ones she trusted most behind Cas. She needed back up if she was to release the Prince, since releasing him meant releasing Cade.

"Princess," Jonah motioned forward with a shake of his head. "The keys."

Of course they had left the keys here just out of reach.

Bastards.

Sol searched around, finding a tiny post on the edge of the makeshift boat. She stumbled to them, nearly toppling over as a rogue wave slammed into it. Water snuck into the wood, submerging the bottom of her boots.

They needed to get moving.

Fast.

As soon as the brothers were free, Jonah tried to call Earth, anything to expand the raft they floated in, but it was no use. Flora denied aid.

"I guess the penalties from the last trials finally caught up to me," he said a bit sadly, holding Phil to him. "We will have to be careful with our movements here."

The cold ocean water seeped onto her clothes, only intensifying her shivers. "How is this thing floating?"

"It's wood from the Driodell forest," Jonah said. "You can tell by the scent."

In between tremors, Sol detected the peculiar smell of sulfur and salt, the same essence as the dirt that lived on her mother's tombstone.

"If someone doesn't get me the fuck out of these things, I will sacrifice myself and tumble this whole raft into the water out of pure spite." Cattya glared at Sol. "And then we are all dead."

"You're insufferable, you know that?" Sol crawled her way, working to unlock her shackles. "Any smart moves and I'll stab you with these keys."

Cattya laughed, but still eyed them. "I would incinerate you before you even knew what was happening."

"Want to find out?" Sol twirled the keys in her fingers, contemplating just how deeply her preaches of mercy truly went.

"For fucks sake, Yarrow, unchain us!" Cade yelled, kicking at the raft. They all shifted with it, and Sol had to kneel to keep her balance. "I think our luck has run out."

Phil and Jonah took her sides, both facing the direction of the Jinn gate. Phil's hand trembled as he pointed at it. "I feel them."

They were ways away from it now, the sea carrying them closer back into Rimemere lands. But Sol still clearly made out the second the multitude of Jinn collectively sank into the water from their shores, the pulse of blue light as they started their hunt toward the raft.

"Sol, get me out of here now." Cas twisted in his place. "Now!"

She threw herself over beside the two men as Cattya and Jonah took defensive positions by the edge of the raft, the Fire Wielder smoking and the Earth Caller unsheathing his weapon. Phil remained behind them, manipulating the wind to get the raft in motion.

"Get me out first or I'll make sure the copper gets into him." Cade glared at her, a horrible smirk on his lip. "Then I'll be sure to drown you nice and slow."

Sol grasped Cas's shackles, breathless and in a spiraling panic. With each attempt to jam the key into the lock, Cade moved, forcing Sol to start over.

Cas watched her silently, and Sol knew he tried to keep calm and not add to the sense of urgency that choked her. The sea around them darkened, the waves now thrashing more violently.

"Princess," Jonah warned. "We need the Prince's Ward soon."

Fuck fuck fuck

"He can't Ward if he's dead." Cade kicked at her thrashing against the pole like a fish out of water trying to distract her.

But this time, Sol was faster.

With a clatter, Cas's' shackles fell to the floor, and he instantly worked on his ankles as Sol sat back to catch her breath.

He tossed the chains into the sea, along with the keys. "You're staying right where you are, Lane," he said, rolling his shoulders. "We will take our chances without a Water Dancer."

"You'll never get us to land on time!" Cade spat, his amber eyes wild.

"We don't fucking trust you," Cattya added. "I would've burned you if it didn't mean burning the wood."

"They're close now," Phil whispered.

The group neared each other, forming a circle in the center of the raft, their backs against each other. Sol pressed Phil against her as they remained in the middle of it.

"Phil, use your wind to shield you and Sol if I fail." Cas reached to his waist band, pulling a dagger from it. He turned to look at Sol. "Don't miss."

She willed herself to breathe as she met his gaze. "Never."

First, the ocean stilled as if it held its breath, the current halting, swaying the raft to a complete stop. Second, the air chilled. It raised Sol's skin and raked a shiver along her bones. It was moments after when the Jinn surrounded the raft.

They circled it like a frenzy of sharks, their lanky limbs gliding into the air like fins.

The sight was terrifying, prompting even Cattya to utter a prayer to Emberdon as she slashed a wound on her forearm. The others followed suit.

"Hey! Corpses!" Cade yelled, kicking at the wood beneath him. "Come and get us! If I'm dying, so are they!"

With an effortless flick of his wrist, a spear of lightning flew from Cas's hands and straight into Cade's chest.

Sol gasped, pulling Phil closer.

The Water Dancer only had a second to glare in disbelief before slumping over himself.

"I'll take the penalty," Cas murmured, shaking his arm. "We had a score to settle."

"Thank the gods," Cattya said, her sword sparking to life. "I grew tired of him very quickly."

Jonah hummed his agreement.

"Who dares wander our seas?" A single head poked out from the waters.

Seeing those soulless eyes again physically made Sol shudder. Her nightmares did not do them justice.

"I smell Wielders," another croaked, emerging beside the first. It smiled. "There's a Fire Wielder."

"I call the Warden." A third one appeared. "Their blood is always divine."

Collectively, the creatures shook the raft with their talons, then let out a macabre laugh when everyone on it they all swayed to keep their balance. More heads manifested along the rolling waves, the sea awakened by their movements.

"Prince," Jonah warned. "Perhaps a Ward would be nice."

"Not yet." Cas kept his attention on the sea, his arms swirling with Shadows.

Sol's birthmark ached, prickling as the Jinn continued taunting them.

The pain spread like hot oil over her back, seeping across her shoulders, and into her chest as she bit on her cheek to keep from screaming.

Phil tightened his grip around her. "There's so many."

Talons slammed into the raft. They gripped the wood, piercing through it, allowing the ocean to rush in. "One of you isn't like the others...what are you, I wonder?"

The Jinn—no, the Mind Slayer pulled itself into their raft boat. It was taller than the one from Yavenharrow. Its skin was violet, waxy as the water repelled from it.

Sol grabbed Cas's forearm as the thing's black eyes flashed white.

He seemed about to release his Ward when a sea-shaking boom to their left had them falling flat to the wood. Instinctively, Sol clung to Phil and Jonah as they grabbed her, then to Cas as he fell beside them.

Sol had only seen a ship so massive once, in the ports of Yavenharrow. It carried exports of fur and gems, both so precious the townsfolk had been blocked from being near the beach for days.

This one was just as grand. Unlike the one from Yavenharrow, it was a sterling metal gray with dark brown carvings along its side. Its sails crumbled in the wind as it raced toward them from the east. And as it neared, its land's sigil showed.

"Finally." Cattya flipped her hair over her shoulder. "I was starting to think they got lost."

The Stone Ledge ship boomed its horn again, causing the Jinn around the raft to howl. The one who managed to climb into it slithered back into the ocean with a low growl, and Sol breathed a massive sigh of relief.

Short-lived since their makeshift boat was quickly sinking.

"You found us a ship?" Phil's face brightened as he stood.

Cattya flared a single flame into the sky. "I found myself a ship, boy." She strode to the edge of the raft as the ship loomed closer. "However, you idiots get back on land is none of my business."

For a second, Sol glared at her, processing the words. She looked from the ship to the Fire Wielder, then finally to Cas as his Shadows flared.

He stood, facing Cattya. "You're a fucking liar."

She shrugged. "I'm an opportunist. Why would I share my knowledge or plans with you when you had no intention of making it to the end with me?"

"You'd leave a child here to save yourself?" Cas seethed.

Sol didn't stop him as he neared the Fire Wielder, his Shadows now interweaving with Wards.

"You said it yourself, Casimir." Cattya didn't inch away from him or balk at the promise of death on his face. "Everyone for themselves, right?"

"Watch out!" Jonah lunged forward before Sol could react before anyone else realized what happened. The boat beneath them shook violently, sending Phil against this brother and Sol nearly overboard. But she regained her balance as she saw what Cattya had done.

Cattya pulled Cas closer. "If you're not with me, you're against me, Prince."

Sol screamed, the sound pulled from deep within her soul as Cattya twisted the key into Cas's side., jamming it deeper into him.

The scene unfolded as if in slow motion, each dragged out second engraving itself into Sol's very being. The way Cattya grinned as Cas realized the betrayal. How the ship pulled closer, ropes thrown from its sides to collect the Fire Wielder. The insane guilt as Sol registered the key was from the ring she used to free them—and made of copper as well.

Her body wasn't her own in that moment. All she saw was the key and the woman who had hurt the one person whose safety was meant to be the only thing she could trust.

The two sides of her fought, one begging her to protect those she cared for while the other reminded her of the promise she made to herself all those years ago, to treat lives with care after seeing the faces of her assaulter's children in pained sobs during his burial.

But she had already killed one person during this mess.

And she was pissed.

Cas pushed Cattya off just as Sol grabbed her by the hair, pulled her into a hold, and with a smooth, deliberate motion, sliced her neck.

CHAPTER THIRTY-NINE

Aquarene's Trial: Part II

Cattya tensed for only a second before slumping into Sol's arms. Sol didn't hold her. She released the woman and let her slide into the ocean, devoured by the waves within moments. The ocean was stained crimson from her blood.

Sol couldn't breathe. Why should she if she had taken the ability for yet another person to? Why should her blood remain inside her if all her victims had ended in it splattered over walls, stones and now oceans?

She stood frozen as Cas pulled the key from his side, then tossed it into the sea.

"Phil, sink them," Jonah said, pointing at the ship. "They'll want to avenge—"

"No." Sol's voice was foreign in her own ears. "No more killing."

Jonah blinked at her with an unreadable expression, his lips tight in contemplation.

"I will change their course," Phil said. "I will send them North."

Sol didn't wait to watch the boy work. She wordlessly sank to her knees beside Cas, searching for his wound.

"Cas," she said softly, pressing the pulsing gash on his side. It nearly missed his reinforced suit. Cattya knew just where to strike.

Behind them, Jonah continued his attempts to Earth Call, reciting sermons for forgiveness from his goddess.

"Out of all the ways we could have died, I truly didn't think copper poisoning and Jinn dessert would be one," Cas said, frowning slightly at the wound. "Very anticlimactic if you ask me."

"We aren't drying," Sol said dryly. "How do I fix it?"

His gaze flicked up to meet hers. "You don't. Copper poisoning is fatal."

"There has to be a way."

"There is not."

"There *must*—" Sol didn't realize she was yelling until he placed a hand over her own, the other on her shoulder. She shook him off. "There must."

This couldn't be it. After *everything*.

The sounds of the ship faded with a caress of the wind, the residue of it accelerating the raft's demise. Sol felt Jonah and Phil's utter panic as they treaded water. Cade's body, still strung to the post, sunk into the waves with it.

Sol sobbed. She pulled Cas into her arms and collapsed against him as he held her gently, his blood already spilling into the sea around them, making the already scarlet water darker. She kicked into the ocean to keep afloat, Cas doing the same.

"It's only copper," she sobbed. "It'll be okay, right?"

Cas laughed slightly against her, pulling back to peer at her. "It's our only tangible weakness as Wielders."

"It's a stupid one!" Sol whined, struggling to keep herself afloat while still clinging to him, unwilling to let him go.

Jonah and Phil swam to their side.

"Not to alarm anyone, but…" Phil's words trailed off as motion resumed beneath them.

Sol shut her eyes.

Would they kill him first now that they've tasted his blood? Cattya's body was nowhere in sight, did they drag her to their lair?

She sobbed harder.

"I must admit, although you look nothing like Irene, you're just as skilled with a blade, Yarrow."

Cas held her tighter, unsheathing his sword with a free hand between the crashing current. Sol didn't miss his grimace, or how the color quickly drained from his skin.

Jonah did the same, shielding Phil.

The Mind Slayer let out a caw of laughter as it floated before them. "Oh, please, you'd be no fun to kill right now." It angled its head, its shorter black hair dipping into the water. "I like my prey to have a fighting chance."

"Speak for yourself, Silas." Another Jinn peeked through the current. "I'll take them all if you want."

Sol wasn't sure how quickly the copper would dull his magic, or how instantly it worked in the system, but the remnants of a Ward flickered around Cas's wrists just enough to make the Jinn flinch.

"Relax, Prince of Shadows," The Mind Slayer—Silas—said. "We aren't going to harm anyone the Yarrow heir is allied with."

The second Jinn swam around them in a circle. "That's a sure way to anger our Mother."

Cas spat as his kicking slowed, the water pulling him under more often than it didn't. Sol wrapped her arms around him with Jonah doing the same, her heartbeat near an impossible speed.

"Just kill us and be done with it!" Sol yelled.

End all this suffering.

"Again, we aren't going to hurt you." Silas reached into the ocean, retrieving a plank of wood just big enough for them to hold. It tossed it their way. "I cannot guarantee the ones on land will be so generous, though. They mostly answer to Lorkin."

Sol barely registered the words as she swam forward toward the piece of wood. She held it beneath Cas.

"Earth Caller," the second Jinn hissed as it returned to the other's side. "Flora will take the tainted offering from your wrist." Before sinking into the waves, it grinned.

With a flash of its light-less eyes, Silas did the same. Then they were gone.

The sea became still around them, no Jinn, or ships or hope around.

"What the fuck," Sol whispered, breathlessly grabbing on to the wood for a repose.

"Do you think what it said is true?" Phil asked.

"Which part?"

Jonah wasted no time in testing the important part out. He took his hand out of the ocean, slashing his right wrist. His jaw tensed as the blood bubbled into the ocean. Sol looked away from it, unable to stomach any more blood.

She smoothed Cas's hair away from his face as they waited. "You better not die out here."

Her panic only increased when his only response was a slow blink.

Jonah gave a small laugh. "It's working."

His blood evaporated into golden shimmers into the air, forming a quick circle before dispersing. Jonah exhaled, closed his eyes, and began to work. The land beneath them, deep beneath the sea shook and shivered for moments, all which passed with excruciating slowness as Sol tried to keep Cas awake.

His skin was ghastly white, his lips violet and breathing shallow. She pressed her forehead to his. "*Please.*"

The water rippled open, revealing patchy paths of stony hills.

Jonah shook his head, his breath quickening as he continued trying to Call more to the surface. "The rest is too deep."

The ocean around them was so red. It was as if they floated not in water, but in a cauldron of blood. And within the sea somewhere were two people who were alive, then weren't, and—

"Hey," Cas said softly. "Don't think about that right now."

"We must hurry" Phil began swimming to the first slope of land. "The Jinn are surely calling others so they may all feast on us."

Jonah nodded slightly to Sol as he pulled Cas forward, helping her. "We must get to land quickly," he said.

Sol's feet touched beautiful, glorious stone. She stood, dragging Cas up with Jonah's help. "I have to save you."

Cas coughed, "Sol, let it go. Leave me here. Copper poisoning takes maybe half an hour at the latest." Despite the obvious weakness, he stood, looking from his wound then back out into the distance. "I won't make it to the shore."

Sol followed his line of vision. She recognized that roof, the color of the architecture. About half an hour's swim away, the peaks of the Gods' Villa were clear, emerging as if from the ocean itself.

"I don't know how much land I can Call, Princess," Jonah braced his hands on his knees. "I—It's too much blood." Phil ripped a sleeve of his shirt, wrapping it around his brother's wounds. "I'm afraid my wind won't do much either."

"I am not moving from this spot until we all agree we move together," Sol said tensely, adrenaline spreading through her. Her birthmark pulsed with it, the scar along her palm seeming to beckon her forward. She met each of their gazes, ignoring how her limbs begged her for rest or how her mind tore itself apart with the events of the last week. "We go together, or not at all." She looked at Cas as she finished the sentence. "No room for discussion."

Cas was able to walk on his own for only five minutes. Sol and Jonah took turns holding him while still trying to maintain as much momentum as possible. His wound had stopped bleeding, but for once it seemed the remedy was for it to continue. Sol begged for antidotes, anything that might help them. The only thing Jonah offered was a total blood replacement, which would require care from healers at the Scholar Towers themselves, weeks away.

He didn't have weeks.

But Sol didn't think about that. They would get to land, and everything would be okay somehow. There was no other option, she wasn't entertaining the notion of there being another.

Fifteen minutes into their walk, Jonah was spent. They had reached the end of the makeshift path, and although it had been unruly and splotchy, it was better than having to swim while pulling Cas. They stood at the edge of the final steppingstone. Ten minutes. That's how far was left. Sol had spent all her summers and free time swimming in Yavenharrow—she would make it.

Swimming.

Water.

Phil seemed to have the same thought at that moment as he glanced down into the water. "This is Aquarene's Trial," he said. "Perhaps an offering for her will help?"

"Even if we have no Water Dancers?" Sol tightened her grip on Cas's waist.

Jonah shook his head. "Wielders can pray to any god—but praying to one that hasn't blessed them won't provide magical benefit."

"Maybe it will bring us luck." Phil shrugged and looked at Sol. "I will do it."

Sol had the instinct to intervene. But Jonah was spent, Cas's blood was poisoned and hers was, as of now, useless.

Solemnly, she gave the boy a tight nod.

The more Sol observed the offerings, the more she admired them. Even through chattering teeth and a staccato heartbeat, she watched Phil work in wonder. The boy's expression was fierce with each movement and chant, truly highlighting the warrior he had been trained to be, even at his young age.

With a final, lethal slash of his arms, the ocean parted. The ground beneath them shook, sending them all into a bow before the division. The uneven space that broke through the waves smoothed into compact sand.

Sol swallowed a lump in her throat as the path to their salvation glowed before them.

It was a slight climb down from their place on the stones to the sand, one Jonah immediately jumped into action to descend. He helped his brother down, then Cas. Sol jumped down, looking up at the walls of water on either of their sides. Fast. They had to be fast.

"You both go on ahead," she ordered. "Call for healers."

Cas stirred in their arms. "Sol—"

"Now, boys." She willed as much power into her voice as she could.

Jonah started the sprint toward the Gods' Villa, and with a single look back, his brother followed. There were too many things against them all, but Sol couldn't focus on any of them. She only pulled Cas forward. Without Jonah's help, the task was more difficult.

"Sol, you have to go," Cas breathed. "Phil won't be able to bleed an offering for long."

"I am not leaving you."

"You are the one meant to survive—not me." He doubled over in pain, falling to his knees.

"No, get up." She knelt beside him. "Get up. Sawyer would kill me if I left you." She tried lacing her panic with humor to lighten the catastrophic situation. Although the effort was obvious, Cas huffed a laugh. "Come on." She stumbled to her feet as Cas shifted to his own. His steps were labored, and slow, but they were moving again.

Phil and Jonah were a ways ahead, and Sol dared a bloom of hope to take hold.

And then the wall of water collapsed.

As if whatever held the passage open snapped, the ocean rushed into itself all at once, not giving Sol even a second of preparation before being thrown into the icy, violent current.

Cas struggled against her grasp, as if he wanted the waves to wash him away. But Sol didn't budge. She held him tighter than she had ever held anything, hooking her arm through his belt quickly before they were sent into another merciless tumble.

Please, Sol begged silently to nothing in particular as she slammed against him and stray reefs. *Please if anyone is out there, let us live.*

As if it had been waiting for that very plea, the ocean stilled ever so slightly. Between the moment of solace, Sol kicked them up to the surface for a breath.

She saw the Villa, now to their right, but closer than it had been. She struggled to pull air into her lungs as water struck her face.

Sol frantically pulled Cas through the turbulent waters, sparing only seconds to sink down and kick the sandbank below them to remain afloat. She tried to just drag him along with her, but with each passing moment he became weaker and less responsive, forcing Sol to propel herself through small jumps instead of fluid swimming, wasting time they did not have. One arm was wrapped around him so tightly it hurt, while the other tried to help them against the current.

With every kick of her legs and lick of salt in her eyes, Sol grew desperate, wishing more than anything for this man to yell at her over her stupid choices instead of being so quiet. She wished Cas would be doing anything else.

"Cas, wake up," she stammered through breaths. She moved to shield him, having them break at her back instead.

She could only hope Phil and Jonah had made it to shore and hoped the Jinn did the opposite and truly meant their blabber about leaving her alone.

Sobbing, she shook him. "Cas, PLEASE."

He didn't respond, his eyes remained closed as water seeped into his mouth and face. Panic coated her throat worse than the sea salt, shocking her colder than the current they struggled in. Using every ounce of strength, she pushed him above the water, praying to any god that would listen to have him hang on.

She kicked her way to the shore, adrenaline squeezing her chest and fire burning in her lungs as her limbs threatened to fail. She willed any ounce of dormant magic within her to listen, to help her in this pathetic situation she had so stupidly put herself in.

She should've just accepted the fight over her. Marry the victor, who would've likely been Cas, but at least they would be safe and warm and *alive*.

Another shuddering sob escaped her while she gripped him harder.

Please don't die.

Please don't die.

"Please, please..."

The tide was stained ruby red as her feet finally found consistent terrain. The shore was mere steps away now, the Villa an unwelcomed relief.

Cas grew heavier in her arms by the time they arrived at the shore. Sol had to sit on the sand, hug him from behind, and drag them both completely out of the water. The hot grains dug into her hands and bare legs, making her grunt with every pull. Cas's head slumped over the front of her thigh, resting on her hip bone.

He was so pale.

"Cas." She coughed and cleared the sea water from her throat, taking only a second to breathe.

Then she saw the Jinn.

Unlike the ones she had seen before, these were animalistic in build, reeking more than the others. One perched near the fence, an elongated beak clicking with interest. Others spread around it. As soon as they began their howls and laughs, she slumped over Cas with a sob.

She would kill anything that came near him. She didn't know how, but she would. Whatever possessed her to do it to Cattya would surely take hold again, and she would let it.

She laid Cas on the sand and leaned over him, unable to stop the tears and shallow breathing, unable to focus beyond the haze of the situation.

"Cas, wakeup. You can't die like this, it's pathetic!" Sol hoped the insult would wake him, that he would roll his eyes and shoot back a remark as he usually did, but he didn't.

She pressed her ear to his chest, listening for something, anything.

But there was nothing.

Keeping one hand on the wound on his side, she closed the other into a fist and desperately pounded his chest. Flashes of the night her mother died swarmed through her mind, lacing the past with the present, taunting her with what would happen if she didn't act quickly. Reminding her what she would lose if someone else she cared for died in her arms.

"Please wake up, Cas. Please. You can't leave me here," Sol cried. "Gods, please. I don't know what to do."

The stench of copper taunted her, from blood and metal alike.

Wielders aren't immortal, Sawyer had told her. *But we are a bit harder to kill.*

Sol continued pounding on his chest. "You're supposed to be hard to kill, damn it!"

The rustling of leaves around her made her look up, vision blurry with saltwater and tears. She hoped to see Jonah, ready with a team of healers or mages or whoever could make this nightmare disappear.

She tore her hair away from her face, greeted by four, lanky Jinn crouching on the sand like toads, a smile plastered on their gods awful faces.

Breath hitching, Sol grabbed a dagger from Cas's belt, holding it over him, and trying her best to seem confident. "Come fucking try it," she seethed.

"Queen of Wielders, we will bargain with you," The Jinn said in unison, unnerving Sol's every instinct. "Leave the Prince of Shadows and we shall let you go."

"*Fuck* no."

Their grins expanded. "We were hoping you'd decline."

The four of them lept, one directly at her, which she evaded swiftly with a stab to its forehead. The creature went down with her knife, leaving her to punch the next one that clawed at her. Sol stood over Cas and punched it again, flinching as her knuckles cracked. The Jinn screeched as it fell on its brother, then snapped its deathly teeth at Sol.

She didn't think she would be as lucky with the other two.

They howled in unison, spit and debris shooting at her face. It was then, as she looked at their decrepit faces and counted her odds, she accepted defeat. She fell to her knees once more, draping over Cas. Sol accepted she would die with him instead of leaving when all noise halted.

The waves seemed to mute, and the air itself stilled. Only the sound of her rugged breathing filled her ears. Then, the pain in her back subsided. Instead of burning, it cooled.

"You three have twenty seconds to flee before I'm forced to kill you." The voice behind Sol was low and brutal, a thousand harmonies laced within it.

Her soul dropped.

She tightened her arms around Cas, the scent of rosewood and sage lingering even after the stretch of ocean they swam.

"You side with the Wielders, Morna? You are the reason we suffer," the Jinn spat, but Sol heard them slide away.

"I side with Mavka, and Mavka sides with the Yarrows," the Mind Slayer said, its voice clanging through Sol's bones. Tears continued to fall.

It had been two minutes. She had to get him breathing. Ignoring the Jinn, she placed her hands over his chest once more and put her weight on them, like Lora had taught her when she was young.

Push.

Push.

Push.

Cas, please.

"Leave. Consider this a final mercy and warning to Lorkin to stay away from the Yarrow Court."

She didn't care what was happening or why the Mind Slayer behind her hadn't torn her to pieces yet. It continued to speak, but she couldn't hear it, not as she continued to work on Cas, even as her arms shook with exhaustion.

"If you manage to get his heart beating again, you will still have to flush the copper, Queen of Wielders."

In front of her, a pair of black eyes clouded her vision.

It was similar to the one from the ocean, to the one in Yavenharrow that had tried to kill her. It blinked at her, its eyes flashing white. "Your blood will purify his."

Sol cried, "Just kill me and be done with it."

It took a long inhale. "I can smell the stars on you girl, that Yarrow scent. But what's the other smell on you, I wonder? How peculiar." The thing laughed, its teeth shining. "I don't wish you dead."

Without further explanation or chaos, it vanished into the waters.

Your blood will purify his.

Against all odds, the creatures had yet to be proven wrong.

She traced a cut to her forearm, carved an identical one on his, and pressed them together.

Her blood spread over his skin, covering his tattoo and scars.

Circulation.

The breeze resumed and the sun pierced into Sol's skin as she looked back down at Cas and crushed her mouth to his.

He tasted of salt and sand, his lips cold as she exhaled a breath into him before shaking him. "Cas, I swear I'll be less stubborn, just please wake up." She leaned down to his lips again, and as she finished her breath, Cas instantly flipped to the side, water spilling from his mouth. Relief flooded through her, so much so that her vision darkened. But she willed herself to focus and rub his back.

Defeated and unwilling to build facades, Sol slumped over him as he braced his elbow on the sand, shaky and breathless, but alive.

Cas pulled her closer with his free arm. She draped her head on his shoulder and pressed her hand to his chest.

The soft beating there was like an answer to all her questions.

Wordlessly, she pressed their forearms together again, hoping all the pieces had been set in motion.

This time, her blood was pulled into his wound, almost as if their arms were wrapped with a band to hold them together.

Cas exhaled a long, shaky breath through his nose as he shifted his face to look at her. He traced every inch of her face with such an intensity that had Sol looking away, back down to their joined arms.

His tattoo darkened before her very eyes, as if it used her blood as ink. It swirled and flowed into shapes she had never noticed before, glyphs of sorts.

"How did you know?" he breathed.

She tore her gaze from it. "You may think I'm insane, but a Jinn told me."

"About the ink?"

"About my blood to flush the copper."

He looked from her to their arms to their surroundings, his chest falling and rising with each labored breath. "This is unheard of."

"I thought you were going to die," Sol whispered. "I would've tried whatever anyone told me."

A small smile pulled at the corners of his lips, the clenching in her chest easing at the familiarity of it. "Let's keep both that and the fact your blood may be more than just royalty, a secret, Princess."

"Your tattoo." She traced it with a fingertip, the ink now depthless and black. "How?"

Cas looked away for a moment, as if contemplating. "It's a long story."

"We have time."

Sol could only gape at him as he told her the truth. As he told her it wasn't just a decorative piece of art, and was instead some sort of Dark Magic enchantment her mother had placed on him to ensure his sentence was completely carried out before he could leave Rimemere. Technically, he could leave Rimemere—but he couldn't leave the Yarrows.

"So...our blood re-seals it?"

He nodded. "Sawyer helped for a very long time, but it seems like yours worked better."

She blushed slightly at the odd compliment. "I—I will help you from now on."

Cas laughed as they finally pulled their arms apart.

"I'm serious." She peered into his face.

His skin was still pale, but livelier than before. Slowly, stars returned to his eyes. "I know, Sol." Gently, he eased strands of hair from her face. "Thank you. I'll be harder to get rid of from now on."

"Promise."

"Swear it."

Behind them, waves lapped the shore, pulling at Sol's feet. For once, she wished to stay right where she was. That nagging desire to flee, and move was silent, her mind blissfully quiet as she sat in the warm sand, her arm still around Cas's waist. Inhaling, she met his gaze. He watched her silently, as if he was also lamenting the impending end of the moment.

Although afraid words would break the moment, Sol whispered, "I don't want to do this anymore." She shivered. "I just want to go home."

Cas gave her the gentlest smile she had seen on him. "Me too. But we have to finish this."

They hadn't gotten instructions or directions for this trial. Jonah and Phil were nowhere to be seen, but Sol begged herself to trust the boys made it back to land.

Turning to the one familiar thing, they slowly made their way back to the Gods' Villa. Sol breathed and pulled every ounce of strength within her to the surface. She slid from Cas's embrace, his absence leaving a jarring chill. She pushed herself to her feet, reaching her hand out to grab his. Wordlessly, he took it. It was peculiar to Sol how quickly near-death experiences could alleviate disputes.

And it felt oddly…perfect.

They neared the sharp right path that would take them to the front of the Villa when Cas tugged Sol to a stop.

"Sol?"

Sol peered over her shoulder. "Hmm?"

"Was I dreaming, or did you kiss me?" Cas's gaze scanned her face, slowly meeting her gaze with a slight smile. Sol held a breath as his silver eyes then slowly moved to her lips.

She continued forward, her grip tightening slightly on his wrist. Cas didn't fight her as she led.

Finally, as they dragged themselves up some steps, she scoffed. "Definitely a dream, Prince."

She was about to continue and comment on the radical idea they stay on the shores a while longer, but all words left her mind as a tug turned her, making her face him.

His attention once again narrowed on her lips before saying, "Then perhaps you shouldn't have woken me."

CHAPTER FORTY

A Kiss for the Keys

Sawyer had to quickly down three mugs of wine before mustering the courage to seek out Fin. He had been gone quite often since the beginning of the Vows, off providing protection to wherever they took place.

It was lovely to have the castle free of his miserable face.

She inhaled deeply, holding the breath inside until it turned to smoke as she exhaled. Raising her closed hand, she tapped on the door. Fin opened it on the third knock, obviously not expecting who stood on the other side.

Sawyer wouldn't deny the man was very attractive—it was his unfortunate attitude that made it difficult to appreciate his physique. He was shirtless and in a casual pair of trousers, his sandy brown hair an unruly mess around his forehead.

His eyes widened then were quickly masked by a haze of challenge. "I see you decided to take me up on my offer."

"I need the keys to my father's study."

He blinked at her. "And you think I'm going to hand them over because?"

"Because I'll tell my father you've been fucking Gina if you don't." Sawyer examined her nails. "He may hate me, but he believes what I say. Quite confusing, I know."

"Hand Gina?" Fin laughed, bracing an arm on the door frame. "The woman is twice my age."

Gods, his *muscles*.

Sawyer shrugged. "So? It's a believable lie."

His eyes darkened. "You wouldn't."

"Try me."

"She would deny it, you know. And the King will listen to his lover before you," he smirked. "And I'm sure when I tell him you're trying to get into his private study, I'll get a massive reward."

"Luckily, Gina is spectating Aquarene's trial," Sawyer said, returning his smirk. "She won't be back for days. And by then, my father would have already killed you to rid the suspicion."

They engaged in a battle of wits for a while, until Fin sighed through his nose. "I'll trade you for them."

Sawyer angled her head, pretending to be interested. "Oh?"

Fin snaked an arm around her waist, pulling her into his room before she could step back. He shifted her to the wall, pressing her against it.

Sawyer resisted all urges to flare as he craned his head down, his breath on her forehead. She glared at him. "Release me."

"A kiss for the keys." His lips grazed her neck as she turned away. "For a little more, I'll stand watch outside until you finish whatever you need in the study."

Slowly, she rolled her head toward him. She looked from his eyes down to his lips. "Enticing offer," she smiled. "But don't ever fucking touch me without my permission again."

Sawyer pulled a dagger from her waist band and jammed it into his thigh.

As he doubled over in pain, she frowned. "Pitty. I was aiming a little higher."

"Fuck, Sawyer." Fin growled as he knelt to take the knife out. "You really should've thought that through."

Sawyer examined his room. It was well organized, way more than her own. It took no effort to find the silver key ring strung along his armor on the wall. She strode to it, the long, ancient keys jingling as she put them into her pocket. "Probably." She stepped over him on her way out. "I should think through a lot of things I do, actually."

She shut the door behind her, turning the knob into a melted mess. "But, alas, I don't care."

The key slid in easily, more so than she remembered. She had always struggled with the old thing as a child, but it took only a soft turn for the door to click open.

The door creaked as it revealed the room.

It smelled of smoke and embers, mixed with dust, so reminiscent of Melisandre that, for a moment, Sawyer felt as if she was back in her home tower.

She shook off the nostalgia with a lung-clearing cough as she stepped into the room.

Unlike her father, the place was organized. Everything had a place and a purpose, most undisturbed for ages. There was a large mahogany desk for writing correspondence, neatly folded parchments and feather pens arranged on its center, and a large window at its side overlooking the rolling hills toward the Dunes of San'ann. A large bookshelf was against the wall parallel to it, but instead of books, it held mostly small boxes or stones, all from different places of the South. The red carpet spread in a strip across the room, making the black sofa and chairs atop it stand out against its brightness.

Now what.

Morna had been incredibly vague, as she usually was.

Sol and Cas had one more trial after Aquarene's, then the final duel. Nina, Sawyer, and Alix had been giving constant offerings to all the gods for their friends' wellbeing, but they had also been searching for whatever lapse in rule Irene used to save Draven and her father, just in case anything unexpected transpired. So far, they've all come up empty.

Footsteps in the hallway behind her made her jump.

"I will not be long," King Semmena said, his voice mere steps from the study. "Gather the rest of the Court in the throne room for an announcement."

Sawyer threw herself behind the desk, pressing herself into the small opening where the chair went.

She pressed a hand to her mouth as boots shuffled against the floors. "Damn idiots," her father muttered. "They had *one* job."

Breathe quietly. Slowly.

She thought she might hurl as the footsteps got closer, then dared a small sigh of relief as the sound of crinkling leather signaled the King sat down.

"What a way to refer to your people, *Majesty*."

The floors vibrated with command in the voice, the low, hollow, otherworldly timbre.

Sawyer felt all the heat within her turn to ice, the air around them plummeting into winter. She didn't dare move or take a single breath as the stench of a Mind Slayer permeated the room.

It was easily distinguishable—it had never left her memory since Morna in Melisandre.

But this one was more rancid, like the leftovers of a bloody battle had been left in the sun for days.

And way, way closer.

"I was not referring to my people," her father said with disdain. "I was referring to *yours*."

The creature growled a laugh. "I told you they would be near the Gate—that's no longer my turf."

There were clacks of talons behind her. Behind the desk.

It groaned as a weight leaned on it.

"They are Jinn!" Semmena exclaimed. "You're telling me they're truly answering to a creature that isn't?"

"Mavka is our Mother, Jinn or not. Most of them will continue in her service despite her insolence."

Sawyer shuddered as the weight on the desk eased, then moved closer to her father. She pressed both hands over her mouth.

"I will not uphold my end of the deal if you do not do yours, Lorkin." Her father sounded clearly impatient, an emotion he usually kept well concealed in public. Whatever was happening here, he had no fear of it getting out to harm his reputation.

"You do not give me orders, Semmena," the creature boomed. "I will do my part when I see fit."

Her father remained silent.

"I have only come to advise the remains of a body were found in the forest. Where your pathetic little games took place a few days ago."

A slight pause transpired before her father spoke. "You found the boy? We retrieved Zeri of Ventry."

"What was left of him, yes." The creature neared the desk once more, forcing Sawyer to shut her eyes for a moment to collect herself. "It was tattered."

The King laughed, "I have intel the Princess killed him. I highly doubt she is so skilled with blades."

"It was tattered by Void magic. Sliced to the bone with the scent of our essence."

Again, the King was speechless. He cleared his throat. "What are you suggesting?"

"That your little Yarrow bitch isn't as helpless as she is fooling you to think." The Mind Slayer rounded the desk, its massive legs sliding into Sawyer's view. Its skin was orange and melting off in chunks, with claws so long they almost scraped Sawyer's thigh.

A tear fell down her face.

"Continue your search, Arnold." The creature stomped forward, coming to a stop before the window. "And I will continue mine." It slid it open, then, without another word, jumped out of the castle.

CHAPTER FORTY-ONE

To Keep a Secret

Sawyer ran down the castle corridors. Her blouse caught on every corner and her boots scraped the marble floors, but she didn't care. Every inch of her body flared with urgency and adrenaline as she hurried down the spiral staircase, down to the foyer occupied by students and servants. Neither paid her much attention except for Francis who furrowed her brows as they passed each other.

Later.

Sawyer would fill her in later.

She catapulted into the gardens, shining blue and silver beneath the moonlight's rays.

Nina.

Nina.

A quick inquiry to a courtier told her Nina was out of the castle with Gaven since midday but couldn't say the reason or when they would return. Sawyer continued her aimless wandering as she couldn't focus on much of anything other than the Jinn's foul smell, its rotting, orange skin engraved to the back of her eyelids every time she blinked.

He's working with the Jinn.

Out of all the insanity her father had done and was surely capable of, she never would have guessed he was working with the enemy. Not only their enemy, but their world's.

Sawyer couldn't breathe. Too many things needed to be spilled into the air or else they would rot within her, but she needed to find Nina.

"Sawyer?"

She swirled around, the motion making her sway. "Alix," she breathed shakily. "H—Have you seen Nina?"

Alix rushed down the hall, signaling for the kingsmen behind him to close the doors. His attention roved all over her. "What's wrong?"

"I—I just need to find her."

"Did you find Samara?"

"I need *Nina*, Alix."

Someone within your castle is lying.

Her breath came in shallow puffs as the room spun. Maybe she shouldn't tell Nina—perhaps no one was safe and she was doomed to carry the worst fucking news herself until everything came crumbling down.

"You're shaking, love." Alix threw his cloak around her. "Are you sure you are alright?"

Someone within your castle is lying.

As Sawyer was about to burst into flames with uncertainty, she felt her.

Nina and Gaven walked through the Castle gates, both sharing similar solemn expressions. Gaven quickly turned right toward the stables, giving Sawyer and Alix a curt nod before disappearing into a cluster of red cloaks.

Nina's ivory skin was pallid, and her usually bright green eyes were muted as she finally stepped up beside them. She looked back and forth between them. "What's wrong?"

"I need your help with something." Sawyer grasped her arm. "Quickly."

She took a couple of steps before Nina eased from her grasp. "Sawyer, I've learned to not go alone with you when you're this erratic."

"Are you sure I can't help somehow, Sawyer?" Alix's tone was laced with concern, his honeycomb eyes narrowing.

"I—Uh." Having two trusted individuals' input might be better, but at the same time the more people dragged into it, the more danger they would be in. Unfortunately, if Sawyer didn't tell someone, she would quite literally boil from the inside out.

"Actually, can you find Penny, Al?" Nina gave him a sweet smile. "She was running some errands for me."

Sawyer arched a brow at her, but Nina merely shrugged. *Later.*

"On it." He gave them a final assessing glance. "Let me know if you all need anything."

Sawyer and Nina were left on the courtyard for seconds before Sawyer resumed dragging her across the lily fields. Mercifully, Nina didn't protest as they maneuvered through the crowds, finally reaching the corner of the yards.

Sawyer looked around for a private place, but the realization no such thing existed on castle grounds smacked her along with a cool breeze. Finally, she swerved to the one place she knew would be empty, a place not even her father dared send spies.

The Pantheon was ominous in the day, but the darkness cast a whole other level of gloom over it. The gates were ajar, and the ground was hidden with fog, forcing Sawyer to slow her steps.

"Sawyer, what in the world—"

"Shh." Sawyer grabbed Nina's hand. "A little further."

They slid around the tombstones and branches until coming to a singular mausoleum with a pointed roof that faced away from the looming eyes of the castle.

"Sawyer, what am I to say if the kingsmen ask why we are in restricted grounds?" Nina braced her hands on her hips, easing from her grasp. "We need to stay under the radar, at least until after the Vows."

"Tell them we finally decided to fuck, Nina, I don't know." Sawyer paced in small steps, digging her hands through her unbound hair.

Why am I even considering something a Jinn said?

"Gods, S. Spill. You're making me anxious."

Fuck it.

Sawyer turned to her, looking her straight in the eyes with the force of simmering embers. "I need you to promise me something first."

Nina furrowed her brows and nodded. "Of course."

"Swear it."

"Sawyer."

"My father is conspiring with the Jinn." The words spilled like poison, hot and deadly. "I don't know for what or when or how it happened."

Nina's chest rose and fell in silence as she processed the information. Slowly, panic flared in her eyes. "How do you know?"

"I overheard him and a Mind Slayer speaking in his study."

"Excuse me?"

"It's a long fucking story, but it's true. The—the thing's name was Lorkin." Sawyer shook her head in disbelief, trying to somehow convince herself today had been a nightmare. She looked to Nina, expecting her to laugh or to ask if it was a joke.

But the Earth Caller was silent.

"You don't believe me." Sawyer sighed, "I know it sounds insane, but—"

"Who's Morna, Sawyer?" Nina's voice took a serious edge, enough to make Sawyer halt her pacing..

Sawyer snapped her head at her. "How do you know that name?"

"Seems like we've both had interesting days."

Nina told her everything. She recounted her and Gaven's encounter at the Jinn Den, starting from the summons from her father all the way to Morna's warning.

The same one she had given Sawyer days before.

Afterward, Sawyer told Nina her own story. Starting from her mother's death in Melisandre and Morna's assistance in her own survival, ending at the day's events. Once everything was out, it was as if a massive weight dissipated from her shoulders. She hadn't shared that with anyone.

The entire time she spoke, Nina's kind expression didn't falter, nor did she interrupt. And once her friend was sure she was done, she only pulled her into an embrace.

"Can't believe she let herself be caught." Sawyer held her tighter. "Because I doubt the kingsmen caught her without her allowing it."

"I'm sorry you carried all this alone for so long, Sawyer," Nina whispered. "I'm sorry if somehow I wasn't trustworthy enough to help the burden."

"No, Nins, it wasn't you." Sawyer buried her face in her friend's shoulder. "I think a part of me just didn't want to recall it at all."

They stayed like that for a while, until the bright calls of the curfew bells sang across the land. Sawyer pulled back, smiling a tad sadly to find Nina in tears as well.

"What now?" Sawyer glanced around, wiping her own face. "What the fuck do we do now?"

Nina shut her eyes. "I don't know. Samara mentioned someone sent out a Mind Slayer to find Sol—"

Sawyer gaped at her. "I'm sorry, who?"

"Um—"

"Nina."

"Samara," said Nina through gritted teeth. She looked away. "Samara told me, okay?"

Sawyer didn't know what she was expecting, but it certainly hadn't been that. Though as she took the moment to process what that statement meant, it somehow made sense.

"Out of all the women—"

"Can we not do this right now?" Nina slumped against the stone mausoleum. "And instead focus on the fact the king is basically that thing Lorkin's proxy?"

"We should've never come back." Sawyer sighed, leaning beside her. "Maybe Lady Lora would have kept us in Yavenharrow."

Nina laughed. "Wouldn't *that* have been something."

A moment of contemplative silence passed, interrupted by another boom of the curfew bells.

Finally, Nina said, "We need Sol. Without her to rival his reign, anything else we do will cause an unwinnable civil war."

"And you think Sol won't cause an uproar? Be real, Nins. We are all hated at court."

Nina looked out to the forest, her lips a tight line. "She has supporters. You both do—the Yarrows do. Yarrows are the reason why Rimemere exists. You're tethered to the land itself. And although Irene left the castle in ruin, she made a difference here. She rounded the Unsettled and the humans, fought for those who had no voice, and stood fierce in her conviction to allow others within our borders for safety." Nina sighed, "Then she and Draven had that fight after her Vows and gods know what happened."

"If the Jinn infiltrate our walls, a lot of lives will be lost." Sawyer peered at her. "We need to figure out where these things are hiding."

"Sol and Cas should be back with us soon." Nina grasped her hand. "We will figure out what to do then. For now, perhaps we should figure out what Semmena has over a Mind Slayer that he gained their allegiance."

Sawyer swallowed a lump in her throat. "I know that answer."

After a moment of silence, Nina said, "What is it?"

The final and third set of bells chimed. "He has Sol."

ACT THREE

*Once upon a time, a girl only had sticks, stones, and bones...
so she built herself a throne.*

CHAPTER FORTY-TWO

Blood, Mud, and Saltwater

Sol wanted to be angry when she learned Gina prevented Jonah and Phil from providing aid. As soon as Cas and her rounded to the front of the Villa, the boys ran to them in tears, their embrace almost knocking them all to the ground. Apparently, the point of the trial was to test the prospect's efficiency against the Jinn and their judgment for quick thinking. Sol had nearly thrown up on the woman's shoes at the statement.

She wasn't the only one utterly disinterested in the discourse. All four of them ambled past Hand Gina and the kingsmen, not caring to listen to their blabbers. Sol remained beside Cas the entire way up the stairs, the four of them leaving the floors filthy with blood, mud, and salt water.

Jonah and Phil gave them both lingering hugs before branching off at the fourth floor to their room. Sol didn't know where Cas lodged, and since her room was the only one on Warrens' floor and there wasn't one for Shadows, she didn't have much of a guess. But he didn't try to stop at any of the other floors, only held her hand as she guided him up, all the way to her room.

She sat him on the floor to avoid the extra task of having to change the sheets into dry ones later. With a sigh, she tossed her drenched boots into a corner before heading to her washroom to turn on the bath. The water was slow to fill, and tepid, but it would have to do.

Sol walked back into her room to find Cas leaning on the side of her bed, eyes shut with the most serene look on his face. She leaned on the doorframe and smiled slightly through heavy eyelids.

As carefully as she could, she walked to him and knelt. "Hey. You must change your clothes."

Cas only groaned slightly.

"I don't think I have anything that fits you," she remarked. "Where is your room?"

He peeled an eye open. "I don't have one. I stayed with Cattya."

The name was like a blade in her skull. She couldn't hide the flinch. "Oh."

"Not like that, Princess." He reached a hand to her face, tracing the side of her jaw. "I was with her because she had intel on the trials. It was never anything more than necessity."

Despite the fact she hadn't asked, the confession placated the unwelcome sense of jealousy the vision of him and Cattya sharing a bed sparked. She cleared her throat. "If you didn't like her, you shouldn't have put up with her, Cas."

"I needed all the information I could get." He dropped his hand into her lap, into her own. "To keep you safe."

It took Sol her entire arsenal of self-restraint to not melt into him. The way his gaze flickered to her lips and his hand interlaced with her own...it almost made her lose all logic.

Almost.

Her breathing quickened, blood pooling in her chest. "Take a bath, Prince. I will find dry clothes for you meanwhile." She tried to pull her hand away, but he only held it tighter.

"You're not wandering this place alone."

"Cas—"

"No."

They compromised with Sol taking a bath first while he went to search for clothes, assuring her door was locked and within reach of his Shadows in case anything came knocking. Sol knew he wasn't worried about the remaining prospects getting to her, but instead of any Jinn that may remain nearby.

Sol let herself simmer in the bathtub for a while longer than she should have, soaking in the lily scent of the oils and the overall peace of the moment. She only got out when the memory of her slicing Cattya's throat invaded. The same moment of finality haunted her for years after the man in Yavenharrow, and the way Ezra stared at her in surprise before he flew over the edge of that cliff had been engraved in her nightmares since it happened.

By the time Sol left the washroom, Cas was once again asleep, this time on one of the sofas. The scent of sage and rosemary hugged her as she neared him. He had likely washed up in Cattya's, to avoid having to wait for Sol.

She looked from him to her bed.

It took her a painful couple of minutes to finally settle on sliding into it alone, even as a part of her begged to call him over.

For the first time in a long time, her sleep was dreamless. No nightmares or strange dreams. Only silence.

By the time the sun's light woke her the next morning, she was starving.

The first thing she did was look at her sofa, slightly disappointed to find it empty. It was alarming at first, until a small tendril of black mist twisted from beneath her door in a beckon to follow.

She brushed her teeth and changed into casual breeches and a blouse, not able to recall if the final trial was meant to be today. If it was, she supposed she would have to brace it in a blouse and breeches.

Her mind drifted to Cas as she followed his Shadows down the stairs, wondering if he was as jolted by the previous day's events as she was. A naive, youthful part of her hoped he was, the part of her that boiled with flutters and desire. The other part, though, the logical one, knew they were both better off returning to their usual, partially tolerating, behavior instead of balancing on whatever line was left between them.

Unfortunately, that logical side was losing.

Sol came to the realization it had been for a while though she couldn't quite locate a tangible turning point. She was Heiress to the Rimemere crown, tasked with eventually eradicating the planet's unholiest threats. She had no time to feel giddy over a boy.

Not even a handsome one.

As the sun's amber rays washed her path in gold, she moved on to the next problem.

Why did that Jinn save them?

Again, that incessant naive side told her maybe it was a genuine desire for their survival. Maybe…maybe there were things yet undiscovered.

Sol zipped her necklace on its chain absentmindedly as she entered the kitchen. A steaming plate of roast with a side of fruit awaited her, a mug of what looked like tea beside it. Jonah, Phil and Cas already picked at their plates, briefly halting the conversation as she entered.

"We figured making breakfast ourselves was the best way to prevent being drugged," Phil said with a small laugh. He and Jonah still had bruises and cuts from the day before but seemed well overall.

Sol sighed with relief before giving Cas a tentative glance. His smile bloomed a flutter in her chest. He brought a cup of tea to his lips, taking a small sip before sitting beside the brothers. "Good morning, Princess."

Sol cleared her throat, hoping the heat on her face wasn't visible. "Hi, Prince."

They finished their food slowly, almost trying to drag out the moment as a kingsman stuck his head into the room to say the final trial would begin in thirty minutes.

Sol wasn't surprised they weren't granted even a day of rest.

Jonah and Phil excused themselves first, leaving her alone with Cas. He exuded an almost radiant aura as if he had the best sleep in the world and not tossed and turned for hours thinking about who else was in the room, just out of reach, and —

"You look well-rested," Sol observed, finishing her tea.

Cas peered at her over a bite of his apple. "I am."

I want to be that apple.

Sol turned away. "Well, I'm glad."

He extended his arm, his tattoo peeking around his wrist. "Your blood healed not only my physical wounds but also worked to calm my nerves it seems."

"Gross, Cas."

He chuckled and gestured her forward. "After you, Princess."

They made their way to the front doors. Today was the day, the questions and riddles could wait. Today she wouldn't let distractions win. She wouldn't fail.

By the time Sol exited the front door of the Villa, Jonah and Phil were already waiting by one of the carriages. The guards wore unusually thick and vibrant attire, every inch of their skin covered by scarlet fabric. Sol eyed them, and the ones posted by the carriage behind, as she halted next to Jonah.

"I already asked why they look ridiculous," he said, a brow raised.

"Did they respond?" Sol asked, working her hair into a braid.

"Nope."

"What do you two think the Fire Trial is going to be?" Phil kicked rocks with his feet. "Emberdon's beginning was from a volcano in Mosorrona."

Sol shrugged. "Won't be surprised if they found one here somehow."

She and Cas rode in the first carriage, the brothers in the other. Mercifully, neither Fin nor Gina showed this time. Sol didn't think she had the patience to stand either of their faces anymore.

They rode through the familiar forest for a while until tin roofs replaced the trees. Sol memorized the layout desperately, scanning the modest cottages that curled over hills and into valleys, looking for the one building she needed to end up in.

Fingers shaking and a bubbling sense of purpose flooding her, Sol closed her eyes once she located it.

It was almost done. Once the trials were over, she would do her Awakening. She would train until she could say she was a Yarrow without cowering and she would finish what her mother started—if not for her, for everyone else.

"You're uncharacteristically quiet, Princess."

Sol fidgeted with her nails. "I have nothing to say."

"You always have something to say."

She shrugged, "People change."

The town's delicate buildings rushed closer, bigger, but Sol kept her attention on the cathedral, the vantage point of her plan. She had to get Jonah and Phil there no matter what.

As they came to a rolling stop by the village square, an unsettling gnawing prickled at her neck. She tapped her fingers against the carriage window.

Something.

"Sol, what is it?" Cas inched closer within the already confined space. "I can't help you if I don't know—"

She turned to him, quickly stopping him mid-thought. His face was lined with worry, raw and intense.

Trust. She needed to learn to trust.

"I—I'm getting them out," she said softly. Cas narrowed his eyes, urging her on. She continued, "I need you to help me get them to the cathedral."

"Sol, this is risky."

"I don't care."

"But—"

"You offered help, so give it, Prince."

A series of knocks from on top of the carriage signaled time to exit and brace the second to last trial. Sol felt her nerves spike and her palms begin to sweat as Cas clicked the door open.

He grinned at her, but his eyes still held a whisper of reservation. "Look at you giving orders."

They stepped into the village with a puff of dirt beneath their feet. Almost immediately after she and Cas were out of the carriage, the guards kicked their horses into a gallop, swirling out of the village and into the forest. Unease cut through her like a blade. The silence was thick, palpable as she looked around the ghost town. Not a single soul wandered. Even the air stilled, like the calm before a mighty thunderclap.

With a sudden infamy, everything exploded.

The blast was deafening. Disorienting. Sol was standing and then she wasn't, thrown to the ground by a second explosion. The cobblestone street splintered and dug into all her exposed skin. Unlike the homes they had seen on their way, the structures around them smelled of scalding wood, giving away the unlikely survival of any as the heat grew, the sound of sizzling flames merging with her breathing. Smoke and the heat of burning air blew around her face as she struggled onto her palms.

"Easy." Hands held her shoulders. "Don't get up too fast."

Sol shook with adrenaline as Cas gripped her against his chest, easing them both into a crouch. As her vision adjusted, her mind raced.

Jonah. Phil. The tunnels. The plan—

Cas coughed. "We have to get out of here—the smoke."

Sol nodded and trailed after him as he navigated them through the compact streets.

As they evaded flames and billows of smoke, Sol looked around for the signal that would mark the start of the trial. But through the haze, she saw nothing, not until they finally reached the edge of the village. Within a cluster of evergreens, a lone arrow marked a path inward, the kind expected to mark the exit.

But no trial, nothing to complete before getting to it.

Sol panted, bracing her hands on her knees as they stopped in front of it. "Where is the trial?"

"I don't think we should question it," Cas breathed. "Let's just get out of here."

The crackling of the raging fire grew closer. "I—I can't leave yet."

Cas met her gaze, his Wards sparking at his fingertips. "Sol, think logically for a second."

"I am."

"You're being emotional."

Sol straightened, narrowing her eyes. "I will not leave them, Cas."

"The point is for us to survive, Sol!" His silver eyes were wild, pleading, as he grabbed her by the shoulders. "Get out of your head!"

She ripped herself from his grasp. "I'm not just leaving, Cas!" she cried. "They're people. Phil is a child!"

"You have to learn to leave people behind in battle, Sol." His eyes blazed silver, the flames surrounding them reflecting back the panic his voice gave away. "You can't save everyone. There comes a time when you have to save yourself."

Sol took a moment to step closer, to breathe out the motivation for enduring the trials and the weight of her identity, and everything else that had been thrown at her in a few weeks.

She inhaled a breath, hot and heavy, then spoke. "When my mother was murdered, she told me to save myself. I got home to her yelling for me to run, to find Lora, and get as far away from the house as I could." Her hands trembled. "So, I did. I did, Cas, and guess what? If I had stayed, I might have been able to save her. I still don't know what happened and I probably never will, but I will never—ever abandon someone I care for again. Even if it kills me."

Her chest heaved with revelation, adrenaline spiking, and begging for more, more truth, more pain to seep from within to cleanse the oozing wounds she had only lazily patched over.

The crackling of buildings crescendo and the air scathed but neither of them moved. Cas watched her as if suspended in the moment, his gaze roving over her. She wondered what he saw looking back at him—did she look as horrible as she felt? Could he see her skin bubbling with the heat, her hair singeing? Could he see how truly broken she felt over that night, how it haunted her every waking moment and influenced her decisions. She was a marionette tethered to the fear of failing someone else she loved.

She hoped he saw her plea to somehow help her cut those strings.

He ran a gentle caress over the side of her cheek, his thumb stroking down to her jaw and said, "We will search for them together, then."

Time raced as they weaved through the streets and buildings, plunging back into the village, and leaving the exit behind. The heat of the flames squeezed and blurred Sol's vision. The bells by the cathedral rang and pounded, a beating reminder of where she needed to be, where she needed to take Phil and Jonah.

All at once, panic set in. She ripped her hand from Cas and bent over, breath fast, heavy, and scarce.

She had failed.

She failed and it wasn't even her fault, though it sure felt like it, as it always did. They were one full day away from finishing these trials. Through blurred vision and tears, she could vaguely make out Cas's form before her.

"Sol," he said softly through the haze.

"I don't know what to do, Cas."

She knew they were running out of time. Though the flames were mostly contained to the wooden buildings, they had started to slither out into the streets, enough so the smell of burnt embers enveloped them.

"I gave you my advice and you said no." He pulled her up from her biceps. "Be strong in your decision, Princess. Listen. Listen, and let the elements guide you." He gestured for her to close her eyes. "They've favored you this far."

So, she did.

Filling her lungs with what little air there was, she closed her eyes and listened.

At first, only the crackling fire consumed her. The smell of ashes and burning wood was overwhelming, and even through her eyelids, she could see the dancing, amber lights.

Her skin itched, begging for cold relief.

She exhaled.

With the exhale came a different sound— the sweet whispers of the wind like a lullaby. The scent of fire was replaced by that of menthol and salve, the kind Lora would rub on her to heal open wounds.

Sol opened her eyes and looked beyond Cas. Slowly, almost undetectably, the flames ahead seemed to part. They bent away from the houses and buildings then flickered as if calling her forward.

When the gusts of cool air blew through her hair, Sol ran with it.

She willed her remaining energy and hope into her legs, begging them to continue. Swinging around corners and making dust drift, she followed the thread. It led her past crumbling storefronts and shriveled trees until the smell of mint and thyme made her skid to a stop.

Behind her, Cas panted. "Sol?"

Sol turned to look at the building before them. It was also engulfed in waves of flame and rubble, but the sign on the window front hung from metal strings, vaguely marking it as an APOTHECARY.

With another cool caress, Sol shouldered the door open.

Plumes of heavy smoke greeted her, making her cough, and shield her face.

But there, beyond the foyer, the smoke parted as if the wind itself tore it aside—

"Phil!" Sol gasped, throwing herself forward. Before she could get inside, though, Cas pulled her back.

"No," he commanded. "I will go."

He pushed Sol outside, though the town streets were beginning to become just as dangerous as the inside of the fire-drenched buildings. She watched him disappear into the smoke, then after some minutes of nothing, almost melted into a puddle of utter relief as he emerged with Phil in his arms. The boy was ashen and covered in black smudges, but clearly lucid as he felt around the air.

"Princess!" he cried, thrashing until Cas put him down.

A sob ripped from Sol's chest as she embraced him, pulling him into her. "It's okay, you're okay," she whispered into his matted hair. "Where is Jonah?"

Phil shuddered against her. "Inside. I tried to shield him with the wind, but it was running out, and he couldn't see—"

Cas dashed back into the apothecary just as the roof began to crumble. The emotions flooding through Sol as the roof caved into itself, as the smoke and flames seemed to breathe before exploding, was mortifying. Fear, panic, and hopelessness all catapulted together until it ripped at her soul, and all she could do was hold Phil closer.

"CAS!" she yelled, torn between running after him and staying with Phil.

A heat hotter than the flames themselves burned at her back, where her birthmark lived, then spread to her throat, down to the scar on her palm, her blood bond, until all at once everything stopped.

Everything.

As if time itself froze, the flames stopped their flaying, and the crackling ceased. Dust suspended in its path, and Sol looked down to find Phil frozen in fear against her, his eyes tightly shut, and tears staining his cheeks.

Gently, Sol peeled away from him. "What the—"

"I will admit, you've needed more interventions than anticipated, Queen of Wielders."

Sol jumped at the melodious voice resonating from everywhere, yet nowhere, all at once. She glanced up, then looked around, until at the end of the crumbling street a figure floated forward.

Its silhouette grew and neared. "In your defense, though, your mother needed even more, and she was supposed to be well-versed in these things."

"Who are you—what is this?" Sol narrowed her eyes. "Don't come any closer!"

An unearthly laugh resonated, spilling like honey. "I was going to send Morna again, but I was closer, and figured it would be a good time for us to meet."

Sol swallowed and clenched her jaw in between bouts of nausea. "Who are you?"

The Jinn smiled. "Mavka. My name is Mavka."

CHAPTER FORTY-THREE

The Mother of Jinn

Mavka moved like a soft current. She floated toward Sol, who was torn between running, yelling, or attempting to fight. She held Phil close, who was still frozen in a snapshot of terror, against her chest.

The Mind Slayer was beautiful. Beautiful in the kind of way the sun was—uncomfortable if looked at for too long. Her skin was a flawless baby blue, nothing like the other Jinn who's waxy pelts rotted from their bones. Strands of jet-black locks tumbled down her back to her waist in thick tendrils, and she wore a lose cloth over her torso and hips in what seemed like a feeble attempt at modesty.

"I quite dislike human fashion," Mavka remarked, crossing past Sol into the tumbling apothecary. "Too many layers."

Typically, Sol was able to formulate plans rather quickly. But this time, she remained where she was, utterly confused. Around her, the space remained suspended as Mavka emerged.

"Your lover and the little Air Caller's brother are safe in there. For now." A smile a degree too reminiscent of the Lower Jinn pulled at the creature's thin, navy-blue lips. "I can maybe keep time frozen for another minute and a half before your planet bursts with the dimensional magic." She picked at her taloned nails. "I would hurry in there if I were you."

"Who are you?" Sol's voice was shaky and brittle, unable to hide the fear. "Why—how?"

"You're asking all the wrong questions, Queen of Wielders."

"Why help me?"

The creature named Mavka frowned. "I have a contractual duty to you Yarrows. Your mother might have broken our agreement, but I never did."

"You knew my mother?"

"Again, wrong question."

Sol shivered as she stood, careful to place Phil in a safe position. "Are you Jinn?"

Sol had a sense that was also a wrong question, but Mavka shrugged, "I am the mother of Jinn." She looked up at the sun, bare and daunting overhead. "Fifty seconds, Queen of Wielders."

"Why here?" Sol squared her shoulders. *Queen. Think like a Queen.* "Why invade Erriadin?"

The creature's laugh reverberated through Sol's very bones. "Oh, no dear. I hate it here. Unfortunately, some of my children disagree with me—as most children do."

The ground beneath them shook, vibrating and sending pebbles jumping around. She had no time to be curious.

"We will meet again, Yarrow Queen." Mavka kicked aside stray rubble and strode back the way she came. "Maybe you'll figure out the right questions by then."

The buildings had begun to shake, and the flames seemed to wink back to life. Before Sol could think twice, she darted into the apothecary.

It was thick with haze and embers, but she spotted Jonah and Cas not far from the foyer. Jonah knelt on the floor with his arms over his face, and Cas was in the process of reaching for his bicep. Sol threw herself forward and grabbed both of their shirts. She pulled them with her whole being, but really only managed to fall back on her heels. Freezing time apparently didn't affect gravity—or weight.

Breathe.

Breathe.

Seconds. They had mere seconds before chaos resumed and the building collapsed. Sol's hand burned like ants feasted on it. Her neck and chest exploded into slashes of hot pain.

Let me in, dove.

This time, Sol didn't fight it.

Everything was blue. Like before time froze, the pain paused and was replaced by a numbing tingle while sparks of blue danced around her. Her exposed skin shimmered like starlight, her hair dancing as if pulled by static.

This time when Sol reached for Cas and Jonah, they easily moved. She pushed them to the entrance, unable to stop to question the off series of events. Just as she collapsed with them beside Phil, in the span of a hasty exhale, time resumed. Coughs erupted from all around, and Sol exhaled sighs of relief.

"Princess—" Jonah reached to her, then to Phil, who instantly sobbed and wrapped himself around his brother.

Sol held them both. "We have to get back to the cathedral."

"Leave me—take Phil," Jonah pleaded, his brows furrowed and voice horse. "They won't let us all leave."

Sol shook her head and pulled him up. "Not all of us are. Let's go."

Mercifully, Cas asked no questions and followed behind them, taking the end of the line to help evade debris and flames. With every step they took crashes resounded behind them as if they went any slower the flames would devour them whole. Finally, the cathedral came into view. Its pointed roof stood tall with the tinted windows reflecting the flames into a show of blood.

Sol pounded against the doors. Over and over, she knocked, each time more frantic than the last. What if they hadn't made it? Sol would have no way of knowing.

And there was nothing else to do if—

The wooded doors flew open, throwing Sol into Cas behind her.

She couldn't remember the last time she had been so relieved to see anyone. But when Penny's little face, eyes wide and full of worry, appeared from behind the cathedral doors, Sol scooped her up into a messy embrace.

"The basement," the girl said against her. "Miss Amana waits."

Sol nodded and placed her back on the safety of the ground before urging Jonah forward.

Sol said, "Come on."

"What is going on?" Jonah's face was smeared in sweat and ashes. "Where are we going? The exit should be at the other end of town."

Sol glanced at Cas who crossed his arms and angled his head. He also waited for an answer.

"I am getting you both out of here," Sol said. "You're both to board a ship North and stay there until things get resolved here."

Jonah's expression went from confused to hesitant, but Phil's was a sentimental joy the whole time she spoke. "They will know," Jonah said finally. "We won't be safe."

"You will. And they won't." Sol gestured them forward to follow Penny. "Come."

Jonah moved forward, his brother still in his arms, and his face clad with disbelief. Penny grabbed his torn sleeves and guided them toward the spiral staircase, one that led down into a basement, interconnected by ancient terrestrial tunnels through the entirety of Rimemere. Tunnels that were almost always guarded by Enchantments.

Almost always.

"The tunnels," Cas said, stepping beside her. "How did you know they ran beneath here?"

Sol shrugged. "Nina."

"How did she tell you?"

"Penny."

"And how did Nina know this trial would be here?"

Sol sneezed. "Samara, I think. I don't know. Perhaps she can read minds, too."

Cas's jaw twitched with a hint of a smile. "You could've told me."

"It was a last-minute plan." Beyond the cathedral wall chaos continued to roar, and she knew they didn't have much time before the flames engulfed the sacred building as well.

She began toward the staircase, Cas closely beside her. "You could go too, you know," she said. "Go North, start a new life. We could meet once a month somewhere for your tattoo—and you'd be free."

He glanced at her sidelong. "Is that what you want?"

"Isn't it what *you've* always wanted?"

They began their descent down the stairs, Penny's sweet voice beckoning below.

He sighed, "For a long time, yeah. I hated being bound to Rimemere."

"And now?" Sol asked.

They neared the end of the staircase, a black tunnel ahead. Cas had no time to answer as Sol spotted red followed by a pair of bright green eyes visible even in the dimness. Sol ran forward and crashed into Nina's open arms.

"Sol." Nina embraced her with such a genuine kindness, that Sol couldn't help the small sob. "Sol, we miss you."

Sol smiled as well, and although seemed impossible after such a short time of knowing them, replied honestly, "I miss you all as well."

"M—Miss Amana," Jonah's eyes went wide, and even Phil shifted to be set down. The boy grinned. "Nina Amana?"

Nina nodded and lowered herself to his level. "That's me! I will be your guide. We must leave quickly."

"How?" Jonah turned to Sol. "How did you know?"

"Jeriyah was easy to put to sleep." Penny giggled. "We slipped some Kerproot into his tea."

"It won't be long before the old fart wakes up, though." Nina pulled Cas into a hug next. "So, I'm afraid we cannot stay long."

Jonah looked from Sol, to Nina, to Phil. "I don't know, Princess."

"I'm not having any of you dying here, Jonah," Sol said. "Please. I know it will be hard to remain hidden and fake both of your deaths, but please. Live," she pleaded. Begged.

Jonah's blue eyes softened, and he reached to grab Sol's hand. She squeezed his palm, gentle and firm.

He brought his free arm over his chest, laying his hand on his shoulder with a set of taps. "Long may you reign, Princess."

Phil looked up at Sol with tears in his eyes. He mimicked his brother's gesture. "Long may you reign."

With a final glance from Nina, the four of them began their journey into the tunnels.

Above them, the roof rumbled and groaned.

Not waiting for emotions to distract her, she didn't protest when Cas swept her back up the stairs and out the rumbling cathedral, the booming of crumbling walls unnervingly close the entire sprint to the exit.

CHAPTER FORTY-FOUR

Dance to the Gallows

They didn't speak on the way back to the Gods' Villa. The pattering of hooves and creaks of the carriage were the only sounds as Sol watched the darkening forest speed by, twilight casting curious shadows and rays of sunshine around the lands. She traced the clouds with her eyes and braced a hand on her chin, the smell of ash clinging to her skin.

Her eyelids were heavy, and body was sore, but she had done it. She had *done* it.

Perhaps she wasn't able to save everyone as she had so stupidly thought during the beginning of the trials, but she saved *some*.

It was the end.

She and Cas had made it. Though they hadn't found a better way out, Cas had already made peace with yielding. And that had to be enough.

By the time the carriage rolled to a stop by the Villa's gates, the moon was high in the sky, and the soft orange tones were replaced with an inky blue night. Cas pushed the door open, and

Sol followed wordlessly. She expected the guards to rush away as they usually did, but one of the kingsmen hopped from the seat.

"Tomorrow is the final duel. You are both to be ready by dawn." The kingsman said as he handed Cas an envelope. "Directives as per His Majesty."

Sol peered over Cas's shoulder as he tore it open.

Then stopped breathing.

"He—he isn't allowing yields," Sol whispered, her voice shaky and hollow. "Why isn't he letting either of us yield?"

The note crackled with violet flames as Cas grabbed the guard by his sleeve. "What the fuck is this?"

"The trial tomorrow is to the death," the kingsman said. "Only one survivor. If the rules are breached, execution for you both will be called."

"My Court will never allow that happen." Sol gritted her teeth. "My uncle preaches tradition then crushes it when it's inconvenient."

"Having one winner is tradition, *Princess,*" the guard smirked. "You wagering yourself doesn't change that."

Cas stared past the man, his demeanor strangely calm as Sol pulled his grip off the man. "Cas?"

"Leave," he said to the kingsman, slow and fierce. "I'm trying to be more restrained with who I kill, but if you idiots aren't off of the Villa grounds in five minutes, I will send my Shadows after you."

The man stepped back. "We are merely messengers, Prince."

"So, I will use you to send one back." Cas's eyes shone. "Leave."

They did.

The kingsman shuffled back onto the saddle and threw the carriage into motion, turning back a few times as they went to ensure the darkness of nightmares didn't chase them. Sol and Cas stood there for a while in silence, the air between them so full of unspoken things. The thought of them going back to their rooms to await the morning's chaos seemed inappropriate, but she wasn't sure what else there was to do.

She looked up at him, "I don't want to go inside."

Slowly, he held his hand out. "Let's walk the beach, then."

Careful to avoid the tumbling branches and stones, they climbed over the wall that separated the sands and ocean. Finally, they sat by the edge of the water, the lazy waves a gentle soundtrack after the day's turbulent waters. Sol focused on it, on the trickle of the tide, and the salt in the air, trying to distance herself from the noise in her mind. The moonlight shimmered against the rolling current, casting the beach in silver flames.

"The moon looks beautiful from here," Sol said, tracing the sand with her fingers.

Beside her, Cas was silent, prompting her to look at him. He watched her with a foreign intensity, a kind Sol hadn't seen him wear so unguarded.

Heat bloomed over her face. "What?"

He angled his head and smiled softly. "Not as beautiful as the sun."

A rouge wave splashed her feet, making her recoil with a small grin. "It takes one of us needing to kill the other for you to be sweet, huh?"

Cas sighed, leaning back on his palms as the wind swayed through his hair. "You'll be fine, Sol. Don't worry about it."

"Your nonchalance is exactly what I'm worried about."

"Me being in these trials was a death sentence from the beginning," he shrugged. "Semmena just waited to make it official to give us hope."

"I'm not going to let you just throw tomorrow's trial, Cas. I..." Sol dragged her hands through her unbound hair. "I don't want to win if it means you don't survive."

"Don't start getting attached to me, Princess. I promise nothing good comes from it."

"Cas—"

"You need to survive, Sol." His voice lowered, "That's it. No argument."

Sol stood. "Just because you don't care about yourself doesn't mean others can't, Casimir."

"You don't know the reason I do things."

"You're right," Sol seethed. "I don't. But I do know we both deserve to live."

He leaned back on his elbows then angled his head toward her, starlight in his eyes. "You should learn sooner rather than later not all human life is worth saving."

"And why don't you qualify?" Her face burned as he stood, never breaking her gaze.

"Sol, why are we arguing about this?"

Sol sighed and tilted her head to the sky, wondering if the moon somehow took pleasure in seeing them bicker beneath its shine. "I just hate the discourse that I'm somehow more important than you. I'm not."

"The whole point of your existence *is* your increased value. You risked yourself during the Fire Trial for people, who in the end, don't matter. That sort of thinking is going to get the kingdom burned to the ground and get you *killed*."

Sol scoffed. "My thinking is going to save lives."

"Likely the wrong ones."

"Then perhaps it's a good thing you're no longer a Prince, huh? You don't have to burden yourself with choosing who the *right* ones are."

His expression change was subtle, quick—but heavy enough to make Sol instantly regret her words.

Slowly, Cas stood. "So, tell me, then." He faced her, hands swirling with static. "If you were given the choice to save your mother or save the world, which would you choose? Which one is the *right* choice?"

They looked at each other in silence, Sol refusing to admit the sentence made her falter in her resolve.

"Exactly," he smirked. "Obviously, the answer is the world. But when you're in that situation, Sol, when the people you love are in front of you and you have to choose to walk away for the greater good, that's when discipline over this matters."

Sol swallowed the ache at the reminder her mother had in fact chosen her and not the world and that was the reason they all suffered. Sol couldn't deny she would have done the same. She couldn't deny she would've given a thousand lives if it meant seeing her mother again, hearing her laugh, feeling her soft smile against her forehead after a day at Leo's farm.

Sol made to turn away, to hide the tears that spilled. "You will not shame me for choosing those I love in moments of urgency, Casimir."

"Of course not. But when those you love stand in the way of something greater, you need to pick your side. Quickly. You say all lives matter, so make unbiased decisions." He strode past her. "I can guarantee if it had been Cattya and Ezra instead of Jonah and Phil, you wouldn't have gone through the trouble to save them."

She looked at the ground, knowing her silence was answer enough.

"And that's fine, Sol. That's what I'm trying to say. Save the people who matter when you can. But it will never be always, especially with your position." His words echoed in her mind as she watched him go. She continued to stare at the place he disappeared from.

A humid breeze rolled through her hair and Sol had the sinking feeling the Prince of Shadows might have a terrible point.

However, she didn't care.

"Cas!"

Sol sprinted into the Villa, the frayed remains of her blouse swaying around her, as she stepped into the darkness. It was so achingly lonely, and although she had managed to save Jonah and Phil, the victory was bitter in light of the other lives lost.

Sure, Sol wanted to be right and keep her pride in front of Cas, but what she wanted more was comfort. To not be left to her own devices, to be told it would be okay even if it was a lie.

"I'm sorry," she sobbed into the dead room, her voice echoing, small and brittle. Everything she should be the opposite of.

She pressed her palms into her face and sank to the floor.

I don't know what to do, Mom.

Sol felt, more than heard, him beside her. The soft crackle of his Wards hummed, the soft violet light shining in the night even through her covered eyes.

"Sol." He wrapped his hands around her forearms, gently guiding them down to her lap. With an edge of worry in his tone, he lifted her chin with his fingers, and said, "It's going to be okay."

She sobbed harder, finally releasing the dam of emotions she had repressed since the trials started. "How are we going to get out of this, Cas?" Sol gazed into him, searching for whatever truth his eyes held.

But, as always, he seemed relaxed, not at all worried about the morning's dance to the gallows. His silver eyes explored every edge of her face, finally landing on her lips. "You will live."

"And you?"

"It doesn't matter."

Sol clenched her jaw. "It *does*."

His features darkened, Shadows suddenly pooling around them. The cool mist was a relief against her warming skin, especially as Cas ran his hand across her cheek to fix a lock of hair behind her ear.

Sol leaned into the touch.

"I distinctly remember saying those you *love* matter, Princess." The word reverberated through her bones, as he continued, "Are you trying to tell me something?"

Breath hitching and heat pooling in her chest, Sol eased back, away from his touch. "I will not raise my blades against you tomorrow."

Cas dropped his hands, but his gaze lingered on her lips. "I'm afraid you already have."

CHAPTER FORTY-FIVE

The Final Duel

It had become natural for Sol not to sleep. She spent the whole night sick to her stomach, opening the windows to feel the breeze, and then wondering if a fall from so high would kill her. She constantly glanced at Cas's own open window stories below, stupidly wishing he would be looking for her too. He'd chosen a room on the third floor, which had been disappointing. Not that she wanted him in her room, but the one next to hers would have been nice.

Keep telling yourself that.

The hope that he would come find her lingered all night, keeping her awake more than the brewing anxiety. But he didn't. Not through his window or her door, not even a single Shadow all night. When the birds began to chirp outside to signal the imminent sunrise, Sol went from being sad he hadn't sought her out to pissed.

It could be their last day on Erriadin, and the man still wouldn't make a move. He had been so sweet, only to leave her with a thirst she had never had the discomfort of feeling before. Sol might be naive and inexperienced when it came to magic and politics, but she knew when someone liked her.

She decided to go in a more tactical outfit for the day, a pair of leather breeches and a flowy white blouse bound tightly by a black chest cover and waist belt to hold her knives. Hopefully, she wouldn't need them.

She was lacing up her boots when a soft knock sounded at her door, making her heart stammer. Cas waited a few seconds before easing the door open.

He wore his usual outfit, an all-black tactical suit with a purple chest band holding his sword to his back. Leaning on the door frame, his gaze roved her over. "Rimemere fashion suits you, Princess."

She continued working the ends of her lace but spared him a slight side smile. "It's grown on me, I guess."

They spent the remaining time before sunrise in the kitchen eating leftover berries, but Sol couldn't stomach much of anything. They made small conversation—nothing as vulnerable as the night before.

That's how she could tell he was nervous.

The carriage was just as somber. For thirty minutes she watched the forest pass, the little animals zoom in and out of the road, and the grass sway with the lazy, late spring breeze. Sol couldn't help the joy she felt when the Rimemere castle finally came into view. Even from a distance it was obvious crowds gathered around the courtyards.

"What is the final duel?" Sol asked. "Like a fight?"

Cas also peered out the window from his spot in front of her. "It changes every time."

They bypassed the castle completely, passed by a large, sinister graveyard then back into the cover of the forest.

Sol fidgeted with her braid. "Do you know *where* it is?"

He exhaled from his nose. "The Colosseum."

The first sign the day wouldn't end well was that Fin awaited them by the Colosseum gates. The building itself seemed to be made out of a mixture of clay, mud, and stone, giving it a rusted color. The ground beneath them morphed from grass to dirt the more they neared it. Past the entrance was a narrow hallway that led to a larger opening, which Sol figured was an arena of sorts based on the circular ground. As they emerged, there were two additional hallways on either side of them.

"Princess to the left," Fin said with a wave of his hand. "Other one to the right."

Sol tried meeting Cas's gaze one final time, but he was dragged the opposite way before she could.

Two kingsmen grabbed her by the arms, dragging her down the corridor, tightening their hold when she tried to wiggle out of it. The last thing she saw as she looked over her shoulder was Fin placing shackles on Cas before they rounded the corner into the depths of the cave.

Sol managed to free herself. "I can walk."

After five minutes of walking, they had reached a small cell. There was nothing within it, and the far wall was solid metal. It vibrated with the sounds from its other side.

"You wait here. The wall will open when it's time." The kingsman motioned her forward.

Sol glared at them, crossing her arms. "I demand to see Cas."

They laughed. "Oh, you will, Princess," one of them drawled. "You will see him plenty out there."

When she made no motion to enter the cell, one of the men pushed her in. Sol yelled after them, but they faded into the darkness of the underground area without so much as a glance back. Chants reverberated across the roof of the cell, giving away just how large the crowd gathered above her was.

Yarrow. Yarrow. Yarrow.

Xanthos. Xanthos. Xanthos.

Sol clamped her jaw shut, sinking to the cell's muddy ground. The only reprieve from her emotional torment was the fact this was the end.

After this, she would Awaken her magic, then take the throne before bracing the gods-awful note her mother had left her.

Breathe.

Breathe.

She traced the dirt with her fingertips, drawing a star then crossing it out. Sol wouldn't fight him. She *couldn't*. There had to be a way other than one of them dying, a way to get them both out of this.

Come, dove.

Sol inhaled. "Lora?"

Let me show you, dove. Come.

It was the third time the echo of her voice rang through her, and each time something happened.

Fuck it.

"Fine," Sol said, utterly defeated. "Show me."

The shift of scenery knocked the air from her lungs. Sol sat in the cell, then she was falling into nothing and everything all at once. It was like home. There were small shops with straw roofs and roads made of soft dirt and cobblestone, even the smell of sweet jam from the bakeries was the same. As Sol stepped forward, though, she realized it only looked like Yavenharrow on the surface, but the liveliness and life her town had was absent. Abducted.

The mirage was wholly silent. Only the stray leaves crunched beneath Sol's bare feet.

She continued down the main road, looking for any signs of souls, of anyone other than her through the otherworldly mist.

But there was no one.

"Sol."

Sol turned. "Aunt Lora?"

Lora smiled softly. "Hi, dove."

Around her, the town echoed their voices, then Sol's steps as she trudged closer. "What is this? Where are we?"

"Somewhere in-between," Lora said, folding her legs beneath her and plopping onto the ground. "Come. Sit. You called me."

As Sol stopped in front of her aunt and bent to sit, she froze.

Lora's skin was hollow and dull, her sandy hair knotted and thin. Just as Sol was about to ask about it, her attention landed on her aunt's eyes.

Her pupils overtook them, then red veins and bruises around her cheeks. Lora smiled. "It's been a bit rough over here, I'm afraid."

"What's happened to you?" Sol's voice shook. "Lora, what is it?"

"We have no time to catch up right now, dear." She blinked, a small twitch pulling at her jaw. "You asked for me."

It took some moments to gather her thoughts, to truly bring herself back from wherever she was. "I—Cas." His name burst from within her. "Oh gods, Aunt Lora. The Trials. The Coronation Vows. I—my uncle made me do them and I joined them, but Cas killed someone, so he had to join too—"

Her aunt laughed. "Ah, Semmena hasn't changed a single bit. I miss the man sometimes if only to laugh when he didn't get his way."

"Lora, I have to get me and Cas out of the final Trial. Semmena is making us fight to the death."

"Casimir will not hurt you, dove."

Sol nodded, picking at her nails. "I know. And I will not hurt him. There has to be another way—I heard my mother somehow had Draven and Semmena survive."

Lora watched her, her onyx eyes narrowing. "Using that loophole will require sacrifice from the both of you."

"Tell me. Tell me what to do, Lora, please." Sol nearly fell forward to her knees in a plea. "Please."

"After Irene's Vows, everyone called her on the loophole. Why do you think we had to leave? The foul play was obvious. Your mother did it for Mel and destroyed her credibility in the process."

Sol felt the time running out. The air began to freeze, her skin shivering and tingling as if she was waking from a dream. "I'll take the risk."

Her aunt watched her for a long moment before sighing, "Rule and Law 5.4 from Stone Ledge states if the final prospects are both on the brink of death, the match gets called a draw."

Sol blinked. "And how do I do that?"

"Our blood bond." Lora stood. "It acts as a siphon. You can draw my magic in short bursts—Call out the law to Semmena and I will do the rest."

Sol could see her breath pooled in clouds by her face. "Magic?"

"Void—Dark Magic. Blood bonds are Dark Magic."

Lora gestured for Sol to stand then grabbed her shoulder. Her aunt's touch was cold. Almost foreign. It made Sol flinch slightly. "You've been helping me during the Trials?"

"Slightly. Although, I promised I wouldn't. I couldn't just feel you suffer."

"Is that...Safe?"

Lora's eyes seemed distant, as if she looked past Sol and not at her. "I will be fine."

"But—Lora."

With a smile too reminiscent of the creatures of nightmares, Lora whispered, "Good luck."

Sol barely had time to gather her wits as her soul, or mind, or whatever that was returned to herself. She lay on the dusty cell floor, then quickly turned away from the wall as it pulled open, the brightness a jarring contrast from the dimness.

She stood on shaky feet.

Dust and debris swirled around as she stepped into the arena, the sun bright and blazing heavily compared to the usual cover of clouds from the east side of Rimemere.

Sol's chest rose and fell with heavy breaths as she looked for Cas though the sandstorms, anxious to assure the guards hadn't somehow taken him somewhere different, that Semmena hadn't found another scheme to hurt him. But her shoulders went slack, and the tension dispersed as Cas's silver eyes penetrated through the tawny dust, then his black suit and hair as he strode forward to meet her at the center of the arena.

Sol hurried her steps, yearning to look around for her Court, for Penny, for all the others who were in their corner. But she knew any distraction now was detrimental.

So, she walked toward Cas as confidently as she could pretend, her fists tight beside her and chin held high through the dirt.

They didn't know exactly what the final trial entailed, no one did. The one with her mother had been a bare duel of blades and wits, according to the stories.

Sol didn't know what she wished for at this point, except for it to be over.

Call out the law to Semmena and I'll do the rest.

As they joined space in the field, relief caressed Sol at the sight of him, unharmed and just as sure of himself as he had been in the morning.

She laughed softly despite the pressure.

Rule and Law 5.4.

Rule and Law 5.4

"Ladies and gentlemen of the South." Sol flinched at her Uncle's voice, a sore to hear after a whole two weeks away from it. "It is an absolute delight to see our final prospects ready to finish the Vows in the name of holy tradition."

Sol looked past Cas to where Semmena sat on a gold and metal throne. Though they were far, the Semmena Court was easy to spot. Samara stood beside her mother who sat on a smaller seat in front of the King Regent.

Jeriyah stood by the shadows, obvious by his tan robes and arms clutching tomes. Gaven was also in the background, and he was the only to give her a small nod when he spotted her watching.

Sol did not nod back.

"As you heard, we will be following the typical rules," Semmena continued. "One winner. Now, I am sure you are all asking yourselves, what if Xanthos wins? The whole thing would be pointless since it was to marry a Yarrow." He finished the sentence with a chuckle, one the arena echoed. "To marry a Yarrow and receive the blessing of the gods. Well, with my dear niece deciding to bend the rules, it seems the outcome must be bent as well."

To the right of the Semmena Court, Sol spotted—

Her eyes swelled with tears at the sight of Nina and Sawyer, Alix a rigid presence behind them. Her cousin gave her a nod, and Nina clasped her hands together, her face the purest despair. She wiggled her fingers at Sol in a small wave.

"They're all there," Sol whispered to Cas. "They're beside Semmena."

He tugged at his sleeve. "They would never miss you beating me up, Princess."

Sol gripped the hilt of her dagger as wailing boomed to her left. Finigan waltzed in from the area entrance, flanked by two guards in full iron armor.

Cas stepped forward. "What is this?"

"No weapons today," Fin said. "Hand them over."

Panic struck Sol. "Weapons are all I have."

"Too bad. Weapons." He held out his hands, flinching as he bounced on his feet. "Now."

Hesitantly, Sol unsheathed her knives and tossed them at his feet, Cas doing the same.

While she worked on getting her smaller dagger free from her ankle, Semmena spoke, "The final trial is Wards. Kill your opponent using only Warren's magic."

"This is bullshit, Semmena," Cas yelled, turning to face him. "It's not a fair playing field. She hasn't Awakened."

Sol yanked the dagger free and tossed it at the kingsman with a glare.

"All prospects are implied to have magic," Gina added. "She should have read the rules beforehand."

"You keep changing the rules!" A voice from within the crowd bellowed. "Let the Princess have a chance!"

The arena filled with unintelligible words and arguments until a flare of fire from Semmena's throne silenced them. "I have not finished explaining the details."

Sol tapped her thigh with her fingers. Something was wrong. Something…Something.

"I have an additional incentive, tailored for the Prince of Shadows himself." The King smiled, slow and wicked. "If the Princess wins, she may overwrite this tradition with whatever nonsense she sees fit. Casimir, if you win, I will grant your official pardon and you may return to Eswin. Your family name will be slashed from the list of Rimemere traitors."

She shifted her gaze to Cas.

His expression changed so subtly Sol would have missed it had she not been looking. But it was clear, clear as day and night, light and shadow, when the words registered within him.

Sol's breath hitched.

This wasn't a duel.

It was her execution.

She glanced at her Court. All three of them stood motionless. Stunned. This was all Cas wanted after all. His home, his name, his people.

"Sol?"

Her attention snapped to him at the sound of her name, like honey and sugar when it came from his lips.

"Yes?"

He grazed her hand with his own as his entire body shone with violet flames. "I'm sorry."

CHAPTER FORTY-SIX
The Magic of Letting Go

Sol ran.

She didn't stop to decipher what he meant, she just ran.

Wisps of lightning chased after her as she sprinted toward the other end of the arena. The ground was uneven and broken, forcing her to jump over holes while trying to not disintegrate into the air with regret.

With regret, disappointment, anger.

Sadness.

He swore he would die before placing her in danger, and she so stupidly believed him. She shouldn't have let her naivety get the best of her. Shouldn't have let her feelings for a boy sway her logic, a boy she didn't even know well.

Sol halted.

But she did know him.

For the overall good, huh?

She turned toward him. And as she did, the anger took hold like wildfire on the driest summer afternoon, bold and scorching, as it spread across her chest.

Cas wasn't running toward her, merely walking with his Wards engulfing his wrists.

His eyes were pure violet.

"You're a hypocrite," Sol seethed. "You preach discipline in decisions, but you turn against me the second your emotional attachments are tugged."

He stopped a few paces from her. "I will never get this mercy again."

"I will give you this and more when I take the throne!" Her anger melted into despair with each passing second Cas didn't look at her directly, with every foreign expression and movement he made. "Cas, please."

It was like a dance. He lunged, but Sol evaded. She ran, and he followed. She didn't know how long they did this, only that it was long enough to leave her entire body shaking. Although she was on the defensive, never once did he truly wield his Wards at her, only enough to keep her swaying from corner to corner. She had no weapons, only wavering willpower—the dance became exhausting.

"Just kill me if you're going to," she yelled at him. "You're holding back."

He propelled forward with a boom of his lightning, this time catching Sol off guard as he tackled her to the ground. Air left her lungs as her back collided with the mud.

Cas pinned her in place, his thighs and knees squeezing her own as he leaned close. "I may be holding back, but you're not even trying."

Sol strained to pull air into her lungs. "I told you I wouldn't fight you–and unlike you, I don't break my promises."

He tapped her necklace subtly. "I won't give you this opportunity again."

She glared at him. "What are you—"

"If we stay like this longer it will be suspicious." His eyes were back to silver, soft and familiar. "Take the kill."

Sol gritted her teeth and shut her eyes. "Never."

She turned her head to the King, her anger flaring at the wicked smirk on his face.

"I call Rule and Law 5.4," she yelled as loud as she could, dirt and wind swirling over her face.

The King's smile instantly fell. His eyes hardened.

Sol looked back at Cas, who still hovered above her. He furrowed his brows at her in confusion. "What—"

"I'm sorry," she said breathlessly, pressing her scarred palm to his chest. She used her other hand to pull him down, pressing them together. Then, like an inhale, the space around them swelled.

Stilled.

And like an exhale, the magic burst.

It propelled from within her palm, unfolding and spreading with a force that pushed Sol back onto the ground.

She expected it to hurt or enhance her already aching body.

But it was the opposite.

For the first time in a long time, her thoughts calmed. Silenced.

The magic fizzled through her, whispering to every ache, and wound to calm, engulfing her in the gentlest embrace.

All pain vanished, replaced with tender waves. She could have stayed there forever. On the ground, looking up at the radiant sun. And she did.

CHAPTER FORTY-SEVEN

Sawyer

The moment Sawyer saw her cousin use Dark Magic, she stalked over to Jeriyah and punched him in the face. She didn't enjoy it, but they needed the Enchantment separating the spectators from the prospects gone.

Fast.

It was a soft hit, more like a push, but the man still went down with a clatter, his book of prayers tumbling to the ground. Sawyer muttered an apology while Samara snapped her head toward them. She expected the woman to lunge or curse at her, but her expression mirrored the urgency Sawyer felt.

Help him.

Nina and Alix were already by the edge of the arena, ready to jump into the field as soon as the Enchantment fell. By the time Sawyer shouldered her way through the crowd to join them, healers already swarmed toward Sol and Cas, both lying motionless on the ground amidst a haze of blue mist.

Nina bounced on her feet, bursts of green pooling around her as her magic begged to help. "Come on, come on."

"We get to them quickly," Alix commanded. "Don't let anyone register what that was."

Sawyer looked around to see if anyone had, but most of the crowd was fixated on the drama and blood, not on what caused it. It had to have been Sol's blood bond. Unless her cousin had known the Dark Spells and not told them.

Or Cas had managed to connect with Loumallet more than he let on.

The Enchantment fell with a crackle.

They jumped over the border, sprinting to Sol and Cas.

"You're more like Irene than anticipated, Niece," her father laughed dryly behind them. "Very much like her indeed."

The healers worked on them for hours with a combination of earth magic and Driodell Forest plants until they finally shared with Nina, Sawyer, and Alix they were stable.

Weak, but stable.

Nina tried to go inside to see them, but the healers advised to let them rest. Now, Nina and Sawyer both sat on the wooden bench outside, watching servants and students roam by, eyeing them with curiosity.

"Can you believe Sol did it?" Sawyer folded her hands behind her head. "The untrained, magicless, small-town girl bested the Vows."

"Shh!" Nina smacked her side. "Don't say anything about magic. The walls have ears."

Sol channeling her Aunt's magic was unexpected. Not only is that a skill honed through years of practice, but the fact Lady

Lora allowed her Niece access to the deadly energy was odd. Dark Magic in the hands of inexperienced souls was as good as throwing them to Loumallet himself. They would have to take Sol to her god's temple to purge, pray, and let out the darkness and hope it didn't take hold. Even if Lora had siphoned the magic, it would still require Sol to purge it from her system.

Again, if that's what had happened.

First, though, they would need to figure out which god was Sol's.

Sawyer rubbed her temples. "I need this day to be over."

"I agree." Nina sighed. "I haven't had so much anxiety since the Wielder tests at the academy. Do you remember those?"

They both laughed at the memory. The four of them had studied the Rimemere texts and practices for weeks, pressured by their Yarrow Court status to pass everything with perfection. Nina and Alix got the highest marks, both on the written and physical magic portions. Sawyer made a hole in the rooftop's training rink arches with her fire, and Cas had thrown his own test to make Sawyer feel better, although he never admitted to it.

"Cas made his Shadows push that one man from the roof, the one who kept bothering you," Sawyer laughed. "What was his name?"

Nina shivered. "Rolian. What a creep."

"Too bad he survived."

"Sawyer!"

Sawyer leaned her head on her friend's shoulder, their laughter echoing before hushing into an aching silence. Despite the attempts for humor, they both knew the turbulent oceans awaiting them now. As soon as Sol took the throne, the true tests would begin. The war against the Jinn would unfold, and it seemed against their own people as well.

"Do you think we will win?" Sawyer whispered.

Nina grabbed her hand. "There is no other option, S."

CHAPTER FORTY-EIGHT

THE IN-BETWEEN

Sol knew this place.

There was a gentle darkness all around her and a peaceful silence as she took the biggest sigh. She walked forward to nowhere, her feet bare and hair loose around her chest. She wore a thin veil of fabric as a dress, and she traced it with her fingertips.

"Sol?"

She turned to the voice.

Cas was dressed in a black suit, as usual. But all the exhaustion the past weeks had drawn on his handsome face was gone, his expression fully awake and radiant, and a relief to see.

She ran to him.

He met her with a crushing embrace, his face sinking into her neck and his arms wrapping around her waist as he pulled her off the ground. Sol wrapped her legs around him, pulling back slightly to peer at him.

His breath was heavy and fierce. Restrained. "Are we dead?"

Sol laughed. "Hopefully, because if not, I think I'll regret this."

She took his face in her hands and kissed him. Like a key sliding into its lock, a sense of utter rightness settled in her chest as he wove his free hand through her hair, pushing her closer with an urgency that left her breathless. He broke away for a moment, but his gaze never left her lips as he said, "I hope you don't." The arm that held her up wrapped around her waist. "I know I won't."

"You Xanthos are always causing trouble for us, you know."

Cas released Sol and pulled her behind him in an instant, the parting of their bodies leaving her with a frigid shiver.

Sol blinked into the darkness. "Aunt Lora?"

Lora smiled, "We must speak, Soleil." She wasn't like before. She was back to her normal self, her smile gentle and kind as it had always been, and her eyes the color of the purest honey. She angled her head at Cas. "Alone, I'm afraid."

Cas's figure shimmered, then in a burst of mist, disappeared into the darkness.

"What—" Sol looked around in alarm.

"He's fine, Sol." Her aunt walked closer. "And you will be too." She held out her hands in a silent gesture to get closer. Sol did. She wrapped her aunt in a hug, the sensation so real it was almost as if she was truly there.

Lora sighed against her. "I'm sorry, Sol."

"For what?"

"For what comes next."

Sol inched back. "Are you okay? Where are we? In that in-between again?"

Nodding, Lora closed her hands over Sol's. "Listen to me. You have a great task ahead of you, Sol. You cannot afford distractions, and I will not be here to guide you." She pulled her into another hug, one that felt too rushed. "Please stay away from Casimir Xanthos."

Sol's head felt like it was filled with cement. It took her several tries to open her eyelids, and when she finally did, the blazing firelight made her regret it.

With a groan, she shut her eyes.

She tried moving her arms, her legs, her fingers, but they were too heavy. The only thing that made her sure she was actually in a body was the fact it was incredibly sore.

"Did you know you snore?"

Cas.

Sol peeled an eye open and let her head fall toward his voice. Although blurry, she made out his outline beside her. He seemed to sit on a chair, and she appeared to be in…

"Where are we?" Sol croaked, voice hoarse, and throat on fire.

"The healer's quarters," he replied, shifting in his seat. "Here."

Sol felt the cool metal of a chalice against her lips. She tried not to moan with delight at the fresh water. Her head was held up slightly by a hand, then gently laid down after she drained the chalice completely. She blinked against the light, struggling to focus. Then, all at once, the memories flooded her.

The duel.

Lora.

Dark Magic.

The dream.

Exhaling a breath, she pushed herself up on her elbows.

"Careful." Cas leaned forward, outstretching his arms in caution. "You're going to feel very disoriented."

He was right. The room swirled and ebbed, but she made out the lifted bare cot she lay on, and the monotonous walls lined with jars of herbs, gauze, and other things she didn't recognize.

"You're alright." For a moment, Sol fought the urge to reach for him, a desire likely brought upon by the bizarre dream. She ached to see if his lips would be as soft here, if his touch would be —-

With an inhale, she sat up completely, resisting the urge to grab his hand. Instantly, Cas took her in an embrace.. Burrowing her face into his neck, she threw her arms around him, not bothering to suppress the bubbling sobs that built in the back of her throat. He felt the same as in the dream, warm, magnetic...safe. She sobbed. They had gone through so much in such a short period of time.

As he always did, he seemed to know exactly what she thought, simply pressing her closer by cradling her head in his hand. "I know," he whispered. "I know."

They stayed like that for a long while, until Sol's tears dried, and Cas ran lazy circles along her back.

Sol sighed and pulled herself back. "How long have I been asleep?"

He gave her some space but remained braced on her cot. "Three days. I was out for one."

Blood pounded at her temples. "Somehow I feel less rested than if I hadn't slept at all." She rubbed her bare arms, startled to find herself in only a small nightgown. Her arms were still covered in bruises and cuts, same as Cas's.

He reached to the table beside them and grabbed a cloak that hung from its chair. He settled it over her shoulders. "Quite a trick you did out there."

With a sigh, Sol told him about Lora and the strange visions of her, deciding to leave out the last dream where they had...seen each other.

"Perhaps the blood bond connected your subconscious as well," Cas mused. "Interesting."

"Sol!" The door to the room burst open revealing Nina, Sawyer, and Alix all holding different sorts of trinkets. Nina threw the bouquet of flowers aside as she rushed to her, crushing her into a hug. "We didn't know what to bring, so I brought flowers, and Sawyer got stew from the human sections."

"It smells really rancid," Sawyer commented, setting the cup on a stool. "But that may just be the typical seafood smell."

Sol smiled and pulled her into a hug as Nina went to Cas.

Her cousin patted her back. "I'm glad you didn't die."

"I only brought extra clothes since I figured you'd hate the healer's robes," Alix said, walking to them. "It's almost as bad as scribe fashion."

Sol looked between them all, a sense of tentative peace settling over her. Perhaps there would be struggles ahead, but as long as she was with them, it would all be okay.

Word that the Semmena Court wished to see them reached moments later, instantly putting Sol in a foul mood despite the glorious success. Although she wanted to rest, the look on the King's face when she slashed the Coronation Vows out of law would be fantastic.

Her Court agreed to let her change into the clothes Alix brought as they were at least more modest than what she wore now, and she had no desire to stuff herself into a formal gown.

They left her alone in the healer's quarters, the lack of anyone beside her rather unsettling after having been around at least one person most of the past few weeks.

Sol took her time to undress, rubbing her hands over her skin. Everything ached. Her bones, her skin, gods, even her fingernails were sensitive. She drew a bath in her mind, decorated with lavender and mixed with oils. She would ask Francis to tell her about the Vows from the castle's view and have her help with tea.

The first thing she did when she emerged from the healer's quarters was hug Alix. The gown he brought her was comfortable against her wounds, but also effortlessly elegant. It was a green so dark it seemed dark in the shadows, the color only shining through near firelights or sun. Nina helped braid her hair into an elegant knot, and Sawyer gave her a medicinal tea to soothe any aches until she could return to bed.

Sol hoped the meeting wouldn't take long, the gloomy feeling of dread simmering at the pit of her stomach as she glanced around. "Where is Cas?"

His absence was jarring, alarming. Her skin prickled with panic, still tethered to the urgency of the Vows, of needing to ensure he was okay—

"He will meet us there," Nina said, placing her hand over Sol's trembling fingers. "He is fine."

Sol swallowed the protests, giving the Earth Caller a nod before following her to the Castle Foyer. She didn't have an expectation of where the meeting would be, but when she realized it was in the Courtyard, the tension melted from her shoulders. Being outside, in the sunlight, and without walls to stop her gave her much needed ease.

Nina, wearing her usual black tactical suit, took her spot to Sol's right, Sawyer mirroring her on the left. Alix gave Sol a courteous nod before stepping in front of her.

Even with them beside her, the people she had missed so much while away, the empty spot at her back ached stronger than any wound.

What if he was taken again? What if a Jinn—

He is a trained soldier, Sol. Grow up.

She clenched her hands into fists, annoyed at herself, at the cocktail of emotions that brewed in the background, tainting her with its future problems.

"Looking for someone, Princess?" The gentle nuzzle of cool mist tapped at her bare back, the dress Alix had chosen leaving her birthmark exposed. A sigh of unfiltered relief loosened her chest as she glanced over her shoulder. She studied his raven black hair, combed back into a messy knot with a leather band. Although still bruised, his face seemed calmer, more relaxed now that everything was over.

When she glanced up to meet his gaze, he was already watching her.

Sol smiled. "Not anymore."

CHAPTER FORTY-NINE

SECRETS FOR THE WIND

Thankfully, there weren't many spectators. Sol had expected a courtyard full of nobles, adding to the nausea she felt as she descended the castle steps. But when she finally looked up to examine what awaited, it was pleasantly empty.

To the right, situated over rows of simple rosewood chairs, was the Stone Ledge Nobility. Cattya's mother—obvious by their identical scowl and blue eyes—glared at her as she passed. Another woman sat beside her, clad in a scarlet gown and a silken curtain of straight black hair. She did not meet Sol's gaze.

Behind the Stone Ledge nobility, the Ladies of Niome greeted her with kind smiles, melting some of the icy atmosphere. The women emitted a calming, collective aura Sol appreciated as she continued cataloging the guests.

On the left side, also sitting on a pair of chairs, was a couple Sol didn't recognize. They were elegant, but not in the obnoxious manner the other Southerners exuded. The woman wore a casual coat and trousers, her plump figure mirroring that of her partner's beside her. They watched Sol and her Court silently as they made their way down the bare middle of the yard. With the way the chairs flanked them, Sol felt like she was walking down an aisle.

Sawyer seemed to feel similarly, as she whispered, "Never thought I'd be walking down an aisle with my father at the end of it."

Indeed, King Semmena and his Court stood beneath the cover of a massive, full tree, its leaves dancing to the ground with the wind.

Samara, Gina, and Gaven stood silently behind their King Regent, Jeriyah seemingly absent from the meeting. Besides a row of kingsmen posted by the gate a few ways away, that was it.

The Yarrow Court, the Semmena Court, and a couple of nobles who seemed ready to hang Sol by her throat.

She supposed it could have been worse.

"I'll admit, the unpredictability of your Vows made them quite entertaining, Niece." Semmena wore a thick, fur-lined cloak over his white tunic, his crown solid atop his head as he watched their every move, up until Sol and her Court was also beneath the shade of the tree.

As Alix came to a low bow in front of him, the rest of her Court dispersed to the sideline.

"Majesty," Alix said. "You must excuse me—High Scribe Jeriyah has requested me in the libraries."

Semmena waved him away. "Go on, Bennet."

Feeling incredibly vulnerable, Sol messed with her fingernails as she clasped her hands behind her back. To the King, she held her chest high—to everyone behind her, she showed her nerves.

And that's how it would have to be for now.

She donned the calmest mask she could muster and smiled. "I like the new gardens."

Semmena eyed the gardens behind them, full of lilies and roses that bled their sweet fragrance into the air.

"Your Royal Hand planted them," said Samara, tossing her twin braids over her shoulders. She looked over to Nina who stood off to Sol's left. "I would have much preferred tulips."

Sol glanced sidelong at Nina who didn't so much as falter in her carefully crafted stoicism. "Fortunately, they weren't planted for you, Lady Samara," Nina said. A subtle shine glinted in her green eyes. "But I will keep your preferences dutifully in mind."

Samara's jaw twitched with annoyance as she cut her gaze back to Sol.

"Casimir, step forward." Arnold Semmena rolled his eyes, utterly uninterested in anything anyone else had to say other than himself.

Cas obeyed, albeit hesitantly. He separated from Nina's side, Sawyer furrowing her brows after him as he stepped beside Sol. They locked eyes for a moment, sharing the confusion.

"Here is the thing," the King continued, pacing along the base of the tree. "There was meant to be only one survivor. One plea granted." He looked between them both, toying with his Wielder ring. "Sol, if you were the sole survivor, the tradition of the Vows would be expunged. Casimir, during the final duel, I promised you pardon if you were the survivor instead."

Semmena crossed his arms over his chest, stopping his pacing beside Gina. The Noble hand wore a navy-blue dress, reminiscent to the one Sol had worn during the Royal Dinner what seemed like ages ago. Her lilac eyes were fixed on Sol, a scowl strung to her lips.

Sol swallowed a lump in her throat.

I have a bad feeling about this.

"But you are both here before me," Semmena said. "And I can only grant one of the pleas."

Sol met Sawyer's eyes. Her cousin looked away.

"So, since you refused the fight to announce a dutiful winner, you will do it here. Now." Gina finished, retrieving a box from a chair on the front row. She opened it, revealing a worn, ancient parchment rolled and secured by a crimson thread. Beside it was a stunning crown, black enough to be carved by the night sky itself. Violet jewels were strung through the peaks, silver vines rolling over them with elegant twists.

Purple, black, and silver.

A shaky breath escaped her lips as she looked back at Cas. His chest steadily rose and fell with calculated breaths, silver eyes dazzling like the heart of a flame as he met her gaze. She could see it then–the same glint of longing he had let slip in the colosseum, the yearning of being unable to return to his people. And although he gave her a chance to end things before she used Lora's magic, Sol couldn't guess what would have happened had she not done so.

Even after the tenderness at the healer's quarter—she would always be second to Eswin.

I don't think the amount of time you spend in a place is indicative of how much you're allowed to miss it.

The words he spoke when they had been in the tunnels at the Gods' Villa echoed. Although Sol had only been in Rimemere for weeks, it filled a hole within her, a rightness nothing else had been able to before. Even with the absolute horror of the Vows and the despicable Semmena court, Sol knew the kingdom was a piece of...

Home.

The way Cas looked away from her in that moment solidified the suspicion he felt the same for Eswin.

"We don't have all day," Samara drawled with a sigh. "Either the Vows are dissolved, or Casimir is Prince of Eswin again. Someone choose—unless you'd rather draw blades."

The nobility around them was silent. Sol wanted to look over at Sawyer or Nina for comfort, for guidance. But she didn't dare tear her gaze from the man before her.

Her attention remained on the Prince of Shadows.

"Cas," she breathed, taking a step forward as the wind whispered a caress through her hair, the same breeze cutting straight between them with a tendril of leaves.

His eyes dulled with resolve. "There is no choice, Majesty. The victory is hers."

The King grinned. "Excellent."

Before Sol could speak, Cas turned away and walked back to the Castle doors, leaving her with the thought that although the Vows hadn't ended in a marriage, something told her they chained her to something else entirely worse.

SAWYER

In that moment, Sawyer didn't know what Cas would say. When her father had announced his scheme in the colosseum, a similar feeling had gripped her—one of total loss.

She knew Cas. She knew his duty to Rimemere, although forced initially, was genuine. She knew he loved them, knew his gentility beneath the rough exterior. They'd grown together, bled together, cried, and cursed the King together.

Surely, he would let Sol win.

But like with any sentient being, emotions are volatile. Sawyer knew it to her core. Something that might have been a priority one second could perish in a plume of indifference the next.

She brags she would kill her father given the chance. But would she?

Cas's connection to Eswin withered when his mother and sister Maya vanished. But did it?

Sawyer didn't have to see Cas's face to know that dissonance was exposed. From where she stood, she could see it in Sol's delicate features. Her lips were pressed into a tight line, brows and eyes pulled close as she watched him, waiting for his answer.

Her cousin stepped forward, stopped by a gust of wind so sudden it was as if Winderlyn himself blew Sol back. "Cas—"

"There is no choice, Majesty. The victory is hers."

As soon as Cas turned away and made his way to the castle, Sawyer went after him.

Shadows spilled from his footsteps, leaving sparks of violet in their wake. She ducked around servants heading to assist the Semmena court, shouldering past the students who had gathered by the courtyards to watch the commotion.

As Cas took the final step into the foyer, Sawyer slammed a hand to his shoulder, whirling him around to face her. "Hey, what was…"

His eyes were bleak. Lifeless. She knew the amount of times he'd been forced to choose between Eswin and Rimemere—between Eswin and the Yarrows—weighed on him. She also knew her father did it on purpose, the horrible, Jinn-loving asshole.

She dropped her hand. "You look troubled."

"I'm not in the mood, Sawyer."

"I have things to tell you, so get in the mood and follow me."

Sawyer didn't wait to see if he complied, only smiled in relief as footsteps and Shadows followed her up to the third floor.

She hurried past the libraries and the lingering courtiers, all surely eyeing how Casimir Xanthos and Sawyerlynn Yarrow entered her rooms just after he returned from Sol Yarrow's vows.

Scandalous.

Giving the remaining audience a charged glare, she shouldered the door open and pulled Cas inside.

She regretted not cleaning, but she didn't do it for herself, and she had no visitors. So, Cas would have to find a spot in the sea of orange peels, blades, and ashes to sit before she spoke.

Because he had to be sitting for it.

Her oldest friend ran a hand through his hair, pulling at the band that tied it back to let it loose. "I want to go give an offering to Warren, Sawyer."

"The god of Souls can wait, Cas." She signaled to her bed which was an unmade mess, but at least had no residue of burnt paper or clothes. When he arched a brow at her, she sighed. "Just sit. I will stand."

When he finally did, Sawyer told him everything. Telling Nina in the pantheon had been a solace she hadn't realized she needed, and now that the truth about her survival in Melisandre was in one of her friend's memories, the others needed to have it too—especially the one who had been plummeted with Dark Magic.

Sawyer recalled the encounter at the third legion's base, introduced him to Morna, then had to go back to the beginning when he looked at her like she had gone mad. As her story progressed, his eyes softened, and by the time she finished telling him about her father and Lorkin, he was standing directly in front of her.

A beat of silence passed through them as she chewed on her nails. "Does Nina know?" Cas asked.

Sawyer nodded.

"Does Alix?"

"I haven't had the chance to tell him. He's been dealing with Jeriyah. The High Scribe has been draining."

Cas hummed, thrumming his fingers at his chin. "Well, Sawyer, it's your turn to sit down."

Sawyer expected Cas to tell her about the Vows. He did—but, to her horror, they had not been the worst thing he and Sol faced at the Gods' Villa. She had a sense he skipped through a lot of it, but when he got to Aquarene's Trial, he went into quieter detail. As if it was a fragile memory, one he didn't want to rouse.

By the end of his story, Sawyer had accidentally burned a hole in her duvet. "Okay, but Sol told you a Jinn told her how to save you from copper poisoning?"

He nodded, kicking aside a clean spot on the floor to sit on. He sank into her orange carpet.

"Is it possible my sweet, fragile cousin was in a state of shock? Or that the key wasn't copper since the only proven cure for it is a total blood replacement?"

There was just no way. Nothing on this dimensional plane could purify Wielder blood tainted by copper. The metal clung to the magic in the blood, eating and eroding it until the Wielder quite literally died.

"No, Sawyer. To both of your questions."

She blinked at him. "What was the antidote, then?"

"It's best not to say."

"Oh, you and Sol have secrets now?"

Cas sighed and shut his eyes, obviously emotionally and physically spent. A pang of guilt punched her in the stomach—he deserved some grace.

"How are your wounds? How do you feel? How's your—" Cold alarm flared in her chest as she cut her gaze to his arm, the one that held his tattoo. It had been almost three weeks since she'd filled it in the cell.

Sawyer stood, knocking over mugs of ale in her haste as she crawled to him. "Your tattoo, it must be—" She grabbed his arm, pulling up the sleeve of his suit, readying her wielder ring against her forearm at the same time. She stopped, glancing up at him. "It's full."

Cas looked past her. "It is, yes."

"What the fuck happened between you and Sol out there, Casimir?"

Sawyer gaped at him as he stood, bringing down his sleeve as he walked to her door. "A whole lot I want to forget. I'll be at Warren's Temple."

He placed his hand on the knob, turning it as Sawyer stood.

"Cas," she said, still unsure of what to make of their meeting. "For the love of all the gods, please don't fall in love with Sol."

CHAPTER FIFTY

Choices for the Dead

No matter how strongly she begged, the healers refused to clear her. Sol had stormed after Cas, a flare of something foreign bubbling in her stomach when she saw he went with Sawyer instead, not sparing her a single look.

Look at me, she wanted to yell. *I'm sorry.*

Nina stayed with her in her healer pod for hours until sundown, promising her a whole week of marvelous rest and pampering starting tomorrow before they took her to Emberdon's temple for her Awakening.

It had to be done by a blood relative, and since Sawyer was the only one, it had to be done on her turf.

The fact Sawyer was her only living blood relative burrowed in her mind for long after Nina left, leaving her with a strange feeling until she finally drifted to sleep.

When Sol awoke, she was alone. The healer's quarters was silent, smelling softly of the ginger and lime tonic by her bedside. The firelights along the walls were extinguished, save for a lonely one atop the healer's main work area in a far corner. Candlewax dripped beside a mess of papers there, landing with a sizzle.

Careful not to disrupt the strange, swollen silence, Sol sat up.

Her body ached in places she didn't know could, and her temples squeezed with a plea to lie back down. But she couldn't. Not as her birthmark pulsed in warning, sending waves of heat to the edges like steel brands.

She grimaced at the pain, but it was nothing compared to the panic that gripped her by the throat as she glanced to the door.

It was ajar—the hallway beyond completely dark.

Please let this be a nightmare. Please.

She sent a silent prayer to Warren, hoping she was already on his good graces as she stood from her cot and faced the open door.

Nina had said guards would be posted outside along with one of them. Surely, if there was trouble, they would have woken her.

Unless they couldn't.

Swallowing the acidic anxiety, Sol looked around, hoping to find something to use as a weapon.

A whimper beyond the door paused her search.

"H-Hello?" Her voice was hoarse and brittle. She inched forward, barefoot, without a weapon, and with the sinking feeling the peace following the two weeks she'd lived had been too much to ask for.

There was no response.

Carefully, Sol pulled the door back fully to peer into the hallway. A useless risk since it was wholly dark. "Hello?"

As she stepped beyond the door, a skittering along the tile raked its noise across her skin. She turned to it.

The temperature plummeted, her birthmark screaming insults at her as she met the gaze of two flashing, bulging orbs.

When the Jinn smiled, its teeth shining in the darkness, she only sighed. "Are you one of the ones for me or against me?"

The smell of rotting flesh inched closer. *"Guess."*

She ran the opposite way.

Darkness engulfed her at first until she burst through the glass doors of the healer's wing and into the castle's main halls, quickly turning to the staircase. She begged her legs to push forward, the splintering pain that wrapped around them leaving her gasping as she came to the foot of the staircase. The silver moonlight shone through the high windows behind her, illuminating the way to the floor her Court resided.

But where others were too.

"Fuck." Sol pulled at her hair as she doubled over for breath.

She couldn't allow it to follow her up. She had to lead it out.

"Your mother had such a wonderful smell, Yarrow." The Jinn's voice wrapped around her temples like a thorny crown, the clacking of talons inching closer. "But you smell so much better."

Sol propelled forward, throwing herself against a random, massive set of wooden doors, fumbling with the hollow, circular brass handles to pull them open.

Where was her Court? Where was Cas?

Tears fell in streams as a whimper escaped her trembling lips. She was no match for a Jinn. Maybe a Lower she could punch, but Sol had no idea what she was against. And she wasn't looking to find out.

The door finally gave to her pleas, shifting open enough to let her through. Sol could melt at the momentary repose as the fresh, late spring air greeted her into its embrace.

The relief didn't last long.

"Noble to choose coming out here alone instead of seeking help, Yarrow."

Sol shook with horror at the voice, worse than any of the Mind Slayers she had encountered until that point. She kept her eyes at the ground, shuddering when she saw the arm's length talons, dipped in black, and connecting directly to webbed, yellow feet. Thick, rancid goo dripped across from nail to nail.

Unable to move, Sol only started with tears in her eyes as the creature bent in half, the contortion making its head hang upside down by its feet.

Its black eyes flashed white, saliva pooling at its mouth. "It was that same stupid little heart that killed Irene."

Sol let out a breathless gasp as the creature's claws plunged through her chest.

CAS

Cas instantly felt her. Even if his Shadows failed to alert him of the Jinn's insidious arrival, he felt her fear like molten metal on his skin.

He was making his way down the staircase, the castle cloaked in night, when the feeling made him stop dead in his tracks.

He ran down the rest of it and thrusted his Shadows out, frantic to locate her. It was his turn to be posted outside her door, a turn he was late too after taking more time than anticipated beneath the castle's main floor within Warren's Temple. He willed his Shadows to search there first, panic itching at his neck when it was empty.

Jumping into the foyer, he stopped. He reeled his Shadows back. The castle was completely dark, as if someone had blown out the firelights, and extinguished the life within.

Cas inhaled, closing his eyes.

Sol.

He narrowed his senses, searching for her voice. For her sweet scent of lavender.

Sol.

Her name pulsed through him like a prayer, encompassing his every thought until she was all he saw.

Sol Yarrow.

When her scream shredded through the foyer, vibrating the ground itself, Cas tore his eyes open. With the sort of calmness before a tempest, he strode to the front doors, letting the full force of his Wards engulf him in violet flames.

NINA

Nina had her sword angled at the Lower Jinn, her nightgown tattered from tearing through her bedroom door. The Jinn thought a copper chain would hold her.

The Jinn was wrong.

The place where the chain had snagged on her legs as she had stepped over it burned, but not as hotly as the fury in her chest.

Looking directly at the thing's flapping, waxy wings, Nina said, "Move."

It croaked a laugh. "No."

To her left, Sawyer's door rattled, also secured by copper chains.

"Move, before Sawyer gets out here." Nina's magic flared at her fingertips, aiding the Fire Wielder with the wooden door. But she didn't need it. The wall beside it shook, rumbling with warning before it ignited in a wall of flame.

Nina smiled as Sawyer walked straight through them, armed with her twin swords and an expression that portrayed just why she was the Royal General.

Sawyer's eyes flared like embers as she turned to the Jinn. "You chose the wrong fucking day to bother us."

CHAPTER FIFTY-ONE
FATE OF FIRE

Sol thought it would be painful, but she felt nothing. Only a pinching and stinging around her chest as the talons sliced through her body, then nothing. She was in total darkness. Conscious only of the fact she was surrounded by night, in an abyss.

No.

As she focused on her blindness with increased attention, she realized she wasn't anywhere, or everywhere, but instead floating within a sea of Shadows. She looked down at her hand, stark white against the tiny particles. She could see her feet, her legs, and her hair flowing down her chest.

Sol's body was only thinly covered by a veil of mist, hanging around her like a loose dress. She touched the translucent fabric with her fingers, but she couldn't feel it. It was as if an additional layer of air prevented her from touching, seeing, or smelling.

Back in the in-between?

A ruffling sounded from behind her, making her tense. She focused on steady breaths as she turned toward the sound.

Sol stepped forward, entranced by the figure that shimmered before her. Then, as if in a daze, took another step.

"Sol." The figure rippled as it came into view, forming from the Shadows themselves.

Sol fell to her knees. "Mom?"

Irene smiled tenderly, a smile Sol treasured and had kept at the front line of her thoughts for difficult days. Her mother looked beautiful, just as she always had. Her black hair was loosely braided into a knot held up by an ivory bandana. She wore a beige dress, spotty with paint and ash. Her sapphire eyes shone, like beacons in the dark as Sol darted forward, nearly crawling toward her.

Irene met her halfway, enveloping her in an embrace. Instantly, Sol began to sob.

She hadn't been able to recall what her mother's hug had felt like. After her murder, she had tried to remember, but nothing comforted her the same. Not keeping Irene's old, unwashed aprons, not tending to her thyme, mint, and lavender gardens so she'd smell like her. Nothing had filled the hole her Mother's death had blasted through her.

But, at least at this moment, Sol felt whole.

"Mom," she whimpered, grabbing the fabric of her Mother's dress. Again, she couldn't quite grasp it, couldn't quite feel everything as fully as she wanted to.

Her mother stroked the back of her head. "You shouldn't be here, Sol."

Sol tightened her grip. "I don't care."

"We don't have much time, Sunshine." Irene pulled away slightly, grabbing Sol's face and caressing her cheeks. She smiled sadly. "You look so much like your father."

"Mom, where am I? Am I dead?" Sol wiped at her face with the back of her hands, trying to clear the tears.

Irene wiped them for her with the edge of her dress. "Nearly. You're somewhere in between." She dropped the dress and grasped Sol's hands. "I don't have much time, Sol. I can't be here. But when I felt you, I—"

The air around them spiked in temperature, and Sol's cold skin protested at the sudden heat. Her lungs, it seemed, disliked the change as well.

Sol coughed. "I don't understand—"

"Sol, listen to me." Irene shook Sol slightly by the shoulders, positioning her so they met eyes. Through painful breaths, Sol looked at her. "I can only assume you being here means they found you," Irene continued. "You can trust them. Mavka's Jinn. The memories they show you will be true, they will not lie to you, they owe you and all Yarrows truth." Her mother scanned Sol's face and body. "Where are you? Are you in Yavenharrow?"

Sol shook her head, for a moment struggling to remember where she was.

"I'm in Rimemere," Sol said finally.

Irene's face relaxed. "With your Court?"

Sol nodded.

She saw their faces in her mind. Did they know she was probably about to die at the hands of a Mind Slayer? She was so sick of near-death experiences. Sol didn't think she'd be as lucky this time.

"Sol, you can trust them. You must remain with your Court, do you understand?" Irene shook her slightly. "Only together will you all be able to defeat this."

Sol shook her head, an icy-hot numbness beginning to take hold of her. "Defeat what? The Jinn gate? Mom, in your letter—"

"I'm so sorry, Sunshine. I'm sorry I couldn't help you with your magic, I tried." Her mother looked behind her, panic suddenly gripping her features. "We are running out of time. I must go."

Sol gripped her harder. "Please don't. Mom, I can't do this. I don't know what I'm doing."

Slowly, her Mother stood and smiled down as she gently pulled her up.

"No one ever knows what they are doing. You will make a far better Queen than I ever did, Sunshine." Irene pressed a kiss to Sol's forehead. "I made mistakes. As a Queen, as a Mother, as a woman. And I'm sorry those mistakes seem to have followed you."

Her Mother pressed a hand to her chest, then the other to Sol's. As heat threatened to swallow them, her hand was a cool embrace.

"But you have the right combination of power to end things. None of us before did."

Sol shook her head. She didn't understand anything. She just wanted this moment forever. But she could feel the end nearing, anxiety and dread pooling in her stomach as her Mother's image faltered. Tears swelled in Sol's eyes.

"Mom—"

"Stay with your Court, Sol. Those three are your strongest allies."

Sol blinked as panic engulfed her, as the air around them heated. "Three?"

"The answers are in Yavenharrow, Sol. Remember that."

Irene's image shook and faltered, but Sol still watched her sapphire eyes gleam one last time. "I love you so much, Sunshine. You're everything I could've hoped for."

Sol sobbed. "I love you, Mom."

Irene faded and Sol was once again thrust into overwhelming darkness. Except this time, the darkness slammed into her like a stone wall. Not a wall, she realized as her cheek throbbed with pain. But a floor.

Sol winced as her body flattened on what seemed to be a smooth, gray floor. She attempted to sit up but resorted to slowly lifting herself with her hands as her body trembled with protests. She rubbed her forehead and looked around her. And instantly froze.

No.

The house was dim, all candles and lights unlit. Sol could smell the mint and thyme, could see her mother's studio through the ever-familiar door that was slightly ajar. She was on the floor at the foot of the stairs, stairs she had run down and up, fallen from, and danced through as a child.

Sol braced a hand on the spiral, smooth railing, and stood.

She knew what night this was.

She knew what memory she was in.

The booming music flowing in through the open windows gave away it was the annual Yaven Port Celebration, a town-made holiday for sailors trademarked by dances and drinks in the Yavenharrow town square which is where Sol had been that night.

The fact her mother stood with her back against the front door, facing the back door, made Sol realize this wasn't a memory at all.

This is what happened after Sol ran.

After her mother had pushed her out the door when she returned for the night, locked it, and yelled at her to find Lora. Sol backed away toward the wall in horror, realizing she would witness what had truly transpired all those years ago.

Her chest felt like it may burst with terror.

Was this what Mind Slayers did? Would she be stuck in this scene forever? Was it her purgatory?

Hot tears burned behind her eyes.

"You are breaching a sacred blood oath by being here," her mother said. Her black hair was in knots around her face, as if she had been running. It blew around her face with each of her heavy breaths and her blue eyes were dimmed with fear as she beheld something past the staircase, past Sol.

As Sol turned, she trembled.

"Too bad we don't answer to blood, unlike you, Wielder filth."

The Mind Slayer was absolutely horrid. It made the ones Sol had seen pleasant.

The one that towered toward Irene was giant, at least eight feet tall, and a door frame wide.

Unlike the ones that crept behind it, the leader had orange, crackling skin, still attached to protruding bones around its limbs. The skin melted off of it like candle wax, and its talons were an unearthly shade of green. It stomped forward, its eyes flashing white, then black, like a lighthouse beckoning its sailors. It had long, stringy black hair that twisted into the gaping holes within its skin.

Sol turned away, suppressing the compulsion to vomit.

Behind it were Lower Jinn, not that it made things any better. The blue-gray, decaying piles of rot were just as paralyzing.

"Mavka won't stand for this," her mother said. She leaned over to her right, fumbling with something behind the wall. She withdrew a sword, angled and ready for a fight.

"I don't answer to Loumallet or his whore," the orange Mind Slayer announced, its hollow voice booming through the house.

Sol stared at the sword as it became engulfed in a kaleidoscope of colors, almost as if doused in an oily flame.

"We answer to the mighty Lorkin," the Jinn on the right added, cackling. This one had a white, festering wound on its forehead.

Irene gave them an unamused laugh. "You all are taking council from that nasty thing?" Her mother eyed the orange creature. "Gods help you."

"Enough banter, Irene," the colossal Mind Slayer growled, getting down on all fours. "Now, where is she?"

The cold smile dissipated from her Mother's beautiful face. "You'll never find her," she whispered.

"Oh, we will. After we take care of you," the creature behind the orange one said, dropping to the floor like a snake. It slithered forward, taking its place at the front, protecting the odd one out.

Sol wanted to scream. To run to her Mother, to launch herself in front of her like she should've done all those wretched years ago.

Her mother had been everything. Everything good in the world.

Sol struggled to move, but she was pinned to the spot, cursed to watch as her Mother brought her sword up in front of her. "Come and get it, then."

They lunged.

The one in the front flew first, directly at Irene in the blink of an eye. It clawed at her, but she efficiently deflected its talons with a sweep of her blade. The creature groaned in pain, the Ward around the blade clearly wounding it. Again, it pounced.

Irene jumped, stomping down on its arm, and with a bellow of fury, slammed her blade straight into the creature's skull. Black blood poured from it, making the gray floors even darker.

"Why even come after her?" her mother heaved. "She has no magic."

The orange monster laughed, a sound that made every inch of Sol recoil. "Did you really think you'd be able to fool everyone, Irene? Do you really think the King Regent doesn't know where you are?"

"Is that who sent you? Arnold?"

The creature cocked its head, flashing a smile full of razor-sharp teeth Sol saw too often in her nightmares. "Perhaps."

"Or perhaps someone else is out for your disgusting family's demise," one of the other creatures snarled.

It didn't give Irene a chance to respond as it lunged at her, teeth clacking, and jaws snapping closed around her ankle.

Sol screamed, the sound echoing her Mother's. Absolute rage flashed over her mother's face as she brought her sword down on the demon's neck, decapitating it before kicking off its head from her leg. Her wound had already begun to bleed.

The orange Mind Slayer inhaled deeply, its eyes strobing. "Delicious."

"Your blood has always been the sweetest, Irene." The final blue creature stumbled forward in a serpentine motion, its forked tongue tasting the air.

"Who sent you?" Irene's voice was low, commanding, a tone Sol had never heard her use.

"You have a lot of enemies," the creature said, angling its head an unnatural ninety degrees to the right. "Which one sent us, I wonder?"

Irene feigned a maneuver to the right, then slashed down left, cutting the creature's skull clean in half.

She shook her head. "Those things were pathetic, Lorkin, even for you."

The thing, Lorkin, rose to its hind limbs, once again a tower in front of Irene. "They weren't supposed to pose a threat, Irene Yarrow Gresnyn."

Instantly, the blood pooling around Irene's ankle shimmered and evaporated, dissipating into crimson droplets. She winced.

"Warren does always demand more of you, doesn't he?"

Lorkin strode forward, its giant clawed feet screeching against the floors. Sol felt her breath quicken, and she couldn't ease the shivering that began from her head then spread down to her feet.

She didn't want to see this.

She knew how it ended.

Yet, her eyes were glued to the scene, as if hands themselves were holding them open. She shuddered.

"No worries. There will be more by the end of this." Lorkin's eyes flashed. "But your Gods don't want blood from dead Wielders, huh?"

Irene yelled and thrust her blade forward, but Lorkin effortlessly evaded with a cold, sinister laugh.

Sol had never seen her Mother fight, but she made her own skills look like child's play. Irene slashed and parried expertly, fluidly, as if the sword was a mere extension of her arm. The rainbow of sparks shone around them, and where they hit the creature, its skin bubbled.

"You'll never Awaken her magic. You'll never get what you want," she breathed through hits, landing a slash on Lorkin's legs.

The thing pulled its leg closer to itself, dragging Irene with it. "Who says we don't already know how?" It smiled, its teeth shining in the dimness.

There were noises beyond the front door, a rustling of trees and leaves that made Irene glance behind her.

The glance cost her.

Sol screamed with pure sorrow and terror as Lorkin plunged its hand into her Mother's chest. Blood sprayed everywhere and her face contoured with pain.

"Mom!" Sol cried, trying with everything in her soul to run to her, to fight for her, to do anything other than stare.

But she couldn't.

"She's going to destroy you," Irene said through tight lips, her breathing labored.

Lorkin scoffed. "If she is as pathetic as you, Irene Yarrow, your daughter will be just as easy to kill in due time."

There was a knock at the front door, frantic and familiar.

Sol screamed even louder at the people she knew would be beyond the door. At the fact she now knew those knocks, the sound of them coming, had distracted her mother.

Irene laughed, spitting in Lorkin's face. "The secrets die with me. I let you win, fucker."

Lorkin removed its claws from Irene, her heart, beating and broken in its hands. Sol felt tears rush out, her face hot, and her lungs refusing to work. She cried even harder when her Mother's body fell from the air, landing in the foyer. Broken, bleeding. Heartless.

Sol watched in horror as Lorkin held up her mother's heart, licked it, then swallowed it whole before hovering over her body. The knocks became frantic. Then, pounding as the people beyond tried to break the door down.

"Yarrow blood has always been the most delicious," it sneered before sprinting on all fours out the back door just as Sol and Leo burst through the entrance.

CHAPTER FIFTY-TWO

Cas

The wood splintered beneath Cas's touch. He stepped over the crumpling debris, his entire being focused only on her.

The weeks they spent together during the Vows were almost binding in a way he hadn't at all expected. Her sureness in herself while holding on to a raw humanity Cas could only hope he still had a shred of made him want to keep her safe, to ensure her light shone in the faces of those who refused to believe in it.

But another very different side of him wanted to keep that light hidden and to himself, safe from those who would abuse it. That side also found itself watching her as she smiled, wishing it would be toward him. Praying to have that dream of her again while he'd been under the Dark Spell.

Cas would take endless blasts of Void Magic if it meant he got to kiss Sol in the dreams they induced.

"Cas!" Nina slid to a stop next to him, grabbing his arm to steady herself.

Sawyer and Alix followed, wearing the same daunting expression he felt on his own face.

"Oh gods," Sawyer whispered.

He saw it then. Beyond the steps of the castle, past the rows of lilies and roses, the Mind Slayer gave them a wicked grin, its thin, needle-like teeth reflecting the moonlight as its obsidian talons held Sol by her chest.

Cas couldn't breathe as he noticed the blood dripping from their pointed tips.

"My, what a rare, rare sight," it hissed. It unrolled from its crouch, coming to its full height before them. It was just as repulsive as all other Mind Slayers he had seen, pallid and rotting, and all that was wrong with the world. Its pupil-less eyes blinked and flashed. "I've never had the pleasure of seeing the great Yarrow Court all together. Lorkin will be pleased."

The creature had Sol suspended in the air but facing away from them. Cas could make the outline of her birthmark, pulsing a subdued blue. He tried not to panic at the blindness, at not being able to see just how wounded she was, though he could barely make out the light rise and fall of her chest to indicate she still breathed. It didn't placate him much.

White-hot rage pulsed through him, his Wards following suit.

"Let her go." Nina's entire body flared neon as the land shook beneath them. Cas struggled against his self-restraint, against every fiber of his being that screamed to kill the demon and grab Sol. But without knowing exactly how deep into the memory transfer they were, it was a gamble he couldn't take.

Not with her.

"Get the people in the castle notified and safe," Sawyer ordered to Alix who gave her a quick nod before running back the way they came. She didn't break her gaze from Sol either.

"I don't think you want me to do that, Ninanette." The Mind Slayer's grin widened as it slowly turned Sol over. It hovered her closer, letting her body slump against its chest. It wrapped its limbs around her, laying its decaying, melting face on her shoulder.

Nina made a noise of either horror or dread.

Sol's gaze was completely hazed, a blinding-white, a mirror to the Mind Slayer's own sinister eyes. Three curved talons were staked clear through her chest. Cas had never seen a memory passage in action. He'd read of it and had nightmares about it. But this...

"We have seconds," Sawyer whispered. "Seconds to take her when it disconnects from her mind."

Nina shook, her magic sparkling and morphing with Cas's Shadows.

He didn't know what to do. They couldn't interrupt a memory passage not—

"We can't sever the connection, Nina." Sawyer held her friend's hand in her own. "We have to wait until whatever memory it's passing is done."

"We don't have time for that," Nina cried, stepping forward. Cas grabbed her shoulder, which she quickly shook off.

"If we sever it now, she dies, Nina. Wait." Sawyer pulled her back further, easing her all the way behind them.

Cas knew she was right. Severing an active memory passage was a death sentence for the captive.

"Oh, you all look absolutely petrified," the Mind Slayer laughed. "I'll make her death quick after this."

Noises arose behind them, surely from the students and other castle dwellers evacuating. Cas heard the distant rumble of metal, signaling the kingsmen were on their way.

"Who do you work for?" Sawyer's face was raw, calculating fury as she stepped toward the creature. "The answer will either doom you or save your miserable life."

"You Yarrows are so demanding," the creature purred. Its limbs twitched. "I'm only showing her what she wanted to know."

"Who do you work for?" Sawyer repeated face stoic and unreadable.

"Why are you talking to it!" Nina said through sobs. "Burn it!"

"I can't. Not until I know who sent it."

Nina was practically on the floor begging as Cas pulled her against him. She was absolutely freezing.

"Tell me, Sawyerlyn. Is it true Morna is your captive?" The Mind Slayer's eyes shone as its grin spread. "All to warn you of something you won't figure out anyway. She's the worst of Mavka's followers."

Smoke curled around Sawyer's shoulders. "You ally with Lorkin."

"And you Ninanette?" The creature's eyes shifted to Nina. "How are you taking the news? It's not too late to come to the winning side."

"I hope you suffer wherever you come from," Nina seethed.

Cas watched Sol. Whatever bickering his Court was having with the thing, he didn't care. All he cared about was the woman before him. With every heartbeat, his blood called to her, muting all other sounds and feelings and thoughts. All he could see was Sol.

Sol.

Sol.

So, at the exact moment her eyes fluttered closed and she slumped against the thing, Cas launched at her.

He kicked the Mind Slayer's arm away with a swift, potent motion, ripping its claws from her chest. Pulling her against him, he willed his Shadows to spread below them as they tumbled toward the ground. He managed to twist her on top of him mid-fall, and a ripple of pain radiated from his entire body as he collided against the pavilion.

"Sol," he panted softly. "Sol, can you hear me?"

Cas didn't wait to see what his Court did as a Ward erupted around them.

CHAPTER FIFTY-THREE

In Cold Blood

Coming out of the Mind Slayer's mental prison was aggravatingly disorienting.

The first thing that returned was Sol's sense of touch. She felt the cold, tiled ground beneath her, pressing on every aching part of her body. Next, was her sense of smell. She could scent the lilies and the soft afterthought of rosewood and sage. The distinct odor of death was also thick in the air, prompting her eyes to pry open. A headache bloomed at her temples.

"Easy, Sol," a soft voice called.

Her vision danced and struggled to focus as she blinked and lifted her hand to her face.

"Sol."

She groaned and looked toward the voice. "Cas?"

His face slowly came into focus, directly in front of her, leaning over her side while his violet Ward shimmered around them.

Sol settled her attention on him. His brows were furrowed, and his eyes were pure starlight as they reflected the colors of his Ward.

He laid a hand on her own, which she didn't realize she cradled against her chest.

"Your wounds, are they deep?"

Sol blinked and looked down at her torso, suddenly aware of the sting. Blood pooled in her hands and stained her thin nightgown completely. That was enough to make her remember exactly where she was.

She could make out muffled noises beyond the Ward and could vaguely see the earth beneath them rumble with power. The remnants of the Mind Slayer's vision flooded into her mind. For the second time in one night, she felt the anger kindle. Had the vision with her mother been real? Or was it another dream, induced by the month's events?

Sol looked at him. "Lower the Ward."

Cas lowered his hand and surveyed her. "What?"

"Lower the Ward."

He remained silent for a moment. "What did it show you?"

Sol braced a hand on the floor below them, pouring her entire remaining energy reservoir into standing as the weight of the month's events threatened to pull her down. Her knees wobbled, but she straightened fully.

Cas stood with her and held her arm "Sol—"

"Lower the Ward." She held his gaze. "That's an order."

They stood face to face for what seemed like minutes as neither of them agreed to break their stare. Ultimately, Cas looked away. "Don't leave my side."

The Ward melted from top to bottom.

The courtyard that had been a poised scene of serenity just hours before was now a chilling mess. The tree they had stood beneath to solidify the end of the Vows was completely uprooted, laying sideways as plumes of smoke rose from its roots. The grass was scorched into ash, and the fountains that had once adorned the hedges spilled in tattered pieces. Nina had the creature locked on the ground, her arms wrapped around its torso as Sawyer lifted a thin blade engulfed in flames. As she made to bring it down, the Jinn met Sol's gaze and grinned.

"Stop," Sol ordered, her voice stern and low.

Sawyer paused.

"Drop your weapon." Sol walked toward them, heavily aware of Cas's unfaltering presence right beside her.

The Jinn's grin widened.

Nina watched Sol cautiously, not flinching against the Mind Slayer's thrashing. "Sol, what are you—"

"Sawyer, drop your weapon," Sol said.

Her cousin's blade extinguished as she lowered it to her side, still not removing herself from where she stood. She also watched Sol with a perplexed expression but said nothing as she walked up to the creature.

Sol looked down at it. "Who is Lorkin?" Her pulse raced beneath the gashes on her chest, her birthmark stinging like hot oil on her back. Still, it wasn't as painful as the emotional anguish fighting to control her.

If only she wouldn't have left.

If only she wouldn't have *fled*.

The Mind Slayer kept its protruding, onyx eyes on her as they leveled. They flashed white as Sol glared. "Answer me."

"The memory hit quite a sore spot, I see."

Sawyer leaned closer, embers crackling around her wrists. "The Princess asked you a question."

Impatience hazed her vision. "I'm growing tired of this."

The sounds of chaos continued all around them, as well as the scraping of metal as what Sol guessed were guards rushed their way. She remained focused on the Mind Slayer as it repeated, "I will never reveal my master's location."

"Then you're no use to me."

There was an overwhelming thirst for vengeance as she stretched her arm to Sawyer. "Your sword."

Wordlessly, her cousin obliged.

Cas tightened his grip around her bicep. "Sol—"

"Although I didn't have a chance to taste her myself," the Mind Slayer taunted as it leaned closer, its breath inches away from her face. The blade trembled in her grasp. "I heard your mother's blood was some of the most *delicious Lorkin* ever tasted."

Sol let out a roar of fury as she stood and used her entire weight to impale the creature in its skull. As the sound of death crackled, Sol saw her mother, fighting to buy her time that night seven years ago. As she brought the sword back up and tears flowed down her face, she saw her mother's pain as the thing named Lorkin suspended her in the air.

As she brought the sword down again and again until the creature's head rolled to the ground beside her. She saw her mother's beating heart devoured by a creature who had wanted her instead.

"Sol, it's dead."

She shouldn't have run. She shouldn't have bothered to knock and just tore the door down instead.

Sol trembled as hands wrapped around her own, suspending the blade above the creature's tattered body. She could no longer see through the tears but vaguely felt the hands remove the blade from her grasp.

"It's okay." Hands remained around her own as a different set of arms gently encircled her waist and pulled her down to sit on the ground. "You're okay, Sol."

She sobbed harder. She was engulfed in a strong, careful hug from behind as she slumped back against Cas's chest. Though his heart was as erratic as her own, his steady breathing began to lull her and willed her to match it. She leaned her head to rest on him as she continued to silently cry.

Cas laid his head on her own. "It's okay, Sol," he said softly. "You're safe."

CHAPTER FIFTY-FOUR

Samara

Samara never got used to it. Granted, she didn't use Dark Magic often, but every time she did she felt equipped enough to handle it.

She never was.

That familiar ache skirted through her bones, making her skin sensitive and sore as she leaned on the wall of the main courtyard. The castle broke into a frenzy as soon as the Jinn signature spread, sending the nobility into a panic.

Idiots.

Samara was on her way to the kitchens for a glass of ale when she felt it, that cold embrace of Loumallet's children.

She watched the Yarrow Princess butcher it through the simple Enchantment, one that hid her in place beside the gardens. The Princess bringing her sword down again and again, even after the creature was nothing but mush, was mesmerizing. It took her whole Court to stop her.

Taking a drag from the Kerproot cigar, Samara shook her head. "One down, I guess."

"Each one counts," Gaven took the cigar from her fingers, leaning on a wall beside her. He stayed behind and in the shadows of the courtyard arches as he didn't have the cover of Void Magic to shield him. "Especially Lorkin's Mind Slayers."

Samara shrugged. "I figured her mother would have at least told her about seeking aid with Mavka. Leave her without magic or knowledge of her best allies?" She motioned for the cigar. "Sol was set up for failure."

She hadn't believed it at first, either. The Jinn, children of the Void itself. Allies? Samara thought Irene was mad. But when she looked through the box the late Queen left her in charge of, her opinion changed.

Quickly.

"Sawyer knows about Lorkin," Gaven said. "Won't be long before they piece together that Semmena is working with the Jinn who killed Irene."

"Too bad that knowledge doesn't do much." Samara extinguished the cigar with a tendril of Shadows. "Not until we figure out who gave him the order to kill her."

Semmena didn't know. He didn't know Samara knew of his scheme, of his own alliance with the Jinn—the ones who shouldn't be allied with.

"And Mavka? Has she said anything?"

Samara shook her head. "Haven't heard from her."

Aside from Semmena's scheming, that was another thing that had Samara on edge. Their one and only Jinn ally was missing.

Behind them, students ran into the halls and corridors, surely curious to see the chaos in the gardens.

"Are you alright?" Gaven neared her. "You've been using a lot of Void Magic."

Samara's eyes burned, the raised veins around her cheeks heated. Keeping Jeriyah's enchantments weak hadn't been difficult—it was the fact Alix Bennet was now reinforcing them that exhausted her. But they needed the enchantments to waver, to quiver and weaken. They needed those tunnels open. "I'll handle it."

The man smiled at her, his brow slightly furrowed. "I will keep you informed."

Samara dipped her chin in agreement before looking back to the gardens. Sol and her Court were gone, but she made out the slight violet outline of her brother's Ward.

"So, what now?" Gaven asked, flicking his brown eyes to her. "Sol Awakens?"

Nodding, she released a sigh to the sky. "And meanwhile, we fast track the reach for the Relics. I don't think they will find them quickly enough."

Gaven nodded and gave her a slight bow, making his way back into the depths of the courtyard.

"And Samara—"

She turned back to Gaven who stood with his hand on the doorknob to the throne room. Wordlessly, he crossed his right arm over his chest and patted his shoulder four times.

Long may she reign.

Samara smiled, crossing her own arm over her chest, tapping it five times in response.

Long live the Yarrow Clan.

EPILOGUE

Weeks passed and Sol had slept for days due to raw exhaustion and sadness. The grief came and went in waves, like the tide at the beaches she once loved. It would sweep over her, leaving her breathless, then recede, leaving her cold and lonely. She didn't eat or leave her bed. Nina had brought her pastries, stews, teas, anything she could think of to get Sol to at least seem interested in existing.

Initially, none of it worked.

Slowly, though, after a week of Sol being in bed like an earthworm, Sawyer dragged her out to the stables to help her with duties there. The rest of her Court was horrified when they found them covered in dirt and manure, but Sol began to feel better that day. She brushed Kahaida until the beast tried to maul her hand, and helped Sawyer chase the smaller mares around the gardens. Nina joined them at some point and took Sol on rides around the human sections.

Alix hunted down all sorts of comfort books for Sol, leaving a new one each night on her nightstand. Sawyer and Nina also settled into her room after Sol kept having nightmares and begged them to stay. The women didn't argue, and though they slept in the living area at first, after a couple of nights, Nina sleepily migrated to the bed next to Sol. Sawyer held out a few days longer before complaining about the awful couches and eventually took up the left edge of Sol's king-sized bed. After a week of that, Sol felt the most rested she had in years.

In between bouts of numbness, she was thankful for them. Out of the four of them, the only one who had maintained a noticeable distance had been Cas. Emotionally distant, because physically he had been closer than ever. When Gaven returned to provide additional protection, at King Semmena's orders, Cas gave him a nasty stare and shooed him away instead.

Which was fine. Sol felt safer with Cas anyway.

But she was disappointed the comfort they reached through the literal death games they survived together seemed to recede. Perhaps it was because she grew so used to speaking to him daily. Or because after the final duel, something changed between them, and she knew he felt it as well. Ultimately, though, he was meant to protect her. Feelings other than that were likely brought on by the stress of the weeks.

Still, Sol missed him.

Finally, after two weeks, Sol felt normal. As normal as she could with the new information, she supposed. Which meant it was time for the one thing they had put on hold to take place: her Awakening.

Sol and her Court stood by the stables as the keepers readied their horses. After almost an hour of arguing with Nina, it was decided Sol would ride with Cas. Her Royal Hand wouldn't risk her wandering so far into the depths of Rimemere without her personal Warden, especially since what happened. A Lower Jinn invading the castle was alarming, but having a Lower *and* a Mind Slayer?

Semmena had been insane with soldiers around the grounds, moving the students to the Gods' Villa to diminish traffic within the castle. Curfew was set and Sol wasn't allowed outside unless she had a small army of kingsmen with her. She hadn't bothered to exit much because of that.

For the Awakening ritual, they had to ride all the way to Emberdon's temple. It was to be performed by a family member, and as Sawyer was her final blood relative, the burden became hers to carry. So, it had to be performed on her turf.

And Sol was condemned to be Warded the whole way. Even so, she didn't mind. She looked up at the sun as the stable hands situated their saddles, soaking up the wondrous, gentle heat.

Lilah sniffed her hand as she stroked her snout.

"Do you want to ride on the front or back?"

She swirled, startled.

Cas wore his usual black tactical suit, with a subtle violet band around his waist holding a set of iron daggers. It was a relief to see his face was nearly free of scars and bruises.

He inclined his head, "I'll choose a position for you if you don't pick one, Princess."

Sol cleared her throat. "I'll ride behind."

At least he wouldn't be able to see her face burn that way.

Without further conversation, Cas mounted Lilah and outstretched a hand to her.

She hadn't dreamt of him since the bizarre vision after the final duel. She settled with replaying the moments in her mind, while he maintained the gods' awful distance when all she wanted was the opposite.

Focus.

"We will take the forest route," Sawyer announced as she stirred Fey to the castle gates.

Nina nodded. "At your lead."

Taking Cas's hand, Sol swung a leg over Lilah and settled into the saddle.

Although the Summer Solstice was still a few days away, the heat was relentless and at full force. Sol opted for her green tactical suit to match her Court, a choice she was quickly regretting as they started a soft canter behind Sawyer.

They passed the gates quickly and steered into the forest.

The trees had become full and luscious, though rather parched at the lack of rainwater. As the humid wind flowed all around them, cooling Sol's hot skin, she traced the swollen clouds with her eyes. In the distance, rolling thunderclouds blanketed the sky above them with a hazy shade of gray.

Next to them, Nina and Alix suddenly exploded into a full-on gallop, the hooves of their mares tearing up the grass as they raced behind one another. Her cousin propelled forward faster, her laugh echoing through the forest.

Sol smiled slightly and shook her head.

Through the sound of hooves and laughter, Cas's Ward materialized around them in a soft shimmer of light, encompassing them like a protective bubble.

He sighed from in front of her. "They do this every time."

"Who usually wins?" Sol asked with an amused smirk.

"Sawyer."

Fitting.

Sol laughed softly and took the conversation as a good sign. "I figured Kahaida would."

"She often stops to chew on the weeds, to Nina's dismay."

Also fitting.

Silence fell, and Sol tried desperately to think of something, anything, to continue the conversation. "Cas, are we okay?"

His Ward flickered. "Yes."

"You're a terrible liar."

"So are you."

Her arms tensed around him ever so slightly. "I'm not lying about anything."

"You lie every time someone asks you if you're okay." He peered back at her, his silver eyes shining. "I know you aren't."

Sol gaped at him, her breath hitching. She truly was feeling better, at least better than a few weeks ago. Was she perfect, though? Of course not.

She tore her gaze from his. "I will be eventually."

Once again, silence fell.

As Lilah came to a stop and the ground beneath them turned into a brown, dehydrated crunch, Sol sighed.

Swiftly, Cas dismounted Lilah, his boots sending the brown leaves adrift around them. He held out his hand to Sol. "We're here."

She took his help and landed beside him, the Ward still rippling and sizzling. Gently, Cas dropped her hand as it dissipated, floating into specks of starlight into the wind just as he released her.

Nina signaled them over from within the cover of trees. "Are you both ready?"

Without so much as a glance, Cas led her into the Fire God's temple.

Sol hadn't visited a temple before, and she wondered if they were all as somber. Emberdon's temple was all shades of gray and black, open to the elements with only the crackling of torches and the groan of the wind as its soundtrack. The trees and foliage around it seemed burned and dull, though Sol supposed it was fitting for the Fire God.

The temple itself was made of obsidian, brittle and crystalline, with thin, crimson ripples of color along the crackling walls. The stone almost pulsed like a beating heart as Sol stepped into the grounds. A statue of the God towered at the end, flanked by pews and benches. In front of the deity was a rectangular stone table with a carved chalice at its center.

She approached the chalice and leaned to look inside it. It was empty, but the darkness inside it seemed endless.

"This temple gives me the creeps," Nina whispered as she strode beside her. "Flora's at least has plants. Live ones."

Sol grimaced. "Let's never talk about that temple."

Beside her, Cas chuckled.

"Emberdon prefers dead things, Nins," Sawyer shared as she sat on a bench. She let out a long exhale and ran her hands along her face. "He especially loves animal sacrifices."

With a disgusted groan, Nina leaned closer to Sol.

The clouds seemed to darken further as Cas and Alix took a stance next to Emberdon. Reluctantly, Sawyer stood and walked their way. "It's quite simple, Sol."

She turned and stretched a hand to Sol, who took it despite the rising nerves enveloping her body. Though she was cautiously excited, she was also nervous to release this final part of herself. Once she Settled, it would be as if her entire life began anew.

"I will utter the ceremonial scriptures and prompt you to say your name when needed. Then, we will join our blood into the chalice, and wait."

Sol focused on her breathing. "Wait?"

"To see which god blesses you," Nina offered, taking her spot on the other side of the stone table. She also seemed slightly nervous.

"Warren is usually quick," Cas said. "It shouldn't take long."

"Or maybe you'll Settle as your paternal line, like Sawyer." Alix cast a taunting glance toward her.

Sawyer rolled her eyes. "Don't even say that or we're back to square one. We need a Yarrow Warden."

The whole thing was making Sol nervous, though she knew she couldn't control any of it. She didn't know what the other side of her blood held, her mother never spoke of her father.

As if sensing her anxiety, Nina gave her a small smile. "It'll be okay, Sol."

Sawyer took her spot in front of the table and chalice, facing Emberdon as Sol stood on her opposite side to face her. Cas and Nina were beside her, and they both took a subtle step closer to her side as she felt herself begin to tremble.

"You ready?" Sawyer met her gaze.

Not giving herself time to say otherwise, Sol nodded.

As if Erriadin itself responded, a soft patter of rain began around them.

First, Sawyer sliced a thin slit along her palm with her iron dagger. She then held it over the obsidian chalice, and her blood slowly dripped into it, the sound of rain merging with it.

"Emberdon, hear me as your daughter," Sawyer began, closing her eyes. She let out a breath. "Use me, Sawyerlyn Semmena Yarrow as your vessel to bless my kin." As her name left her lips, her blood began to vaporize in golden shimmers. She looked to Sol. "Say your name."

For a second, Sol hesitated. Not due to lack of trust, for once. But due to the finality of the situation. There was no going back once she told them. She would break the one rule her mother left her.

"S...Soleil," she said. She held her cousin's gaze. "Soleil Monserrat Yarrow."

As soon as Sol uttered her name, the rain stopped. The wind halted, the birds stopped their songs. It was as if the world took an inhale and held it. Sol did as well.

Especially as absolutely nothing happened.

Sawyer took her hand and gently cut along her palm to match her own wound, then joined their hands to hover over the chalice. Her cousin's blood had been dripping gold before, but as soon as it mixed with Sol's, the magic seemed to recoil.

No one spoke. For a second, they all just watched the chalice. Sol didn't know what to expect, but it hadn't been the stillness that transpired.

Then, she heard it.

Like that day so long ago when they confirmed her lineage in that ancient conference room, voices filled her head. She braced her free hand on the table as her temples tightened.

"Soleil Monserrat, you lie," the voices chanted over and over in her head in an unsettling crescendo, growing angrier and louder with each passing second. *"Soleil, speak your proper name."*

Sol tore her hand from Sawyer's and grabbed her head in agony as an incessant ache spread from her forehead down to her shoulders.

"Sol." Cas instantly grabbed her elbow to steady her as Nina stepped closer.

"Soleil of the Yarrow clan, tell us your full name." The voices ebbed and echoed with relentless fury.

Sol groaned as she sank to her knees.

"What are they saying, Sol?" Sawyer rounded the table and knelt beside her.

Soleil Soleil Soleil.

Sol knelt all the way forward and pressed her forehead to the ground, aching for the cool stone to calm the throbbing.

"Sawyer, close the ritual," Nina ordered. "Now."

Sol vaguely heard her Court call her and murmur other things through the haze that clouded her thoughts. It wasn't until a damp cloth was pressed to her bleeding palm that the voices halted.

Life and rain resumed beyond the temple, and Sol released her held breath as well. She slumped to the ground, completely drained of all energy and motivation to stand.

Cas carefully lifted her head off the ground and held her shoulders. "What did they say, Sol?"

She closed her eyes and muttered, "That I was lying."

A beat of silence. "That you were lying?" Sawyer asked.

"To speak my proper name."

Tentatively, Sol sat up and leaned against the table stand.

Nina frowned. "Why would they say that?"

"Your full name, paternal included, is irrelevant. You should only require the Yarrow, since it's the oldest bloodline." Alix added, running a hand through his hair. He knelt beside Cas. "The other original bloodlines that predate the Yarrows were all annihilated throughout the years."

Sol didn't have much to offer the conversation. Her mind was blank and foggy.

"What if she does need her father's name?" Sawyer's jaw tightened as she looked down at them.

Sol shrugged. "I don't know it."

The silence that followed her statement was heavy with terror. Her primary duty as queen was to close the Jinn gate—something she couldn't do without magic. Her blood was useless.

Useless.

She clutched her chest. "Oh gods, what if I need it?"

"There is no way—" Alix stood, pacing around while the rain recoiled from him. "There is no *way*."

"Who the hell did Irene tangle herself with," Nina whispered. "Where would we even begin the search?"

Yavenharrow.

Sol looked at her to say so but stopped.

The pain was unlike any other. It was slightly like when her birthmark flared, also reminiscent of the way her body ached like the days after the final duel.

But it was hotter, doused with oil and lit on fire.

Sol clutched her hand and screamed, falling back on the ground. Her palm felt like it was dipped in hot metal, in an inferno, as if Emberdon himself grabbed it.

Then, all at once, it stopped.

Sol opened her eyes, the ringing in her ears making her unable to decipher what her Court said. Just as Sol tried to sit up, Sawyer pointed at her palm.

Lora's blood bond was gone.

Coming
March 2025

FRAGILE HANDLE WITH CARE

Of Seas and Storms
By: Melanie Mar

OF SEAS AND STORMS

SUNS AND SHADOWS: BOOK 2

Yavenharrow smelled like blood and salt. Leo didn't know if it was an after effect of the Void Magic or if it was a consequence of the corpses mixing with the ocean. He and Mina had tried to bury as many as would fit in the town Pantheon, but they could only be out during the day—and time went by quickly when digging graves.

As Leo sprinted through the alleys, the sun mocking him as it lowered to the horizon, he began to panic. It gripped his throat and ignited his lungs as he cut sharp corners and jumped over bloody puddles, clutching the last bag of bread he could find against his chest. The once lively Old Square was tattered and broken, holding only vague memories of the lives that wandered it mere weeks before. A dusting of frost coated the bricks, the ghost town invaded with a cold so severe not even the oldest trees survived it. With each leap he took, the sky muted, growing dimmer as the menacing nighttime mist unrolled from the shadows, reaching for him like ghastly limbs.

Just a few more strides. A few more seconds and he'd be at the foot of his cottage where Mina surely waited by the front door in a cloak of dread. She had told him not to be out so late. Leo hadn't planned to, but he had been so close to infiltrating *her* base this time. He had been halfway through the sea of webs, blood, and illusions before the dwindling sunlight through the Archive's windows warned him nighttime approached. It was the furthest he had gotten.

Still, it had not been enough.

The wind that pushed against his every stride grew colder the closer he got to his cottage. It splintered against his face until all he could see was the mist of his labored breath. The sun fell beneath the hills as Leo pounded his fists on the wooden door. "Mina!"

He stumbled through the entrance, caught off guard by his sister's immediate response. Mina caught him by the bicep as she slammed the door shut, throwing the bolts into lock, and the wooden planks over it in reinforcement before pressing herself against the door.

All the lights were off. Beyond the single crystal door leading to the backyard, Leo noted the barn was shut, not even the stray sounds of the animals echoed into the fading dusk. Lungs burning with effort and clothes drenched in sweat, Leo threw the bag he held to the floor and bolted to her side.

The aged wood creaked behind them, unfamiliar with the weight of petrified, trembling bodies stacked upon it. Leo glanced at Mina, who seemed to struggle more than he was at retaining any air. Her chin-length, ebony hair was wild and clung to her forehead, her cotton dress torn at the skirt and sleeves.

He frowned, pulling at the ribbons of fabric. "What—"

She slammed a shaking hand over his mouth.

The wind howled against the boards of their home, the sound akin to talons on pavement. As the final shreds of sunlight faded, casting their living room into total darkness, Mina turned to look at him. The snapshot of terror on her face made Leo's stomach plummet.

She's outside.

"Leon," the creature taunted, her voice clear as a silver dinner bell. "Leon, where is my niece?"

Leo took Mina's hand in his own and clamped his jaw shut, closing his eyes as if it would somehow make the world darker, as if it would hide them from the thing that had been haunting their town and hunting its people.

A soul-stirring melody rang beyond their walls, her voice carrying in the breeze and through the shadows, beckoning them to reveal themselves.

But they wouldn't.

Leo and Mina had endured weeks of this—they knew keeping utterly still, quiet, and away from the outdoors would keep them safe, at least until they had the protection of sunlight once dawn broke through.

They remained motionless a the melody inched closer.

Mina squeezed his hand.

Leo squeezed it back.

The song, a melancholic tune interwoven with many tones and timbres, hovered directly behind them. The melody thrummed in his ears like a caress he knew would end in bloodshed.

All at once, it stopped.

Leo and Mina remained in stunned silence against the door, their heavy breaths the only sound. Heat pooled in Leo's chest. Adrenaline stung across his skin. He let his eyes flutter closed as a single, serrated claw trailed the door's carved designs from the outside, leaving a line of shivers in its wake.

"Soleil will come home," the creature said, no longer masquerading beneath the bright, lively tone of her song. It pulled at Leo's chest—she sounded more like herself than ever.

Softly, so softly that Leo had to press his ear against the door, Lora said, "And when she does, it'll be me who kills her."

ABOUT THE AUTHOR

Melanie Mar is a Social Worker along with being a mother to an incredibly active infant and two equally demanding fur babies. When she is not combating adulthood duties, she enjoys exploring the outdoors (when it's cold), watching horror films, reading romantic fantasies until 3 am, and spending all the time she can with her family.

Melanie lives in Texas and her Bachelor of Science in Psychology gives her a unique perspective on human behaviors, helping her craft three-dimensional, relatable characters with their own ways of overcoming struggles. She participated in AWP's 19th Season of W2W as a Mentee and was published in her local university's magazine.

She is currently working on her debut romantasy series and spending all her free time living within its world.

Made in the USA
Columbia, SC
11 May 2025